A
PROMISE
OF
LIES

A Promise of Lies

Copyright © 2024 by Clare Sager.

First published in Great Britain in 2024 by Clare Sager, T/A Wicked Lady Press.

All rights reserved.

No part of this book may be reproduced in any form or by any electronic or mechanical means, including information storage and retrieval systems and AI training, without written permission from the author, except for the use of brief quotations in a book review.

Without in any way limiting the author's exclusive rights under copyright, any use of this publication to "train" generative artificial intelligence (AI) technologies to generate text is expressly prohibited. The author reserves all rights to license uses of this work for generative AI training and development of machine learning language models.

Dust jacket, paperback, and ebook cover designs by Maria Spada.

Under dust jacket cover illustration by Nate Medeiros @mythicmountain.

Opening character illustration 'Wicked Lady & the Serpent of Tenebris Diptych' by *Bus Stop Shop @s_holdthebus*

Opening 'Storyscape' by Charlie Arpie @charliearpie.

Closing character illustrations, 'An Ending Diptych' by Agnieszka Gromulska @AseriaArt.

Map created using brushes from the Map Effects Fantasy Map Builder @mapeffects.

A PROMISE OF LIES

CONTENT WARNINGS

Please read safely—this book contains adult themes and scenes of a sexual nature as well as the following content that some readers may find distressing:

- Death, including execution, some graphic.
- Threat of sexual violence.
- Violence and murder.
- Prejudice and discrimination.
- Misogyny.
- Alcoholism.
- Fat shaming (not by MCs).
- Loss of a loved one.
- Familial abuse.
- Pregnancy (not FMC).
- Infertility.
- Dealing with trauma present and past.

For the women who got tired of waiting for a hero.

KATHERINE

WICKED
LADY

BASTIAN

SERPENT
OF TENEBRIS

TENEBRIS

LUMINIS

PROLOGUE
BASTIAN

Blood coats my hands. It's my own. My chest feels like it's been ripped apart. I don't know how I'm still standing—I can *feel* my insides pressing on the thin wall left holding them in.

My father's eyes are wide on me. They flick down to my stomach. He pales.

It's bad.

I suck in breaths, tighten my grip. I'm dead. It's just a question of when exactly I drop.

But I can't give up until I stop him.

"Bastian," he begins.

"Why?" I swipe, and he turns my sword away with ease.

"I..." He grits his teeth, takes half a step back, like he doesn't want to finish me off. "I didn't mean to, I..." He shakes his head, glancing at the bloody mess he's cut through me.

"I don't mean me, I mean..." My head swims. Now he's backed away, I chance a look down. Raw and red, the dark crimson of muscle, the light yellow of fat and flesh where he's sliced clean through my leather armour. It's bad, but...

But there should be more blood.

I should be on the floor, a breath away from oblivion.

He should be striding past me to do what he came here with a naked blade to do.

"Why do this?" I choke out. "Betrayal. Treason." The words others associate with him, but that I never have.

And yet here he is, come to kill the queen. The queen he betrayed the other side for all those years ago. The queen I thought he had chosen.

I'm not supposed to be here today. It's my day off. But there's been something strange about his behaviour and yesterday I caught him cleaning his armour. I knew something was wrong, but...

I thought I'd get here and find him facing some enemy, that I would help, and we would fight side by side to protect the queen. Not *this*.

"I don't—"

"You don't understand." He straightens as if realising I'm not about to drop dead. In his old armour, unworn for centuries, he looks every bit the legendary general. And when he speaks again, it's as the general. "Step aside, Bastian. Get to a healer while you still can. Let me do what must be done."

"So you can plunge us into chaos?" I laugh, humourless and bloody, and the cut in my lip stings. It's a pale pain in comparison with the agony of my chest and stomach, spiking with each heartbeat. Darkness pulses on the edge of my vision, like my own shadows ready to rush in.

But I can still move, can still grip my sword and straighten.

"Not chaos." His brow tightens. "Step asi—"

"No." I'm clumsy with pain as I sweep my sword up and across. He's going to catch it, but if I delay him just long enough, someone will hear the sounds of our fight. Someone will come.

But as time draws out like a bowstring stretching longer, thinner, less real somehow, the darkness of my Shadowblade cuts through the air and no steel rises to meet it.

He lifts his chin, bronze-brown skin catching the light like he's a statue and can't fight back.

My heart clamours, pain pounding through my entire being. It understands before I do.

I can't stop. My sword slices through flesh, grinds on bone. I think he makes a sound, but I can't hear anything except my thundering pulse.

Blood splatters me, mingling with my own.

He staggers under the weight of an injury that matches mine.

He could've stopped me. Should've. Why...?

Never blunt your blade. It's been drummed into me a million times—never hold back. No quarter given. No mercy owed. And certainly never damage your sharpest weapon.

Even now, the voice in my head barking the instructions is his.

Yet as he falls to one knee, he catches himself on the tip of his sword like it's a walking stick rather than a blade to be kept honed. The ring of metal on stone cuts through the roaring in my ears.

He nods once, pain crinkling his features, then his weapon clatters to the floor, steel sparking unheeded.

My shadows rush in to cradle him.

For a long moment, all I can do is stare. "Why didn't you block me?"

A faint smile curls his lips. "I can't kill my son. Not even for this."

"*Baba*, you..." I shake my head. "You could've stopped me. You could've..."

"Today you stopped me." He nods like this is right, and his breathing rattles. "Tell your *athair*... to remember..."

I drop to my knees and try to press on his wound, but I can see parts of him I shouldn't and his blood slicks my hands. He shouldn't be bleeding this much, not with the willow knot that lives in his pocket—a guard against a single mortal blow, gifted by one who loves him. A gift from my *athair*. "Your charm... where is it?"

"Tell him to remember... our promise..." His hand rests on mine, not quite closing, and as he blinks, his dimming eyes rest on my cloak.

I touch the pocket hidden in its folds and find something that crumbles, giving off a charred scent. I know the smell.

Ash. His charm used up saving me.

"You..." I shake my head.

He dips his chin. An admission.

He slipped it in my pocket instead of keeping it to save himself. Already the weakness from my injuries is abating. My throat is raw, so I can barely croak out the word, "Why?"

He knew I'd try to stop him. He knew I would betray him... or stay loyal to the queen. Two sides of the same coin.

"You are worth dying for. Worth fighting for." His voice is barely more than a rasp in his chest. "Worth everything." He smiles. "My boy."

He gives me one more order, which just might be the hardest to obey.

And then he says nothing.

His mouth, his chest, his eyes—they're all empty.

He's gone.

I am alone.

The strength rushing back through me from the charm's magic drives me to my feet, but I want to kneel. I want to die.

I should have died here. He is—*was* more experienced, more skilled, more *everything* than I am.

But I'm the one left standing and I can't stay here and mourn my father. I have to turn away and get to the queen. I have to stride through the palace, finding a gaggle of loyal guards who stare at the state of my armour but follow my orders at once.

And all the while I wonder—how the hells am I going to tell *Athair* what I've done?

I

BASTIAN

I blinked at my hands. They were clean. No blood, only what was rushing through my ears. But when I rubbed my fingertips together, I could *feel* the ghost of it slick upon them.

"Bastian." Asher's voice, low with warning and close.

It was only then I registered the other voices—whispers in a crowd—and understood where I was. *When* I was.

The throne room. The final moments of the eclipse. Now, not back then. Years separated me from my father and his final order.

You must live.

I'd tried. Good gods, had I tried.

But here I found myself dying in the throne room once more, insides spilling as another person I loved was taken from me.

No.

Not this time.

There was no blood, but the world was red and my veins burned.

I heard nothing of Braea's words before she disappeared back into Dusk, ready to succumb to Sleep once the moon finished crossing the sun. But I saw the smirk on Cyrus's face as he inclined his head and followed the guards as they ushered their "guests" away into Dawn's side of the palace.

When I'd taken my father's life, I'd been a boy, powerless to change things. But now...

I strode across the throne room, not towards Dusk, but to Dawn. My body was not my own, but some machine driven by terrible fire. Shadows surged with me, smoky and thick.

The crowd parted, and I dimly registered fearful expressions, but my eyes were fixed on that door where I'd seen Kat and Cyrus disappear.

He was responsible for this. He'd taken her.

Well, he damn well wasn't going to keep her.

Pale armoured guards tried to bar my way.

Tried.

I charged through them, my shadows and I working as one to pass through the group like they were ghosts.

Perhaps I was the ghost. I moved as easily as one. I barely slowed as I stepped through the lodestone doorway and into Dawn. A second clutch of guards scattered as I shouldered through them.

I caught the glint of golden hair topped with a matching crown and bellowed, "Cyrus!"

He turned, eyes widening for a moment. I wasn't meant to be in Dawn. Good. Let him be shocked. Afraid. Let him shit his fucking pants.

I was going to kill him.

That fire throbbed in every fibre of my being, making my scar ache.

Then I was face-to-face with him, still striding until my fingers bit into his collar and he slammed against the wall. Metal rang out as his guards drew a dozen weapons.

I didn't need a weapon. I was going to do this with my bare hands, and, in the meantime, my shadows would hold the guards at bay.

Cyrus gestured for them to stay back, then, slowly, he smiled. "Careful, Bastian. I'm king now."

I spat out a laugh as shadows simmered around us. "Do I look like I give a shit?" My voice didn't sound human anymore —it was a feral growl, low and lethal. "What do you think you're going to do?"

He shrugged around my grip. "I won't do anything... to *you*." There was a dangerous lightness to his voice.

Despite my fury, that tone registered—a needle pushing through me.

He fluttered his lashes, head cocking to one side. "Katherine, on the other hand..."

If his tone was a needle, his words were a punch. The roar of blood in my ears exploded, leaving them ringing, then a solid silence.

I wasn't the boy I'd once been, no. I had power now. I was the Bastard of Tenebris. The Serpent. I'd served my queen, my country, in a thousand ways big and small. I'd saved lives and taken them.

But I was no king. And with Katherine in Cyrus's control, I might as well be nothing.

He could have her killed with a word. Hang her with a gesture.

I couldn't act on instinct. I couldn't—or at least *shouldn't* go racing after Kat or rage against her being taken, even though every part of me, body and soul, demanded it.

"Now, what was it you charged, *without permission*, into Dawn for?" Cyrus arched his eyebrows and peered down at my fist bunched in his clothing.

I yanked my shadows close and clamped them into submission as I unknotted my knuckles. Taking a step back, I had to swallow down the shards of my rage before I could reply. "Nothing."

Another slow smile, then he nodded. "That's what I thought." He stepped out from between me and the wall, then moved into my space until we were almost nose-to-nose. His smirking amusement disappeared as his eyes locked with mine. "Run along, Bastian. I have new toys to play with. You'll have to find something else to entertain you."

THE PALACE and the city passed me by in a hot haze—a strange, distant surreality—as I made my way to the Hall of Healing. I didn't realise my destination until I found myself staring up at its marble columns. Thank the Stars some part of me was still sane.

They'd gathered the bodies from the attack here for sorting and inspection. Victims' families—by blood or choice—would come here to identify and claim their loved ones.

But the body I sought wasn't a victim.

At my terse demand, a younger acolyte nodded and directed me to a staircase that spiralled down.

I followed it round and round, mind and soul spinning faster, further, like they were going to catapult off the planet and disappear into the nothingness of space.

Kat was gone. Taken. Given.

Given *willingly*.

The knowledge burned. I was a fool.

I thought I had control. I thought I knew the pieces on the board and controlled at least some of them. I *thought* I had an ally in my queen—someone who would work *with* me to move the other pieces.

But she had sacrificed the person most precious to me.

Dizziness had hold of me by the time I reached the bottom of the spiral staircase, and I had to grip the handrail to stay upright. I emerged into a dim space that stretched on into darkness.

It took a moment for everything to stop spinning and for me to realise what the shapes were on the floor. Row upon row of bodies.

Elthea's cream braids swayed above one as she unbuttoned its clothes. A cluster of lights drifted at her shoulder.

Shit. Would've been better to do this alone, but at least the cool air eased my head and heart. By the time she looked up and raised her eyebrows, I had some semblance of calm.

"What brings the Serpent down here to play with the dead?"

"Is that what you're doing? Playing?" I took my time approaching, pretending I was just glancing casually at the arranged bodies. But I had my eye out for one with his head caved in.

I'd ensured no one would recognise my other self's face, but there hadn't been enough time to disguise the tattoo covering our back or the scar down our front. All afternoon, I'd been stuck in the palace, so this was my first chance to retrieve him and stop anyone from discovering my ability to split.

Besides, despite my exhaustion, I needed distraction more than I needed sleep.

Elthea's soft snort drifted into the room's echoing darkness. This mortuary filled the space under the Hall of Healing and, judging by the pillars stretching into the distance, it had to extend even further than that.

"Not playing, *working*. Look." She held up a lock of the dead fae's hair—almost as black as mine. "And yet..." With surprising gentleness, she pulled open their trousers enough to reveal the hair there. "Blond." Frowning, she knelt back on her heels.

I took the opportunity to skim the bodies nearest us. The ones behind me were all wrapped in shrouds, with clothes folded in a neat pile; those ahead still wore their battle clothes. Black hair, dark armour, slashes across bellies and chests, blood crusted around the throat. No crushed heads.

"That one"—she pointed to the wrapped body next to us— "had light brown body hair. That one"—she pointed to the next—"had green."

I blinked from my search to her. "But the Ascendants' hair was all black."

She took a long breath and sighed it out. "And I thought the Serpent was meant to be so cunning and clever."

The instant her scornful look hit me, I understood the relevance. "Dyed. Their hair was dyed."

"I believe so." She rolled the body over, checking its back. "I'll be examining some of the attackers more closely to confirm, but it certainly looks that way. I found dark residue caught in their ears." She nodded towards a hard leather case containing tiny jars and vials. Their varied contents included a black waxy substance, clippings of different coloured hair, pale flecks, crimson liquid. Specimens.

"You think they'll tell you more?" I went back to searching for my other self.

Lifting the hair off the neck of the body before her, she gave a cool smile. "They may not wish to, but I'll make them."

"Chilling." I scoffed in an attempt to hide my reaction as I spotted a familiar shape a couple of rows over. The neck disappeared into a pulpy mess.

If she got to that one, peeled off its clothes, and turned it over, she'd find a *very* distinguishing tattoo on its back. Hells, she'd probably recognise the scar upon our chest before that. After all, she was the one who'd treated that wound and had let it scar rather than healing it completely.

At least when I'd died in Innesol, the Horrors had consumed my other self's magic, leaving the body unrecognisable. Not that I was going to rush back into Horror territory to search for it.

"I didn't expect the Serpent to be so affected by death— after all, hasn't he dealt out plenty of it?"

I jerked my attention from my body and found Elthea looking up at me, one eyebrow arched.

Hadn't I told Kat to never reveal her heart? Now here I was trying to kill Cyrus one minute and staring after the corpse I was meant to be hiding the next.

"That doesn't mean I enjoy it." I shrugged one shoulder, nonchalant. "You have a lot of bodies to examine on your own."

"Everyone else is helping with the injured and the families. I can be more useful here, however."

As if on cue, a couple emerged from the spiral staircase and an acolyte walked them to one of the shrouded bodies.

"I could help."

Her eyes narrowed. I hadn't played it nonchalant enough. "*You*, help *me*?"

"I could use the distraction." Physical work would help, even if it was a task that didn't require the attention of the Night Queen's Shadow.

Slowly, she looked me up and down, and I could feel her mentally cataloguing me. "Hmm. I suppose it would be hard not to form an attachment. She has her charms, I'll grant you." She canted her head, and I swallowed as I realised she was speaking of Kat. "You shouldn't worry so much. Her resilience is impressive... for a human." Wiping her hands, she rose. "Very well. You can help. I'm looking for tattoos, scars, any other identifying marks on the civilians, defenders, or attackers."

I kept my expression neutral at the mention of scars and tattoos, nodding like an obedient assistant.

"Write a note and leave it with the wrapped body. The civilians and defenders are being set aside so families can collect them for burial."

Returned to the soil, where their magic could seep back into the land. Elfhame would be stronger, but we were weaker after today.

I'd heard humans used cremation, but we considered it barbaric—something was lost in the burning. But the Convocation had agreed to burn the attacker's bodies—a last resort to rid ourselves of the enemy taint. And it would help me hide evidence of my secret.

Elthea indicated several wrapped forms that had been offset from the row. "I'm not so interested in them. The Ascendants, though... They could prove to be a treasure trove of information."

I huffed through my nose. Only Elthea could see a room of dead people and think "treasure."

"Check their pockets for personal items and search for signs of dye. I could do with more samples of that residue for testing. I want evidence to confirm my theory, and if I get enough, I'll be able to work out what dye they used."

She handed me a pad of paper and a pencil before pointing out the empty jars and the small metal implements used to scrape up the residue. In a cart nearby lay folded linens, waiting to be wrapped around bodies once they were undressed and checked.

When I got started, I didn't make a beeline for my other self's corpse. Instead, I went to the nearest body in that row—an attacker. Just as I'd observed in the palace, he had black hair and the Hydra Ascendant insignia that didn't quite match the one Sura had given Kat. No tattoos or notable scars. Yet, as Elthea had observed, his body hair didn't match. In this case, it was a straw blond—more Dawn than Dusk.

Doubts might've trickled in after the fighting had stopped, but Kat had to be right. This was a group mimicking Hydra Ascendant, and alongside the insignias, this was another piece of evidence. As I noted the hair colour, I wondered what Sura would make of the fact someone was impersonating her group to cover their own motivations.

More pressingly, how was I going to broach the implications of the hair dye with Elthea?

If I suggested this was Dawn Court trying to look like Dusk, it would sound like I was trying to shift blame from my own people.

Then again, if she had noticed the dye and was investigating it, did I need to say anything? Better to leave her to identify the truth herself. It was more likely to be accepted coming from Dawn Court, especially such a highly regarded healer known for her scientific approach.

I tried not to think about what her "scientific approach" had led her to do to Kat.

I tried not to think about Kat at all.

But my exhausted mind was a treacherous thing, and as I wrapped the shroud around the body before me, the form seemed shorter, rounder, softer. The phantom scent of spring crept around me.

It isn't Kat. It isn't Kat.

I gritted my teeth and told myself over and over.

I was grateful to turn to the next body until I saw this one wore no armour, just the elegant outfit of a servant. Steeling myself, I took in her face. She was familiar, though the last time I'd seen her, she'd worn a warm smile and welcomed me to the royal wedding.

The hot thing that had been slithering through me since Kat's name had been announced finally quenched. Ice crept into my bones.

An innocent went to work today, likely said goodbye to some loved one, maybe even promised to raise a glass later to celebrate their prince's marriage. And hours later, here she lay, cold and still, never to keep her promise.

Slowly, I raised my head and the rows stopped being bodies—these were people. Every one of them, even the attackers. I might be Dusk and many of them Dawn, but they were *all* my people and there were precious few of us left before today. Now...

Our dwindling numbers bent my back.

Hadn't we learned our lesson from earlier wars? We

couldn't afford to fight amongst ourselves. Not if we wanted to survive.

With a deep breath, I blinked away the burning in my eyes and continued my work. Cataloguing identifying marks, noting names where folk had inscribed jewellery or paperwork in their pockets, checking for evidence Elthea might find useful. Finally, I shrouded each of them as carefully as I would've wrapped my own father, if I'd been allowed to.

I didn't have any feelings left by the time I reached my other self. Or perhaps I had too many and they'd all become one churning mass that I couldn't raise my head from. I didn't catalogue the scar. No paperwork was better.

As I wrapped him, still clothed, I vaguely wondered if I should feel some discomfort from handling what was essentially my own body. But there was no space left for that, not when fear for Kat and grief for the dead filled me so completely. It would be two or three weeks before I could split again, but the delay was better than dying outright.

By the time I'd wrapped my other self, I was as cold inside as the bodies surrounding us.

"I know this one," I called over to Elthea. "I'll take him."

She glanced my way and took in the blood soaking into the shroud. "Ah, the one with the crushed head. He's a defender, then? Hmm." She nodded and noted something in her book. "I assumed he was one of them. It was a quick death."

When she sucked in her lips in what was almost an apologetic smile, I realised she was trying to be comforting in her own odd way. Not quite "sorry for your loss" but close.

In return, I cleared my throat and nodded. Not quite "thank you" but close.

An acolyte helped manoeuvre the body into a compartment that would lift it to the ground floor, and from there into one of the Hall of Healing's charnel carts. I declined their offer of a driver and promised to bring it back when I was finished.

Steering out of the stable yard, I set my face into a hard look that invited no questions and urged the two hinds through the darkening streets.

Then, upon a hillside overlooking the city as it turned to Tenebris, I burned Bastian Marwood.

2

BASTIAN

After, I made my way back to the palace, stopping in to check on Vespera. I was waylaid as various guards and servants stopped me to talk about the day's events. Eventually, I managed to reach the queen's rooms, ready to make my report to her now the sun had set.

Except I wasn't ready. Not to see her face, calm and relaxed, like this was just another evening and just another report. It heaped fuel on the smouldering embers that had flared at Cyrus.

"How could you?" I bit out, like part of me didn't want to speak, but the words were an overwhelming storm.

She looked up from picking out her clothes for the night. At first her eyes widened, but gradually they narrowed as she canted her head in question.

"How could you give her to them?"

She watched me a long while, like she had spotted something new and couldn't decide what it was. "I assume you meant to include a 'Your Majesty' in there."

My shadows stilled, like they were waiting to see what I would do. I bit the inside of my cheek until a coppery taste flooded my mouth, reminiscent of standing over my father as our blood mingled on the floor.

Just like that night, I needed to take a step back.

"Your Majesty, Albion won't let this slide. Katherine is their subject. You sent me there for *months* to reforge that alliance. Now you've given her to Dawn as a hostage—they won't be happy." *I won't be happy.* Hadn't that crossed her mind?

She cleared her throat and returned the sheer blouse to the drawer. With a solid *clunk,* she closed it and straightened, lifting her chin. Despite wearing a dressing robe, she was now every inch the Night Queen. "First of all, she isn't a hostage. She's an esteemed guest, just like those from Dawn are."

Semantics. But I ran my tongue over the jagged cut inside my mouth and kept quiet.

She stalked closer. "Second"—she jabbed a finger into my chest—"*you* took her on missions. *You* asked me to let her stay indefinitely. *You gave her a ring.* You know that has meaning." Every accusation was punctuated with a poke.

I felt every rebuke and the unfurling implications—barbs inside my chest.

"She is yours and you are hers. Did you think no one would notice? Did you not think about how that might give the Albionic queen a hold over you and me a hold over the girl?"

I could barely shake my head. I had caused this. Allowed it. Helped put her in the line of fire. My rage turned upon itself, hot and bubbling like I was going to be sick.

"Or did you only think with the contents of your trousers?" The queen curled her lip, and for a second I felt what it was to be her enemy.

It was not good.

Not when I'd spent my life serving her. As her Shadow, as a member of the Queensguard, and before that as a stable hand who dreamed of being more.

Now, for a moment, I stood outside. In the face of her look, everything I'd ever done crumbled away.

It was as though I'd been thrown from my home into a blizzard with the door slammed shut behind me. And just like shelter in a snowstorm, I needed her. The realm needed her. She was stability, a constant. She and Lucius had delivered us from the terrible wars of succession and we'd had peace for a thousand years. Now he was gone and only she remained.

She huffed a long breath and her cold fury thawed into frustration. "You are not in Albion, however, and the human girl is here in *my* realm. She may still be a subject of Albion, but your actions have made her a subject of Elfhame, too."

And there it was.

The agonising truth.

This was my fault. By showing Kat favour, I'd exposed her, but I hadn't taken enough steps to keep her safe.

"Cyrus wanted her," Braea went on, a little more herself than the cold queen. "I couldn't deny him."

Fuck. *Fuck!*

I should've given her more than a ring—I should've sworn myself to her. Properly. A marriage. Then they wouldn't have been able to separate us. Cyrus wouldn't have been able to take her.

I swallowed back the bitter taste licking its way up my throat.

"Considering the attackers were from Dusk, I was on the back foot when it came to negotiating. If he'd asked for you, I'd have been hard pressed to say no." Braea sighed as she turned away.

She yanked the blouse from a drawer and found some trousers to pair with it, then disappeared behind the dressing screen.

When Elthea raised the hair dye, our position might improve. That was some minuscule comfort. In the meantime, I had to bite my tongue and stick to my plan of letting her share her discovery.

By the time Braea emerged, I stood in a tight pool of my own shadows. It felt more like I stood in a pit.

She buttoned the cuff of her pale blue blouse. "Maybe it's for the best." She looked up just in time to see me twitch at the comment. Brow knotted, she gave me a pointed look. "You don't need any more distractions. There must've been signs of this attack. You missed them."

I'd failed her. Myself. Elfhame. Katherine.

I fell deeper into that pit as my thoughts spiralled, as dizzying as going down to the mortuary. Only now, I kept going down, down, down into the unfathomable hells that waited below.

"Oh, Bastian." Braea squeezed my shoulder. "Remember, it's only temporary." She blanketed her earlier harshness with a soft smile. "And who knows? Perhaps her links to Albion will keep a leash on Cyrus."

I managed a grunt and a vague nod.

Another squeeze before she let go. "Get to bed. You're dead on your feet and you stink of bonfires."

I didn't even have the energy to argue. Without another word, I made my way back to my rooms. I shrugged off my jacket, caught up in the simple routine of hanging it up and stretching in the living room doorway, ready to crawl into bed. Without thinking, I called, "Kat?"

But there was no answer.

The jolt of remembering cut through my exhaustion.

My gaze fixed on the settee where she liked to curl up and read. Despite all my magic, she didn't appear.

I held my breath and listened. There was no hummed tune as she ran a bath or showered.

This was it. She was gone. Truly gone. And not only had I been unable to stop it—I had helped cause it.

My chest heaved as that terrible, searing heat from earlier broke over me. "Fuck this." I swept an arm across a side table, sending trinkets flying.

They smashed against the wall, and it felt good. Hot and awful and destructive, like the thing inside me that didn't deserve anything better.

I threw the side table across the room. Glass tinkled. Wood cracked.

I barely knew what I was doing. Barely understood my own thoughts as they spun further and further from control, and I gave myself over to feral rage.

My bellowing became wordless as the room became shards and splinters.

Fuck Cyrus. Fuck Dawn. Fuck me for letting this happen.

Only the Stars knew how long I erupted until, finally, I searched for the next thing to break.

And found nothing left.

I held a chair leg like a club, muscles tight and ready. But there was no enemy to strike and no object to crush into tiny pieces.

I met my own gaze in the shards of mirror still clinging to the frame. My hair was a mess. My eyes glowed like some kind of unholy fire above the dark circles that gathered underneath.

But my shadows only pooled around me. They hadn't

joined in the destruction as though I was doing exactly what they would, given free rein.

Surrounded by a kingdom of ruin, I looked every inch the wicked, wild unseelie everyone feared.

Grimacing, I turned from my reflection. I could carry all this into my workroom. Tomorrow, I would begin fixing it.

But no, they were just things, and I was a fool to think I could achieve anything by fixing them.

I flung the chair leg into the fire, sending sparks flying.

"Are you done?"

3
BASTIAN

I whirled, glass cracking under my boots, and found Faolán in the doorway. Rose, Ella, and Perry peered around him, and I spotted the dark gleam of Asher's hair in the antechamber beyond.

I dragged in a breath, calming myself, and used my shadows to sweep the worst of the destruction to the edges of the room so my friends could enter.

"What's the plan, then?" Faolán asked, like it was that simple.

Rose gripped her hands together and nodded with fierce determination, despite her eyes gleaming like she was fighting tears. "Whatever you need—I'll help."

I blinked from one to the other. "You mean... a rescue?"

"Of course." Faolán raised one shoulder as if it was obvious. "We march in and get her. You have secret passages and other spy stuff, don't you? What's the point in all that if you can't use it in a moment like this?"

"Bastian." Asher picked through the fine debris left on

the carpet, sparing Faolán a pointed look. "Remember who you are. You know better than this. We have to be more subtle. We'll spirit her away the moment she's in a lodestone."

At his shoulder, Perry gave a soft, sad smile, brow crinkling. "I know it's hard to wait, but it gives you plausible deniability. We can make it look like a kidnapping."

"And how long do we have to wait for that?" Faolán's tanned face bunched up in a glower that would've made a weaker person piss themselves. But, to his credit, Asher stood firm, even as the shapechanger took a step closer and growled, "We can't leave her there."

As their argument went on, Ella remained silent, arms folded. Although she was half Faolán's size, it was her glare that forced me to look away. It was something that had been honed to a fine point—the kind that could find a gap in even the strongest armour.

At that moment, she hated me.

And it was deserved. She understood what had dawned on me during my conversation with the Night Queen. She knew I was responsible for her friend's current position.

What I was about to say just might make her hate me more. But it was the best thing we could do for Kat right now.

I drew a long breath like I was about to dive deep, deep underwater and maybe never surface. "No."

Faolán whirled. "What?"

"There will be no rescue attempt."

"*What*? You can't be serious."

Rose paled, but a muscle in her jaw solidified.

Asher sighed, nodding. "It isn't easy, but it's the right decision. If we wait until the perfect moment, we can form a plan that—"

"No." I cut him off. "There won't be any sneaky kidnapping, either."

His dark eyes went wide, but it was Perry who spoke. "Then... what do we do?"

"Play the game," Ella's voice cut through the quiet. Her gaze still bored into me as though the others didn't exist. "Whispers. Subtlety. Stick to the rules, but twist them so they're barely recognisable. Isn't that what fae do?"

She made it sound like something sordid, though it was just what we were. Bargains ran through our veins, each with laws to define them.

I bowed my head. "It is."

"Good." She bit out the word. "Because if you don't play the game, Kat will pay the price. And you've done a shit job so far."

"Ella!" Rose took a step forward. "That's a bit harsh on Bastian. He—"

Ella cut her off with a look. "It's true, though, isn't it? Especially after that little show in the throne room this afternoon. I may be relatively new here, but one thing holds true across human and fae courts—*never reveal your heart.*"

I flinched: my own words used back at me were a punch to the gut.

She stalked closer, apparently unconcerned that I dwarfed her as she pointed a finger in my face. "*Your* queen let him take her. Hells, for all we know, she volunteered Kat."

"No. She told me Cyrus wanted her."

But Ella snorted. "And you don't think she could've twisted the truth?"

"She wouldn't." That was more Sura's style—she'd made it sound like Braea had killed Nyx, deceiving Kat without uttering a lie. I shut my eyes and drew a breath, shoving those thoughts aside.

When I looked again, Asher was frowning, gaze distant and troubled. Faolán stared at Ella, mouth open. Rose worried her lip and wrung her hands. At least some of them thought Ella's accusations might be true.

Finally I inclined my head, thoughts under control, body no longer humming with anger. Instead, a buzzing ache settled behind my eyes. "You're right. Not about the queen, but I do need to play the game."

Remember who you are. I'd spent years building the persona of the Bastard of Tenebris. Now I had to use it to keep Kat safe.

"Though I'll need your help—all of you."

They leant in with murmurs of agreement.

"We'll pretend she was just warming my bed. She's of less value to my enemies if they believe I don't care about her."

Ella scoffed, though she was no longer pointing at me. "You think you're that good an actor?"

"I swear to you"—I held her shoulders—"I will do everything in my power to keep Kat safe. *I swear.*"

Normally she looked away from my gaze, unnerved by the glow, but this time she held it. Finally, she inclined her head. "Don't make me have to go mining for that hunk of iron, Marwood."

Once before, she'd threatened to forge her own iron blade and use it to hunt me down if I ever hurt Kat. I didn't doubt she'd follow through on that promise.

"I wouldn't dream of it." I squeezed her shoulders before releasing her and taking in the whole group. "Help me spread those rumours. We need to use any allies we can in Dawn—not that there are many." I had my spy, possibly Elthea, though it was hard to tell what side she was on in any given situation. I suspected she cared only for her experiments.

Asher tapped his lower lip. "What about Caelus?"

I couldn't help wrinkling my nose.

"Yes, you dislike him." His eyelids fluttered like he resisted rolling his eyes. "But he seems to like Kat, and he's never been a fan of Cyrus. He has an interest in keeping her safe, even if it's because he thinks it might earn him some... gratitude."

Dislike wasn't quite the word for Caelus. He didn't seem like a bad person, but... "I'm not sure we can trust him."

"Not with our lives, perhaps," Perry added. "But with Kat's? I think we can."

Asher took a step closer to her, perhaps unaware he was doing it. "At least consider it."

I grumbled and pinched the bridge of my nose as the pounding in my head grew. "Fine. I'll think about it. But for now, can you all get out so I can go to bed?"

Rose chuckled as though relieved at the tension deflating. "Subtle hint taken." She gave me a quick, hard hug before leaving. The others clapped me on the shoulder or squeezed my arm as they made for the door until there was only Faolán and me left.

"Even if it's not a rescue, we'll get her back," he said, voice more gruff than usual, as though he was having to force it. Jaw and lips tight, he nodded, then pulled me into the kind of enveloping hug only he could give. "Trust her," he muttered in my ear. "She's strong. She can survive this."

I squeezed him, eyes burning. I didn't trust myself to answer, so just nodded against his shoulder.

He slapped my back and pulled away. "Get some sleep, Bastian. You look like shit." But he tempered it with one of his half smiles before heading to the door.

"I love you too, Faolán," I called after him.

He dipped his chin, then left.

I trudged to my bedroom, scrubbing my hands over my face. I was going to have to tidy as best I could tomorrow, then formulate a major apology to the cleaning staff. Gifts, a bonus, an extra day off—nothing quite seemed enough.

When I dropped into bed, those thoughts drifted away, and I called for the lights to fade.

In the darkness, I reached for the other side of the bed, but there was nothing.

4

KAT

Wherever I was led, I went. I was vaguely aware of the lavish decoration, though everything seemed to float past, not quite real, not quite obeying the laws of gravity.

Then again, laws seemed unimportant when Cyrus had done this... when he was now *King* Cyrus.

I managed to paste a faint smile in place, like I wasn't concerned about being in Dawn's side of the palace. Like this would all be fine and I was perfectly safe because I trusted my host implicitly and there was no reason for them not to trust me.

All perfectly fine.

Everything was absolutely, entirely, positively, utterly fucking fine.

But my heart knew the truth, hammering too hard and too fast, making it feel like something was caught in my throat. Or maybe I was going to be sick.

Still, I smiled, and I walked.

Cyrus caught up with our little procession of guards and guests, swaggering to the front. The golden crown of Dawn glistened under the fae lights. He hadn't been officially crowned yet, but that didn't seem to matter—he wore it, and I had to admit, he wore it well.

This was reality, a glint of it breaking through my stupor.

I fixed my gaze on that glittering metal, and gripped my hands hard even though it crushed my fingers painfully against Bastian's ring. I clung on to those reminders of reality. I couldn't afford to go away, however tempting it might be.

Maybe the new king felt my gaze, because he glanced back and when he caught me staring, he smiled. Sharp, white teeth shone almost as much as his crown.

I dipped my head—an obedient girl who didn't dare be so bold as to meet a king's eye.

Obedience would serve me well here. I could retreat to those well-worn paths.

Out the corner of my eye, I spotted the old king's assistant, Adra, slip into place at Cyrus's side and say something.

"The time?" Cyrus's voice filled the corridor as he tossed his head. "Why the hells should I give a damn about the time?"

"Your *Majesty*, the Sleep." Her ashy blond hair bobbed as she widened her eyes at him.

"Fucking Sleep." He stopped and spun on his heel, giving us a dazzling smile. "My dearest guests, forgive my terrible hosting, but I must leave you now. I am sure you will all be most *intrigued* by all that Dawn Court has to offer." He spread his hands as if welcoming us to a party rather than to a prison, and his gaze paused its passage over the group, resting on me. Without looking away, he angled his mouth to Adra's ear and murmured something.

Particular attention. On me. Shit.

If he realised I knew he was the one who'd killed his father, I was dead.

So I forced my smile a little wider, a little brighter, and told myself it was a good thing when he gave Adra an approving nod before sweeping away.

My churning stomach kept me anchored in the here and now as Adra led us through the corridors. We passed pale servants and courtiers whose red-rimmed eyes revealed they'd been crying.

They were in mourning... and they were also in danger, even if they didn't realise.

Cyrus had staged this attack. He'd had all those people killed—*his own* people. All in order to kill his father and take the throne. What was it—he'd grown bored of waiting?

Whatever his reasons, these fae were expendable in his eyes.

How long would it take their numbers to rebuild after today?

My chest cracked at the memory of Bastian's sorrow as he'd told me about their wars, the lives lost, and how their population had never recovered. I could see his face, the grief in it, the desperation to never allow something like that to happen again.

Meanwhile, Cyrus did this and was all smiles and swagger.

"Katherine? Katherine Ferrers?"

It took a moment to yank myself out of my racing thoughts and realise we'd stopped. The other "guests" parted so Adra could look up from her notebook to me. "You'll be in here for tonight."

A servant opened the door as Adra turned to another guest and assigned them the room opposite.

I was ushered inside, the lock clunked behind me, and like that, I was alone in Dawn.

Darkness obscured the room, and I blinked into it, welcoming the nothingness after the day's sensory clamour.

But it was short-lived as a familiar voice came from outside. "I'm here to see Lady Katherine."

Caelus?

"Let me through."

"I'm afraid not," a woman replied. "The prince—uh, the *king* has said they're not to have any visitors."

A glimmer of hope kindled in me. "Caelus," I called through the door.

"Katherine?"

Metal clinked outside—I recognised the sound of spears clashing together, and I could picture guards blocking his way.

"Sun and Stars, I'm not about to break in there, you idiots," he huffed. "Calm yourselves. I'm sure His Majesty's orders didn't specify she couldn't speak to someone through a door, did they?"

A moment's silence, followed by Caelus, "I thought not." Then, louder, "Are you all right?"

Despite the hope lighting in me, calming my nerves, I bit my tongue. Could he be an ally in Dawn? Possibly?

He'd helped me before. So, probably?

Then again, I had given him *arianmêl* and taken advantage of its effects to get answers about unCavendish's pearlwort necklace.

Either way, anything I said now would be heard by the

guards and anyone else close by. This wasn't the time to seek comfort and confess my fears.

"I'm... I'm fine."

But that word broke me.

It was as though saying it let all the adrenaline seep away at last, leaving my body shaking, throat closing.

I was alone. Separated from Bastian and my friends by a different plane of reality.

I was trapped. Penned in with Cyrus and gods knew how many fae who hated Bastian and had no doubt seen us dance today.

I was unsafe. Perhaps the most unsafe I'd been in my entire life.

Because these were fae. They'd had centuries to dream up cruelties I couldn't imagine. They had power that made my magic seem like a pathetic candle flame against an inferno. They could only be killed by iron, aconite, or fae-worked weapons, while there were a thousand inventive methods that could end my life.

"If you're sure?" Caelus called back. "I'll speak to His Majesty—I'm sure he'll let me see you."

"Great. Night." I couldn't form any more of a reply with that, fighting against the way my chest wanted to gasp every breath as I pushed my palms against the door.

Hardness. The wood. *Focus on those things. What can you feel? What can you see?* It was Bastian's voice in my head.

The smooth lacquer. Dampness on my cheeks.

Three more things. That would bring me back from this spiral.

I sucked in a breath, held it, then managed to choke out, "*Lumis*." Fae lights sprang into existence.

Moss green carpet. Gold-green trim on the door, the colour of aspen leaves.

I managed to take a steadier breath, then another, before pushing away from the door and hugging myself tightly.

My arms around myself, hands squeezing my biceps.

Five things. Real. Here. Now. Like Bastian had showed me when I'd been so afraid and broken in his rooms back in Lunden.

I needed him to wrap me in a towel and squeeze me close. I needed to know he was nearby, ready to tell a rude aristocrat to keep my name out of his mouth. I needed...

I needed *him*.

But...

That was impossible. A powerless wish.

He wasn't here.

I took a long breath and held it.

Perhaps I could channel him—do for myself the things he would. I squeezed myself tighter and nodded.

He would check the room over like he had on our journey to the Lady of the Lake. Entrances, exits, spy holes.

I should do that.

A yawn seized me and weariness swept in from a day of...

I scrubbed my too hot eyes. The wedding, the attack, discovering King Lucius dying, helping Bastian search the palace for attackers... the throne room. Had that really been just one day?

I would do my security check after a moment sitting down —that wouldn't do any harm. It was a small bedroom, though carefully decorated in shades of cream and green. The bed at its centre called to me. I sat on the edge, unable to stop myself sighing as the covers puffed up around me, making it feel like I sank deeper and deeper with each second.

Just a moment's rest, I told myself as I yawned and kicked off my shoe.

5
KAT

I woke up on top of the covers, one shoe still on, the curtains open to the rising sun.

So much for a quick rest.

Rubbing my eyes, I checked the room. It was small, simple, almost plain—certainly nothing special. No hidden doorways or spy holes, just a door to a small chamber with a toilet and sink. Maybe I wasn't being given special attention.

That suited me. Keep my head down and stay out of trouble until this was all over.

I was washing over the sink when servants arrived and set out breakfast. Amongst the fruit and pastries, I found an invitation to a month of celebrations of King Cyrus. It started today with tea accompanied by the other guests and some select members of Dawn Court.

Who knew being held hostage could be so civilised?

They also delivered a chest of clothing, though it wasn't my own. It contained gowns in various shades of pale lilac and pink—pretty, but the colours made me look sickly.

I dug through the whole chest before I found a sap green dress. I put that on, tidied my hair, and paused at the door of my room, tugging at the neckline.

Since arriving at Riverton Palace all those months ago, I'd grown used to revealing clothes. But this gown was a little too small and much too long, like it had been made for a tall fae woman, rather than a short human one. I'd pinned the skirts, creating a cascading effect that seemed almost deliberate. With each movement of my shoulders, I had the distinct and unpleasant feeling my tits were about to burst out.

Ariadne and Blaze were truly masters of their art if they could make daring outfits for my generous bust without the danger of it spilling over.

The back of my nose tickled. How long would it be before I could see Ari? Sitting in her atelier while she worked and Rose chatted and Fluffy lay across my feet, warming my toes. It might be a simple pleasure, but it was one I longed for.

I swallowed back another useless wish and set off.

At once, a guard in pale whispering grey fell into step at my shoulder, and when I threw her a glance, I recognised the sharp look she returned. Amandine—the fae who'd tried to stop us crossing the bridge into the palace my first day in Luminis.

Great.

Brusquely, she informed me that she'd been assigned for my safety and would be accompanying me everywhere. She looked far too pleased when she said "everywhere."

Ah, so she was the kind of "guard" assigned to keep an eye on me as much as to keep me safe.

Every gesture was sharp, and I could feel the way her gaze pierced me as we walked on. The scene at the bridge wasn't a one off. She hated Bastian and, by extension, me. I'd find no help here—probably not in Dawn, full stop. Caelus might've tried to see me, but he would soon realise being my ally would bring him nothing but trouble.

My only hope lay with the other guests from Dusk.

I tried not to tug at my dress. It was a losing battle as the sleeves rode up to my armpits and the waist rucked up, made for someone whose body was longer than mine, their arms more slender.

By the time we reached the room where tea was being served, it felt like I was fighting my own skin, stuck in a misery of discomfort.

It's the clothes that are wrong, not you. I tried to remind myself, but it felt like reality didn't agree.

Still, I plastered a smile on my face as the door opened. It was like Bastian had warned me—*your heart is your greatest weakness.* Any sign of a chink in my armour and they'd peck at it until I was dead.

Instead, I sauntered in—my gait designed to avoid making the neckline bust open (*bust* being the operative), but it made me look unhurried and confident.

Time to make some alliances.

I was embarrassed to admit I hadn't taken in much about them yesterday, but I had the chance to rectify that now.

As I smiled around the room and found five cool looks undressing me, assessing me, calculating how much I was worth, I realised my mistake.

From Dusk or not, they would sell me out to secure their own release.

At best, they feared I would do the same to them.

A petite man with hair almost as dark as Bastian's leant in to the woman at his side and whispered something. Watching me, she nodded, and the way her top lip curled took me back to the party the Night Queen had held in my honour.

Oathbreaker. I'd heard someone say it and Bastian's name on the same breath, but hadn't been able to identify the speaker at the time. But in the crowd, I'd spotted this woman, lip curled in the same way. I would bet my estate she was the one who'd uttered the insult.

Keep his name out of your mouth. I wanted to hiss it in her face, maybe lace the words with a touch of poison, but...

No. Head down. No trouble. Inoffensive and unnoticeable. That was my best strategy. Especially as there would be no easy alliances.

And joy, the sisters with rose gold hair who'd been part of Dawn's contingent in Albion were here too. The elder one had removed my pearlwort necklace, leaving me delirious from Bastian's charm—not a night I cared to remember. Now she murmured something to her sister, who gave me a cruel smile, which I returned tenfold. They were not the kind of allies I needed.

Then I spotted a face in the corner that made my stomach turn. Uncle Rufus.

Uncle fucking Rufus.

He smiled like a chess player whose opponent had just made the fatal mistake that would win him the game.

I glanced at my guard—surely she'd step in if he touched me or I looked suitably distressed? She waited by the door, eyes fixed ahead.

Maybe not.

Surely he wouldn't try anything in front of so many people. I was safe... *ish.*

So, I approached a table laden with pots of tea and coffee, cups and saucers. There was even a sugar dish in the shape of a fish pond, complete with a red and white carp poking its head up out of the sugar. On smaller side tables stood cake stands covered in tiny savoury and sweet pastries and an array of cakes.

"Good morning." I nodded to the group as I took a clean cup and poured myself coffee with sugar and a generous dose of cream.

One of the Dusk guests with violet hair, and a couple of the Dawn fae nodded back, barely glancing my way. The two remaining Dusk guests, a woman with an eye patch and a fae with startling lilac eyes, continued their stilted conversation about the decoration on the tea service. I could feel the edges of their attention on me, and as I sipped my coffee, I caught the woman stealing a glance over the rim of her cup. The younger of the rose-gold-haired sisters watched me. Her nails had been filed into points, which tapped against her cup.

I firmly ignored my uncle.

At least there was cake.

I perched at the end of a chaise longue with my coffee and a small but carefully balanced plate. I'd chosen coffee sponge, lemon drizzle cake, and a small raspberry tart topped with cream and gold leaf. No one eyed how full my plate was.

Yes, I will have my cake and bloody well eat it, thank you very much.

When the tea service conversation sputtered out, one of the men from Dawn nodded into the silence and I could practically see him searching for a topic. "The wedding yesterday was... quite something."

Murmurs of agreement filled the room. One of the Dawn fae seized upon the topic, running through the particulars of the music and the ceremony, the clothing and decor, the choice of an eclipse day.

Somehow, she avoided the topic of how the wedding had ended. I let myself drift away on the comforting sing-song of her voice, the rest of the world fading.

This place, this situation—they weren't safe. Especially with the lack of allies and an enemy on the throne. Make that enemies on both thrones. If Braea hadn't volunteered me to go to Dawn, she at least hadn't protested when Cyrus had asked. She'd been only too happy to see me go.

I needed to speak to Bastian. Not about Braea. I wasn't sure how to explain the way I *felt* her enmity in a facial expression, or heard it between the lines of an apparently innocent conversation about her daughter Nyx. But he didn't know about Cyrus and I couldn't trust that information to a message. I needed to get away from here and back to him.

Maybe that wasn't far enough. I could run away to the estate. Its quiet solitude was certainly appealing. It was mine, for now at least. The queen still hadn't responded to news of Robin's death to say it *wasn't*, and there was no word about surviving relatives.

If my guard was always going to wait outside my bedroom as she had this morning, I could climb out the window. I'd go to Bastian and beg him to leave. He could come and live with me on the estate. Or we could sell it and buy our own.

As long as I could escape, I didn't care.

The chaise longue dipped, pulling me from my plans.

"My dear niece, we have some matters we need to discuss." Uncle Rufus smoothed the wool of his trousers, voice dipping below the rest of the room's conversation. "If I didn't know better, I'd say you've been avoiding me."

I swallowed, mouth suddenly dry. An obedient niece didn't avoid her uncle, especially not if she wanted to escape punishment.

But I wasn't sure how much obedience was left in Katherine Ferrers anymore. Maybe I'd used it all up obeying Bastian when it was my choice and to my benefit.

Still, the chill in Uncle Rufus's voice made the cakes left on my plate about as appetising as stale biscuits iced with sabrecat shit.

"Uncle Rufus," I managed to say around the lump in my throat, "I'm sure you and Father taught me better than that."

"I'm sure we did." His gaze drilled into me, though I couldn't meet it. "At least now we're both in the same court—*together*, as family belongs."

Meaning, I wasn't only stuck with Cyrus, but with him. My coffee threatened to make a reappearance.

"Speaking of family," he went on, "in light of your husband's untimely death, we need to discuss Markyate Cell."

My cup clattered in its saucer as I jolted upright, though the arrival of more guests smothered the noise. "My estate?"

An instant's wrinkling of his nose told me he didn't like hearing it called that. No, it was easier for him to think of a dead man owning it than a living woman.

The rebellious part of me grew bold, and I found myself saying, "What could we possibly need to discuss about *my estate*?"

His nostrils twitched and the redness flaring over his cheeks was a warning flag, making my throat tight.

"Lady Katherine," a bright voice cut through my uncle's stiff silence. "What a gorgeous dress!" Zita stood over us, a wide smile in place, though something sharp glinted in her dark eyes. "There's room for me, isn't there?" Before either of us could answer, she inserted herself in the gap between Rufus and me.

"Princess Zita." I bowed my head.

"None of that, Katherine." She squeezed my thigh. "It's still just Zita. Though perhaps I can call you Kat now?"

"Of course." I barely got out the words before she was fingering the neckline of my gown, touch skimming my bust.

"Such lovely fabric. One of Ariadne's creations? I heard she dressed you almost exclusively."

At the far end of the chaise longue, on the other side of Uncle Rufus, stood Prince Sepher. Folding his arms, he rolled his eyes and muttered, "Are all human women like this?"

I wasn't sure how to answer Zita. Admitting I didn't have my own clothes could be an admission of weakness. Ari was known for sewing spells into cloth—if everyone thought my dresses were made by her, they might think twice before crossing me.

But Zita was known for her taste and style. She'd spent years on the stage, where it was her job to be looked at—she had to see this dress didn't fit.

In which case, the compliments were false. Though there was no barb in her tone, like I was the butt of a joke. Then what was she up to?

Uncle Rufus muttered to Sepher about the flighty frippery of women.

The prince made noncommittal sounds in return. His comment didn't match with what I'd seen of his behaviour with his wife. Wearing a hunter green shirt that perfectly suited his colouring with a neckline cut low to show off his physique, he obviously cared about his appearance.

Had they stepped in to save me from Rufus? Or was it simply that now I was away from Bastian, Zita hoped I would take her up on her earlier offer to join them in bed?

If the latter, letting them think it was possible might win me the allies I needed in Dawn—powerful ones, at that.

I smiled as Zita continued her very hands-on examination of my gown. "Not on this occasion. I thought one of Ariadne's creations might be overkill for tea."

She laughed, waving a hand at Sepher and blocking Rufus out in one movement. "You see, my love? I told you she was a fucking delight."

Perhaps this *was* a rescue attempt. Uncle Rufus certainly looked pissed off.

I was laughing politely as a delicate *ahem* sounded at my shoulder.

Adra, once King Lucius's assistant, and now apparently King Cyrus's, inclined her head. "Katherine." A pleasant smile curved her lips, but her eyes retained a professional disinterest. "You are required."

Saved from Uncle Rufus, but was I now in trouble with the king?

6

KAT

As Adra led me away from tea with my guard trailing us, I wondered about Zita's potential help and what it might mean. Hadn't I been searching for an ally? But could she and Sepher be trusted? He was Cyrus's brother, after all.

We weaved through corridors, not heading back to my rooms, I soon realised. Although there was something familiar about the route. I must've gone through this part of the palace during the attack.

We passed servants cleaning rooms, removing broken furniture and supervising mops that seemed to move on their own. The lilting hum of their magic spilled from open doorways into the hall.

At last we reached a set of double doors that opened into an antechamber containing a huge gilt mirror. Leaving my guard outside, Adra led me in. "His Majesty apologises for the lowly condition of your accommodation last night."

So these were his personal rooms—that explained the

oversized mirror. I could picture him practising heroic poses in front of it.

As funny as I found the image, he was king now, and all the more dangerous. I swallowed and straightened, preparing for a private audience with His Majesty. Appear the calm, unthreatening human woman. Nothing more. Nothing less.

Adra continued into a sitting room furnished in shades of cream, with marble panelled walls veined gold and pink. If there had been any doubt I stood in Dawn's side of the palace, the fireplace would've quashed it. Made of the same marble, it dominated one wall of the room, carved rays spreading from the pink-tinged fire, like it was the rising sun.

Certainly grand enough for a fae king, and for once I was grateful for the strict teaching of my father and countless governesses, as it helped me avoid fidgeting.

"We had to vacate their previous occupants, but new rooms have now been prepared, which we trust will meet with your approval." Adra spread her arms in presentation.

I smiled. I blinked. I slowly, horribly understood.

These were *my* rooms.

Not the cosy little room that spelled out how unimportant and barely noticeable I was, but an entire suite, lavishly decorated. She started to explain how it had two bedrooms, a study, a private dining room, and three well-appointed bathrooms.

I swallowed down my heart, which was trying to punch its way out of my throat with each beat. Magic tingled over my skin, though I held my power on a tight leash. "The king is far, far too generous. This isn't necessary. I'm sure—"

"I'm sure Lady Katherine will get almost as much pleasure from her using these rooms as I will." Cyrus's voice came from behind me, making even my clamouring heart fall still for a long moment. "That will be all, Adra. I can show the lady around. Besides, we have a small matter to discuss."

"Your Majesty," I managed to say on a breath as I turned to him and bowed. I kept that pleased and appeasing smile on my face—unCavendish had enjoyed my fear and I had a feeling Cyrus was the same. If I showed any, it would only encourage him to try to frighten me further.

I had to play the part of the perfect guest.

"It is such a pleasure to see you here, Katherine." He smirked down at me. Power hummed from him—the tingling I'd felt earlier—far more than before, like he was gaining strength now he ruled Dawn.

"Allow me to show you around. I chose this suite for you, especially." With a glint in his eye, he led the way, seeming to watch me expectantly.

To appease him, I widened my eyes at the size of the rooms and exclaimed over the decoration, though I preferred the cosiness of Dusk's side of the palace. Dawn was too bright, too light, too much like a great cloud that I might drift away on and never come back.

All the while, something crawled along at the back of my mind. Something familiar about the space, something in the look he gave me.

"And this completes the tour." He spread his arms, standing at the centre of the main bedroom.

The strange sensation crawled down my spine as I eyed the huge bed with its gauzy drapes.

"It's beautiful. Your Majesty does me too high an honour— such a gorgeous suite of rooms *and* a personal tour. I'm sure I'm not deserving of such attention." I looked down, perfectly humble.

"Oh, but you are, aren't you?" With a slow smile, he sauntered closer. "You're special in so many ways—kept by the Night Queen's Shadow, a human who not only survived poison, but gained magic. Quite incredible."

In the long pause that followed, I could feel his close attention, but I didn't dare return it. I'd used my gift enough that it was no surprise the news had reached him. Though I noted he considered me "kept" by Bastian rather than some other word like "beloved."

"Which brings me to that small matter." He reached into his inside pocket and produced a flat box, similar in shape to a jewellery box, except this wasn't covered in velvet but a dull, grey metal. It clunked open, more like a prison lock than a trinket box, and revealed a solid, hinged bracelet and a tiny key. He stiffened and took a long breath.

Then I felt it. The taint of iron.

Even coated in silver, it made my magic scatter, agitated. My chest constricted.

"I'm sure you understand why I can't take any chances with such a... deadly power in my court."

He meant to block my magic.

"Of course, Your Majesty." My voice sounded remarkably level.

"Then allow me to do the honours. Just to be sure it's secure."

I held out my wrist, fixing the smile on my lips, while he donned gloves and removed the bracelet from the case. With a soft *click*, it fastened around my wrist, and the constant vibration of magic around me vanished. It was like I suddenly couldn't hear, and I found myself swallowing, trying to make my ears pop.

He turned the tiny key, causing another *clunk-click*, then

smiled. "*There.*" His shoulders sank, and I was shocked to read relief on his face.

For all I'd been putting on a show, hiding my fear, he'd...

It seemed ridiculous, but he'd been afraid of me. He knew I could poison him with a thought. Maybe I should have done so —fuck the consequences.

Except that would most likely lead to war between Dusk and Dawn—not to mention my own death.

He held up the key and inspected it. "Such a little thing, yet so important." His gaze slid to me. "And now it's *mine.*" He dropped the key into his inside pocket and patted it. "I'll be sure to keep it close."

Sickness rose in my stomach, and I barely had time to mutter "Excuse me" before running to the bathroom to throw up. How had I grown used to this disgusting stuff before?

After splashing water on my face, I emerged. Cyrus wandered around the bedroom, touching the chest of clothes that had been brought from my previous room, running his fingers over the hairbrush on the dressing table.

I swallowed down another wave of nausea as he fingered a silky dressing robe set over the back of a chair. I could deal with the iron. I'd done it before and could do it again. With deep breaths, I pushed away the twisting sensation in my stomach—it was a distant thing that didn't matter.

"The perfect room for the Serpent's little human." Cyrus flashed me another sharp smile before sauntering over to one of the high windows.

Daylight haloed his golden hair and crown, gilding his skin. I couldn't deny it was a breathtaking sight, but hadn't I always known? Fae were at their most dangerous when they were most beautiful.

That earlier urge to run away hit me again. I could climb

out the window, grab Vespera from the stables, and ride south over the border.

Except then I'd be in Albion. My uncle could easily follow me, and Robin might be dead, but that place was full of men like him.

How many women hadn't managed to find that piece of broken glass? How many had been killed by their own Robins?

Once again, I couldn't change my circumstances, only survive them. I only ever moved from one pile of shit to another. And Cyrus was just the latest.

Running away to Albion wasn't the answer. It was just as dangerous as Elfhame. Neither kingdom kept its people safe.

What had Sura said? Peace had a cost, paid by those it didn't serve.

Then again, violence had a cost, too, I realised as I watched Cyrus gazing out over the city he'd gained through it.

The problem was the people on the thrones—or the thrones themselves. Perhaps Sura was right—the system was broken here and in Albion.

As though he could feel my stare, the king turned. "That's an intent look." His eyelids lowered, smugness clear in his smirk as he lounged on the windowsill.

He thought I was enjoying the view *of him*.

I managed to avoid wrinkling my nose—barely. "Ever since I got here and learned about the palace's unique construction, I've been wondering—what happens if you climb out a window?"

He made a soft sound of surprise. "Planning to escape my hospitality so soon?"

I laughed like I'd be foolish to do such a thing. "More wondering how safe I am when my guard waits at the door.

Someone could climb in. Or, if they were particularly daring, leap out of a Dusk window and in through this one."

"I wouldn't recommend it. They aren't structured lodestones. Your body would pass through an unstable channel between the different planes. It's sturdy enough to admit fresh air and light, hence being able to see Luminis." He gestured at the spires outside. "As you pointed out, making all the windows stable passages would be a security risk."

"So, what would happen to your body?" The risk just might be worth it.

"You'd be forced through the gaps in the planes. Best-case scenario, you might get through unscathed, but that would be a miracle. Worst-case scenario, you would be disintegrated."

I swallowed. "And middle scenario?"

"*Bits* of you would be disintegrated. Chopped up by fragments of the veil between the planes, like meat through a grinder. No, more like something soft forced through mesh." He said it impassively, despite how horrifying it sounded.

He glanced out the window, giving me a chance to wipe my sweaty palms against my gown and breathe past the sickly feeling in my stomach.

"Well," he said at last and rose from his perch on the windowsill, "I have important, kingly things to do as I'm sure Adra is dying to remind me. But I trust you find these rooms much more fitting for such an esteemed guest." He smiled, not quite benevolent, not quite smug. He gestured towards the window. "I thought you'd appreciate having a familiar view. I'll leave you to enjoy it."

He nodded, and I barely managed a bow before he swept out, my mind still caught on what he'd just said.

I stalked towards the window and it was as though the spires outside pierced my chest and not just the sky.

Because I knew this view from the palace.

Two sides, both identical, divided only by the thinnest barrier. You could be in the library in our version of the palace at the same time someone else is in Dawn's library, and you'd never know the other person was there. The same space but on different planes.

These were Bastian's rooms—the Dawn version of them, anyway. He could be standing right next to me in Dusk and neither of us would ever know.

7

BASTIAN

The sun beat down on the square before the royal balcony, like it knew today, Cyrus's first public appearance as king, was a day for Dawn Court. The Convocation had met and agreed he'd make a short, reassuring speech, followed by the most influential folk gathering in the throne room to pledge fealty to him. It was all designed to show his power and support, deterring anyone who might move against a brand new king.

Boring but necessary, and entirely in the way of me working on my plan to get Kat home.

I scowled in the shade that pooled along the balcony's edge. My shadows hazed like mist, partially obscuring me. Below, Dusk fae gathered in clusters, wide gaps between them and those from Dawn Court. Each threw mistrustful glances at the other. The air felt prickly, making those looks palpable.

Even members of the Convocation had grouped by court. The Chancellor and the Marshal of the City near me. The Mistress of the Vault, the Master of Magic, and the Marshal of the Field stood over in the sun. Mouth a tight, thin line, Elthea stationed herself off to one side, not far from where Sepher towered over almost everyone else, including Zita.

Faolán guarded the doors to Dusk. Asher, as one of the last remaining members of our royal family, was beside me, showing we stood in solidarity with Dawn. On my other side, Ella and Perry represented Albion and the Pirate Queen, respectively—more solidarity in case accusing eyes should turn to them.

At last, the doors from Dawn swung open to great fanfare and out swept Cyrus, hair blazing even brighter than usual, while his retinue followed. Amongst them, flaming red hair snagged my attention, even though it was barely visible past the taller fae.

My entire being strained towards her, looking for every little gap between the bodies that I might snake through to find clear air between us. My shadows slithered through the crowd, but I yanked them back before they got far.

Never reveal your heart.

I chanted the words in my mind and forced my gaze away from trying to catch a glimpse of her face. He'd brought her and the other guests here. Why?

His eyes narrowed as he searched amongst his retinue. With a slow smile, he said something I couldn't hear, but it looked like, "There you are." He disappeared for a moment and emerged with Kat, his hand at the small of her back as he paraded her across the balcony.

Every muscle in my body coiled so tight, I thought they would pop clean off my bones.

I stood there, rigid, torn between wanting to stride over and tear him apart with my shadows and hands and the need to not murder a reigning monarch.

She looked pale in a pinkish shade of lilac, but she held her head high, and my heart could've exploded from pride. She was strong. The fear of what Dawn might do hadn't broken her.

I would get her home soon. I *would.*

She skimmed the crowd gathered in the lodestone and my chest seized when she found me. I wanted to ask if she was all right, but all I could do was widen my eyes in question. She nodded, once, small, and my heart fractured that bit more to see her so contained.

I flinched as something jabbed me in the ribs.

"Can you *please* stop fucking her with your eyeballs?" Ella hissed.

I tore my attention away. *Play the game. Pretend she doesn't matter. Remember who you are.*

"She seems remarkably calm," Perry whispered.

That was my Kat. She only had to keep this up a little longer. I'd woken in the night with a plan that would bring her home in a matter of days. Not a rescue, but something that used the rules to our benefit. Something Cyrus would never see coming.

Reaching the balustrade, Cyrus waved and tossed his head, sending sun sparkling off his crown. He wore white with a grey sash and belt—a nod to mourning, while still looking bright and shining like some mythical knight.

Classic Cyrus, making a show. I stopped myself from rolling my eyes. Barely.

The other guests huddled to one side, close to the balustrade. Below, the folk from Dawn seemed to calm a little, as though the sight of the hostages was a welcome reminder that Dusk wasn't going to be allowed to get away with this.

"Good people of Luminis—*and* Tenebris." Even from the

side, his smile was dazzling as he surveyed his people—his city. "I stand before you as your new king to reassure you that the events of earlier this week will not be allowed to happen again. And your friends, family, loved ones—*our* people—they *will* be avenged."

Much as charm didn't work on other fae, Cyrus had a kind of glamour to him, and the crowd below raised their voices, under his sway. This was what they wanted from a king—someone who stood in the sun and looked every inch the hero.

When their cheers died down, he went on, explaining a version of events at his brother's wedding, "in order to quell rumours and mistruths." The attackers were described as "dark-haired."

"Hmm." Asher bent closer and whispered, "No mention of hair dye?"

I glanced over at Elthea. She kept her eyes squarely on Cyrus, but her lips pressed together.

"Apparently not. Question is, did she keep quiet to protect Dawn or did she report it and someone above silenced her?"

"She reports directly to Mored, so..." Asher spread his hands as we both glanced at the Master of Magic.

"Or someone above him." I indicated the new king. Did he know about the dye and was keeping quiet? "It would be useful to know where the information was cut off." It would tell me who my enemies were—those willing to sacrifice the truth in order to protect Dawn. Even those who might be involved in the conspiracy to impersonate Sura's organisation.

Cyrus continued painting a picture of a bloodthirsty attack on the palace designed to destroy the entire Dawn royal family.

"Well done, by the way," Asher murmured.

I cocked my head in question.

"You didn't leap on Kat the instant you saw her and only needed a little reminder from Ella."

I scowled at his teasing. "This isn't the time."

"I'm serious. It's hard to hide how you really feel."

He wasn't wrong.

I itched as Cyrus went on and on, conveniently leaving out the hair dye. If I said anything, it would look like I was grasping at straws, desperately trying to point my finger back at Dawn to protect Dusk. Tensions were high enough already. Instead, I gritted my teeth and made a mental note to visit Elthea.

Inwardly, I groaned as Cyrus painted himself as an injured hero. Had the crown made him more insufferable? I never thought it possible, but here we were five minutes into his speech and no end in sight.

"If you had to guess, who from Dawn would you say stood to gain from Lucius's death?" I leant close to Asher, voice little more than a breath. My own thoughts were too busy and far from unbiased.

"Is this a hypothetical or do you have reason to think they're more nefariously involved than the picture His Majesty is painting? Something to do with this elusive hair dye you mentioned, perhaps?"

"Just indulge me."

"Well, who's already gained the most?" His gaze flicked to Cyrus. "But that might be too obvious—son kills father, leaps on his throne. I'd like to think even Dawn is more subtle than that." He shrugged. "Perhaps it's a longer game. It's brought Prince Sepher a step closer to the throne. Though I'm not sure that's something he wants."

With only his profile visible, Sepher gazed out over the city, eyes half closed. He certainly looked disinterested.

"Newly married." I made a thoughtful sound. "And to a human."

"Much more likely to produce heirs—secure the royal line."

I found myself nodding. He seemed to have genuine feelings for Zita, but that didn't mean she wasn't *also* an advantageous marriage choice. "Could be part of a play for the throne."

"Mm-hmm. It'll be interesting to see if Cyrus marries quickly for the same reason. If he gets an heir in place, it pushes his brother further back in line. If not for the throne, why else might someone want Lucius out of the way?"

An excellent question.

I scanned those gathered on the balcony—the most influential people in the realm. The Mistress of the Vault and the Marshal of the Field stood close together, having their own whispered conversation.

"Members of the Convocation?"

Asher twitched at my side. "I suppose they'd keep their position no matter who's king."

Barring treason or some other major disgrace, their seats were for life. "And they might see Cyrus as easier to manage than his father."

"The self-indulgent prince could easily become a puppet king, giving them more de facto power. *Interesting.*"

"Then there could be a more personal angle." I stood straighter, shoulders easing as my mind whirred along familiar paths—strategic and logical, rather than seeing only Cyrus and my rage at him. "See if you can find out about Lucius's enemies in his own court." I would ask my spy to do some digging of her own.

Cyrus spread his arms and the crowd fell into an expectant hush. "It's obvious Hydra Ascendant was responsible for this attack, but rest assured, your new king is a man of action.

Where my predecessor stood still, not keeping his people safe from threats, *I* will not allow our enemies to get away with their crimes."

Asher winced and inwardly, I did the same.

Oblivious to the stir rippling through those gathered, Cyrus went on. "With immediate effect, membership of Hydra Ascendant is forbidden, as is the display of any and all hydra iconography."

I kept my face still, but my spine stiffened. This wasn't part of the agreed announcement. I glanced at the other Convocation members, but they watched him, expressions as neutral as mine.

How did he plan to enforce such a law? It wasn't like Ascendants carried membership papers.

"Furthermore," he intoned, voice deepening, "there shall be no unsanctioned gatherings of more than six people in private dwellings, and no groups of more than four in public."

I suppressed a groan. This was even less enforceable.

"These measures are to keep you safe, preventing treasonous elements from meeting and plotting against us." He pulled his shoulders back, no longer the foolish prince playing at soldier. "Be clear, good people of Luminis, it was my father who was killed, but Hydra Ascendant mean harm to our very way of life. You saw how many were taken from us that day— we still mourn them."

Below, the crowd murmured and nodded.

"And Hydra Ascendant aren't the only ones to face justice. No." Solemnly, he shook his head, pausing for effect. "There was treachery in the throne room that day. You are aware that I myself did not escape unscathed." He rested one hand on his side like his injury was still causing him pain.

What a pile of shit—he'd been healed perfectly, without so much as a scar left.

"My own servant and onetime friend, Krae, stabbed me in that very room, spilling my blood upon the sacred marble floor."

From one side, I caught his bitter smile. "But then again, that's what you get for trusting a shapechanger."

The crowd's muttering rose, though I couldn't tell if it was in agreement or opposition. As Cyrus announced an astronomical bounty on Krae's head, I had to force my head not to turn to Faolán. It would only draw attention to him.

"Furthermore," Cyrus went on, "to counter the enemy in our midst, all shapechangers will register in this book."

With perfect timing, a plinth drifted forward, and Adra placed a huge ledger upon it. The thud silenced all whispers on the balcony.

"It will allow us to ensure they adhere to a strict curfew."

Blaming all shapechangers? And a curfew just for them? Even more untenable than the gatherings. How were people supposed to live and work with that? Faolán was going to lose his mind. I made a note to take him to the training yard so he could take it out on an unsuspecting practice dummy.

Truth be told, I could do with blowing off steam, since throwing Cyrus off the balcony was out of the question.

"And, of course, not even my family is above the law. Therefore, the first name in the ledger will be my own brother's." Cyrus stepped aside with a flourish and let the plinth float into place between him and Sepher.

The air stilled as Sepher's yellow eyes bored into him. Zita was a statue.

My pulse sped, readying my body for action. At my side, Asher stiffened, and Perry adjusted her stance. I caught a glimpse of Kat, partially blocked by Cyrus. She fiddled with something on her wrist, and I had to clench my fists against the need to get her away from the royal brothers.

"You understand, in light of these threats, certain elements of society must be monitored." Cyrus said it so smoothly, it sounded like the most reasonable thing in the world. Again, his voice dropped as he added, "For everyone's safety."

This time, a few of the Convocation members met my gaze. The Marshal of the City shook her head, and the Chancellor's surprise was clear on his face. They hadn't decided this in some secret meeting.

Sepher's tail twitched from side to side before he finally smiled. Though it wasn't a reassuring thing but a ghoulish one, like he'd just pictured exactly how he was going to crack his brother's skull open.

I couldn't blame him.

"Of course it is." Sepher swept up the pen in his clawed fingers and wrote in the ledger under Cyrus's smug scrutiny.

In turn, Zita watched Cyrus unobserved, her dark eyes smouldering. My spies told me she'd tried to assassinate Sepher at their first meeting, and I could well believe it.

She pointed at Cyrus, hand shaking, and hissed, "May you always have the justice you deserve."

On the balcony, silence rang out. The only movement was Cyrus squaring his posture as gazes shifted from Zita to him and back again.

Adra cleared her throat and widened her eyes at Zita, prompting her to explain herself.

Zita gave a half-hearted shrug, then added, "*Your Majesty.*"

Cyrus looked to Adra as though for guidance, a waver in his confident exterior.

No matter who she was married to, I owed Zita. Seeing Cyrus off-balance was a fucking delight.

"Sepher?" he said at last, a faint waver on the second syllable. "What did your wife just do?"

She smiled sweetly. "It's a blessing—ensuring your reign will be as long and just as you deserve."

Sepher spread his hands. "My wife *is* gifted."

"Hmm. Well." Cyrus nodded, as if trying to convince himself that everything was all right. He flashed a brief, stiff smile and backed away as he waved at Sepher to continue filling in the book.

Interesting. All this suggested the tensions between Sepher and Cyrus ran deeper than merely squabbling brothers.

"There." When Sepher finished, Cyrus gestured like this was a job well done.

Applause drifted up from the square below, quieter than earlier.

A flickering frown marked the king's brow, as though the response wasn't as enthusiastic as he'd expected, but it soon disappeared behind another smile. "Who's next?"

Faolán went to step past me, the tightness of his jaw visible through his beard.

I caught his arm and muttered, "Hold off." Stepping forward, I let my shadows sink to my feet. Down in the square, I picked out the groups with Dusk colouring. Their heads lifted, and I felt their attention turn to me.

"Dusk will manage their own registry," I announced. That would buy me time to discuss this with Braea as soon as she was awake tonight. "We wouldn't want Dawn to do all that work alone, especially in a time of mourning. Dusk will gladly carry part of this burden."

It wasn't a cheer, but the voices below rose and many folk

nodded, while a muscle in Cyrus's cheek twitched, even as the smile remained on his face. He couldn't decline such a reasonable offer—not without looking like a tyrant or a fool.

At my side, Faolán made one of his trademark wordless grunts, this one more growly than usual. At least Rose was technically a werewolf—a human who had been changed—and not a shapechanger. That term only applied to fae who were born with the ability. She wouldn't need to register, so I only had one wolf to worry about.

Finally, Cyrus inclined his head. "Such a generous gesture from the Bastard of Tenebris." His smile turned into a sneer for a moment before he turned to the crowd below. "Good people of Luminis and Tenebris, let today's proclamations reassure you that I have your best interests at heart. We will be strong against these threats—whatever that demands."

I bit back a groan. So much for a puppet king.

8
BASTIAN

As the group on the balcony dispersed, my mind was already racing ahead to my report to Braea, though I dared a glance at Kat. The tension ratcheting her polite smile mirrored what was running through my body.

"Well, that went worse than I expected." Asher sighed.

"Absolute shit-show. Let's go home." I turned to go.

"Home?" Cyrus chuckled, and for a moment I thought he'd overheard us, but he was looking from the register to his brother. "You've written your home address in here. You're not planning to leave the palace, are you?"

Catching Asher's arm, I lingered.

Sepher stiffened in that way only a prince who'd rarely been denied could. "Why not?"

"Despite what you are, until I have a child, you're my heir." Cyrus canted his head as if this was all obvious and expected. "And we can't have any harm befalling my *dear brother*, can we? We need to consider safety more than ever after Father's tragic demise."

The shapechanger's shoulders strained against his shirt as he started towards the king, when another voice rose.

"Surely Sepher can go home." From the far side of the balcony approached their mother, Dowager Queen Meredine. She gave an appeasing smile, though her cheeks were pale. Her deep green hair didn't seem as smooth as usual, as though it missed the crown she'd worn for so long. It had been removed after Lucius's death and sat somewhere in the Dawn coffers, awaiting Cyrus's consort. "No harm is going to befall him in his own palace."

"*No harm*? The man was almost assassinated there mere months ago. Or have you forgotten?" Cyrus shook his head, beckoning Adra.

Sepher huffed like the whole thing was ridiculous.

"It wasn't that serious," Meredine tried to argue, but Cyrus's attention was on his assistant.

"She had an iron blade, Mother." He turned back to her with a slow, sad smile and patted her shoulder. "But I can't blame you for not understanding. Adra, kindly ensure my mother is escorted back to her rooms. I've overlooked her care. After all, her husband has just been brutally murdered. The poor woman mustn't be strained with such affairs of state."

A sickly feeling rose in my stomach as Meredine opened her mouth and managed a "but" before guards flanked her. She exhaled, shoulders sinking, and let the guards escort her away.

Fucking hells. Not only was the peace between Dusk and Dawn tenuous, but Dawn was nowhere near as stable as it had been under Lucius. At least he'd known to put on a united front within the royal family and keep their problems private. That was why he'd sent Sepher away when he'd lost the ability to hide his gift. The undesirable trait swept under the carpet.

What a fucking mess.

All we needed now was for Sura to make her move and then we'd have a full house of disasters. It would be perfect timing for her and the worst for us.

Ironic that a fake Hydra Ascendant attack might be the thing to pave the way for the real thing.

"What did you do that for?" Sepher towered over Cyrus now the guards had moved away. "It *wasn't* 'almost.'"

Cyrus eyed Zita, scoffing. "An earnest attempt, though. I'd much rather have you here when I can watch over you personally. For your own safety, of course."

This could be a chance for me to get Sepher out of the way —and owing me a favour.

I sidled over, gritting my teeth as coming face-to-face with Cyrus made my blood simmer. "Your Majesty's concern is commendable, but his palace's remote location makes it easy to secure. He's safer there than he is wandering through Luminis."

Sepher's eyes narrowed as his attention slid from Cyrus to me.

"We *believe* we've cleared the city of attackers," I explained, spreading my hands, "but there's still the possibility some are holed up within the walls."

Smooth smile in place, Cyrus turned to me. "Marwood, you misunderstand," he said louder than was necessary. "I'm confident your attempts in the city have driven away any such threats. However, we've all heard today how one of his kind is responsible for the murder of our beloved father. Anti-shapechanger sentiments are running high. I wouldn't be surprised if there were reprisal attacks. You see, the register isn't just to keep innocent folk safe—it also allows us to keep an eye on shapechangers."

Sepher's jaw went solid, and his hand found its way to Zita's shoulder.

"It would be a shame if something were to happen to you or your lovely wife because a well-meaning but misguided subject thought they could curry favour with me by avenging their late king upon your kind."

It was only then I realised why he was speaking at such a volume. This was a continuation of his announcement.

Sure enough, the three of us were on display, close to the balustrade, and below, the crowd had stopped filing from the square. Hundreds of pinpricks of attention were on us.

The sickly feeling doubled, a knot in my stomach tightening.

This arsehole had just given the idea of attacking shapechangers to anyone who wanted to win his favour, making it even more dangerous for Sepher and Zita... and for every other shapechanger living in the city.

And the register would give them a checklist of names and addresses to work through. It only took one corrupt official or a guard with a grudge—they'd gladly give anyone a look through the pages.

Sepher had gone very still. He understood the barely veiled threat. Zita watched the crowd below, seeming to pick up that this was still part of the show.

"There's no need to worry. I'll take care of you." Cyrus slapped him on the shoulder, a broad smile making his teeth flash in the sunlight as he turned to the city. "I'll take care of you *all.*"

9
KAT

A couple of days after the announcements on the royal balcony, I had dinner with the other guests from Dusk, as well as Cyrus and his favourites from Dawn. Much to their annoyance, he placed *me* at his side, like I was a prize he wanted to show off. The Shadow's human, stolen out from under his nose.

But he still wasn't used to his new limitations as the Day King. It was only when Adra came and reminded him of the time, just as he called for dessert, that he realised the sun was about to set. Cursing, he hurried away.

I suspected he didn't want to fall into his enchanted Sleep in front of us—that would be an unacceptable display of weakness.

After, Amandine and I made our way through the palace without a soul in sight. Until, that was, I turned into the corridor leading to my suite.

For once, I spotted him before he cornered me. Red hair,

tall—for a human. Heart lurching, I stopped dead and ducked out of sight, causing Amandine to give me an odd look.

Uncle Rufus, hanging around near my rooms. Whatever reason he wanted me alone couldn't be good.

"I need you to keep him away," I told her. "He's... dangerous. To me, at least."

She cocked her head, eyes narrowing.

"*Please*," I whispered, throat clenching around the word.

She surveyed me with a frown and eventually inclined her head. "I see." With that, she marched on ahead.

Sagging with relief, I backed away from the corner, unable to stand the sound of my uncle's voice as she caught up to him.

Amandine coming to my rescue. It was quite the contrast with this morning when she'd stopped me leaving the palace to take Vespera for a ride—one that would take me past Kaliban's house and Ariadne's atelier... perhaps even somewhere I could bump into Bastian.

The thought of him was a constant barb. Or perhaps the place where a barb had once been and now was only the tear where it had been pulled out.

I had to turn from that longing, since my attempts to leave the palace had been foiled. I couldn't even leave Dawn's side of the palace. Amandine had blocked me from the grand hall lodestone, stating with a smirk, "King's orders."

I'd hoped Cyrus would at least pretend I was a guest and allow me—

A hand clamped over my mouth. Sharp nails dug in to my cheek as I tried to cry out, but their grip was tight. Pulse pounding, I reached for my magic, but there was nothing.

That fucking bracelet.

When I tried to twist away, something dug into my back, perfectly placed just below my ribcage. I froze.

"There," a feminine voice breathed in my ear. "You understand now. Silence. Obedience. That's all I want from you."

Those two words made my whole body leap to obey. They were etched on my bones.

"*Urgh*." The form behind me shuddered. "Iron." There was a faint rustle, then darkness fell over my eyes. The point of a weapon still against my back, she gripped my arm and compelled me onward.

Had Cyrus sent someone after me? Did he know? If I was killed by an intruder, he could claim innocence—the perfect way to get rid of me.

We walked for several minutes. I strained to listen, but there was no sign of another person or hint of where we were, just the muffled pad of my feet on carpeted floors.

The threat of panic lingered in my throat, a lump I couldn't swallow down.

I tugged on the bracelet, but it held fast.

Definitely no magic.

And no weapons. I yearned for my pistol or bow, for the moth-hilted dagger. We'd had our weapons taken upon entry into Dawn, and Bastian's orrery along with them. The best I could do was some hairpins—they'd cause some damage if I could get a good shot at her eye or throat. The soft bits, as Faolán would say. I had to wait for the right moment.

If she took me somewhere quiet and cut my throat, the knowledge that Cyrus was behind the fake Hydra Ascendant would die with me.

We stopped and there was a faint grinding sound, then cool air wafted over me.

Outside. She was going to kill me in the gardens—neutral territory, less blame on Dawn.

As soon as she took this hood off, I'd grab my hairpins and—

Soft golden light revealed a courtyard I knew well, and as I reached for my makeshift weapons, I froze, because that light touched a face I knew even better.

Charging forward, I made a sound that was trapped between a laugh and a sob. "Bastian."

Eyebrows peaked together like he didn't dare hope I was real, he met me halfway and swept me up. I caressed his cheeks —warm, spiked with stubble, exactly the shape I'd held a hundred times before—his neck, his shoulders. I buried my face in them and clung more tightly to him than I'd ever clung to anything.

I soaked him up. The scent of cedar and bergamot and work. The warmth that seeped through my clothes. The gasping rise and fall of his chest as he crushed me against it.

It felt like an age and yet still not long enough by the time we eased apart.

His gaze skimmed over me. "Are you all right? Have they—?"

"I'm fine." I nodded, smiling even though my eyes burned with unshed tears. "Are you—?"

"Infinitely better for seeing you." He let out a shaky breath, like some part of it had been held for a long time, before kissing my brow and squeezing me close again. At least a few of my tears soaked into his shirt. "Wait." Shuddering, he pulled back. "What's—"

His gaze snapped to the bracelet. "Iron. And he's *locked* it on you." A growl edged his words, reverberating into me.

I held the sensation in my chest, something I could keep when we were parted again.

Straightening, he looked past me. "Did the guard see you?"

"She was distracted by the uncle," my abductor stated. "I'll give you some privacy."

There was something familiar about the feminine voice, but when I turned, the speaker had disappeared behind Dawn's door.

"Who is that?"

"My spy in Dawn. She'll escort you back, too, though probably with the hood." His mouth skewed to one side as he watched the door shut. "Better for her and you that you don't know her identity."

That practicality kick-started my mind. I needed to tell him about Cyrus. The possibility of an alliance with Sepher and Zita. The fact I wasn't allowed to leave—

"I have a plan to get you home."

I blinked up at him, a hundred words caught in my throat. A plan. *Home.* With him and Ella and our other friends. Escape from Dawn and Cyrus. Thank the gods.

Thank the fucking gods.

Every muscle in me sagged and I would've fallen if he hadn't caught my shoulders.

"The taboo worked against us for long enough, but now we can use it to our benefit." A smile threatened on his lips as his gaze skipped between my eyes. His throat rose and fell, long and slow, then he took a deep breath and dropped to his knees.

"Katherine Ferrers." He said it like my name was a complete sentence—a complete story in its own right. Silvery eyes piercing me, he held my hips. "Marry me."

10

KAT

I heard the words. I played them again in my head until I finally understood what they meant.

Marriage to Bastian.

My stomach dropped, and at the same moment, my heart lurched into my throat like they were trying to run away from each other.

"If we're married, they can't keep us separated. It's taboo, even for a king." He squeezed my hips, prompting. "You'll be able to come home right away. They can't keep a wife away from her husband."

Wife. Husband. My skin flushed hot then cold at the words as nausea coiled in my stomach, vines knotting tight.

The man I loved was on his knees, proposing, and I was supposed to feel... happy. My heart was supposed to leap with joy, my stomach somersault, my eyes fill with tears.

But I could only gape at him, unable to breathe, as my head shook, slowly at first, then growing faster. "No. I—I can't."

He frowned and caught my hands as they clasped together,

giving them a little shake. "Kat. I understand it's not the most romantic proposal, but we need to be practical about this. I've thought of all the ways to get you home and this is the quickest and the only one guaranteed to work. We need to get you the fuck out of—"

"I can't."

"No, Katherine, *I* can't. I can't watch you living in Dawn. I can't keep you safe. I can't bear knowing you're in their clutches and that we could fix it so easily. You do understand Cyrus won't hesitate to use you to hurt Dusk—to hurt me?" His frown deepened, the lines scoured dark by a passing fae light. "He must know how I feel about you. And that aside, he would hurt you just for the pleasure of seeing your pain. You heard what Sepher did to Zita, how he humiliated her. Cyrus is worse. So much worse."

His frown slackened and something different crept onto his face—something I only remembered from drifting in and out of consciousness, half mad with pain.

Fear.

"Say yes and come home. Don't let your pride keep you in danger. I'll ask you a million times, each more romantic than the one before, but right now, I need you *home*."

"Pride?" I bit out the word as anger roused me from my threatening panic. "*Romance*? Don't you know me at all, Bastian Marwood? You think it's *pride* that keeps me from saying yes?" I yanked my hands from his grip. Good gods, I could've slapped him.

And maybe he heard that in my tone, because he blinked and jerked back as though I had struck him. It was like he finally saw me as he took in my trembling hands and the delicate hair on my arms straining to attention.

"What is it? What's wrong?" His voice softened, the frustration fading with each word, but it was still there, hard beneath the syllables like rock beneath soil. "Talk to me. Help me understand. Because right now I can't see why we shouldn't marry. We love each other. This will get you home. It will keep you safe. I cannot see a single reason against it."

I bit my tongue, trying to dampen my anger, because he sounded so reasonable. Yes, I did love him, and I wanted to get out of Dawn. And yet...

He rose slowly, like he didn't want to spook me further, and cupped my shoulders. "You can tell me."

Nodding, I released my tongue. I had to remember who this was—he may be frustrated, but I was safe. He wasn't about to throw half a dinner service at me. "I love you, Bastian, but... I can't marry you."

The creases deepened, like he was fighting to understand. "If you don't want to *be* married to me, that's fine. We can marry, get you home, then dissolve it as soon as you're safe. It doesn't have to... we don't have to tell people it means anything."

I huffed, which helped loosen my chest. "You just tried to say, 'It doesn't have to mean anything,' didn't you? And you couldn't."

His flattening mouth was all the answer I needed.

"It's not that I can't marry you. I can't marry *anyone*. The whole idea is abhorrent to me. Surely you can understand that."

His eyes shifted away, though his shoulders remained square and tight.

"I choose you, Bastian. I have chosen you a hundred times before tonight, and I'll choose you at every chance I get. But I will not ever choose marriage, and I won't be forced into it again."

Eyes wide, he exhaled a short, sharp breath as though I'd hit him—a punch to the gut this time. His shoulders sank, the last of his frustration evaporating. "Shit. Fuck." He screwed his eyes shut and scrubbed his face over and over. "Forced. Of course you won't. *Of course.* I'm sorry—I hadn't even stopped to... All I could think about was getting you home. I'm so sorry."

I caught his hands and pulled them away. "You're going to damage your face if you keep that up. And I'm quite fond of your face."

A chuckle huffed from his lips as he shook his head. "I'm glad of it. And I'm truly sorry for being a thoughtless idiot." He slid his palms against my cheeks, fingertips into my hair, and kissed me.

I shivered at the slow overwhelm of his lips on mine, like he was an entire world and not just one person. It had only been a week since we'd last kissed, but it might as well have been glacial ages where ice had carved me hollow.

Too soon, he pulled away and pressed his brow to mine. "Stars above, what did I do to deserve you?"

I slipped my hands over his and squeezed. "I thought we always said, 'Fuck deserve.'"

He scoffed. "Maybe that's why we say it. If I only got what I deserved, then I wouldn't have you. And I'm not noble enough to give you up."

"There's my villain." I kissed his palm, savouring the salt of his skin.

He made a sound low in his throat. "I am. Always. And I will plot and scheme to get you back." He led me to the bench and pulled me into his lap, talking through avenues we might try to get me home soon.

"I could offer Braea a bargain. She demands your return,

and I offer her... I don't know, *something* as payment. Though I'm not sure what I can give that she doesn't already have." While he traced circles on my back, he scowled at the court-yard's fountain as though that had stolen me away. "I hate this dress, by the way. His choice, I'm guessing." His gaze flicked to me, then back to the fountain as he went on with other ideas.

Yet none of them would work. Not really.

It had become clear, not over the past few days, but over months and perhaps even years. For all I had been obsessed with safety, I had never actually been safe.

Before the queen's summons to Lunden, I had hidden from the lion, but I hadn't been free from it. Now, living in Dawn Court, I found myself living with one. All fawning had done was appease it with a tasty morsel—for now. Next time it was hungry, I'd be in danger once more.

As a child, I'd heard a story about a man who pulled a thorn from a lion's paw, so later the lion spared his life. A sweet tale, but mercy didn't come into Cyrus's vocabulary. This predator needed to be removed entirely.

"Bastian." I stilled his touch on my thigh, as though that might still his thoughts. "None of these plans will work—not because they aren't good plans, but... because me returning to Dusk isn't the answer."

He turned from the fountain to me, eyelids fluttering. "*What?*"

"Even if I come back, there will still be the danger of Cyrus hanging over us, won't there?"

"At least you won't be in his court. That will stop him from—"

"He's behind the assassination. And I have evidence of it—or, at least, I've *seen* the evidence." If I had it in my hands, life might be easier. I explained what I'd seen as I'd bent to kiss

Cyrus's knuckles—the gold and scarlet thread that perfectly matched the fake Hydra Ascendant insignias. "It might not be enough to prove it to others, but I know it was him. And if that evidence exists, then there *must* be more."

Bastian scowled, gaze distant as he went back to tracing patterns on my thigh.

"If I come home, we'll be together—and believe me, I want nothing more—but Cyrus will still be on the throne. He killed his own father, along with countless innocents from his own court. He's far more dangerous than Lucius."

A low rumbling sound came from Bastian's chest. "Because he doesn't give a shit about the established rules that maintain the peace."

"Exactly. He's capable of anything. We need to prove his guilt and get him off the throne."

"You think we'd be better off with King Sepher?"

"Maybe?" I bobbed my shoulders. "In this instance, I'm willing to take an unknown quantity over Cyrus."

Bastian gave a deep sigh, pulling me closer like he only wanted to keep me safe and fuck everything else.

I couldn't blame him. It was mighty tempting to lose myself in his hold, in our courtyard, and pretend nothing else existed. Eyes shut, I wrapped my arms around his neck and indulged in that fantasy.

It lasted for only a second before I stroked a finger along his ear, making him jolt. Hopefully, it pulled his attention back to the wider world that stretched beyond the circle of our arms. "He might know about the Crown and go after that. Now he's had success with one monarch, he might assassinate another. There are a dozen things he could be plotting."

"You don't know that."

"Exactly. *We don't know.* And other than whoever he

worked with, I'm the only person in Dawn who knows he's behind the attacks."

A muscle in his jaw twitched. "What are you saying?"

"It's safer in the long run to solve this bigger problem. To get to something better, we have to go through this struggle, even if it upsets your courts." I didn't quite *say* "silly little courts" but the sentiment ran through my tone.

The muscle went solid. "You think there's a problem with our courts?"

"You don't? Can't you see how the separation breeds mistrust and exactly this kind of plot? Didn't Cyrus design the attack to make it look like Dusk was responsible? Honestly, it's a miracle the system has lasted this long."

His eyes went wide, but I was too tired and too comfortable with him to mind my tongue. Thoughts that had only wafted around my head half formed spilled out. "A country is meant to serve its people as much as they're meant to serve it. It's meant to ensure they're safe. Yet Cyrus is responsible for how many deaths? And now he's pointing the finger at Dusk and at shapechangers. He's dividing your people even further, so no one ever thinks to look at him."

"What are you saying? You want to get rid of the courts?"

"That's not what I said." But did it lie between my words? I shook my head. It was too big an idea and impossible to achieve, even if I did want it. Another wish that wasn't worth considering. "We need to get rid of Cyrus. That's the pressing issue. If I can get evidence of his guilt, that will do it, right?"

He tensed under me and made a noncommittal grumble. "Why do I feel like I'm going to hate what you're about to say even more than the idea of getting rid of the courts?"

I soothed the soft skin of his earlobes until his eyelids drooped. "I was employed to spy not so long ago, and I might not have been very good at it—too distracted by a rather handsome fae lord with a thoroughly wicked tongue —but now I have another chance. I'm going to spy on Cyrus."

Despite my work on his ears, he made a low sound of irritation, and I was sure he was going to forbid me from doing any such thing. But he said nothing, as though considering the idea.

"I'm stuck there, anyway. He makes sure I sit near him when we all eat together. I'm sure I can get closer to him."

Bastian remained very still, but I caught the minuscule flare of his nostrils. "I *do* hate this idea more than dismantling the courts."

"But it's a good idea, isn't it?"

With a groan, he wrapped around me. "That's why I hate it."

As I stroked his back, the door to Dawn ground open. "She'll be missed," his spy called through.

Under my cheek, his chest rose and fell in a deep sigh. "A few minutes more."

Eyes stinging, I gritted my teeth. I'd been so caught up in us, I'd forgotten this was only a temporary reunion. With a tight smile, I pulled back. "We'd better make some plans. I'm going to need lock picks. I think Ella has some."

"You think I don't?" He raised his eyebrows, affronted, as he pulled a set from his pocket.

"Yes, but do yours look like hair pins? Ella has a set that can be disguised."

Grumbling, he conceded and rubbed my wrist, right beside the bracelet.

I went on, "We also need to find Krae before the guards do."

"Mm. If Cyrus gets hold of them first, they'll end up dead before they can be questioned."

"Exactly. I'm sure they're involved, but I don't believe for a moment they masterminded the plot *or* killed Lucius."

He nodded slowly, watching the burbling fountain. "Cyrus has turned on them, setting them up as the scapegoat."

"If that's the case, it makes them a weak link. They're in fear for their life, and we can offer safety in exchange for information."

They'd already shown they believed in repaying a debt— I'd saved them from the snare and they'd saved me and Vespera from falling in the sabrecat race. It suggested they worked on fair exchange, which made me doubt they were working for Cyrus out of loyalty. More likely, it was just a job— or Cyrus held something over them.

Bastian gave me a sidelong look. "Maybe we'll make a good spy out of you yet."

I elbowed him in the ribs, tossing my head. "Bastian Marwood, I am going to be the best spy you've ever had."

"You're already my favourite. Unfortunately, there isn't time to *have* you. Next time."

"You keep making these promises. Don't think I've forgotten what you said while we were dancing at the wedding."

He fixed me with a look so intense, I could've sworn it burned a path right through me. "Oh, I'm counting on you remembering every word of that promise, love."

The door ground again, and I huffed, my desire cooling. "Planning, Bastian. *Focus*."

"Somewhat challenging considering where you're sitting."

Sure enough, I wriggled and felt something harden against

my backside. "I *see.*" Clearing my throat, I shifted to one side. "Sepher and Zita."

That barely quenched the fire in his eyes. "What about them?" He shifted in his seat, distracted.

"They tried to leave the palace today and were stopped. Cyrus isn't fucking around. But... they approached me the other day and I can't be sure, but it *felt* like they were trying to win me over. I might be able to make an alliance of some sort. My enemy's enemy..."

He flatted his lips, focus sharpening. "You should stay away from them. Sepher may hate his brother, but he hates me, too. Although... I did find out Cyrus is the one who broke his tail when they were younger."

I winced. I'd seen the scar on the prince's hairless tail; it stood out pale against the smooth, striped skin. "I remember you saying Cyrus had turned against him when his power woke. I didn't realise it was that bad."

"I don't know for sure that it was deliberate, but after what I saw on the balcony, I'm willing to bet the ill will between them is stronger than I suspected and very much current. Still" —his brow furrowed—"I don't want you caught between royal brothers. It's far too dangerous."

"More dangerous than having no allies in Dawn at all?"

He fell silent, gaze sliding away as his jaw worked side to side. "We just need to make you seem unimportant to me. I've got Ella, Rose, and Ariadne helping spread rumours that you were merely warming my bed." He gave an apologetic smile.

I couldn't help kissing its corner. "Using the humans to spread lies. There's my Bastard." Perhaps there was more we could do with that—more Ella could do, in fact. A plan unfolded in my mind. "I have an idea..."

II

KAT

Buoyed by seeing Bastian, I set to work the next day. At lunch, I was my most charming, my most attentive, my most fawning with King Cyrus. Rather than trying to disappear, I laughed at his jokes and praised his stories. It was grotesque, but I found myself smothering a smirk rather than a sneer.

Because I was going to fucking destroy him and he would never see it coming.

However, as lunch went on, I noted something guarded in him, and that was enough to quell my satisfied smirk. Maybe he did suspect. Already? Was I being *too* perfect?

No. It was the change. Too sudden and too extreme. As far as he was concerned, I was Bastian's and loyal to him. Of course my fawning was suspicious. I needed to convince the king that I'd turned my back on the Night Queen's Shadow.

The question was, how? If I suddenly started making disparaging comments about him out of nowhere, it would seem even more suspicious. I needed an opportunity to *show*

84

His Majesty that an insurmountable barrier stood between us, and not just because I was in one court and he in another.

And no, the irony of now wanting the king's attention when I had so desperately tried to avoid it was not lost on me.

After lunch, I was left to my own devices, save for my constant shadow, Amandine. Feigning boredom (though it wasn't really a lie, since I had so little to do—no friends to visit or magic to hone), I asked her to show me the library.

Like Dusk's, this one was huge. The ceiling vaulted overhead with walkways at different levels, providing access to the higher shelves, and a maze of bookcases threading deeper into the cavernous room.

I worked my way around the shelves, which contained all sorts from thrilling adventure novels to ancient tomes of history. Amandine stationed herself near the doors, which gave me the opportunity to thread between the shelves and dip out of sight for a short while. By the time she came looking for me, I had a thick anthology of fairy tales. Just some "frivolous" reading, as my father would've called it—but tucked inside was a smaller book of ancient legends.

I hadn't forgotten about the Crown of Ashes. We'd scoured Dusk's archives, but here was a chance to see if Dawn had more information.

So I tucked myself into an armchair and read, searching for any mention of the mysterious item.

OVER THE FOLLOWING DAYS, this became my pattern, including Cyrus remaining aloof. That problem was on my mind as I made my way to a break in this new routine. With Amandine hovering over my shoulder, we walked through the sky blue and gold corridors of Dawn, heading to the gardens where yet another celebration of *great King Cyrus* awaited us.

I'd spent all morning in the library and had eaten lunch at his side while he only smiled cooly at my best efforts to be winning. I needed that opportunity—the sooner, the better.

"Are you ever going to tell me where you disappeared to?" Amandine's voice broke through my thoughts as we reached the door to the gardens and her grip locked on the handle.

I gave her a questioning look.

"When you sent me after your uncle." Her brow tightened. "I wouldn't mind, but I really thought you needed help, that he..." She shook her head. "But you fooled me—just another lying human."

She looked... *hurt*. Like my deception was a personal affront.

Still, her question was one I couldn't answer. "I... I know I disappeared, but I swear what I told you was true."

"I hoped you would volunteer the answer, but it's been days and nothing. Now I ask and you still won't say." She scowled and loomed over me. "If you don't tell me, I'll tell the king how you disappeared off somewhere."

Shit.

Fine. She thought she could threaten me. It was time she learned I wasn't so defenceless.

From within her shadow, I thrust out my chin and returned her glare twofold. "Please do. I'm sure His Majesty will be *thrilled* to know you didn't obey his orders and keep a close eye on me."

She rocked back on her heels, eyes round, as though she hadn't expected me to strike back. She huffed out a breath as I threw the door open, and we went on our way in a frosty silence that was at odds with the sunny day.

Bright music accompanied the dancers and acrobats dotted through the gardens, but my attention skipped past them. With the city's warmth enhanced by magic, roses had emerged early in a riot of pink, yellow, and white. Frivolous, like Father had called those books, and yet... I couldn't help loving them.

As we approached a gaggle of guests admiring the dancers, I fingered the fine velvet of my dress, imagining it was the soft touch of petals. Someone from Dusk wore the deep violet colour I'd once dreamt of breeding into my roses.

Like any party, I was offered a drink, which I accepted, but I ended up drinking it alone, save for Amandine lingering at the edge of the crowd.

I was Dusk in the middle of Dawn, so none of Cyrus's people would talk to me. The Dusk hostages kept to the cool distance they'd established on day one. And although other fae from Dusk were here, since this celebration was open to both sides, they only glanced my way with stiff nods and apologetic smiles.

We might be in the same place, but that didn't mean we could mix. I was off-limits, spelled out harshly by the pastel pink dress I'd been forced to wear. I was running out of options that (barely) fitted.

I bit back a sigh and took the smallest possible sip of my drink. I needed to keep my head, and it was hard to gauge the strength of fae drinks.

Then I spotted something that made me want to gulp the rest of it down.

Impossibly dark hair cut through the crowd. Bastian. He

looked bored, eyes half hooded as he spoke too softly for me to hear. Ella clutched his arm, leaning close.

My heart tripped and fell.

"Oh, Bastian!" Ella swatted his chest and fell into him. He caught her effortlessly, a faint smirk curling his lip. "You're positively incorrigible!"

Eyes turned their way. Heads bowed together. Murmurs snaked after them. Glances flicked towards me.

I couldn't blame them—Bastian and Ella were putting on an excellent show. It was only because I knew them so well, I caught the strain in Ella's voice and the tightness of Bastian's smirk.

I'd suggested Ella pose as Bastian's new lover. What better way to convince everyone he didn't care about me?

Despite that, the response in me was physical—*real*. It swirled the tiny amount of alcohol I'd consumed, leaving me feeling like I was one jolt away from throwing up over the nearest performer.

But that physical response at spotting them could prove useful. If I harnessed it, this just might be the opportunity I'd been searching for.

I skimmed the crowd, checking Cyrus was nearby. Yes, that golden hair and cruel crown glinted just over there. Perfect.

Breath held, I clenched my fists around the crystal glass as I stared at Bastian and Ella. I kept up that tension until it trembled through me and my pulse pressed at my throat and face. My skin must've flushed by now.

Remember that horrible sinking feeling, I told myself and flung the glass to the ground.

Its tinkle brought all eyes my way, and that was my cue to charge.

"How could you?" I burst at Bastian before turning to Ella.

"And *you*? I thought you were my friend." I couldn't quite summon tears, but I made my voice waver convincingly.

For a single beat, Ella blinked at me, then her eyes widened as she caught on. "How dare I? Are you truly that self-absorbed? Can you not imagine a world where he might want someone other than *you*?" She laughed, lip curling in this cruel way that was wholly un-Ella. "You truly think you're so special?"

Bastian made a faint sound of derision, but he was less helpful in this subterfuge, since he couldn't directly lie. "Did you expect me to wait and not touch a single person while you were gone?"

"Now, now, Bastian, darling." Ella's voice went higher, needling. "We should be honest, my love. This isn't new. We were just waiting for you to be out of the way."

Oh, very good, Ella. Sticking the knife in further, making it seem they'd been fucking behind my back all along. She might be even more devious than I was.

I tried to believe it, imagined how that would feel, threw myself into its darkness. I wallowed in the frustration that I was being kept away from the people I cared about and the one time I got to see them, we had to put on this stupid pantomime.

My vision swam with tears, and I looked up at Bastian.

He froze.

"No," I said in a stage whisper. "Say it isn't—"

"Stay away from him," Ella growled, and the next thing I knew, I was flying through the air, her arms wrapped around me.

Bloody hells, I didn't realise this was going to be a contact sport.

The gasps surrounding us were certainly the effect I'd

hoped for, but I wasn't supposed to be on the floor with Ella on top of me.

"Sorry about this," she whispered as we rolled around. "You'll never touch him again," she cried out before lowering her voice again. "I've hidden the lock picks. Thought I could use this to get close enough to tell you."

Two birds, one stone.

Well, we couldn't leave our audience with a bad performance. I used my weight to swing on top of her. "You think I want to touch him now I know where he's been?"

Ella flashed a short sharp grin, then grabbed for my hair. She took a good handful, and I followed where she lead as she brought my ear close to her mouth. "Bench by the great trees, under a mossy stone, six inches wide."

I gasped and reared back like she'd whispered the worst insult imaginable in my ear, then pulled my arm back for a slap.

Before I had to work out how to deliver a convincing strike without hurting her, a strong hand wrapped around my wrist. I blink up at the face cast in shadow, backlit by the sun. He gave a gentle squeeze, and I understood who it was before I could see clearly. Bastian.

It had been almost a week since we'd last touched, though it felt more like months.

"I won't have anyone harming what's mine," he said, a growl edging his words as he hauled me to my feet with ease. And for a moment, barely the blink of an eye, there was this desperate tightness to his features that told me how much he meant it. He meant one thing, while everyone else heard something different.

To them, he was saying he wouldn't have me hurt Ella.

But the truth was something else entirely.

No matter the distance between us—even a different plane of existence. No matter whose domain I lived in. No matter the dangers. He would do anything to keep me safe.

Including pushing me away, which he did now. His thumb rubbed over the soft skin of my wrist for a fraction of a second before he let go.

It was the safest I'd felt in so long, and I held on to it like a drowning man to a lifeline. Behind me there was the sound of someone else helping Ella up as I glared up at Bastian like he really had replaced me.

He towered over me, glaring. "I think it's time you accept the truth about my feelings, Katherine. Ella is at my side now and you embarrass yourself."

I clenched my jaw, chin wobbling, then huffed, spun on my heel, and flounced out of sight towards the Great Yew and the Great Oak.

It had all been a lie, a ridiculous performance, but my heart pounded like every word had been true.

I fixed my gaze on the two trees. They dominated the sky— the oak's new foliage emerging yellow green and the yew's constant needles a cooler blue-green.

The Great Yew stood for Dusk Court. Its trunk had split in two centuries ago, struck by lightning as Ari had once told me, but instead of dying, it had grown tall and wide.

At its side, Dawn Court's Great Oak seemed fresher and more vigorous, its single trunk thick and unblemished. The newness was merely a trick of the bright spring leaves unfurling.

Nearby stood a bench. Perhaps because the trees were sacred, no performers had set themselves up here. It worked for me—I had the area to myself, and I was out of sight of the other partygoers.

I spared a glance back. Amandine. Damn. Not *entirely* alone. I needed to be subtle. Never thought I'd find myself longing for wide skirts, but they certainly would help hide what I was doing as I retrieved the lock picks.

When I turned towards the bench, I found myself face-to-face with Cyrus.

I gasped and clutched my chest, drawing attention to my cleavage. Fae women tended to have more slender figures, and I'd caught plenty of fae eyeing my curves. Exotic. Enticing. Tools I could use.

"Your Majesty!"

As I bowed my head, I bit back a curse. Amandine keeping an eye on me *and* Cyrus blocking my way. I would have to come back for the lock picks.

Slowly, Cyrus smirked. "Katherine." His eyes flicked to one side. "You're dismissed." He waved his hand, shooing Amandine away. "What an interesting party this is proving to be."

My heart tripped over itself. Did he know what I was up to? If his fae hearing had picked up Ella's whisper...

Eyelashes fluttering, I cocked my head like I had no idea what he could be referring to—certainly not the lock picks that were mere feet away.

"The exchange between you and the Serpent and his new human."

I huffed out a breath, gaze dipping away so he wouldn't see the flash of relief. Instead, I frowned, letting him think my harsh sigh was over Bastian and Ella.

When I dared look up after long seconds of silence, he was watching me, his attention sharp enough to cut. The glint in his eye made me want to squirm, but it gave him away.

He'd enjoyed our little show. He'd liked seeing the supposed rift between us and the way everyone had stared.

I wondered how deep his enjoyment went. Time to test it.

I made my chin wobble. The poor human, so affected, so close to tears.

Almost imperceptibly, he leaned closer and one corner of his mouth rose.

He'd enjoyed our show, but he *loved* seeing me upset and weak.

Good to know.

That lift at the corner of his mouth twisted. "Missing the dashing Night Queen's Shadow?" His mocking lilt raised my hackles, and I channeled the feeling into my performance.

"Not anymore." I looked away, shaking my head.

"Oh?"

"It's so strange, even before all that, I... now I'm away from him, I feel... different." Hopefully that would cast my recent behaviour in a different light. If he thought Bastian had charmed me, it would help explain my sudden change of heart.

He made a thoughtful sound. "Almost as if you were... compelled. Did he ever—?"

"My kingly brother, there you are." The first thing I saw when I looked up was Sepher's broad smile, showing off his sharp, sharp canines.

Zita sauntered up next to him, glancing my way with the briefest nod.

"Sepher," Cyrus said with a sigh. "What a... Well, I was going to call it a delight, but the word just won't come out of my mouth. *Here you are*—that's true enough for me to say."

"I'm so glad we feel the same." Sepher's gaze skewered his brother, and the promise of violence made me want to shrink away. "I have a bone to pick with Your Majesty."

"Your guards won't let us leave the palace." Zita's voice was no less dangerous than her husband's look.

Cyrus's face screwed up. "That was a week ago. Why are you bothering me with this now?"

I hated to agree, but he had a point.

Sepher took a step closer, towering above Cyrus—he was tall enough to tower over Bastian and might've even stood taller than Faolán, though he wasn't as broad. "Because if I'd seen you that day, I would've ripped your pretty little head off your shoulders with your crown still intact."

"Of course"—Zita gave a smile as sweet and sharp as a poisoned lemon tart—"if you'd prefer not to talk about it with Katherine present, I'm sure I can persuade my husband to take this somewhere more private."

I held my breath and tried to look nonchalant. If they went elsewhere, I'd be free to go after the lock picks.

Cyrus huffed. "I can see you're determined to have this discussion now. Just don't expect me to thank you for not ripping my head off. Remember who's king, Sepher." He flashed his teeth in a sneering smile. "Lovely Lady Katherine, I must apologise that our conversation has been cut short just as it was getting interesting. You'll excuse me."

"Of course, Your Majesty." I bowed my head, humble and demure... and definitely not excited to get on with my mission.

Cyrus angled closer, crowding in. "I look forward to the next time I have you to myself." With that, he turned and swaggered away, calling for his brother to follow.

Sepher squared his shoulders and took a deep breath. "Hmm?" He scented the air, nostrils flaring, nose wrinkling as he searched for something. At last, he spotted the iron bracelet. The disgust was plain on his striking features as he made a low sound before stalking after his brother.

Even though it was silver plated, he'd scented the iron. Faolán's sense of smell was even stronger than most fae's—the same had to be true of Sepher as a fellow shapechanger. Perhaps I could use the fae's distaste for iron to my advantage. Worth noting for the future.

Zita laughed softly, shaking her head. "I can't believe he's done that to you. The coward."

"I've put up with worse."

"I bet you have." She said it like she knew—truly knew what it was like. And though I'd only had a handful of conversations with the woman, for that moment we shared something.

"You have the place to yourself." With a nod, she backed away, and I could've sworn she winked as she did so.

Amandine was nowhere to be seen, so I ran to the bench, flipped over the stone Ella had described, and retrieved a small roll of black velvet.

As I tucked it away under my gown, I had to wonder whether Sepher and Zita's distraction was a coincidence that happened to benefit me or a deliberate ploy to help.

Whether they were allies or just had good timing, I would use whatever opportunities came my way.

12

BASTIAN

"They still haven't made the hair dye public." I scowled as I stalked down the corridor at Braea's side.

"Of course they haven't." She rolled her eyes and stifled a yawn.

It wasn't long after sunset, but we had a Convocation meeting, so I was giving my "wake up" report to her while we made our way there. Not ideal, but neither was a meeting so early in her day.

"And unfortunately," she went on, "there's nothing we can do about it. We're not saying anything until we have evidence in our hands. We'll look like fools grasping at straws and things are shaky enough as it is right now."

It was comforting to hear my own words reiterated back at me. I was right, and she agreed. My earlier questions about Kat had been forgotten, and things between us were smooth once more.

It also put my mind at ease over keeping Cyrus's guilt from

her. I didn't want to come to her without proof, not when it might affect her behaviour towards Dawn and we had nothing to back it up. The fewer people who knew, the less danger rumours could come out before we were ready with a case against him.

Braea pursed her lips as we rounded a corner. "Well done for getting the information, though. Someone is trying to frame us *and* Hydra Ascendant. But this business with the dye means there's evidence somewhere—we just need to find it."

I'd been to the Hall of Healing a few times since Cyrus's proclamation, but Elthea was always with patients or not there. The longer she avoided me, the more suspect it all became.

"Cyrus must be suppressing it. He's cleverer than I gave him credit for," Braea muttered. Then, with a wave of her hand, she glanced at me. "Leave Cyrus to his machinations for now. I want you focused on those *ashes* we spoke about." She arched one eyebrow meaningfully.

It was all I could do to keep up with the fallout from Lucius's death and the changes in Dawn. I only had resources to pay the barest lip service to searching for the Crown as well.

"Top priority, remember," she said with a lilt like I was a teen who needed to be brought back on track. "If we have it, we have more power, then overgrown princelings and silly little splinter groups won't be a threat."

"Of course. I've asked Lysander for help, too. Eyes outside the city."

It was true in a way—I'd asked him to help search for the fox shapechanger Krae beyond the city walls. Living on his own estate, Lysander's comings and goings weren't under scrutiny, whereas it would be noticed if I left the city—by the queen and others.

Yet I felt a pang of guilt at Braea's look of gratitude. "You asked him? I know you don't have the easiest relationship, so I appreciate your sacrifice all the more. I should've given more credit to your commitment."

The request had stuck in my throat. There had always been friction between us—I suspected my shadows reminded him of the whispers about unseelie heritage in his own bloodline. He was a shadowstepper, after all, able to disappear into darkness and reappear elsewhere. But I'd needed help, and he was the person best placed to do it.

With this many troubles piling on top of each other, I couldn't afford to be picky.

Stars willing, we would find Krae and they would have the evidence we needed to prove Cyrus's guilt. When that happened, Braea would have as much gratitude for my minor deception as she did for the "sacrifices" she thought I'd made searching for the Crown of Ashes.

We turned one last corner and found ourselves facing the double doors to the Convocation chamber as they opened. Beneath the domed roof that was one third day, one third night, and one third the twilight in between, a large oval table housed the other Convocation members. They acknowledged our entrance, inclining their heads.

"Your Majesty," the Mistress of the Vault, Deema, said, "thank you for joining us at what I know is such an early meeting for you. From Bastian's report, it sounded like we had plenty to discuss, so I thought it best to schedule as much time as possible." Her pastel blue hair glinted in the light coming from the starry wall sconces as she gestured to the pots of tea and coffee set up to one side.

The delicate pastries stacked on platters made my heart ache for Kat. She wouldn't have been able to choose between the raspberry frangipane tart or the chocolate and hazelnut swirl, so she would've taken one of each. Then she'd have spotted the swirled cinnamon buns drizzled with icing and grabbed one of those, too.

"It may be early for you," Deema went on as we took our seats, "but it's late for us, so I hope you'll forgive us for any yawning. I had some food sent up in case you hadn't broken fast yet." Her smile was so charming, I found myself returning it as I attempted to shake off thoughts of Kat.

"Yes, yes," Mored, the Master of Magic, huffed with a dismissive wave of his hand, "all very cosy, I'm sure. But we have business to attend to, Deema, and Her Majesty's time is precious."

As others murmured agreement, I was sure Mored muttered, "As is mine."

The Chancellor, Lucan, twisted the delicate handle of his coffee cup between his fingers. "Well, I believe the first order of business is one raised by Her Majesty. In light of the—*ahem*—subject matter, we thought it best to carry out this meeting without Prince Sepher."

"Actually, it was Bastian's item." Braea gestured that I had the table.

The Marshal of the Field, Tor, regarded me and gave what looked like a nod of approval.

I planted my coffee cup and outlined the points we'd worked on. In short, Cyrus's new laws were impossible to police, unfair to shapechangers, and potentially damaging to anyone who might be accused of being a member of Hydra Ascendant. They opened up far too many opportunities for old enmities to lead to false accusations. We'd already encountered one case where so-called evidence of membership had been planted on a neighbour.

For the most part, Tor and Lucan kept their reactions in check. No clues if they agreed or not. Deema wore a tight little frown that I couldn't decipher, but I caught her nodding once or twice. The Marshal of the City, Galiene, kept glancing at Lucan. Every time I caught her, she shot upright and fixed her eyes on me like she'd been paying attention all along. Mored outright scowled.

As always, with the Convocation, this wasn't going to be straightforward.

"What's more," I went on, "these laws won't even make anyone safer. As the case with the warring neighbours shows, this is likely to make folk *less* safe. Not to mention the potential for the register to be abused. We all know how many still hold prejudice against them for nothing more than what they are."

Braea leant forward, elbows on the table. She'd rolled up her sleeves at some point, giving her the air of someone ready to pitch in. "My Shadow speaks for me in this. I must hand it to Cyrus, he's surprised me. I always thought he'd be much more interested in erecting statues of himself and throwing elaborate parties than introducing new laws." She shared a smirk with the group. "He's a loose cannon."

Lucan gave a soft chuckle, echoed by Galiene. Both came from Dusk, who were marginally outnumbered in the Convocation when Dawn's representative was here. An odd number meant no stalemates when voting. But having both Braea and me in attendance without Sepher or Cyrus gave us the advantage for once.

Braea spread her hands. "With the current landscape of the courts in mind, what can be done?"

Galiene gave a long exhale as though gathering herself. "This *is* a delicate matter. His Majesty acted unilaterally in his speech." She grimaced as if reliving the moment. "However—"

"*However,*" Mored cut in, "this is clearly just a case of youthful exuberance. He wants to stamp his mark on his new rule."

I clenched my jaw against replying with a reminder that Cyrus was the same age as me and yet I didn't run around acting like a fucking prick. Well, except for running after him into Dawn.

But it was no surprise that Mored, from Dawn, was supporting his king.

"'Youthful exuberance' is no excuse to damn a whole segment of the population." Deema spread her brown hands on the table, piercing Mored with a look.

He held her gaze, but his normally pale cheeks flushed.

Before either of them looked away, Lucan waded in. "After what happened to his own father, it's no surprise he feels a need to act. And, besides, shapechangers are animal half the time—perhaps it's best not to trust them."

Lucan's tone was gentler than Magic's, as if to soften the blow, but it still stunned me. His attitudes I expected to hear out in the backwaters, but he, a member of Dusk Court, was agreeing with Dawn on this. And Deema had agreed with us. This wasn't split along court lines.

With an apologetic smile, Galiene canted her head. "We do tend to arrest more shapechangers relative to their population levels. They're just more inclined to violence and other animalistic tendencies than normal fae."

A low growl came from me—one Faolán would've been proud of. Yes, he was capable of ripping apart a kelpie with his bare hands—Rose had witnessed it—but in my father's memories I'd seen atrocities committed by dozens of fae who weren't shapechangers.

All they'd required was permission from leaders who made

their enemies less than people and the goading of their peers. Who can kill more? Who can make their victim scream the loudest? Whose mutilation is the most inventive?

Coffee churned in my stomach as the memories gripped me so hard I couldn't speak.

If they were "normal" fae, give me abnormal any day.

Tor cleared their throat. "There's been talk of shapechangers leaving the city."

"Perhaps it's for the best," Galiene murmured. When Deema and I snapped our attention to her, she straightened, pushing her dark brown braids from her face. "For their safety, I mean."

Tor scowled, their brow furrowing so fiercely they reminded me of my *baba* for a moment. He'd once occupied that seat on the Convocation—before the wars of succession, long before he'd been branded a traitor.

"*Not* for their safety or ours," they said. "Many of my best people are shapechangers—scouts, fighters, leaders. It's short-sighted to let your petty prejudices cloud your judgement. Galiene, I'm particularly disappointed by your assessment— I'm sure many invaluable members of the City Watch are shapechangers. How will the city fare if they all leave because they're afraid?"

Mored snorted, leaning on the arm of his chair. "If they're so fantastically skilled, what do they have to be afraid of?"

The general leant forward, lips flat, but it was Deema who stepped in. "Aren't false accusations enough for you?" Her voice was soft, like an approaching storm. "Last week, there was an altercation. Someone attacked a shapechanger, crying out treason, calling them a murderer. Someone else accused them of eating babies." Her gaze cut its way around the table. Even Mored looked away when she reached him. "*Eating babies*." The quiet fury in her voice trembled like that storm was coming closer. "Others stepped in to protect them, but still more joined the attack. It ended up as a fight in the streets with a dozen dead."

That struck the room to silence.

"We can ill afford to lose so many." Lucan inclined his head.

"I'm not finished." Deema's teeth flashed as though she'd like nothing more than to sink them into the next person to say a word. "I woke up this morning to find a threat painted on our door."

Galiene's dark eyes widened. "Your door? I've heard no report of this. I didn't—"

"And why would we report it to you?" Deema laughed humourlessly. "After all, isn't it 'for the best' if my husband gets out of your city? That will make it pure for all the 'normal' fae, won't it?"

Another silence yawned open, filled with fidgeting and downcast gazes.

I already knew Deema's husband was a shapechanger, but it seemed the others didn't. I made a mental note to have someone watch their house going forward. I trusted my people not to harbour foolish prejudices more than I trusted the City Watch.

"I'm sorry," Galiene said at last. "I'll look into it personally."

"It is... unfortunate," Lucan added.

Deema looked like she was going to give a barbed reply, so I intervened. "I'm sorry things have been allowed to escalate to this point, Deema, for you, your husband, and all the other shapechangers who call Tenebris-Luminis home. This has clearly become an issue already—one we must act upon."

"Bastian is right," Braea said, leaning forward with her fingers steepled. "We need solutions, not a debate."

Lucan winced. "I'm not sure repealing these laws so quickly will be possible. Not in the current circumstances."

"Besides," Mored muttered, "imagine the paperwork."

Tor shot him a stern look. "Unfortunately, the current situation we find ourselves in is something of a tightrope. Forgive me for saying, Your Majesty, but I'm sure you're aware the attackers were all of Dusk descent."

"Allegedly." I couldn't help myself. When they turned to me with raised eyebrows, I took a sip of coffee, like this was only idle gossip and not an attempt to plant a seed of doubt. "I heard a number of the attackers were found to have dyed their hair."

A laugh burst from Mored. "Oh, really? They're impostors now, are they? You can't trust everything you hear, Marwood."

Galiene twisted her mouth. "Unfortunately, reports from that day do seem to be a little muddled. An early one I received stated that one of the bodies had a tattoo of the Celestial Serpent, suggesting they were from Dusk."

Shit. I took another sip of coffee, composing myself behind the cup. That had to be my other self's body—someone must've seen the tattoo before I could remove him from the morgue.

Galiene went on, "I can't see a member of Dawn Court doing something so permanent for the sake of impersonating Dusk. True or not, we couldn't confirm the presence of that tattoo on a later re-inspection of the bodies."

Braea gave a deep sigh that invoked all her many centuries. "That's it, then, isn't it? We can't undermine the new king in such a public way."

Lucan's dark hair gleamed as he canted his head. "I'm afraid it isn't advisable. At least not in the current climate."

I squeezed the arms of my chair, wishing they were Cyrus's throat. He was the one responsible for *all* of this, from the attack and assassination to the shitty laws he'd enacted in response. Stars help me—I was in real danger of punching him in the face the next time I saw him.

Shaking her head, Braea scooped up her tea cup. "The poor boy must be half out of his mind after everything he saw."

There was some general muttering about how terrible the attack had been, though no one seemed to pick up on Braea's phrasing. No one would ever have referred to King Lucius as a "poor boy."

"These laws make it impossible for shapechangers to live and work, though." I shared a look with Deema—her husband must've encountered similar issues to Faolán. I raised my hands, fending off objections. "I understand we can't repeal the law. I get that. But what if we... add to it?"

Braea paused with the cup halfway to her mouth. "What did you have in mind?"

"Deema, what's been the hardest part of the laws for your husband to deal with?"

She exhaled slowly and I could see her composing herself. At last she replied, "The curfew. Everyone knows where we live now—it's too late to put that back in the bottle. But the curfew affects him every day. He struggles to get back on time from looking after his mother. He can't visit his friends. We can't go out for dinner."

I nodded slowly. "One of my operatives is in a similar position. His life is suffering for it, and if you care about nothing else, so is his work for the crown. The man can't do his job if he's only allowed outside for a handful of hours per day."

"Perhaps it's best he isn't allowed to roam freely," Mored muttered behind his coffee cup.

Braea shot him a look so cold it burned. "I'm sure you're not casting aspersions on one of my employees, *Mored*."

His throat bobbed slowly as he blinked. "I—uh—of course, I would never dream of—"

"That's what I thought." She gave him a smile just as frosty.

"You know"—Galiene nodded—"I think we could do something about the curfew. People could apply for a permit to be exempt."

"That's... actually an excellent idea." Lucan sat up, and Galiene's cheeks flushed.

As they turned to the topic of how the permits could be put in place, who'd be allowed one, reasons they'd be denied, I sipped my drink. They didn't need to know I had every intention of granting one to everybody who applied.

Braea leant over to me and said in a conciliatory tone, "Try not to worry about Cyrus. He can be managed. Just give his paranoia a little rein and everyone will come around to our way of thinking."

I narrowed my eyes, giving her a sidelong look. "You want him to look foolish?"

She raised one shoulder. "Would it hurt?"

"Some people, yes." Hadn't it already hurt Deema and her husband? Those dozen dead fae she had mentioned?

She dismissed my comment with a tilt of her cup before sipping from it.

I frowned. How far was she willing to go to make Cyrus look foolish—unstable, even? What would she let him do before she intervened?

"I see that look. Aren't you always cautioning me to think

of the stability of the courts? That's exactly what I'm doing. We can't undo what's been done. Not yet, anyway." She put down her cup and placed her hand on mine. "Patience, Bastian. Patience."

I scrutinised her, throat aching. Words tangled there, but I couldn't pick apart what they were. I swallowed down the fragments and pushed out my reply. "I hope you know what you're doing."

"There is always an opportune moment to act. When it comes, we'll take it."

When she squeezed, my shoulders eased. She was right. This was a strategy, as the courts so often demanded—it was no different from the pretence with Ella.

We had been backed into a corner. I just hoped we would find a way out before Cyrus hurt anyone else.

13

KAT

The chill sickness of iron jangled through me with every step. In the couple of days since my fake argument with Ella, I had spent every moment possible practising and now I could pick the tiny, fiddly lock on the bracelet. I'd been doing just that when Amandine had arrived with a summons to Cyrus's office.

It had taken every deceptive bone in my body to smile and nod as I hid my wrist. I'd managed to click it back into place as the door to my suite closed, disguising the sound.

But after just a few minutes without the bracelet, the side-effects of iron hit me afresh, mingling with the question of what Cyrus might want with me.

The day of the fight, he'd sent Elthea to check if I had any injuries. She'd told me he understood humans were "fragile."

Since our encounter in the gardens, I'd worked every day to make myself as pretty as possible. Hair oil, delicate perfume, subtle make-up. I'd chosen clothing that made my light tan skin look pale. He liked weak, and I made myself look as *fragile* as I could.

We arrived at the door to his personal office, not the official one that had been his father's. My stomach bubbled with iron and anxiety.

Please don't be sick.

Adra gave a perfunctory smile and cut Amandine off. "You can wait there." She gestured at an alcove near her desk before showing me into Cyrus's office as I held my breath.

I needn't have bothered—he wasn't there.

"His Majesty will be with us shortly." Another efficient gesture towards a plush chair.

She intended to wait with me. Which didn't really work with my plans. I couldn't let a chance to snoop around Cyrus's office go to waste.

So I smiled broadly and instead of heading towards the chair, I approached her. "Thank you *so much*, Adra. I truly appreciate your attentiveness and everything you do to keep Dawn running so smoothly." I reached out and squeezed her shoulder, and at once she wrinkled her nose and shuddered out of reach.

Her wide eyes settled on my hand and trailed to the source of her disgust. The iron bracelet.

My smile remained cemented in place.

Ashen, she cleared her throat and backed away. "I think I'll wait outside." The door slammed after her.

At least this bracelet was good for something.

I wasted no time celebrating, though, and made straight for the desk. It seemed the most likely place here for Cyrus to store private information. At least until I had access to his bedroom. Rifling through the top drawer, I wrinkled my nose at the thought.

Pens and ink. Sheets of paper and sticks of wax. Nothing of interest, though for a moment I considered stealing a small pair of scissors and hiding them under my clothing. Fae-worked scissors would kill a fae as surely as a dagger, right? But I couldn't afford to be found with something that suggested I was anything but captivated by Cyrus and glad to be in his court.

The next drawer revealed screwed up pieces of paper, which I unfolded. Sketches... of himself... on a plinth. Designs for a statue? I rolled my eyes and continued searching.

At first, I thought the bottom drawer was empty, but when I groped inside, I found a folded letter caught in the joints.

Interesting. I didn't have Cyrus down as the sentimental, letter-keeping type. Though perhaps this one had been missed when he pulled other papers out to throw away.

It was the kind delivered by a messenger—no address on the outside. The seal had broken off, leaving crumbs of white wax. It was written in an elegant, sparse hand.

Dearest Cyrus,

I regret that we can't meet quite yet. There are those at court who wish me ill, so I cannot reveal myself to you until circumstances change. Though I would certainly feel safer with you on the throne. You're so clever, I know you'll understand.

Just as I understand your frustrations with your father. Many criticise him as too friendly with Dusk. But you're right—it's your duty to act against any enemy.

However, you're focusing on the wrong people.

If you turn your sights closer to home, you'll have the power to do whatever you wish... and you won't have to wait an immortal lifetime to do so.

After all, he was once Her Majesty's ally in the wars of succession—can he really be trusted to do what's best for Dawn alone?

Yours ever watchfully.

I blinked at the letter. I read it again.

Was this person hinting...?

I took a deep breath and gave it one more read.

Cyrus had killed his father... but somebody else had given him the idea?

I swallowed and found myself looking for someone to show this to, for someone to ask if they saw the same things I did. Ella or Bastian would read it with level heads. I still felt half sick from the iron bracelet and didn't trust myself.

But I was the only one here. The only one left to trust.

Assuming I was right, then, what else could I learn from this letter? It was unsigned, so I checked the outside once more. No watermarks or other distinctive markings on the paper. Not even a partial seal, just the remnants of white wax.

A strange thing to commit to writing—encouragement to kill a king. Then again, it sounded like the writer hadn't met Cyrus, and the letter, frustratingly, contained nothing to lead back to them.

Though it read as though this wasn't their first message. There had to be more.

Just as I bent to feel at the back of the drawer, voices filtered from outside, one deeper. Cyrus.

I cursed the rustling paper as I refolded the letter and

shoved it back in place, but I could've fallen to my knees and kissed the rug as it muffled the sound of me running towards my chair.

Too late. I spun on my heel just as the door opened.

I gasped, not entirely faking it, and he eyed me, then the seat Adra had offered. "Is the chair not to Lady Katherine's taste?"

My throat wouldn't cooperate and even I could see my hand tremble. I needed to gain control of this situation *and* of myself. He couldn't find out I'd been rummaging through his desk or all this work would be for nothing.

Perhaps a grain of truth would help sell my lie.

Shaking my head, I visibly gathered myself. "Your Majesty, it's not the chair that's the problem but *me*. I was just so..." I fanned myself with my hand as if searching for the right word. "Well, it's not every day you're summoned to a king's private study." My voice lowered on the word "private" and I intensified my look.

It was only a moment, chest heaving as I watched him watching me, but it felt like a decade, having cast the dice and waiting to see how they would fall in this dangerous game.

"Hmm." His mouth curved as he approached. "This is the effect I have on you?"

Eyes widening, I took a small step back as though half afraid of him. The curve deepened. I lifted my chin and swallowed slowly so he could see. "Your Majesty wished to see me?"

"Hmm? Oh, yes. I wanted to check how you were feeling now you're rid of that..." He flicked his fingers as though getting rid of a fly. "Undesirable magical affliction."

"Your Majesty is too kind. Truly, it's a relief. Such magic is too powerful for an untrained human—I was always so afraid

I'd accidentally unleash it." It had been true, once, and I put myself back there, afraid of what I might do. I thought of Kaliban's encouragement and sarcasm-edged patience, of how he hadn't given up on me. And I cursed the fact I couldn't visit him. How was he? Did he have food? Company whose thoughts weren't too loud?

Did he think I'd abandoned him?

My eyes stung as I looked up at Cyrus. "It's more curse than gift." Oh, the irony of saying that as a lie, when once I'd truly felt that way.

A small frown etched between his eyebrows as the slightest pink tinted his cheeks. "It is, isn't it? You poor little thing." He came closer, as if transfixed by my vulnerability, but jolted to a stop, gaze catching on my wrist. "And the bracelet is working? No ill effects?"

"It blocks the magic. And it makes me feel a little sick and weak at times, but it's a small price to pay for peace of mind, isn't it? I'm sure you know best."

At that last part, he straightened like I'd paid him the greatest compliment.

He liked me not only weak, but submissive, and I couldn't help but think of Bastian in that moment, though I hated myself for making any comparison between them. Bastian may not like it when we argued, but he liked my fire and strength. He only enjoyed it when I submitted in the bedroom, which I could understand—control was his version of safety.

Cyrus, though? I could see it from beneath my lashes—he wanted to feel strong and powerful. A god playing with ants.

I bowed my head and curled in on myself, then glanced back up to confirm.

Sure enough, his head rose and that subtle flush of his cheeks intensified as his pupils blew wide with pleasure.

The weaker I was, the stronger he felt.

He might not find me the prettiest or the most attractive—I was no match for fae beauty—but he loved how fragile I seemed.

If that was what it took to lure in a monster, so be it.

His eyelids fluttered as though he remembered himself, and he rubbed his hands together as he approached the desk. "I'm so glad you think so. As long as the bracelet is effective in the long term, that's all I wanted."

Damn. Dismissed so soon? This was the most time I'd had alone with him since coming up with my plan.

"If I may add...?" I tilted my head in question and waited for him to turn back to me. "Thank you for sending Elthea to check on me personally the other day." I looked away as though embarrassed, but I *felt* his attention sharpen on me now he was reminded of that moment he'd enjoyed so much.

"The fight. Mm, yes." He stalked closer, backing me against the wall.

My skin crawled and every instinct shrieked at me to look up and run away, but I squashed down the urge. Let him think he was the hunter and I was some poor, unsuspecting prey.

He only stopped once his toes were almost touching mine. For a second, I was back with unCavendish, and the ghost of his hand threaded through my hair. But there was no yank, and no part of me was so desperate for touch that it wanted any attention, even bad.

So, instead of freezing, I counted out three seconds as my chest heaved as though I was overcome by his nearness. Only then did I look up.

This prick had forced me away from my friends, my love, my home, yet I managed to moisten my lips and give him an inviting smile. Because unlike my encounters with unCavendish, *I* was in control of this situation and using it to *my* advantage. I wasn't the one being used but the one doing the using.

He leant closer, arm against the wall, bracketing me. "And how *are* you after your argument with the Serpent and his new human?" His voice dropped to something more intimate—one person speaking to another, rather than a king to a subject. "You weren't wounded, were you?"

I snorted softly. "Just my pride." Then I looked away, as though struggling to joke about the topic because of the great hurt lying beneath.

"What is it? Tell me." It wasn't quite an order.

I swallowed. Time to confide in him the lie I'd hinted at before. If it worked, it just might be the last thing I needed to get him to believe I had well and truly severed all ties to Bastian.

"I... feel so different now I've been away from him a while. I think he might have been using charm on me. He once said I was susceptible..."

"Oh." The sound came out of him laced with a laugh. "The great Bastian Marwood had to charm you." Out the corner of my eye, I could see him wrestling with a grin. He cleared his throat, apparently winning the battle, and went on more softly, "He must have—it's the only thing that makes sense—and now you're wearing iron, he can no longer do so. He was holding you back, and I've set you free."

Holding my breath was the only way to avoid laughing. He was really painting himself as my hero. Good fucking gods.

If stroking his ego would help me get close to him, then so be it.

I touched the bracelet, then blinked up at him. "You saved me."

I could actually see him puffing up. Any further and he'd explode. The smug pride was insufferable, and I was this close to choking on laughter. Just a little longer—I could burst once I was alone.

Slowly, his eyes narrowed and the smug smirk grew devious. My insides fluttered, caught between victory at capturing his attention so closely and dread at whatever was going on behind that cruel smile.

A rap sounded at the door. "Your Majesty is meeting with the Convocation in ten minutes," Adra called through.

Cyrus made a thoughtful sound. "This is to be continued." He pushed away from the wall, opening up my path to the exit.

I made a show of gathering myself and smoothing my dress before setting off.

My fingers closed around the door handle, when his voice reached me. "Oh, and Katherine?"

Putting a coy smile in place, I stopped and turned.

"Remember, curiosity killed the cat."

The dread inside me won, cold and heavy like lead. A warning. Much as he enjoyed my show of weakness, he hadn't *entirely* believed my excuses. He suspected I'd been poking around in his office. I bowed my head and left, but the feeling clanged through my bones, a distant bell tolling.

14

BASTIAN

"**N**eed I remind you how many died in the attacks on the city and palace?" Braea snapped as she paced her office. "And didn't your report say the human girl saw an armed shapechanger shortly before the assassination?" She sighed and shook her head, tone softening. "The more I think about it, the more I think the boy has a point."

I had to grit my teeth and squeeze my hands into fists before I could reply. "And what about Faolán? He's my most trusted operative, and he's been nothing but loyal to you and to—"

"Yes, he's one of the good ones." She patted my shoulder. "But you can't be so naïve to imagine they're *all* good."

I dragged in a breath. It felt like every conversation about this went around in the same dizzying circles.

Tonight it was because several shapechanger families had been rounded up in mass arrests ordered by Cyrus. From what information I'd gathered, they had committed no crimes, yet they sat in the dungeons far beneath our feet. This afternoon,

Faolán and I had beaten each other for two hours in the training yard. It had become habit now, training harder than we ever had before, all to let out our frustration.

"Remember, Bastian, I have your best interests in mind. I know you're fond of the fellow, and I'll ensure he's kept safe."

I pinched the bridge of my nose to try and force the thought out, but it crept in. Yes, Braea had pulled some strings to keep Faolán's name conveniently out of any register. But he was safe, not because of who he was and his service, but because he happened to be my friend.

We went on in circles a little longer until eventually she sighed. "I can see you're getting another headache and we're not getting anywhere. Go and get some air."

I made my way downstairs, off balance. The world only righted when I stepped out of the palace's side entrance and took several deep breaths in the cool night.

Being in conflict with Braea made everything askew—just by a few degrees, but enough to give a deep sense that something was wrong.

Coming here and looking across the gorge to Tenebris helped though. The city's size and the infinite heights of the night sky above gave me perspective, reassuring me that we'd find a solution. While this entrance, which so few people used, gave me that rare thing: quiet.

"There you are." A low purring voice swept that away, shattering my inner quiet, too, because I knew exactly who that voice belonged to.

"Sepher." I turned and it was only when he moved that I picked out the pale streaks in his hair amongst the darkness of the low trees and shrubs hugging the palace walls. "Skulking around, I see." I was too tired and frustrated to hide the disdain in my voice.

He snorted. "Rich coming from a man who wears shadows like a fashion accessory."

"Hilarious." I rolled my eyes. So much for peace. I might as well go to the Hall of Healing looking for Elthea. At this point it was clear she'd been avoiding me, but that was less frustrating than spending another moment around him. "Good night, Sepher. Go and find something else to catch."

But as I set off towards the bridge, he caught up to me. "I've been waiting for you for hours. Don't you want to know why?"

"Not really."

Apparently that wasn't an acceptable answer, because the next thing I knew, seven feet of shapechanger blocked my path.

I couldn't help the growl that rumbled in my chest. Recent events had eroded my patience to a fraying thread and I'd sparred with Faolán enough times to not be intimidated by Sepher's towering presence.

At the edge of my vision, I noted his twitching tail. He reminded me of a cat getting irritated because they were trying to sleep and someone kept bothering them. But *he* was the one harassing *me*.

"I've got something for you," he bit out. Before I could reply, he glanced around and thrust a cloth-wrapped package into my hands.

"If this is a prank, I'm throwing you in the river."

"Such ingratitude. Open it, idiot."

I spared him a long, cold look before pulling back the cloth. A piece of wood—what was I meant to do with that? I flicked him a glare, but he widened his eyes at the object. "Have a proper look at it before you set your shadows on me."

Wide and flat, it might've been a thin book, except it was

covered in bark. And, curiously, that bark had two different textures—one more craggy, the other slightly smoother, both familiar. Although it had clearly grown that way, it wasn't natural.

It reminded me of an old stone tablet—we had some in the archives, inscribed with ancient texts. There could be words hidden in the bark. I tilted it, peering at an odd formation at the point where the two types of bark met, and had to smother my reaction when the oval shape coalesced into a recognisable object.

A burning crown.

The Crown of Ashes—had to be. Did this mean Sepher knew of it? And he knew Braea was on the hunt? This "gift" could be an attempt to buy his way out of the palace—if the king wouldn't let him leave, maybe the queen would. It would explain why he'd waited for me personally rather than entrusting this to a servant.

I turned it over like I hadn't just spotted something so intriguing. "What makes you think I'd want this?"

He shrugged. "I don't give a shit about it. But my brother does. One of my people found a large group of his lackeys searching ruins not far from my home. It piqued their curiosity so they had a little search of their own and intercepted this. I'm not sure what it is, and frankly I don't care, but if it's important, I don't want my brother to have it." His teeth flashed in a wide grin—a predator realising he had the advantage.

"So you're choosing me over your brother now?"

He wrinkled his nose. "Not much of a choice, is it? I would've given it to Kat—she's much more pleasant to deal with than you, but she's in my brother's clutches, so you seemed a safer bet to keep it out of his reach."

I kept myself very still, focusing on the object rather than the image of Kat anywhere near Cyrus. Sepher might prefer me over his brother, but that didn't mean I trusted him with the truth about Kat. I needed to maintain the pretence.

Shrugging, I made a faint grunt. "Most things should be kept out of reach of your brother. Thanks, I suppose." As I turned away, I re-wrapped the wooden tablet.

I was several strides away and tucking the package into my jacket when Sepher called, "I always thought fae-touched humans were immune to charm."

My steps faltered as my mind raced. He was right. This had to relate to Kat. She could be using charm as cover—making it seem like she was under Cyrus's sway. We had limited communication, so I couldn't know her exact plans.

Or it could be Sepher's assumption. He'd seen Kat and me together before—he'd even joked about us marrying. He had an inkling about what we really meant to each other. He wouldn't believe Kat had *chosen* to get close to Cyrus.

Shit.

My pulse raced against my thoughts. Kat wasn't an experienced operative. This was too advanced a mission to let her take on. Not to mention dangerous. She had little to no support in the field—we couldn't risk the communication. What had I done?

I swallowed down my worries and turned. "Since I doubt you're talking about your wife, I assume you're talking about Katherine Ferrers." I shrugged one shoulder. "She isn't fae-touched or fae-blooded. Her magic is... the result of an arcane accident. I'm not sure the usual rules apply." I knew full-well she was immune to charm, thanks to the ring I'd given her, but none of what I'd just said was a lie. If she needed to rely on charm to make her plan believable, I couldn't snatch away that safety net.

"Hmm. Interesting." He watched me for a moment, eyes narrowing in calculation until his gaze was a pinprick. "It must be *killing* you to see her at my brother's side. He's taken quite a liking to her."

Play the game.

Again, I raised one shoulder like I couldn't even be bothered to shrug fully. "She was good at warming my bed. And you'd know as well as any how intriguingly rare red hair is for us. I recall it netting you more than your fair share of lovers. Besides, I was planning to share her eventually, anyway." True, just that I was planning to share her with my other self.

He didn't let up with that intent look. "Then she's just collecting powerful fae and you've been traded for a king." His smirk turned cruel. "I look forward to seeing what she does next"—he nodded at my chest—"and what you do with that."

Which would be precisely nothing.

The Crown was dangerous. Our balance was already a mess and it would only make things worse. If I had my way, it would remain hidden forever. My loyalty lay with Braea, as it always had, but in this instance, that loyalty meant protecting her from herself.

She wouldn't learn of this bark tablet from me. Loyalty or not.

15

KAT

Despite Cyrus's warning, my act in his office seemed to do the trick. The next day, Amandine wasn't posted outside my rooms, so I decided to test the length of my new leash. I spent the morning walking through Dawn's side of the palace, realising that the layout was similar to Dusk's, but not quite identical. Not once did I catch sight of Amandine. Good.

Perhaps I could see some of my friends—Rose and Ari wouldn't ruin my cover. Being seen to confide in them about Ella's *terrible betrayal* might make it more believable. But guards stopped me before I could reach the grand entrance hall lodestone and told me I had to wait for Amandine before going into the city. Less good.

Still, at least I knew where these new boundaries lay.

At lunch, Cyrus leant towards me on the arm of his chair, delivering all his best lines in my direction. He even took a morsel of dessert from his plate and fed it to me. I hated being fed like I was a lapdog, but when I reminded myself that this was all part of my plan, it was enough to tame my anger.

"Such a pretty little thing," he murmured, swiping a crumb from my mouth.

I fluttered my lashes and let the pressure of his touch pull my lips apart. *Gods, grant me sharp fae teeth so I can bite off his fucking thumb.*

Just like unCavendish, his gaze lingered on my lips, which had been perfectly rouged before the meal.

As in Cyrus's office, I didn't feel frozen or cowed into snivelling compliance as I always had with unCavendish. Instead, I leant closer as though my spine turned to jelly in his presence. It was no accident it also gave him a great view down my dress.

The situation was different, but also... *I* was different.

With a deep breath, I bit my lip as if holding back a smile and was rewarded by his low hum.

I was not a pawn on the board for him to sacrifice. No, I was going to take this fucking king down.

AFTER LUNCH, Adra took Cyrus away for an urgent discussion, and, buoyed by my success, I took my chance. With both of them gone, his office would be clear.

I needed another look at that letter. I might even borrow it, give it to Bastian, then sneak it back into the drawer, but that was much more risky.

One thing at a time. First, I needed to get into his office.

The gods were on my side, because the whole corridor leading to it was empty without a guard in sight. I hurried towards the door to Adra's outer office.

Locked. No surprise there. But I pulled the picks from my hair and set to work, Ella's lessons fresh in my mind. A simple mechanism, it took no time to get through as I kept watch along the corridor.

Inside, however, was the greater challenge—the lock to Cyrus's office was more complex. Now I was out of the corridor, though, I could crouch by the door. Biting my lip, I set the tension wrench and moments later, I had the first pin lifted. The second followed shortly after. A few more to go.

"Interesting," came a voice, right behind me, making my heart fucking explode.

I froze, every part of me focused on that thundering pulse.

Move, Katherine. You have to move.

Slowly, I straightened and turned.

Arms folded, one ankle crossed over the other, Prince Sepher lounged against the wall, just inside the door to Adra's office. I blinked, hoping that might get rid of the terrible apparition, but, no, he was real.

Shit. Shit. Shit.

"Good luck." He raised one eyebrow. "You're not getting in there. At least not like that." He cocked his head, gaze turning distant for a second. "Yes, I can hear my brother coming this way."

Fuck. *Think of an excuse.*

But there was no possible reason for me to be here picking the lock.

I barely registered he'd pushed away from the wall when his huge hand closed on my shoulder. "Come along, my sneaky little friend." Then he was leading me out and along the corridor. Towards Cyrus, ready to tell him what he'd found me doing.

My gaze skimmed over the gilded ivy leaf design on the walls as my mind raced through possible plans.

If I could get my bracelet off, I could poison him and run. Not that it was the best idea to murder a prince and I didn't want to rob Zita of her new husband, but I didn't exactly have a host of options. Regardless, my hands shook too much to get my lock picking tools into the bracelet.

We rounded a corner and I searched for some other escape.

There was none. I was trapped in Dawn, and Sepher was its prince.

And, oh great, even better, this was a dead fucking end. Maybe he was just going to kill me himself. I'd have to stab him with my lock picks, right in the soft bits.

At the end of the corridor, Sepher spun me around and leant in, almost nose-to-nose. "The former lover of Dusk's spymaster comes to Dawn and starts flirting with my brother. And then I find her trying to break into his office. What game is she playing?"

I blinked. If he wanted to talk, maybe I could reason with him or at least buy myself time to come up with an excuse. "You do understand people have died, right? This isn't a game."

He threw his head back and laughed. "*Everything* is a game. It's simply that in some games the stakes are higher." With eyes narrow, he watched me, tail swishing behind him. "I think you might've taken a seat at the wrong table if you don't realise what you're playing for."

"You assume I got to choose the table."

"Hmm." His lips pursed and he surveyed me for long seconds, as my pulse slowed to something approaching normal. "So you're just *pretending* to be under my brother's thrall?"

I held my breath. Admitting my ploy meant trusting him. Denial wasn't believable—not when he'd caught me. I doubted he'd believe the story that I was trying to leave Cyrus a surprise gift.

Trusting Sepher didn't seem like the brightest idea—at least not according to Bastian. Yet hadn't he and Zita stepped in between me and Uncle Rufus at tea? And in the gardens, they had lured Cyrus away, leaving me clear to retrieve Ella's lock picks. I'd put it down to coincidence, but maybe he was trying to work me out.

I lifted my chin and glared at him. "Why do you care?"

"Because if you're not charmed by him, you might be useful to me."

A huffing laugh escaped me. So *he* was also looking for an ally... or a tool.

He glanced back the way we'd come before stooping and pushing a decorative ivy leaf. What had appeared to be just a painted design pressed into the wall, followed by a click so soft, I questioned whether I'd really heard it. Then a section of wall swung away into darkness.

A secret passage. I knew they existed in Dawn, just as they did in Dusk—I'd even travelled down them to the lodestone courtyard with Bastian's spy. She'd refused to reveal the entrance, muttering, "Can't have you giving me away." And I'd had no luck in finding it on my own.

"This leads to my brother's personal suite... amongst other places. Best not to go to his rooms though—wouldn't be possible to explain that away, now, would it?" A slow smile showed off his canines. "*Unless* you're absolutely certain he won't return for a while."

Why did I get the feeling he was going to ensure that wouldn't happen?

"But," he went on, cleaning his claws, "if you *do* find your-self there, I wouldn't be upset if you were to fetch me the gold fountain pen he keeps on his bedside table. I'm sure it'll help keep me quiet about finding you sniffing around."

Ah, so there it was. Helping me was just a means to help himself. It didn't necessarily mean he could be trusted.

"Why don't you do it yourself? You know about these secret passageways and you can move much more quickly and silently than I can."

"He would smell that I'd been there. But he's had you sitting at his side all week—I daresay his clothes smell of you anyway."

"And what if I bump into Cyrus in the passageway? I'm sure that would go down well."

He snorted, glancing down the corridor as though he expected to see his brother any moment. "And I thought you were smart. Do you really think the golden child had any need of hidden passageways?" His amusement faded as old anger wrinkled his nose and drew his brows low. "My brother grew up with the privilege of not needing to know about things like secret passages. I did not. I have a feeling you're more like me than him in that regard."

Escape. That's what secret passages would've meant to me if I'd discovered those as a child. I'd have taken Avice with me and we would've waited out Father's rages somewhere hidden.

"Go left and keep straight. Oh, and watch your step." He nudged me towards the entrance, calling a single, dim fae light and sending it to follow me.

I entered, looking back as he pushed the hidden door shut. His face appeared in the last sliver of light. "Know that if you're caught, I won't help. You're on your own."

Then the door shut, leaving me in darkness.

16

KAT

The fae light was so dim compared to the main corridor, it took a long while for my eyes to grow accustomed to the gloom. The passage stretched left and right, so narrow I could touch one side with my shoulder and the other with my elbow. It had to be hidden within the walls.

It was slow going in the low light. Following his directions, I trailed my fingertips along the wall. With long, deep breaths, I placed each step carefully, even as cobwebs tickled my face. Stopping, I wiped them off in silence. I couldn't risk making a noise and attracting attention from someone in one of the rooms I passed.

Muffled voices broke the quiet, and I sucked in a silent breath, pausing, listening. I couldn't make out the words and it quickly became clear they weren't here in the passage with me, but in one of the rooms beyond.

I edged onwards and the voices grew clearer.

"—must be a reason the spymaster hasn't made themselves known to me." Cyrus's tone was clipped, edged with impatience. "It's been two weeks since I ascended to the throne. You must've told them."

"I don't know who they are, Your Majesty. And what would I tell them? I helped you as my prince before you were my king. That's all." A woman's voice I recognised, but couldn't quite put my finger on.

I crept closer. My pulse grew deafening in my ears. While Bastian was widely known as Dusk's spymaster, the identity of Dawn's had always been kept a secret. Whoever they were, it sounded like they were also keeping it secret from their new king.

"And you didn't betray my father?" Cyrus barked a laugh. "Silly me, I must be misremembering. Because *I* thought you'd taken my money and planted my spy at the human court. Are you calling me a liar, Adra?"

I froze. *His* spy. UnCavendish?

"No, Your Majesty. Of course I would never."

She went on, trying to appease him, but I was spinning, falling under the weight of what Cyrus had just revealed.

I'd known Adra had helped procure the pearlwort necklace unCavendish had given me, but as the former king's assistant, I'd assumed that meant Lucius was behind the changeling.

Adra had been working for Cyrus all along.

The foolish prince who preened and tossed his hair like a boy playing at hero had been plotting far more deeply and for far longer than I'd ever imagined.

But it made sense. Lucius had understood the delicate balance between Dusk and Dawn. He wouldn't have risked that by having Bastian poisoned, even in Albion where he could've blamed a jilted human lover like yours truly. No. He'd been far more patient, far more prudent than that.

But Cyrus?

Yes. That was absolutely something he would do. No wonder unCavendish always had it in for Bastian—he was acting on the orders of a master who *hated* Bastian.

Shit. I needed to warn him. Despite the fake Hydra Ascendant attacks, I had the impression Bastian still didn't take Cyrus entirely seriously, but in light of this, he needed to be careful.

I shook my head and leant into the wall, hungry for more. The conversation was so clear, there had to be a spy hole or hidden grate somewhere to let the sound through.

When I extinguished the fae light and looked off into the darkness, I caught in my periphery the faintest sliver of light. I groped for it and found a heavy velvet flap hiding a spy hole. On tiptoes, I peered through.

Cyrus sat at his desk, feet on it, arms folded, glaring at Adra, who stood with her head bowed. But she wasn't shaking and her face showed no fear, rather she seemed to be patiently waiting.

"Enough," Cyrus huffed. "I see I shall have to continue waiting for our spymaster. Perhaps they are simply tardy with making themselves known for me. I'll ensure they're punished for such insolence. You would do well to remember the price for revealing our earlier arrangement."

"Of course, Your Majesty."

"Good." He sat up as though ready to get down to business and I pressed against the spy hole, ready to hear more secrets. "As for other matters, we need to—"

A knock sounded at the door, reverberating through the walls.

With a huff, Cyrus called, "Enter."

And in walked Sepher. "Adra." He nodded in greeting, then

jerked his chin at the door. "My brother and I have a lot to discuss. Bring us some drinks, would you?" His eyes turned straight to me, and my breath caught. "I suspect we'll be occupied for some time."

Meaning Cyrus's suite would be empty and this was my chance to explore.

I lowered the velvet drape and whispered for the fae light to return before continuing along the dark passage.

Sepher really was helping me. If he wanted me in trouble, that would've been the perfect moment—I'd have been caught red handed.

As he'd hinted, turnings went off to my right, but I ignored them and continued straight, though I did peer down one, sending the fae light ahead to reveal it. Even narrower, it continued for maybe fifteen feet, then two more passages branched off. Further ahead it branched again.

This place was a labyrinth.

Calling the light back to me, I resumed my course along the main path, trying not to think about getting lost in the walls. I hadn't seen any other doorways yet. This place could easily become a tomb.

The passage turned and as I batted more cobwebs away from my face, it took me a long moment to realise my foot hadn't connected with the ground. I gasped so hard, I choked. On instinct, my arms shot out, and I somehow wedged myself in place.

The fae light drifted around me and I blinked into the gloom, trying to make sense of my surroundings. My heart jolted as I understood what the shapes meant.

A sheer drop stretched below me into pure darkness. One foot hung over the gap, while I held my weight on my forearms, pressing into the walls.

Dread stole over me, colder than ice. For a second, I was dangling over Dia's grave, the scent of damp soil filling my nose.

I squeezed my eyes shut, like that would help blot out an image that was only in my mind, and pressed harder into the walls, the stone unyielding and rough against my fingertips as I searched for a handhold.

I'm not there. That was a long time ago.

Rough walls. The cool, still air. Sweat trickling from my armpit down my side.

Here and now.

The threatening memories ebbed away and I drew a long, steadying breath. Shoulders burning, I eased backwards until my weight was on the foot left on solid ground and I could step away from the pit.

I sagged against the wall. "Fucking Sepher," I panted. *Watch your step?* Good fucking gods, that was *not* enough of a warning.

Thankfully, the pit wasn't wide, easy enough for me to jump over, but just big enough that someone fumbling along in the dark who didn't know the passageways would fall victim to it. That "someone" had very nearly been me.

I shuddered but picked myself up, dusted off the cobwebs, and jumped across the gap.

Prince or not, next time I saw Sepher, I was going to murder him.

I continued along the passage without further incident until I reached the dim outline of a door in the stone wall. Some squinting and feeling around revealed a small sun carved into the stone, which indented under my fingertip, just as the ivy leaf had under Sepher's, and sent the door swinging out into a lavishly decorated bedroom.

If there was any doubt about whose room this was, the huge, golden sunburst radiating from the headboard would've laid that to rest, along with the cloud-like drapes hanging around it. I took a moment to admire the way the fabric billowed like real clouds. Fae magic would never grow old to me.

Not trusting the secret passage after the pit incident, I wedged a marble statuette in the door to stop it closing behind me and only then did I set forth to explore King Cyrus's rooms.

17

KAT

I surveyed the space first, since I had no idea how many rooms there were and where might be best to search first. The huge bedroom seemed strangely empty, like no one really lived there, though there were clothes in the armoire and drawers. It took no time to find the golden pen Sepher had asked for. It winked in the sunlight streaming through the windows. I grabbed it and tucked it into my bodice. At least now I could focus on my search.

In contrast with the bedroom, an expansive lounge was very full, with gold and crystal ornaments glistening on every surface, and a ceiling mural of the sky with clouds that skimmed along as though it was open to the real sky above. Spare bedrooms. The three bathrooms gleamed with mirrored tiles, spacious showers, and one had a bath big enough to swim in.

He had two dining rooms. One with white marble columns and a long table large enough to seat twenty guests, and another much more intimate with a round table that seated four. The smaller dining room's floor to ceiling windows looked out to the east, perfect for viewing the sunrise's lingering colours once Sleep loosened its grip on the Day King.

And that was when I realised.

There was nothing personal here. No signs of Cyrus, only of the king. Certainly nothing that screamed "Search here for all my secrets!"

Still, I had one more door to try.

If this was anything like Bastian's suite (albeit much bigger), this would be the equivalent of his workshop. I held my breath and turned the handle.

Boxes. Lots and *lots* of boxes.

But not stacked in order like a storeroom, more like…

I sidled between the stacks and found glass cabinets and a set of many, tiny drawers covering one wall, with finely made cupboards lining the other.

More like someone was partway through unpacking these boxes and putting everything away in their new homes.

I glanced back towards the bedroom. Servants had put away all his clothing but not the items in here.

An open box beckoned me closer. Half hanging off the edge, as though it had been taken out, then hastily discarded, a deep frame housed a dozen butterflies. There was something sad about their little bodies pinned to the board, their iridescent wings doomed never to flutter again. I peered into other boxes stacked around this one and found other insects as well as collections of pelts and pale skulls perfectly cleaned.

Something tugged me back to the butterflies, though. That lingering sadness, perhaps.

When I stood over the frame, I realised… their wings *were* moving. Slowly, they folded open and closed, showing off the beautiful faceted colours. Their legs extended and bent as though they tried to walk, despite the pins impaling them. My stomach turned at the thought of living in a glass cage, pinned in place, yet somehow still alive.

I didn't know what I planned to do, exactly, but I grabbed the frame—their prison—and felt a snatched second of buzzing before there was a clink and it fell silent, as sudden as a thunderclap.

The butterflies twitched, then went still. Truly still this time.

The frame must've been enchanted to keep them alive and I'd somehow broken it. A dull gleam at my wrist winked at me. The iron bracelet. It had hit the frame and blocked the magic for a moment—the silence after the buzz.

Shit. If Cyrus realised I'd been here...

But if the frame had broken on its own...

I propped it on the edge of the box, then nudged it off. Glass tinkled on the floor, and a satisfying crack opened up at the corner of the frame. He'd left it precariously balanced and it had simply fallen off. No snooping humans with iron bracelets involved.

I sighed with relief that was as much for the butterflies as for myself and removed the bracelet. Magic flooded me, its resonance overwhelming, and I had to catch myself on the curiosity cabinet. Once I could see straight, I left the bracelet by the door and turned my back on the boxes of broken animals before trying another stack.

These boxes contained various items I couldn't link together. An orb full of smoke. A music box whose tune hurt my ears. A locket containing shimmering opalescent hair. All sorts of strange objects whose magic buzzed and purred over my skin.

This felt like Cyrus's personal collection. Something he

didn't trust anyone else to put away. Not quite what I was looking for, but close. How long would Sepher keep him occupied? It would take all day to search every box—maybe longer.

I wandered between the stacks, hoping for some sign or for instinct to kick in and tell me to look in *this box—this is the one.*

But I reached the back of the room and nothing had leapt out at me. With a huff, I sank into a chair surrounded by smaller boxes, as though Cyrus had sat here sorting through items.

This was impossible. There was too much. I'd have to try my best for a while longer, then sneak back in another day.

I spun slowly on the chair, surveying the room. There had to be something. And failing that, the first thing that caught my attention, I would investigate.

Fae lights clustered in wall sconces, casting warm light on the dark wood panelling of this back wall. It was a much cosier space than most rooms in Dawn. If not for Cyrus's unsettling collection, I might've liked it here.

My gaze snagged on a a dark scar marring the perfect decor. A knot in the wood? Or a hidden button? It seemed this palace was full of secret doors if you only knew where to look.

Squinting, I approached. But it wasn't a smooth, carved button disguised as decoration or even a knot, but a dent, raw and splintered, as though something had smashed into the wall.

And below, half hidden behind a box, a mirror glinted at me.

Gingerly, I fished it out, expecting to find it broken, but there wasn't so much as a mark upon the ravens decorating the frame or a crack upon the brittle glass.

Interesting. Its edge matched the gouge in the wall, and yet it was perfectly undamaged. Why had Cyrus thrown it? I was pretty positive that was what had happened.

Like many of the items in here, it resonated with magic, though this was a deeper hum than anything else in the room. When I held it up, I couldn't see myself. Frowning, I moved around, trying to catch the light, but still couldn't find my reflection. And something about the frame seemed... not off but... meaningful. The design was more Dusk coded than Dawn, with moths and spears gathered between the birds, so why was it here?

It had to have some personal relevance for him to have such an emotional reaction. It certainly felt more personal than the other curiosities.

I backed away from the gouge in the wall until I found an open box. The tissue paper discarded on top looked like it had housed the mirror. Inside, I found a bundle of letters.

"*There*," I breathed, scooping them up. More from whoever had encouraged Cyrus to bump his father out of the picture.

But when I opened the first one, the words "my darling" caught my eye. *Love letters*? I didn't think Cyrus capable—from all I'd heard, he changed lovers as often as most people changed underwear. He had no attachments. It was a good reason to draw out my flirtation with him—desperation to have me would keep him around for longer. If I gave in too soon, he'd discard me.

Setting the mirror down, I plonked myself in the chair, then set to work on the letters. Arrangements to meet. How much they couldn't wait to see him next. How wonderful last night had been. Standard love letter stuff. Unlike the letter I'd found in his office, the seal remained on these, but it was a plain disc of grey wax.

I tried to summon the image of the other letter to work out

if the handwriting matched. But I'd only seen it for a minute. I couldn't be sure.

Still, this stack of letters was in the same box as the mirror. Did that mean he was in a relationship with someone from Dusk? I knew enough of fae culture to understand that would be shocking, but I doubted it would be enough to help dethrone him.

"More's the pity," I muttered as I flicked through the remaining notes. No clues about this lover's identity.

Careful to leave them as I'd found them, I returned the letters to the box and found myself drawn to the mirror again. Perhaps it was that the silvery surface reminded me of Bastian's eyes.

Missing him was a constant physical sensation—a splinter that just drove deeper.

I sighed, breath misting on the mirror's surface as I thought back to last time I'd seen him, silhouetted against the sun, helping me up from the ground, then pushing me away.

Something tickled at the back of my neck. Something close to sensation of being watched.

And when my eyes refocused, I found the mirror had cleared and showed, not this room, but a different place entirely.

Dark and grey. Lacquered wood. I peered closer. Was that the inside of a cupboard?

The rumble of a man's voice came from somewhere nearby. I froze, eyes wide. I couldn't see the door from here, too many boxes blocked the way, but I listened so hard, I thought my eardrums might burst. My time was up. Cyrus was back.

The voice sounded again, muffled, so I couldn't hear the words. But it didn't come from the corridor.

It came from the mirror.

I'd heard of scrying mirrors that could see the past or the future or places far away. This had to be one. I opened my mouth to call through. Whoever it was on the other side would—

A door slammed. Not from the mirror—from behind me. Somewhere in this suite.

"Shit."

I couldn't be found here.

I muttered more curses as I hurried to the damaged wall and slid the mirror back where I'd found it. My fingers caught on something, and I hissed at the stinging pain of—

Great, a paper cut. On the back of the mirror, a folded slip of paper sat tucked under the hook. I'd been so consumed with the front, I hadn't spotted it.

I didn't have time to stop and think. I grabbed it, shoved the mirror in place, and fled the room, scooping up the iron bracelet on the way.

Voices drifted from the lounge, and my pulse drummed in response. It would be bad enough if a servant found me here where I very much didn't belong, but Cyrus?

I'd be dead.

And that was one hundred percent his voice coming from just the other side of the door.

As quietly as possible, I hurried through the hall, thankful for the thick carpet muffling my steps.

Please don't come this way, I chanted internally. It was painful to ease open his bedroom door rather than flinging it wide as quickly as possible, but I had no choice. I needed silence as much as speed.

Once I had the door shut behind me, I allowed myself a deep breath and hurried to the secret passage. Marble statuette back on its plinth, then into the darkness once more.

Working my way to the entrance, I kept my sweaty hand closed around the slip of paper. Somewhere along the way I'd lost the dim fae light Sepher had sent with me, so I had to keep every ounce of focus on feeling my way in pitch black.

Aside from the butterflies, had I put everything away exactly? The question tortured me with every step.

After I turned the corner, I edged forward until I located the pit, leapt over that, and ran the rest of the way to the door. Someone had been good at planning, because they had a spy hole at the entrance, perfect for checking the main corridor before emerging from the hidden passages. My eye burned at the sudden light, but the way was clear.

I stepped out, dusted myself off, and strode to my rooms.

Only once I was in my bedroom with the door shut did I unfold the slip of paper.

Just two sentences covered it in a messier version of the handwriting from the love letters.

I'm entrusting this mirror to you. It was my sister's and I fear what my mother will do if she gets hold of it.

Oh, gods.

I knew that mirror. I knew who the sister was. And yes, her mother would be fucking *furious* if she found out.

18

KAT

The rest of the afternoon, I paced, the knowledge buzzing inside me.

Cyrus's lover was Sura. That mirror was the one Nyx had used to contact her unseelie lover.

It haunted me all night, too, merging with nightmares about unCavendish, except his face kept flickering between Cavendish and Cyrus.

The next morning, when the orrery on the mantlepiece whirred to eleven o'clock, I slipped out. There was a particular garden room Sepher and his friends had taken to occupying. It seemed the best place to find him, so I could give him the fountain pen that sat in my pocket, evidence of my theft from a king. I needed to get rid of it. Clipped footsteps marked my route through the palace.

Could Sura be behind the letter from Cyrus's office? Even if the writing was different, she might've dictated it to a secretary or disguised her handwriting or...

I shook my head, the possibilities crowding in.

Did Cyrus know she was alive?

And the mirror. Could that be used to contact Nyx's lover? He had every reason to hate Braea—could he be an ally against her?

I didn't know for sure that she'd offered me to Cyrus, but I wouldn't be surprised. At best, it seemed likely she'd worked *with* Cyrus to select me. He got his hands on Bastian's lover, while she had me out of the way.

After the veiled threat she'd given me outside the palace's side entrance, I had no doubts she would welcome any opportunity to remove me from the board.

I turned the corner and a shadow loomed from an alcove. Tall and red-haired, for the briefest second, I thought Sepher had found me. But this hair was paler, and the smile that greeted me was far colder.

"Here she is at last, my elusive niece." Uncle Rufus blocked my path.

"Uncle." His timing was so irritating, I barely managed half a fake smile. It was growing harder to pretend to be an obedient niece when I had much bigger problems and much more powerful villains to contend with. "How good to see you. I was just on my way—"

"To see me, I hope. I've been trying to get hold of you for over a week. Surely you received my messages?"

I'd burned them, unread. The thought of having something in my possession that came from him made my skin crawl. Blinking, I cocked my head as though confused. "You know, it doesn't appear I have. My guard is rather zealous about what —and who reaches me." I glanced around as though Amandine might appear at any moment, and for once I wished she would.

He made a sound that was part thoughtful, part dismissive. "Then we need a more in-depth conversation than I realised."

Lifting his chin, he stepped into my space, until I had no choice but to back into the alcove. "About Viscount Fanshawe's estate." His slow smile made my insides squirm, as I pressed against the wall. "Your late husband and I had an agreement that would alleviate his financial woes."

I stiffened. *I* had been the one to suffer Robin's financial disasters. *I* was the one who'd worked her fucking arse off to solve them. What the hells was he doing making agreements about what would happen to *my* estate?

"We agreed I would purchase the land for a large lump sum and rent it back to him at a fair rate for the remainder of his lifespan, with the understanding I would leave it to any legitimate offspring that might arise from your union." His gaze trailed down to my belly, and a sneer spoiled his benevolent smile.

Well, no offspring were ever going to happen with Robin. But my mind snagged on the "remainder of his lifespan." Now he was dead, what did that mean?

"And do you have a signed agreement to this effect? Did he sell to you before he died?"

He flinched, eyes skipping back to mine. "It was a gentlemen's agreement. No money had changed hands."

That was something. But it still left more questions. Where did Uncle Rufus get that kind of money? And why would he help Robin?

Viscount Fanshawe.

Of course. *That* was why. The estate came with a title. Wasn't that what Uncle Rufus had always wanted? The second son who'd spent a lifetime aggrieved that his brother had inherited. Buying Markyate Cell was his way to become, at last, a lord with a title, an estate, and unbridled access to the very highest echelons of Albionic society.

He was so predictable, I could've laughed.

"Unfortunately, Uncle Rufus, without a written contract or any exchange of money, your verbal agreement died with the Viscount Fanshawe, and Markyate remains *my* estate." I smiled innocently, like I was merely reciting facts and not enjoying every word.

His face grew red and he lurched closer. Every fibre in me squirmed away as my hand flew to my throat, afraid—so, so afraid he would grab me again.

Stupid girl. I had to remember my place. What he could do. And most of all—the fact that, without my magic, I wasn't untouchable.

"You have nothing. You *are* nothing." His voice boomed, echoing off the alcove walls, no longer kept quiet by the veneer of gentlemanly civility. "Or do you need another lesson in duty?"

"That's not a very nice way to speak to one of my brother's guests." Sepher's voice cut through the air, making my uncle jolt upright.

Rufus took a step back, turning, and we found the prince behind him, lounging against a statue, cleaning his claws. But unlike when he'd snuck up on me earlier, there was a thread of tension thrumming through him, like a bowstring released a moment earlier. He glanced up from his apparently idle work, but his claws caught the light, all of them unsheathed.

A reminder of what he was and the fact he needed no weapon.

"Your Highness." Rufus gave a brief, tight smile. "This is a family matter." He turned back to me, blocking Sepher out.

"You misunderstand the way things work in Elfhame, little man." A growl edged the prince's words as he loomed over my uncle. "She is Dawn's before she is yours."

Rufus blinked, swallowed, turned, and I found myself holding my breath.

"You might make your little deals, trading our goods to your people," Sepher went on, voice terribly low. "You might even have made yourself very rich by human standards. But don't think that makes you a person of importance. You have no place in our court. *You* are nothing. You're only here as long as we suffer your presence, and right now my patience is in short supply. Get out of my sight before it runs out."

Again, my uncle's throat bobbed and the raging pleasure of seeing his brow sweat bloomed in me, fierce and hot like a desert flower. He paused as if waiting for Sepher to step back and give him space to leave the alcove.

Sepher didn't move.

Instead, Uncle Rufus had to squeeze past as he had made me do so many times. He glanced over his shoulder with a look that said this wasn't over, but in that moment, I could've kissed Sepher.

I leant against the wall. "Thank you."

He raised his eyebrows. "What for? I can't stand the man. He fawns over my brother constantly and he is in-fucking-sufferable. Getting rid of him was a favour to no one but myself." He shook off that thrumming tension, like a sabrecat shaking off irritating flies, and stepped back. "I'm guessing you have something for me. Come on." He opened the door to the garden room and ushered me inside.

19

KAT

Inside I found Zita and Celestine, pale-faced. Celestine was a tall fae with the kind of willowy figure my Dawn clothes had been designed for. She and Sepher had been close since childhood, but otherwise I knew little about her. She tended to look a little sickly, but not normally this ashen.

I frowned from them to Sepher. "What's wrong?"

Zita straightened, lips pressed together. "It's Adra—Cyrus's assistant, and my father's before that."

Celestine's eyebrows pulled together as her eyes went bright, while Sepher dropped into a chair and gestured for me to do the same.

From Celestine's reaction, I had a horrible feeling I knew what was coming before Zita's next words. "She's dead."

"What happened? I only saw her yesterday."

Celestine sat forward. "She..." Her voice cracked as her lip trembled, and she shook her head, unable to go on.

Sepher's large hand dwarfed her delicate shoulder as he comforted her. At my querying look, he cleared his throat.

"When we were children, she was the one my father would send to summon us. She always had sweets in her pocket that she'd sneak to us, even if we were in trouble."

"How did she...?" I didn't want to upset Celestine, but the question gnawed at me.

The faint smile that had stolen over Sepher's face as he'd described his childhood memory of Adra faded. "An accident. Apparently."

Still stroking Celestine's back, Zita scowled. "She fell down the stairs and broke her neck."

"What?" I stared from her to Sepher, then back. "That can't be true. When have you ever seen a fae so much as stumble?"

Zita bared her teeth. The ferocity suited her, since her canines were elongated like a fae's—the mark of her fae-touched magic. "*Exactly.*" She glanced at the door. It was closed. "She was found at the bottom of a staircase with a broken neck, but I don't believe she fell for a fucking second."

Aconite, fae-worked weapons, a broken neck. I added another cause of death to the ones I knew worked on fae.

"It's obviously murder." Sepher scowled into the distance, rubbing his lower lip. "But who and why?"

Remember the price...

Cyrus had threatened her not twenty-four hours ago. She'd been working for him before Lucius's death: it was conceivable she knew something about the assassination plan or had grown suspicious. Cyrus absolutely would have someone murdered to keep his secret. Had he ordered one of his personal guard to kill her or done the deed himself?

And he'd announced Krae's guilt, ensuring they would find no peace and be arrested or even killed on sight.

He was tying up loose ends. Anyone who could spill his secret.

And that included me.

For several seconds, I couldn't breathe.

Cyrus could never find out that I knew he'd assassinated his father. He couldn't even have the slightest inkling. He was not above killing me, *just in case.*

"Kat?" Zita touched my knee. "Are you all right? You've gone an odd colour."

"It was Cyrus." I swallowed and nodded, trying to shake off the fear that threatened to suffocate me. "I can't tell you why, but I'm sure of it."

Celestine made a soft, dark sound, like she'd kill Cyrus with her bare hands if he was here. Zita held my gaze a long while as if trying to read my thoughts.

"My brother, of course," Sepher muttered. He gave a long-suffering sigh, then raised an eyebrow at me. "Bad news aside, do you have something for me?"

"You're the one who delivered the news. But yes, I do."

His eyes narrowed as he glanced down at my empty hands. "And, of course, humans never lie. How do I know you really have it?"

"You two have been trying to help me ever since I arrived here. Blocking my uncle just now and on my first day here. Getting rid of Cyrus in the gardens."

Sepher's face remained impassive, but it was Zita who gave him away by straightening and glancing at him.

"*Why*? You don't get this until you tell me." I fished the pen from my pocket and dangled it in the air so there would be no doubts that I'd followed through on my side of the hastily struck bargain.

In a blink, Sepher was standing before me. I'd never seen someone so big move so fast, not even Faolán. He bent over me, hands planted on the back of my chair, teeth bared in a vicious smile. "Or I could just take it from you."

But I didn't sit idly. I'd practised so I could work the lock on my bracelet by touch alone. In a moment, it clunked to the floor. "Oops. How clumsy of me. But at least it allows me to do this." I flashed my teeth back at Sepher as I lifted my hand and let the purple poison creep over my fingers. Magic tingled through me, like the blood flowing back in after pins and needles.

With a snarl, Sepher took a step out of arm's reach.

Celestine gasped, eyes wide on my hand. "Aconite," she murmured, expression creasing into a glower.

Sepher's tail swished left to right, and although he'd backed off, he still towered above me, body taut with readiness. The moment I lowered my hands or quelled my poison, he would take the pen and maybe even my life.

But I'd had enough of being threatened by men who were twice my size and thought their strength meant they could do and take whatever they wanted.

I held his gaze, even though his slitted pupils unnerved me.

After long moments of crackling tension, Zita sighed. "Sepher, darling, don't be a dick. You threatened her first. Sit down."

He shot her a sharp look, then me an even sharper one, but eventually plopped onto his chair, arms folded.

Celestine eased back into her seat, nodding her approval. "I think you can admit the truth to our new friend here." She threw me a brief, wary smile.

Sepher made a low, grumbling sound. "I have my own reasons to be... less than pleased with my brother. He made too many years of my childhood... unpleasant, and now he's fucking up my adulthood by making me fill in his stupid book and stay in his palace." His gaze flicked to Zita and lingered. "I wouldn't be angry if he were to become more acquainted with justice."

Celestine watched as though expecting him to go on, but he said nothing more.

Maybe they knew Cyrus had killed Lucius but weren't sure if I did. Under fae law, since Sepher was so closely related to the victim, it was his right to take Cyrus's life. The problem was the evidence. If Cyrus's guilt wasn't proven, the rest of the world would consider it murder rather than a just execution.

Eventually, he shrugged. "I assumed you were under his charm. It was the only way I could explain you going anywhere near him. But it seems I was wrong. And I don't know exactly what game you're playing, Kat, but if someone's toying with my brother, you can bet I'm going to help. If he's going to keep me confined to the palace, it's only fair he deals with the consequences."

That didn't sound like he wanted Cyrus dead for the assassination. He didn't know.

Still, I chuckled at what Sepher had said and held out the pen. "May he reap the rewards of *all* his actions."

"It's all right. You can keep it." He stood, making no move to take the prize. "I didn't really need it. Asking you was just a test."

"*What*? You sent me there just for *a test*?"

"I got my answer about whether you were really for or against my brother. And I'm sure you found some answers of your own."

Zita rose and squeezed his arm. "What my husband is trying to say is, we would welcome an alliance with you, Katherine Ferrers. Us against him."

He made a thoughtful sound, tail finally calming. "Do you accept?"

An alliance with a fae prince? That had to come with all sorts of unexpected strings attached. "I'll think about it."

Zita flashed a grin. "I understand." As Celestine stood, Zita started for the door, Sepher at her side, though his long-legged stride slowed as he scented the air with a frown.

It was only when I turned to watch them leave and felt the air prickle that I realised my gaze kept skipping over an area by the door.

Orpha, the half wraith operative who worked for Bastian. I'd met her in passing leaving Bastian's offices, introduced by his assistant. Now, she lounged against the wall, clearly waiting for the others to leave. Her wraith blood made her hard to see. Not exactly invisible, but she could pass unnoticed.

I smothered any further reaction, and Zita and Sepher walked right past her and out into the hall.

"Oh." Celestine made the soft sound as she drew level with me, and Orpha froze. Celestine was staring right at her, lips parted, eyes wide. A pink flush blossomed on her pale cheeks.

Orpha shot me a look that said "Oh shit" and slammed the door. She took three strides forward before I realised her weapon was drawn.

"It's all right," I blurted, stepping between them.

"No one can know I'm here," Orpha gritted out between her pointed teeth. "It breaks all the agreements between Dusk and Dawn."

"Celestine can be trusted. Can't you?" I threw a desperate look over my shoulder and found her still staring at Orpha.

She blinked, swallowed, then nodded. "Oh. Yes. Of course." The corner of her mouth curled as she stepped out from behind me. "No one will learn of this visit from me."

Orpha paused, dagger turning in her hand as she eyed Celestine from head to toe, lingering on the embroidered hem of her gown. "Fine." She returned the weapon to its sheath and jerked her chin at me. "If she breathes a word, you deal with her."

I didn't exactly want to poison Celestine, but I nodded, praying it wouldn't come to that.

"I suppose I should excuse you two." Celestine gave a self-conscious laugh and circled around Orpha, not taking her eyes off her. At the doorway, she paused. "Celestine. My name, that is."

Orpha barely glanced over her shoulder and shrugged. "Great. Good bye, Celestine."

Nose wrinkled, she waited for the door to click shut before speaking again. "I never had you down as someone with such... *princessy* friends."

I winced at the casual dismissal of another woman. And for someone who said "princessy" like an insult, Orpha was eyeing the jewelled details of my gown very closely.

I didn't really know Celestine, but she hadn't done anything to merit my dislike nor Orpha's. If anything, she seemed more friendly towards Orpha than she'd ever been to me. Offering your name was meaningful in Elfhame. "She's also rather friendly and beautiful. Did you notice that?"

A furrow scored between Orpha's eyebrows. "I came to deliver a message, not comment on the beauty of the women I encounter. Bastian's had no joy looking for Krae in Dusk. Faolán and Rose tried to track their scent using the dagger used to stab Cyrus. There was no sign of them on the bridge, so..."

"They're probably still in the palace."

"That's the suspicion. He's still searching the secret passages on our side, but there's a lot to get through."

"And he can't come to Dawn's side without risking—"

"A *lot* of shit." She nodded, pale eyes wide. "There was so much chaos that day, Krae could be hidden somewhere in Dawn. He wants you to find an entrance to the passages and search on this side, but only if it's safe."

I laughed a little. It still felt like a novelty having someone else as worried about my safety as I was, when it had been solely my obsession for so long. "I already have a way in. I'll begin searching today."

Carefully, I thought, picturing the pit I'd almost fallen down.

She eyed the door, clearly ready to leave, but I caught her arm as she went to turn. Her gasp was so sharp, I flinched, worried I'd hurt her.

"Sorry, I—"

"It's fine." She rubbed her arm, eyebrows bunched together. "Not many fae want to touch someone with *any* wraith blood. I'm not used to it. Is something wrong?"

I gave an apologetic smile. "Can you tell me anything else? I don't get much information about the outside world here. My friends, are they all right?"

She blinked at me as though my questions were as alien to her as affection, and my heart squeezed in empathy. Not so long ago, I'd been starved of touch. Now here I was missing it, because it was something I'd grown accustomed to.

"Rose has been a little sick, but it doesn't seem like anything serious. I hear humans get ill quite frequently. The rest are fine. I think the blond one misses you most."

"Ella." The back of my throat ached suddenly, and I had to

swallow past it. "And beyond the city walls? Bastian's work—*our* work?"

Her lips pressed together. "I'm not sure I should share business matters so openly."

Good gods, I was trapped in Dawn because of the machinations of fae courts—this was *my* business.

I bit my tongue. What had Bastian told me about Orpha? He'd once grumbled about having to pay her an extortionate bonus for lugging a large quantity of books back from some ruins for him, so she had a mercenary streak.

"I could make it worth your while."

Her gaze panned from the door to me. "How worth my while?"

"I'll give you my next booking with Ariadne." That was something money couldn't buy and, to a fae, worth more than anything else I possessed. Besides, it wasn't like I could go and see her at the moment.

Orpha's eyelids twitched. Tempted, but not quite enough.

"*And* I'll foot the bill." Bastian had paid me and aside from sending money to Morag and Horwich back at the estate, I didn't have much to spend it on.

She grinned, showing off her full mouth of sharp teeth. "You have a deal. Bastian's had a few of us checking on Hydra Ascendant's activity... but there's been little. No signs of large groups mobilising." Her mouth twisted to one side.

"And? There's something else."

"They seem too quiet, if you ask me. I don't think they're planning a full scale invasion, but they're up to *something*."

"Of course they are." I sighed and thanked her, before giving her the time and date for my next appointment with Ari so she could take advantage of it, but my mind was tangled up in Sura and what she might have planned.

What had she planted in my mind and then locked? She'd told me it would save Bastian's life, but there could be more to it—something that might help us now... or something dangerous.

But the blank space in my mind remained, a spot my thoughts slipped around when I tried to remember.

I hoped it wasn't a deal I'd live to regret.

Whatever Hydra Ascendant was up to, I couldn't help uncover it—I had a king to deal with.

I'd once read an old story that included a curse I hadn't understood in childhood.

May you live in interesting times.

Now I understood it all too well.

20

KAT

A few days after my conversation with Orpha, I walked back to my rooms from an early dinner. Late sunlight shafted through the windows lining the corridor, warm and bright. The gilded edges of the clouds painted on the walls glistened and glimmered as I passed. Moments like these brought it home that I lived in a literal palace—for now, at least.

But, of course, it could all come crashing down any moment when Cyrus discovered what I was up to or if Sura made her move.

Joy.

With that gloomy thought dogging my steps and a false smile on my lips, I returned to my suite. It was only when I closed the door, I could let the smile fall.

No sooner had I kicked off my shoes than I found another reminder of the lie I was living.

A small box of chocolates sat on the coffee table. A gift from King Cyrus.

I would've preferred cake, but these would do for eating my feelings.

I took a bite from one of the carefully crafted chocolates.

And immediately spat it back out. The floral flavour still clung to my mouth and nose though.

"Fucking violets." I ran to the bathroom and rinsed my mouth out with water. Who the hells liked violet flavoured anything?

I wrinkled my nose in the mirror before pushing a smile in place. "*Thank you* for such a delicious gift, Your Majesty." I batted my lashes.

Gods. I almost convinced myself.

Just as well, since my life depended on the charade of a woman half in love with a king.

Piece by piece, I shed it. The smile first. Then a pair of heavy earrings he had given me that made my earlobes sore. Next, my gown in dusky rose.

I stood naked in the bathroom. Myself at last.

Yet I still felt this stickiness on my skin. A taint from his touches and my lies.

I found myself squeezing the potion bottle necklace as I turned the taps on full blast and ran a bath. I would scrub him away and sleep clean, for tonight at least.

I would be myself. Mine. Bastian's.

Who I chose to be and who I chose to give myself to.

While I waited for the bath to fill, I wandered naked through the suite, checking there weren't any other gifts I'd missed.

It was a habit Cyrus had taken to. Flowers. Jewellery. The box of chocolates. A lovely idea, if they'd come from anyone else, but always generic rather than tailored to me. Something he'd heard women wanted. Or maybe I was just ungrateful because of the giver.

I froze when I caught voices out in the hallway—my guard questioning someone who approached.

"I've just been with the king, and she's been summoned." Caelus.

As they knocked on the door, I grabbed a silk robe and tied a hasty knot. "Yes?"

Caelus entered, wearing a long dressing robe. Fae fashions were different to human ones, and I'd seen folk walking the corridors in various states of undress, robes included. But no one had come to my door in one.

"It appears we match." My light-hearted tone rang hollow in my ears.

"I'm meant to tell you to ready yourself for the hot springs." His gaze skimmed down me. "But I see you already are."

I smiled, but my insides jolted together, like prey animals herding tight to avoid being the one taken by a predator. Caelus followed as I turned off the taps gushing into the bath.

Cyrus had summoned me to the hot springs beneath the palace. He'd charmed me. Given me gifts. And now he intended to have what he'd paid for. Ella had told me about men like that—they believed a few presents and some compliments gave them to right to something more.

In a daze, I followed Caelus away from my suite.

I would go away. I would let him do whatever he wanted to and I would be far, far away.

My stupid eyes burned, blurring the corridors we passed down. This was a matter of practicality. What needed to be done. It would save me, save Bastian, save Elfhame, and gods knew who else.

Sometimes a piece had to be sacrificed to take down a king.

Caelus spoke with a smile that tried to be reassuring, but I couldn't take it in over the ringing of my ears.

I dimly registered the sun outside getting low outside before we started down the first staircase. If I could drag things out long enough, Sleep would claim him.

But that would just be putting off the inevitable.

These were simply consequences catching up with me. Once upon a time, they'd been the consequences of flirting with Caelus, with my uncle dragging me to him. Now Cyrus, with Caelus leading the way. What a horrible full circle.

We descended through every level of the palace. I passed through churning nausea to a numb stillness that teetered between determination and hopelessness.

At last, we reached the doors to the hot springs. Caelus nodded to the guards, who eyed me, but stepped aside to let us pass.

There was a momentary dizzy tilt to the world as we stepped through. A lodestone. I'd forgotten the springs were shared by the two sides of the palace. I clutched my stomach, almost losing my dinner.

"Are you all right?" Caelus murmured, catching my shoulder.

I wanted to flinch away from his warm skin through the thin silk, but I reminded myself I should get used to unwanted touch. Instead, I swallowed down the sick feeling and nodded.

"This way." He ushered me down a narrow corridor that closed in, suffocating and dark.

I blinked when it opened up into a cavern, and I sucked down a greedy breath. Raw rock and crystal shards enclosed the space, glistening in the gold and lilac fae lights. It stretched on in near darkness, disappearing into clouds of steam, far larger than I'd expected.

Caelus led me past several pools of various sizes to the furthest—a large square one with a glittering black pillar at the centre. He gestured to the steps leading into the steaming water.

I shrugged off the robe. Better to get this over and done with. I couldn't see Cyrus yet, but I could feel Caelus's attention and the way he tried to bend it around me. Despite his efforts, I caught him watching as I descended into the dark water. He swallowed, but it was as though he couldn't drag his attention away.

I had power over him.

The reminder allowed me to pull my shoulders back as I slipped into the warm water.

Even if I didn't want this, it needed to be done. I was using what advantages I had, just as men had used their physical strength over me. This was no different.

If I told myself enough times, maybe it would be true.

At the bottom of the stairs, I glanced back at Caelus. Where was his king? He nodded me on, and I made my way further into the pool, water lapping at my breasts.

"We're here," Caelus called, lowering himself to sit at the edge, feet trailing in the water. Why wasn't he leaving me alone with Cyrus?

From behind the pillar, a dark figure emerged. At first I could only see shadows, but as they dissipated into the steam, I let out a low cry.

Bastian pushed through the water to me, hands in my hair, lips on mine before I fully understood what was happening.

The scrape of stubble on my chin. The bruising intensity of his kiss. The paths his fingers traced on my scalp, like they were the ones that would always lead him to me. I knew them. I knew them all so well. Bastian had called me here. Not Cyrus.

It took too long to realise—Caelus had never said Cyrus had summoned me here. He'd said he'd just been with the king *and* that I'd been summoned. He let the guard—and me—link the two things and assume it was the king who had also done the summoning.

Fae had truly turned deception into an art form.

When Bastian released me, I sank from his kiss, clutching his arms, taking long breaths of that familiar smell, though I could've sworn his shoulders had grown broader. "I thought..."

"I know what you must've thought." He stroked my hair, his touch soothing. "I'm sorry. We couldn't risk Caelus saying anything in case anyone heard." He kissed my brow, then fixed Caelus with a level look. "*Thank you*. He has to stay. The guards at the entrance know Cyrus isn't here. If he leaves, they'll know you're here alone."

I sighed. "Which isn't allowed. I'm to be accompanied at all times outside of Dawn."

His mouth flattened.

I gave Caelus a tight smile before turning back to Bastian and pinching his nipple, making him yelp. "I could murder *you*, though."

He caught my hand, kissed my palm, then placed it to his cheek. "I'm sorry. Truly. I needed to see you alone, and, besides"—the corner of his mouth tilted, a little wickedness creeping in—"I can't stand seeing you in the clothes he's chosen, and this was the quickest way I could think of to get rid of them."

Despite myself, I laughed, but I still prodded him with my elbow as he lead me to the far end of the pool. I pulled the picks from my hair and shed the bracelet, leaving the tools and iron on the pool's edge.

We stopped by a shelf carved into the rock where the water lapped only a few inches deep. He ran his hand through the shallow water, but his silvery eyes took their time trailing over me. "I hate to bring up work when you are so gloriously naked, but..."

"It's a rare chance to actually talk about it rather than only leaving messages." I understood, but that didn't stop me gathering my hair over my shoulder, leaving one side of my body bared. I'd intended to seduce someone I didn't want this evening and I wasn't going to pass on the chance to at least tease the person I *did* want.

With Caelus on the other side of the pool, and the lapping water covering our voices, I told Bastian about my adventures in Cyrus's office and suite, which I hadn't trusted to a written report or relayed message. Bastian nodded when I told him I suspected Adra's death was Cyrus's work, tying up loose ends.

"Cutting them off, more like," he muttered with a glower as he looped an arm around my waist and pulled me closer. "You've done well, love. Though I feel sick to think of you sneaking into his rooms. If he found you in there..." A shudder rippled through him, bringing us closer still.

"Hmm, that reminds me." I pinched his nipple again, but he only flinched this time. "That's for not warning me about things like *pits* in the hidden passages."

At least he had the good grace to wince. "Ah. Yes. Sorry. I know all the paths so well, I don't even think of them anymore. And I didn't know you were going to find a way in there so quickly."

I stuck my nose in the air, as cocky as Sepher. "Of course I did. I'm resourceful."

Bending closer, he chuckled against my neck. "You *are*. Impressively so." His lips grazed my throat, making me squirm in barely contained delight. "And you found that letter. I wonder who's stirring things... and what else they might have planned. Do you think you can get it for me?"

I let my head hang back, giving him better access to the sensitive skin he was teasing. It was a challenge keeping my thoughts straight when my body was so occupied in waking from the slumber I'd forced it into on the way here. My nerves lit up, ready to soak up every breath upon my skin, every grazing touch, and the way his fingers dug into the soft flesh of my hips as though reassuring himself that I was really here. But he kept that other hand in the shallow water, like it was an anchor stopping him drowning in me entirely.

Somehow, I managed to string a sentence together. "I'll try."

I never said it was a complex sentence.

There was one more thing I hadn't shared yet, distracted by the way his body slid against mine, slippery from the water yet perfectly familiar. "The mirror."

"Hmm?" The sound reverberated from his lips up my throat as he trailed kisses to my earlobe.

I swallowed and tried to fight the flames he fanned in me, but it was a losing battle, and my reply came out gasping and desperate. "I recognise the descript—*ah!*" I couldn't bite back the sound as he nipped my earlobe.

A dark chuckle followed. "Do go on with your report, soldier."

I dragged in a breath, but that pressed my breasts into him, and since being pierced my nipples had grown almost unbearably sensitive. The pleasure shot through me, making my knees tremble.

Catching me, he pulled back with eyes darkened. "You seem distracted. Let me help." Except his help involved manoeuvring me against the wall and crushing me against it. "Continue."

Even with his hardening cock poking me, I would be professional and get out what I needed to say. I *would*.

I stretched my arms out to the side and pressed my hands into the edge of the shelf behind me. *Focus, Kat.*

"I have a theory. It was Nyx's. The one she used to contact her lover. And I found a note on the back in his lover's handwriting asking him to take care of it. It referred to the mirror's owner as her sister."

He sprang upright, eyes wide on me. "Sura was... No." He shook his head. "*No.* Dusk and Dawn don't mix like that... not at their level, especially."

"Sura and Cyrus." I nodded, firm. "Her daughter..." I raised my eyebrows, prompting.

"Oh shit. She *does* look like him."

"Exactly. And wasn't she talking about uniting the courts? Wouldn't a child of the two royal families be the perfect figurehead for such a plan?"

His chest heaved as though he could barely contain himself and his expanding thoughts. "And if she encouraged him to kill Lucius, it would leave Dawn destabilised enough that folk would welcome a new regime."

"If they were lovers, that means she knows him well enough to know his desires and frustrations and thus exactly how to manipulate him."

He raised an eyebrow. "Should I be concerned?"

"Are you saying I'm manipulative?"

Face screwed up, he made a sound that wasn't "no."

I mean, I *was* in the process of manipulating a king into

letting me close. "That's fair. But we're talking about Sura, not me. She's planning to rule with Cyrus and their daughter as one big happy family. She's the person most likely to have written all the letters." I frowned, trying to remember the one from his office. "It said she couldn't reveal herself yet, how it wasn't safe. And it *isn't* safe for Sura to reveal she's alive—not with her mother still around and very much in power." After all, wasn't that exactly why she'd made a bargain with us—our freedom, but we couldn't tell Braea of her survival?

"It was the same writing, then?"

I squinted, trying to picture all the notes I'd found. "I can't be sure. I'd need another look."

He nodded. "All the more reason to try and get hold of the letter from his office again. But *only* if you can do so safely. Understood?"

"When have I ever been anything but careful?"

His eyes narrowed as he pursed his lips. "Do I need to list the occasions you've flung yourself into danger in the time I've known you, *Katherine*? Let's see. There's drinking poison. And the sabrecat race. The—"

"All right. All right." I pressed my fingers to his mouth, though the fact he cared so much made me feel like something precious—like some*one* precious.

Throat suddenly thick, I pulled my fingers away and replaced them with my lips. "I get the picture," I whispered. "I'll be careful. No unnecessary risks. I promise."

Eyes screwed shut, he kissed me back once, then leant his brow to mine. "Don't make promises you can't keep, love."

No. I would stay as safe as I could. Wasn't that what I'd always lived for?

But I loved him for wanting my safety almost as much as I did.

"You worry too much," I murmured. "Let me distract you." I tiptoed to his mouth, using the shelf behind me for stability, bundled up as much of that love I could and put it into the kiss I gave him. Long and deep. Comforting and warm at first, then a fire leaping to life, as I slid my tongue into his mouth.

A low sound reverberated from him into me, and suddenly the molecules of distance between our bodies pressed together was still too much. I arched into him as he crushed me against the wall. I needed to be him. To feel him. To contain him. I needed something imprinted on my skin to remember when I returned to Dawn.

Caelus was here, but fuck that. It hadn't mattered before. Let him watch. Let him see that I adored this man and that, no matter what I had to do, I chose him.

I fucking chose him.

I reached between us and ate up the groan Bastian gave as I slid my hand along his cock.

"He's watching," he breathed around kisses.

I spared a glance for Caelus. He sat at the other end of the pool, lips parted, gaze skipping away from us. But he couldn't hide how his robe bunched up in his lap, tenting on his hard length.

I had no power to escape Dawn, not yet, but I had the power to do that to him. I had the power to make Bastian shiver as I ran my thumb over the smooth head of his dick.

Here. Now. In the golden gloom, I had this small measure of power.

I drank it down. Every heady drop.

Head spinning, I called out to Caelus, "You can watch. There's no shame in it." *No shame in sex*, as Bastian had once told me. "You have my consent."

Slowly, he turned back to us, cheeks flushed. I smirked at him as I stroked Bastian, making their breathing ragged.

Bastian took advantage of the permission I'd given, hands skimming up my sides and around my breasts. He teased his way closer to my nipples as his attention skipped from me to glancing over his shoulder at Caelus. "Do you want him to show you how much he's enjoying seeing you, love? Shall I tell him to touch himself?"

My skin burned with each word until I had to lift myself partially out of the water, using Bastian's shoulders. The steamy air was cool in comparison, but it still took me a few seconds to form the simple word: "Yes."

Bastian flashed a wicked grin, and he called over his shoulder. "You heard the woman, Caelus. *Show her.*"

I'd been forced to release his cock in order to escape the water, and it seemed that had allowed Bastian to regain his composure, because he slid one hand under my backside and lifted me clear.

Now he had better access to my breasts and took full advantage of it. Just a graze of his lips on my nipple had me gasping as the sensation shot through me. When he closed his mouth around it and sucked, I cried out at the pleasure racing to my centre, eyelids fluttering shut. If not for his strong arms, I'd have fallen back.

When I regained myself, I found Caelus's taut body on display, the robe discarded. Moisture made his skin gleam in the golden light, catching on the muscles of his arm as he slowly slid one hand down his length.

"I know this isn't what I promised you," Bastian murmured in my ear, "but it will have to do… for now."

What he'd promised? I blinked, mind only drifting to the

answer hazily. His double. He'd promised to give me both parts of himself. But he couldn't reveal his secret with Caelus here.

I gave him a lazy smile and traced the edge of his ear in the way that always made his breath catch. "I suppose I can forgive you."

"Good." There was a finality to it. A line drawn that said *this* was the beginning. Of what, exactly, I wasn't sure, but my pulse raced, eager to find out.

He squeezed my thighs, fingers grazing my edges, so close to where I throbbed for his touch. "Are you ready?"

I swallowed but still couldn't get my tongue to work. All I could do was nod.

And, with Caelus's gaze searing into us, Bastian began.

21

BASTIAN

I lifted Kat onto the pool's shallow shelf, enjoying how pink the heat had made her tan skin. Her tits heaved, so tantalisingly close.

I'd never been much good at resisting temptation—at least not when it came to her—so I bent my head to them and sucked each nipple into my mouth in turn, gripping her thighs so she couldn't squirm. I sent shadows to help me, clasping around her arms and middle, holding her hair back, so I could reach any part of her skin I wanted.

And I wanted it all.

Her nipples pulled tight under my ministrations, and when I flicked my tongue over them, she arched against my hold, whimpering.

"So many things I've missed wrapped up in one person," I murmured, voice thick as the taste of her, the feel of her, the sound of her threatened to overwhelm me.

Every night I'd reached across our empty bed, and every

night it had been empty of all these things that were so utterly her.

Her eyes grew bright, but I didn't want her to be sad or think about our time apart. I was going to erase that with the moment we had.

Not just erase it—obliterate it.

So, gently, my shadows laid her down, and I eased her thighs apart. Her crimson hair floated on the water, spreading around in a glorious, flaming halo. My shadows slithered amongst the strands, serpents who had found their equal and opposite and wanted nothing more than to be close to her.

The lights clustered close, like they too wanted to be near and light up the curves of her body, the planes of her face, all the shapes that I had been starved of for too long. They orbited her, glinting in her green eyes as she blinked slowly.

I was staring. No one could blame me, though. Not when I got to have this.

Though I wasn't the only one who was supposed to be enjoying the view. The water rippled as I stepped to one side, letting Caelus see my ember in all her glory. His lips parted as his cock strained in his hand.

"See the effect you have on him, love?" My shadows supported her head and shoulders, letting her watch him watching her as I teased her inner thighs, working my way slowly higher.

My balls clenched as her pupils grew wide, taking us both in. I needed to be buried in her. I wanted to lose myself in her. Forget all the shit that waited for us outside this chamber.

Part of me wanted to show Caelus that she was mine, no matter what Cyrus thought, no matter the awful argument we'd faked in the gardens.

And another, deeper part of me needed to prove it to myself.

When my shadows were biting into her soft skin because she strained against them so hard, desperate for my fingers to touch just a little higher, I smiled down at her. "Was there something you wanted?"

She let out a frustrated little huff.

Teasing her was so sweet, and it made her eventual pleasure all the sweeter. "Hmm?" I edged higher, very nearly at her glistening wetness.

"Please."

A low rumble came from my chest. That word from her lips would never grow dull. "See, that wasn't so hard, was it?"

She gave me a murderous look, but it was quickly replaced by her eyebrows peaking together as my thumb glided over her entrance and up to her clit. She arched against the restraints, eyelids fluttering shut as she gave a deep groan like she'd been waiting a lifetime.

"That's it," I murmured as I lifted and spread her thighs wider, testing her limits. Tension trembled through her, building with each circle I made. Shadows crept over her, teasing her nipples, squeezing her breasts, winding her tighter still.

My heart thundered, harder and louder with each whimper she let out. My love. Mine.

I looked back, a feral smile baring my teeth as I saw Caelus had come closer. His hand pumped his length now, thumb sliding over the glistening tip. He could think about her all he wished, but she was mine.

I watched him as I slid two fingers into her pussy, thumb circling a little faster, and was rewarded by her cry as she tightened around me and came undone. She pulsed around my fingers, as Caelus gripped the pool's stone edge, knuckles white.

I had done that to her. Her pleasure was mine. Her body was mine. But most of all, her heart was mine. She'd given all of herself to me and I would work to prove myself worthy of such a precious gift.

Cheeks flushed dark, Caelus met my gaze as I continued working her towards a second climax. He wanted to be where I stood. He wanted to feel what I felt. He wanted her.

I'd been forced to trust him to get her here, but maybe part of me had wanted this. The part of me that had been jealous seeing Cyrus near her. The part of me that had rebelled against our false argument. The part that had relished in shoving Cyrus against the wall.

My shadows grew as though feeding on my jealousy and twisted mercilessly around her nipples, sending her over the edge once more. Caelus gave a hoarse cry as he came.

I gathered Katherine up as she trembled through the after-shocks. "You're so good at that, love," I murmured in her ear, sending goosebumps chasing over her skin. "Did you see what you did to our friend? My ember always does so well."

She smiled into the kiss I gave her, arms loose as they looped around my neck. Her eyelids drooped like she was half asleep.

Caelus had watched me make her come at the party back in Lunden, but he hadn't seen more than that, and I needed to check what she was comfortable with. "Do you want to leave it there or...?"

Her eyes sprung open. "You'd better be about to fuck me, Bastian Marwood."

I chuckled, cock twitching at her eagerness. Shrugging, I shook my head. "You give such mixed messages."

She gave a warning grumble, then ran her tongue over my pierced nipple, sending a shockwave through my nerves.

"Fuck," I blurted.

She only smirked as I laid her in the shallow water, on her side this time.

I slid behind her, cock aching at the sight of a waist shaped perfectly for me to hold and her backside so delightfully cushioned for me to pound against. "You're in a lot of trouble for that," I growled in her ear and soaked up the shiver that ran through her.

Roughly, I grabbed her thigh and lifted it, pulling her flush against me. My dick slid between her buttocks, and I barely bit back a groan at the feel of her. I continued forward, gliding along her entrance as I slipped one arm under her and brought her face to mine.

I claimed her mouth as I claimed her pussy, and she arched into both. Fuck, she felt like... like everything.

Tight and sweet. Slick and warm. Sunshine and comforting darkness. Spring growth and autumn rain.

"Lift your hips, let Caelus see how well you take it."

She obliged, and I caught her watching him, biting her lip at the way he watched her tits bounce with every stroke.

Mine. Fucking mine.

I squeezed her, fingers digging into her thigh and breast, needing to hold her, have her, feel her close, closer, closest. My hips snapped against hers, edging the line between controlled and feral. My tongue delved into her mouth, meeting hers, twisting with it, tasting chocolate and something floral.

I explored every part of her I could reach, needing to remember that this was us—this was real, not that argument. Needing to be the first to so rigorously map the precise curve of the roof of her mouth. To be the first to find the exact spot in the front of her pussy that made her cry out and drench my dick in the evidence of her pleasure. To be the first to know her love and to give it back to her a hundredfold.

Because there was something more important than her being mine.

My breathing grew frantic, consuming as I pressed my cheek to hers. Our wet bodies slid together, perfect pleasure in movement. "No matter what, I am yours, Kat. Yours."

She whispered back. "*Mine.* All mine."

That was what sent me over the edge. The thrumming tension in my belly exploded into her, obliterating, pure white hotness that blinded me. My low cry echoed from the cavern walls, mingling with the ones I drove from her.

When I could understand the world again, I kissed her once, twice, a hundred times. "Sorry," I murmured in between. "I meant to get you there again." But I'd been too consumed with that word she'd given me. *Mine.* She'd claimed me even more thoroughly than I'd claimed her.

Softly, she chuckled and shook her head. "You are a wonderful idiot. No apology required."

Another million kisses. I couldn't stop raining them down on her. But I would have to. Because she had to go back to Dawn and me to Dusk.

When I finally managed to pull myself away, I found Caelus's eyes boring into us. I was still inside her, but he watched our faces, eyes wide, and when I met his gaze, he turned as though suddenly ashamed to be caught staring.

I slipped from her and washed her clean before going right back to the same position. I held her as long as possible, arms around her, her hands squeezing mine. It had to be past sunset now, and every second ticked into dangerous territory.

Eventually, Caelus cleared his throat, and I looked up to

find him wrapped in his robe, holding out Katherine's. "We really should—"

"I know."

Kat's hold on me tightened and for a moment she screwed her eyes shut. I shared that moment of denial.

This was real. The going back was not.

But she disentangled herself from me and rose, each movement cracking my heart. I helped her into the robe, helped pin her hair with the lock picks, and even snapped the bracelet around her wrist—anything to put off the inevitable.

Caelus went ahead, waiting by Dawn's entrance.

We stood at the edge of the pool, lights drifting around us, glistening in her overbright eyes.

"I'll see you later," she said, voice thick, belying how casual her words were.

I swallowed back the gritty, hot feeling in my throat and nodded. "You will. I'll be there in bed with you, just the other side of the veil. Lie on the left side and place your hand in the middle. I'll hold it all through the night."

Her chin trembled, and I stood ready to hold her and let her cry as long as I dared. But it lasted less than a second before she inclined her head, once, firm. "And listen for me telling you how much I love you."

"I will." My eyes burned, and I screwed them shut as we kissed, hard and slow like we could stretch time itself. Even after she pulled away, I didn't dare open them.

It was like waking from a wonderful dream into a living nightmare—as soon as I woke, it would be real and the dream would disappear.

When I opened my eyes, she was gone.

THE NEXT DAY, I did feel better. I slept more deeply than I had since Kat had been taken, and I swore I could still feel the ghost of her touch when I woke.

My assistant Brynan even commented on my good mood when he caught me humming as I tidied my desk. Stacks of paperwork weren't unusual, since there was always more of it than I could keep up with, but they had grown unruly even for me, threatening to spill to the floor if I passed too quickly.

Clearing some space gave me room to breathe and made things seem better. Sure, Dawn's throne was occupied by a self-serving megalomaniac with a particular dislike of me *and* the woman I loved as hostage, but we weren't entirely helpless.

My mood had improved so much that when Orpha appeared in the doorway, unseen for long moments, and asked for some time off to deal with a family matter, I waved her off and wished her luck.

I was just tackling the last pile of paperwork when Faolán swept into my room. The dark furrow between his eyebrows made me stop, mid-signature.

Even worse, he just... stood there.

Faolán wasn't a man of many words, but those he had usually came without this much trouble.

Now, though, he opened and closed his mouth, licked his lips, clenched and unclenched his fists.

"What is it?" Slowly, I stood. "Is it Rose? Has something happened?"

He shook his head, gaze sinking from mine. "It's your father."

22

KAT

I sat at Cyrus's side, still smiling faintly at some joke he'd made, when a servant handed me a plate of chocolate cake. Something else, though, dug into my palm beneath the plate. A tiny, folded piece of paper.

My heart dipped as Cyrus grabbed my hand. I barely managed to slip the note between my fingers. *Please, gods, don't let him notice it.*

He held my gaze as he pressed a kiss to my knuckles, like a knight in a tale of old when chivalry ruled and women were prizes to be won.

"*Oh.*" I made the sound as though overcome and looked away. Across the table from me, I caught Caelus's eye for a beat, and my face grew hot. At least the blush would help sell the story that I was so affected by Cyrus.

"Such a sweet little thing." The king smirked, placing my hand on my own thigh before covering it with his own. His fingertips grazed through the light silk of my skirts, and I forced myself still, even though every shred of muscle in me screamed to get away. "So innocent-seeming, and yet I bet you're much more fun than you let on." He leant close, blue eyes like a cloudless winter sky. "I can't wait to peel back all the layers of stuffy human civilisation you dress up in."

I needed to keep as many of those layers for as long as possible. But I also needed to let him see tantalising little glimpses to keep his interest.

So, I bit my lip and looked up at him from beneath lowered lashes as though both frightened and intrigued by his words.

The rest of the meal, he leant close, watching me eat the cake, smirking when I licked a crumb from my lip. It was only when I finished that I excused myself and went to the nearest bathroom to read the note.

To the dungeons.

Just three words, but they were written in Kaliban's hand. What the hells was he doing writing to me here? And *summoning* me to the palace dungeons?

Shit. What had happened? Had he been forced to go out and been overcome by other people's thoughts? Maybe he'd hurt someone by accident, lashing out as he tried to escape. He'd come to rely on me and now I was stuck here, unable to help him.

The cake sat in my stomach, heavy, but I hurried towards the only stairs I knew that led to the dungeons. I ran down them, sweaty and half sick by the time I got to the bottom. Panting, I stared at the black stone door before me.

No guards.

Strange. The dungeons were meant to be a lodestone, or so I thought. Lodestones were always guarded.

I wasn't going to kick this piece of luck in the teeth, so I hurried through. That was where I found the guards, and I stiffened as they eyed me in the flickering lantern-light. But these weren't Dawn's guards. They wore the mid grey of a dull day, and as many of them had Dusk Court coloured hair like black and deep twilight blue as Dawn colours like green and golden blond.

They also didn't try and stop me, just indicated a corridor to the left and stared ahead.

I followed their vague directions, the hair at the back of my head on end. Any moment, they were going to turn on me. This had to be a trap. It felt too easy.

There was no decoration here, just bare stone and wall lanterns with flame rather than fae lights. I passed doors with metal bars and the sickly feeling in my stomach doubled. They had to be iron, just like prison bars in Albion. That explained the use of fire rather than magical lighting. The sweat from hurrying down here grew cold.

At the end of the corridor, a pair of guards stood at the top of another set of stairs. They nodded me onward.

Three more levels I passed until at last a guard pointed me towards the cell at the far end, then turned and left. Down here, the lanterns were less frequent, with darkness pooling between them, and the cells were set back from the corridor, leaving shadowy recesses at their entrances.

Dread an icy cloak around me, I approached the final cell. I knew what I would see before I got there, but it was still horrible seeing Kaliban's pale face the wrong side of the bars.

Someone else had beaten me here, a form in the shadows.

"Wait—*Bastian*? What are you doing here?"

He turned, doing a double take. "What am *I*...? What are *you* doing here?"

We spun on Kaliban, who spread his hands. "Well, this

isn't how I planned to tell you both, but... Kat, I'm Bastian's *athair*. And, Bastian, yes, I know your beloved and I approve. Greatly, in fact."

Bastian's father. The one whose dreams of Innesol and the Horrors had infiltrated Bastian's memories. That meant... The carved wooden stags and hinds on the shelves. The extra pair of slippers. They were his dead husband's, who'd bred deer in the palace stables and taught Bastian all he knew of them. Who Bastian had killed.

I rounded on Kaliban. "You *knew* who I was with and you *didn't tell me?*" I said through gritted teeth. "If you weren't locked up, I'd be fucking fuming with you right now."

"You *sound* rather angry with me as it is."

I gave him a level glare. "Imagine how much worse it could be."

"What the fuck have you done?" The words came out of Bastian with quiet fury. "If I find out you've hurt her, I'll—"

Kaliban gave a derisive snort. "Not everyone is as out to get you as you believe, Bastian. We don't have time to dwell on the good fortune that brought this fine young woman into my life."

I didn't know whether to be touched by his words or concerned that he was being nice rather than sarcastic. Whatever he'd been arrested for, it had to be bad.

"But," he went on, "rest assured, none of it was so I could cause her any harm." He met my gaze and gave the slightest nod.

It was for me to decide what I told Bastian.

I squeezed his arm, ready to give him a shake if he didn't calm down. "We met by chance. Kaliban helped me with my magic."

"And now"—Kaliban nodded—"I need *your* help."

Bastian blasted a sigh. "You can say that again. He was caught 'consorting with shapechangers' and now they're accusing him of having a part in Lucius's assassination."

Kaliban clicked his tongue. "Not for that. I need you to fetch something from my house. The magic there knows you—it will let you in."

I shifted, unsure of the idea of entering without him.

"You're being loud." He raised one eyebrow and I smoothed my thoughts in the way that made it more comfortable for him.

Bastian gave me a sidelong look but remained silent.

Kaliban came to the barred window in the door, careful not to touch them as he gripped my hand. "Under the rug, you'll find a squeaky floorboard. Press it while saying 'Sylen' and it will open for you. Inside you'll find a few items. I need you to bring those here as quickly as possible." He squeezed. "Stop for no one. Speak to no one. Especially not once you have the items. You must come back here at once. Do you understand?"

"But Dawn's guards. I'm not supposed to—"

"If you go out through Dusk's exit, they'll let you through." Bastian stared at Kaliban, brow tight with a frown. "No one from Dawn will know you've left the palace."

"Won't the prison guards stop me?"

"They become neutral when they come to serve in the dungeons. There is no Dusk and Dawn down here, only justice." He finally turned and gave me an encouraging smile, but there was something tense about it. "You'll be fine. There'll be something warm in the cloakroom by the side exit we use. Take a coat from there—preferably hooded."

"And take that thing off." Kaliban frowned at the iron bracelet. "I don't want you contaminating my house again."

23

KAT

I followed Bastian's instructions, the dread in me warring with the momentary relief of stepping through a lode-stone into Dusk. The air felt different here compared to Dawn. Cooler, like fresh sheets, and scented with jasmine and other night-blooming flowers I didn't know the name of.

But it was short-lived, as I hurried out of the palace, a borrowed cloak wrapped around me, hood pulled up. The guards nodded as I crossed the bridge, no doubt assuming I was a servant rushing to do my master's bidding.

I barely registered the streets I hadn't seen in weeks as I made my way towards Kaliban's home. But the city's magic filled me. It was like my chest had been constricted so I could only take shallow breaths, but now I could *breathe*.

As I turned a corner, I found myself caught in a crowd. Various fae craned to look at something, and I had to shoulder through them. Thankfully the iron bracelet seemed to help, as folk grimaced and edged out of my way.

I half fell out of the huddle and spotted what they'd come

to see. Smile dazzling, hair perfect, crown golden and glittering, Cyrus worked his way through a select group of fae. The Kingsguard held back the rest as he shook hands and doled out gifts of jewellery and perfume.

As he clapped one man on the shoulder and shook his hand, he looked out at the crowd, as if posing, and his gaze reached me.

I froze, breath caught in my throat.

But he passed over me, eyes distant.

He hadn't seen me. Didn't even pause on the red hair I couldn't stop spilling from the hood.

I almost laughed as I realised. He didn't see these people. He only wished to be seen by them. Loved by them. Admired. Worshipped. Adored.

Turning, he continued on his way, eyes flashing when he saw a woman with a little boy of maybe five years old.

"Well, look what the gods have brought us!" Cyrus spread his arms and snatched the child from his mother, holding him high.

"I can fly!" The boy squealed in delight, winning a cheer.

Their pride was palpable. For them, children were a precious rarity—Cyrus had chosen well. They would associate him with that good fortune.

He knew it, holding the boy close for a long while as I worked my way through the edges of the crowd, and watched him from the corner of my eye.

I'd almost made it through when the child starting crying and wriggling. "Ow. It hurts. Too tight."

As if nothing had happened, Cyrus's smile remained in place, but he turned his head and whispered in the boy's ear. The child's eyes widened and his tears stopped. One corner of his mouth rose, but it didn't warm my heart.

I knew fear when I saw it.

Wondering what he'd threatened the child with, I hurried away. At last, I reached Kaliban's home. The magic bristled, on alert, but after a second, it calmed and let me in. With the door shut behind me, I flipped back the rug and opened the secret compartment as he'd instructed.

A blood-stained bundle greeted me. The fabric was a rich, midnight silk, with pinpoints of glittering stars scattered across it. Even amongst fae, it had to be an expensive cloth— the kind you'd find a way to clean.

My earlier dread returned. It felt as though I hadn't chewed that cake at all.

Swallowing, I took the package. I wasn't expecting whatever was inside to be so heavy, and it slipped from my grasp and out of the silk, landing with a solid *thunk*.

An astrolabe as big as my palm and dizzyingly intricate with discs and dials nestled together to chart the movement of celestial bodies.

I'd gathered from Bastian that orreries and astrolabes were deeply personal items gifted for special occasions like coming of age or passed from parents to children, just as his orrery had come from his *baba* Sylen. Did Kaliban mean to give this to Bastian now? Did he think he was going to...?

I shook away the thought and grabbed the astrolabe, standing as I did. I needed to get back. For protection, I placed it face down on the silk together with a note that had also fluttered out of the package.

The air went thick as I blinked at the astrolabe's back. Inscribed in the gold surface was Dusk Court's crescent moon and nine-pointed star with a crown above. The royal family's insignia.

I blinked again, though it seemed to take an age as pressure built in my ears.

The note. I stared, unable to make sense of it, but the words "my baby" leapt out at me, and it was signed, in a wandering hand, "Nyx."

Pain as sharp and sudden as a stick breaking in a silent forest cracked through my head.

My face tingled. I stumbled and shielded my eyes, the world too bright.

"What's...?" But my voice came from far away as a ringing sound blocked my ears, rising in pitch with each moment.

The memory of Sura's voice reached me but I couldn't make sense of the words. I reached for them, but found myself falling, falling, falling.

Blood. Fresh, not from the shawl. Drops on my hand, on the astrolabe, on the floor.

My blood.

A woman on the bridge, hands cradling her round belly.

I was dying. The pain. Fuck. *The pain.*

It was opening me up. Blasting me apart.

She falls, arrows piercing her body.

The floor jolted through me at last, but the rich, dark wood had turned grey, and my blood was black. Darkness haunted the edges of my vision.

The river rips at her. She curls around the little life inside. But the rocks are cruel.

Each image was a gunshot. Fragmenting. Obliterating. Only a circle of light remained, showing the leafy pattern of Kaliban's rolled up rug.

She washes up on shore at last. Alone. Soaked. Stomach heaving as though it wants to flush out anything that might hold her back.

Help.

Help me. I tried to cry out. Something was wrong. My head —splintering.

The pain racks her body. She bites on her leather belt. If she screams, they'll find her. There's no hope for her, but maybe...

My last pinhole of light fractured and the shards slipped away into darkness.

24

BASTIAN

I leant against the wall, waiting for Kat. The cold hard stone matched the sold tension in my body. Kat had known my father all this time and neither of them had told me. He must've lured her in somehow. But to what end?

I shot him a glance through the barred window. He waited, crouched, back against the side wall of his cell. It wasn't a relaxed stance, but one I knew from war—from *his* war. The kind of stance that was ready.

Pinpricks of his other memories needled me. Innesol's town square, empty save for a child's shoe. Arguing with Sylen about the Horrors. Throwing up after feeling the thoughts of one of their victims.

Kaliban wasn't meant for war. He should've had a peaceful life in a quiet cottage near the sea. No one around to make his magic overwhelming. No terrors to sear themselves on his mind so they ended up bursting from him when he slept, infecting others with his nightmares.

But he'd been born at the wrong time.

And now, a thousand years later, he was caught up in more strife. Arrested for involvement in an assassination.

This had to be Cyrus's work.

In so many ways, Kaliban had chosen the wrong son. It was my fault he was alone. And it was my fault Cyrus had done this.

I rubbed my forehead, another tight headache closing in. I didn't need this—the worry about him *or* the sensation of failure that he could instil in me with just a look.

What was worse—he didn't even speak to me in that sharp way he usually did. It was like he thought he had to be nice so I would help him.

Whatever had happened before, he was my *father*. I would help him without his sudden act.

"Why did you call me here? *And* Kat?"

"It will become clear when she returns."

We waited in silence for a long while. It was as uncomfortable as the stone, as uncomfortable, until I cleared my throat. "This is a mistake, you know. You'll be released soon. I'll make sure of it."

He snorted and shook his head. "We didn't raise you to be so naïve. Dawn has chosen me as a scapegoat, and they chose well. My past makes me an easy target. And the fact I'm your *athair* makes me a prized one. Whatever they need to make stick to me, will."

I opened my mouth to argue, but couldn't. He was right. After Sura's coup attempt, they hadn't been able to prove anything against him, so they'd been forced to let him go. Still, he'd been marked as a traitor. Guilty by proxy. How couldn't he know what his husband was up to?

And that made him very sticky for this.

I never understood why he hadn't moved away after that.

To the clifftop cottage I'd imagined for him. Away from the city, he would've had a better life.

For whatever reason, he didn't. And now he was here, in the perfect place to become Cyrus's scapegoat alongside the elusive Krae.

What better way to strike at the heart of Dusk? The only way it could've been better was if we still had a close relationship.

"Then," he said, eyebrows rising, "it would only be a short leap towards accusing my son of involvement, too."

I flinched, slamming shut the doors in my mind. I'd been away from him for too long, was too tired, too stressed to watch my barriers. "Sorry," I muttered. Keeping my mind shut should've been second nature.

But he'd called me his son. He hadn't acknowledged me as such in a long time. Not after what I'd done.

"Besides," he went on, "I'm not entirely innocent."

My head snapped up.

He held up his palms. "Not of *that*. But I was seen with shapechangers. I've been helping them get out of the city."

"You mean you put yourself at risk? Now who's the naïve one?" He'd given them ammunition. "How could you be so foolish? Didn't you always tell me—"

"I have a lot to atone for." He said it as matter-of-factly as you might say the sun rose in the morning.

I kept any more thoughts of Innesol squashed down, but I couldn't argue with him.

At the end of the corridor, someone cleared their throat, and I looked back, expecting to find Katherine. But it was one of the guards.

She cocked her head. "Everything all right? Just... you've

been a while. People don't tend to want to hang around down here."

I checked the watch in my pocket. Kat had been gone for over an hour. My heart sank. She should be back by now. Even if she wasn't hurrying—*she should be back*.

I reassured the guard, who left, then I turned on my father, shadows rising. I gripped the bars, letting them sear, filling the air with the smell of burning flesh. My shadows stuttered and disappeared. My sense of magic in the world vanished. "What have you done to her? What trap did you leave for her?"

His eyes went wide. "A trap? Why the hells would I hurt her?"

"To do to me what I did to you." The words choked out of me like water bubbling up through a spring. White hot pain screamed along my nerves, but it was nothing compared to the guilt inside me. "I took the one you loved most in all the world and now..."

I tore my hands from the bars and took two paces towards the stairs when I heard the approaching footsteps.

With a guard's arm around her shoulders, Kat staggered in, eyes wide, hair wild like she'd been tearing at it.

"Kat?" I was already at her side, taking over helping her. She leant against me heavily, hugging herself like she was trying to hold parts of herself together. "What happened?"

The guard frowned. "She was like this when she came back. We tried to take her to the Hall of Healing, but she screamed until we turned around and started in this direction."

"Thank you. I've got her now." Something must've frightened her, and she wouldn't reveal it until we were alone.

"Knew," she whispered as the guard left. "Knew. He knew."

"What did he know?" I smoothed hair from her face,

gasping when I saw blood below her nose. My body went on alert, energy spiking through me. "Kat? What happened? What's—?"

"Bring her here," Kaliban called from his cell.

As I walked her over, she muttered to herself, unintelligible. She wouldn't meet my gaze and gave no answers to my coaxing questions.

A deep, dark dread crawled through my bones.

"The bridge." She shook her head over and over, eyes glassy and distant. "Can't... can't think."

What the hells had happened?

When I glanced at my father, I found him pale—as pale as he'd gone when I'd delivered the news that I had killed his husband. "Katherine," he said slowly, "did you get it?"

"The truth," she mumbled, more blood oozing from her nose. "I got it. Right in... right in my brain. I got it. The bridge. That night."

"Kat?" I cupped her cheeks and tried to make eye contact. "You're not making sense, love."

Gently, I wiped her face clean as her eyes skipped left and right like she couldn't keep still. I tried to anchor her—to be that stillness, even though my heart hammered. I'd never seen her like this, even when her uncle had terrified her so much.

"Slowly," I murmured. "What's happening? Where did this blood come from?" Her face didn't look bruised or swollen, so I didn't need to go and destroy someone for hurting her.

"The bridge. That night. What the queen did." She pressed her lower lip and chewed it. "The bridge. That night. What the queen did. My head. *My head*." A tear trickled from the corner of her eye. "I can't."

"It's all right, love." I prised her hand away and pulled her lip from between her teeth before she made herself bleed. "You're safe now. I'm here."

"The bridge. My head. They broke it." She stopped hugging herself and held out a small package. "They broke it. I found it."

"Oh shit," he hissed. "*That's* what they hid."

"They broke it." Her breathing calmed as her lip trembled. "*I found it.*"

There was something very wrong. A stroke? I'd heard of people's minds changing after suffering one—words coming out wrong, not being able to speak.

"Come on, love." I slid an arm around her shoulder, ready to usher her out. "I need to get her to the House of Healing."

"No." She yanked away. "*No.*"

My father took a long breath before he inclined his head. "The item I sent her for. Seeing it has broken something in her mind. Not my intention, but it makes sense now."

"*What* makes sense?" I snapped, stomach tight and sickly seeing her like this. "Because none of—"

"Quickly, give me her hand. Before more breaks." The way his face crumpled as he looked at her stole my breath. He'd looked at me like that once. He loved her like a father. How had I missed that?

He reached out between the bars, careful not to touch them. "Kat, my dear, give him the package, then take my hand."

She obeyed, trembling all the while.

Something hard bit into my fingers as I gripped the silk-wrapped parcel, watching my father close his eyes and reach for her mind.

I kept my walls in place, letting him soothe her. He didn't need my worries crowding his work.

Something had broken in her. She sounded... I'd never heard her ramble like this. How much could he do? Could he fix her? Would she be like this forever?

Turned inward, the thoughts choked me, and I found myself squeezing the package to my chest. If it came to that, I would find her somewhere safe and quiet. Somewhere with a garden. Somewhere she wouldn't be stared at, where I could look after her. I would leave my job. Leave the city. Whatever she needed.

A soul-deep sigh brought me back from contingency plans as Kat sagged against me. I caught her. "Love?"

"Bastian." She nodded, leaning into me. "I'm... back."

But she'd gone an unpleasant colour, and she held her head when I eased her into a sitting position.

"You need to tell him," she whispered, massaging her temples. "I don't know if I can."

My father swallowed. His colour wasn't much better than hers, but when he met my gaze, his was firm. "Open that."

Frowning, I pulled back the bloodstained silk. A gold and silver astrolabe, beautifully wrought, perhaps the best I'd seen. Braea had one similar, just as intricate, though slightly larger. This was easily its match in quality.

"Look, you're not going to die in here." I held it out to him. "You don't need to give me—"

"Check the back."

I turned it over. The royal insignia glinted back at me. "Did you *steal* this? Is it not enough to be arrested for—"

"Read the note."

Beneath the astrolabe, half hidden in the silk, I found a piece of paper. Its folded edges were tattered, like it had been read often.

The soft cream of the paper and its weight felt familiar, and when I unfolded it, I understood why. My father Sylen's writing. This had been torn from the ledger he'd kept, tracking bloodlines and characteristics of the deer he bred. This page recorded that a fast hind had been bred with his strongest stag, both his most intelligent animals, though they'd failed to breed in the royal stables to date. His notes ended without recording whether they'd succeeded this time.

"What has this got to do with—?"

"Turn it over." His voice had gone very soft, little more than a whisper.

The writing wandered, so weak in places, ink barely registered on the page, and there were bloody fingerprints at the edges, but it was mostly legible.

These are the final wishes of Nyxis Nemesine Voltarin, the Night Princess, daughter of Queen Braea. To Kaliban and Sylen, I entrust my most precious one, my baby, heir to Dusk, born of love between seelie and unseelie. I name him Bastian.

25

BASTIAN

I stared at the torn out page. Read it again and again.

"We found her on the banks of the river, a tiny baby in her arms. She was soaked and so pale we thought she was dead at first. But she was clinging on, desperate not to leave her boy alone in the world. The river had washed the blood from her clothes and snapped the arrows."

My father's voice was distant, an accompaniment to the note as I read it over and over—a compulsion I couldn't shake.

"She wouldn't tell us what had happened, her focus was entirely on her baby. She begged us for paper. Begged us to take him and keep him safe. She wanted to give us proof and she wanted to give him a name. To give *you* a name."

I name him Bastian.

I name him Bastian.

I name him Bastian.

It wasn't possible. It wasn't...

"But I..." I shook my head, grasping for words other than

what was in the note. "The woman who was attacked... she's my..."

"We let everyone think that. You know how useful assumptions are. The timings lined up—you were born when she was nine months pregnant. But you weren't conceived that night. You were two months premature—that's why you were always such a small child. A little miracle."

I couldn't think straight. There were so many arguments against this, so many reasons it couldn't be true. But all I could do was finally tear my eyes from the note and look at him, at Kat, searching for signs that this was a joke or a hallucination or *something*.

Tears streamed down her cheeks as she wept in silence. "It's true."

And with those two words, the world shifted. I was one thing one minute, something else the next.

Just like that.

A breath in. A breath out. The two moments worlds apart.

My knees thudded into the stone floor.

I was the son of Princess Nyx. Braea's grandson. Sura's nephew.

Did she know? Was that why she had refused to kill me, even though it would've been the smart course of action?

"Sura planted the information inside my head," Kat went on when I remained silent. "She locked it away so I couldn't reach it. She was afraid everyone who knew would die before you could be told, but she knew you'd keep me close. I was meant to remember if she died, but seeing this must've..." She shook her head.

"It broke the lock. Forcibly. Thank the Stars above, I managed to fix the worst of the damage." Kaliban watched me. I'd never seen so many lines on his face. We didn't age like humans, but today he looked ancient, as though worry wore him thin like old clothes.

"So..." I stumbled into more silence, too many questions falling over themselves to be voiced. "She survived? Nyx is still alive?"

But my father shook his head. "Only for a short while. The arrows... they were too much. There was nothing we could do. Maybe if one of us had been a healer, but... She knew it was coming. That's why she was desperate to leave something for you. She wanted you to know where you came from and that you were born from love—love that reached across the veil between here and the Underworld and didn't care that your father-by-blood was unseelie. She made us help her write it, kissed your little head and told you she loved you, then she closed her eyes."

Goosebumps crept over me, and my eyes burned.

I'd always understood the woman who'd given birth to me didn't love me. I could deal with that. It was old knowledge, long accepted. Familiar in a way. But this?

I turned away from it and planted my feet on a more practical path, checking Kat's nose had stopped bleeding. "How did she die? You said arrows—whose?"

He exchanged a look with Kat. "She wouldn't say how she got three arrows in her and ended up in the river. She was entirely focused on keeping you safe. But..." He took a long breath and his gaze slid to Kat again. "She made us give our word that we'd never tell her mother the truth."

Her hand slid into my lap and she gave my leg a comforting squeeze. "Remember what Sura told me about how Nyx died? She needed to keep you safe from Braea... and from anyone who might try to put you on the throne when they discovered Braea had killed Nyx."

I flinched, shutting my eyes against that lie. If Sura had planted that information in Kat's head, she could plant lies too —she didn't have to say things out loud to put them there. That could be a way around the law that bound us.

Instead, I frowned at my father. "Why didn't you tell me? All these years and nothing."

"We swore to protect you. If you'd known as a child, that was one more person to let slip. The only ones who knew were us and Princess Sura. Three was already too many. But your father and I trusted each other, and Sura... to her you were all she had left of her sister. She would do anything to keep you safe."

I hated that it made sense.

"Her coup wasn't to gain power for herself. It was to remove Braea from the throne. It took her years to gain support from the right people—Sylen and me included. But she never forgot her sister or what Braea had done to her. She hoped taking the throne would make you safe."

"But the queen loves me, she wouldn't—"

"Braea locked up Nyx because she couldn't control her. Don't you understand? She murdered Nyx because she couldn't stand the thought of having an unseelie heir—*you*. She had Sura executed. Do you think she would hesitate to kill you if she found out?"

He was wrong. He didn't understand. But arguing with him was pointless. Once he'd made up his mind, it was set.

"Sylen knew it." He leant as close to the bars as he could without touching them. "That was why he never wanted you in the Queensguard. He was afraid that if you got close to her, Braea would recognise who you really were."

I searched through my memories, filtering them through the lens of this new information. Had he dropped hints?

I kept landing at the day he'd died. The day *I'd* killed him. The day *he'd* let me.

"Why didn't he tell me? Why didn't he stop me? If I'd known..." Would I have let him take the throne for Sura? How would I have weighed Braea's stability against the truth? What did all this mean for his death? For the first time in fifteen years, I wasn't sure I had made the right choice, however painful.

My father gave a sad smile; it was the kindest look he'd given me in a long while. "His blood may not run through your veins, but you and he were cut from the same cloth. He would've done anything for the realm—for *your* future. That included giving his own life."

"The willow knot charm. That's why he put it in my pocket."

His eyes gleamed as he nodded. "He knew there was a risk you'd run in headlong, trying to save the day. It would keep you alive until you could be healed. He *probably* intended to keep you out of the fight with the injury, but *of course*"—his mouth twisted in a sardonic smirk—"you refused to even look after yourself and insisted on saving the queen first."

The back of my throat ached. All this time, I'd wondered if it was an accident or if he meant to protect me if Braea lashed out due to his treachery.

"He couldn't kill you, because the coup was meant to make you safe, just as he'd sworn. Just as I have stayed away all these years in order to protect you."

Again, the world shifted. This time it jolted away, leaving me in free fall. "*What?*"

"I'm sorry that I've played the part too well, but it was necessary."

"No, you were right. I took him away from you. I betrayed

you both. I understand." His anger at me was fair—righteous, even.

"Oh, I was furious. But at *him*, not at you. He'd left me when we'd promised to be together always." When he blinked, tears fell. "After the coup, there was so much suspicion on me and if I kept you close, I knew it could easily fall on you. I hated myself for it, but when I turned my back on you, I was doing as Sylen bade me. I was remembering our promise."

I'd repeated his message, even as my own heart lay in tatters and I broke Kaliban's. I'd had no idea that promise related to me.

"I never stopped loving you, Bastian. How could I? My boy. The son I didn't know I wanted—I *needed*. You saved me. Having you..." He shook his head as the tears reached his lips. "It was starlight in the darkness of my own guilt—a guiding point when I was lost. And I know I failed you. So many times. My dreams... I let them imprint on you. I hurt you with them—"

"That wasn't your—"

"I still did it. The first time it happened, I should've found a way to stop them or at least protect you. But I was too comforted by having our little life in the stable quarters—a normal life where I could wake up with your father and make you breakfast. So, yes, I failed you. But I have never—*never* stopped loving you."

I had to wipe tears from my own cheeks, and this time I leant into Kat's comforting touch on my arm. All these years, I thought he hated me. I thought I'd never achieve his forgiveness, so I was unworthy of it.

But he had forgiven.

He still called me son.

He was still my *athair*.

"Why didn't you tell me?" I could barely choke the question out as I held myself together.

"It was part of protecting you. Knowing puts you in danger —even now. It's much easier to keep a secret when you don't know it. But..." He spread his hands. "They're going to execute me. This was my last chance. At least I thought it was." He gave Kat a lopsided smile. "I didn't realise Sura had locked the knowledge in Kat's mind."

I scrubbed my face, a last ditch effort to wake up. But the calluses on my palms bit into the skin around my eyes, telling me there was nothing to wake up from.

"All this time you left me on my own to... to think you *hated* me."

He bowed his head. "If Braea thought there was even a chance you were working against her, influenced by me, she would've had you killed." He took a deep breath before meeting my gaze, his eyebrows knitting together. "You don't understand the lengths she will go to."

"No. You misunderstand her. She treads a tightrope." The same as me. "It isn't easy to keep the peace between two courts... To do what must be done."

"Don't you think I know that?" He laughed mirthlessly. He'd done what needed to be done. It still burned him. "The— the..." His jaw went solid as he squeezed his eyes shut. "The... the..." His face went red. Sweat beaded his brow, which scrunched up in... it was either pain or effort. Or both.

Kat reached through the bars, touching his shoulder. "Kaliban?"

He huffed out a sigh. "I can't speak of it. There's a... a..." He waved his hand.

"Geas?" I offered.

There had to be one in place, because he couldn't even nod

to confirm. An obligation that had been placed upon him, in this instance that he couldn't communicate about a particular topic.

A geas placed a great deal of strain on its subject, and required even more energy from the person placing it. They weren't spoken of lightly and few were put in place. Even threatening one was considered serious.

He spoke his next words slowly, as if testing the boundaries of his restrictions. "That infernal book of hers."

I swapped looks with Kat, who shook her head, clearly as puzzled as I was.

He'd been nursing his hate of Braea for a long time now, and if he'd been conspiring with Sura about the coup, who knew what poison she'd dripped in his ear about her mother.

There was nothing I could do about any of that. I certainly wasn't going to act on what I'd just found out. I couldn't even bring myself to think the words.

"Whatever happened in the past, we're going to get you out. This is all... nonsense." Both the arrest and some of what he'd said, too. "I'm going to fix this."

As I helped Kat up, he shook his head. "Whatever you need to believe, Bastian. But just in case you're wrong... just in case this is the last chance, I need to tell you one more thing."

"Please, no more surprises." I rubbed my forehead. There was too much new information in my brain. Too many things falling over each other as I tried to process—or ignore—them.

"I've seen you in Kat's thoughts"—he gave her an apologetic grin—"before she learned to stop them bleeding out. My boy..." He came up to the bars. "For too long you've blamed yourself and felt the guilt and responsibility for things you didn't do, all because you remember them. *I* did those things. *I* am the one who deserves punishment. Not you."

I stared at him, frozen by the shock of being perceived. He and Kat had seen me, understood me, pulled out the quiet things I kept to myself.

I suddenly understood how prey felt when it was caught in the hunter's gaze.

"You need to stop torturing yourself for what you didn't do. You need to stop thinking that you're undeserving of any brightness because of my darkness, skulking in the shadows, while your queen stands in the light." He took my shoulder, his words echoing in my mind, easing the old memories so they were indistinct ink spills rather than crisply drawn diagrams. "You need to be the prince, the king, the *leader* you were always meant to be."

26

BASTIAN

I spent the rest of the day in a daze, short-tempered and glowering whenever anyone pulled me from my thoughts. For a long while, I sat in my office staring off into space rather than at the report in my hand. Still, none of what my *athair* had said would process.

It didn't make sense.

It made too much sense.

It was impossible.

And yet it was true.

Instead, I tossed the report away and stalked to the training yard. There was no sign of Faolán, so instead I took on three recruits at once and told them not to hold back while the other fetched my friend.

We fought away the time, until the sun set, chilling the sweat that coated me.

Even Faolán huffed, hands on his hips as he caught his breath. "Cyrus again?"

I grunted in response. It was too much for me to take in,

never mind explain to anyone else, and I was too busy trying to avoid the whole damn business.

But now Dusk was ascendant, there was something else I could do. I clapped Faolán on the shoulder and thanked him, went and washed, then reported to my queen.

"I need you to free Kaliban," I said, as soon as the niceties were over.

Eyebrows raised, she looked at me in the mirror as a servant finished pinning her curls back. "I heard you visited him." She dismissed the servant and waited for him to leave the room before turning to me. "While it's understandable you would want to check on him after he was arrested, it isn't wise to be seen growing close to someone facing such a serious accusation. Doing so would be a danger to you *and* to Dusk."

For a moment, I could barely breathe past his words bubbling to the surface. *You don't understand the lengths she will go to.*

But Braea looked as she always did. Patient in a way that was only possible after living so long. Firm but caring. She treated me with tough love sometimes, but it was still love. She'd helped me in so many ways, lifting me from nothing, a stable boy, to her guard and now to one of the highest positions in the realm.

And I'd done so much for her. Whatever was necessary to achieve what we'd always worked for—the safety and security of Elfhame.

It was only thanks to her that I was respected. It was only because of what she'd given me that I'd ever been able to help Kat. And now I needed to help *Athair.*

She was my queen. Whatever he said, I couldn't see her any differently.

His view was clouded by his own biases. That didn't mean she was what he thought.

And Sura? She wanted the throne. Maybe she told herself it was because she wanted me safe, but there was no geas on fae that said we couldn't lie to ourselves. She would twist the truth whatever way helped her achieve her ambitions.

"Bastian?" Lines crept between Braea's eyebrows. "Are you all right?"

I'd been staring, trying to see what my *athair* had insisted was there.

But he was wrong.

I shook off his warnings. "It's been a long day. Dealing with Kaliban has this effect on me. But... for all he gave me as a child, I still need him freed."

She looked at me a long while, concern still etched on her smooth features. Eventually, she sighed. "You know I would look weak if I tried to help someone who once worked against me. Even if that was a thousand years ago—you know our memories stretch back further."

I gritted my teeth, desperate to say that he hadn't plotted against her. But, of course, it wasn't true. My very existence was only thanks to such a plot.

Her brow lowered, the lines deeper and fiercer now. "If I immediately free the person Cyrus blames for assassinating his father, how will that go for Dusk, do you think?"

The way she snapped the question was a punch in my gut. Mostly because she was right. Springing to his aid would seem like confirmation that Dusk was behind the assassination and protecting its chief operative. People would say I'd asked him to do it.

Then Cyrus would have the perfect excuse to strike back, and that would only escalate.

Braea sucked in her lips, inclining her head. "I understand you're upset." Her tone soothed me, familiar and gentle. "Whatever his crimes, he once meant a great deal to you. I know how difficult it is to let go of someone like that."

A deep, deep breath heaved through her, reminding me: hadn't she been forced to let go of someone she'd cared for when Sura had tried to overthrow her?

She understood me. She'd been there after I'd killed Sylen and Kaliban had turned his back on me. Even though I now knew why, at the time I had been devastated. She had been there, helping me. Directing me. Comforting me with a hand on the shoulder and encouragement to take some time for myself.

How could that same woman be responsible for my mother's death? The woman I'd trusted for so long. Who I'd fought for. Killed for. Dedicated half of my life to. If she was what my *athair* said, what did that mean for all those things I'd done? All that time?

She squeezed my shoulder now. "Cyrus is under pressure to show some results, since he's been unable to find this Krae person after pinning all the blame on them. Let him have this victory—for a while at least. There aren't any scheduled executions and he hasn't even had a trial yet. We have time to investigate. *If* Kaliban wasn't involved, I'll see him freed."

I found myself nodding, leaning in to her familiar comfort. She was right. Cyrus wanted to show he'd solved the crime quickly and was a great leader and now we could all go along our merry ways with him on the throne.

"See? You understand." She gave me a little shake. "You remember what I said after you prevented Sura's coup? I made you my Shadow to aid me in upholding the true and lawful rulership and assure the stability of Dusk Court and all of Elfhame. You didn't doubt me then. What's changed?"

Wincing, I had to drop her gaze. I'd let other voices creep into my mind—ones that had their own agendas.

Whatever her mistakes, she kept our central mission at the forefront of her mind. Prevent a catastrophe like the wars of succession from ever happening again. When it came to ruling Elfhame, nothing else mattered.

It was selfish of me to push her to help my *athair* when it would ripple out to the courts, with the potential to cause a tidal wave.

I'd been weak, letting Bastian Marwood's feelings cloud the work the Bastard of Tenebris had to do. "Forgive me. I... seeing Kaliban."

She nodded in understanding. "Then you trust me still?"

It took only as long as I needed to draw breath to answer. "I do. We will resolve this, but in the right way."

27

KAT

When a pounding headache stopped me going to dinner the day of Kaliban's revelations, Cyrus sent Elthea to my rooms. She frowned as she checked me over, noting things in her book. Cyrus had to make an appearance himself to remove my bracelet with his little key so she could use her magic to investigate what had happened inside my head and do what she could to ease the lingering pain.

In the days that followed, headaches continued to plague me, but they gradually faded, and Elthea left me medicine to take when they grew unbearable. Most nights I took it to help me escape the thoughts circling my mind.

Bastian was Braea's grandson. Nyx's son. Heir to Dusk Court.

There was no one I could speak to about this. Amandine accompanied me every time I left the palace and I wasn't allowed to visit Dusk streets, so I hadn't been able to visit Ariadne, Rose, or Ella. I had, however, left letters for my friends under the stone by the Great Trees—it had become my drop point with Ella and the only way I could communicate with her, aside from fake glares from a distance. One day, she'd even left a note there pointing me to a hidden spot in the gardens where I found a parcel of her beauty concoctions.

I took advantage of my freedom within Dawn to slip into the secret passages as often as I could, charting where I'd searched and where the dangers were as I looked for Krae.

In my mapping, I'd found another entrance in the library, and that was where I waited now. This hidden door was easier to access than the one Sepher had shown me—guards patrolled that corridor, whereas the library tended to be clear.

Except for today. Hence the wait. An older fae man sat near the fireplace, throwing me disapproving looks. If he found my presence so distasteful, why didn't he just bugger off?

With an over the top sigh, I went back to reading a letter from Ella that I'd hidden inside the book. I considered using our drop point to get some information back to Bastian. I could never tell when Orpha was going to pop up—her visits were generally a matter of opportunity, and I hadn't seen her since Celestine had managed to spot her.

During my time in Dawn, I'd worked my way through a fraction of their library, but I focused on the older section. I figured that would be the best place to find information about the Crown of Ashes. And so far I'd been rewarded with a brief mention.

One book referenced the translation of another book written in an early form of High Valens. Annoyingly, I couldn't find a copy of the older book in the library, so I only had a few quotes to go on. "The Crown lies beyond the gauntlet." Whatever that meant. There was an even more vague comment that the gauntlet "lies in the world beneath" and "can only be found after shedding skin." In a cavern or dungeon, perhaps? An underground passageway?

As I screwed up my face, staring off into the distance, movement broke through my thought.

Slamming his book shut, the disapproving reader rose. He clicked his tongue and glared at me as he returned the book to its shelf and stomped out.

Apparently my thinking face was too offensive to him. *Good.*

As soon as the door shut, I leapt up and hurried to the secret passages. This one wasn't opened by pulling out a certain book, as I'd read in dozens of stories, but instead by touching a volume called *The Book of Ways*, tucked at the bottom shelf of the bookcase opposite. The doorway swung silently open and I called for one of the fae lights to follow me into the gloom.

The dusty darkness had grown familiar, but it still made me jump whenever a spiderweb clung to my face as I entered an uncharted area. Before I set forth, I checked the book with the Crown reference was safely in its hiding spot just inside the entrance. If it wasn't in the library, that meant Cyrus couldn't read it—assuming he hadn't found it already. It was a small thing, but any measures to keep the Crown and information about it out of his hands was worthwhile.

Grabbing the stick I'd left with the book, I pulled the map out of my pocket and held it under the dim fae light. I'd disguised my map as an embroidery design, just in case anyone found it on me. I'd checked a large area to the left of the library and had started along the right, but there a central corridor I hadn't ventured down yet.

This place was labyrinthine—not just easy to get lost in, but huge. I started to the right with the plan to extend my explorations that way. I'd tackle the central section once this side was mapped.

With the hand-drawn map, I could go confidently at first, but once I hit new territory, I had to slow. Anything that looked suspicious, I poked with the stick—it had already revealed another pit hidden beneath stone that fell away under the slightest pressure.

Despite my light, the darkness pressed in, making time feel strange. I couldn't say if it had been twenty minutes or two hours since I'd left the library. Each minute merged together in stone and shadow and measured steps.

With a pencil, I catalogued the turns and junctions. Sometimes short, steep flights of steps led up or down—passing over or under a corridor in the main part of the palace, I suspected. A few times, I came across ladders that were so slender, I feared placing my weight on them. But they were fae-worked, so I needn't have worried—they held me without so much as a creak.

Despite the chill air, sweat built on my brow as I climbed my second ladder of the day, cursing whoever had designed this place. Still, when I stopped to draw in the section I'd just walked, I smiled when I spotted just how much I'd added to my map today.

This labyrinth would reveal its secrets to me whether it liked it or not.

I grinned to myself, tucking the pencil behind my ear and calling for the fae light to follow. As I turned the corner, still smug, a shadow reared from the darkness and slammed into me.

Bones jolting, I hit the wall.

I tried to push away, to swing the stick at the figure

looming over me, but then the steel kissed my throat and I froze.

"I told you, I didn't owe you anything anymore," my assailant hissed.

The fae light drifted to my side, and it was only then I saw the coppery hair and the pointed features. My skin tingled as I realised who it was. Krae.

"You should've brought better equipment to hunt me with." Their nose wrinkled in a snarl as they knocked the stick from my hands. It clattered to the stone floor. "No one would know if I killed you now. You'd just disappear."

I caught my breath, trying to gather my scattered wits. But my hands were quicker than my mind, already working on the bracelet.

Sepher had threatened me in the garden room, but I'd never felt in real danger. He was a boisterous sabrecat who needed to be taught not to throw his weight around. But Krae?

The steel they held at my throat felt like real danger.

Slowly, I swallowed, the knife pressing harder against my skin. When the bracelet clanged to the floor, though, I smiled. Magic hummed through me, and I pulled on the most delicate strand of its melody. "Do you think I'm completely defence-less?" Poison wafted through my words, not powerful enough to kill, merely a warning.

Eyes wide, Krae darted back, the steel gone from my throat.

It was a small triumph to see someone else afraid of me, rather than being the one who was afraid. For a moment, I was powerful.

But they soon mastered their shock, replacing it with a glower. "I still don't owe you."

There was that transactional reference again. Everything

was owing and deals with them. That could be my route to getting their help.

"And I don't owe you," I countered. "I can hand you over. *Or* you can help me and I'll help you."

Their eyes narrowed, glinting in the gloom.

"That's how you operate, isn't it? Transactions. Give and take. What's owed and by whom. What about Cyrus? What do you owe him?"

They drew a sharp hiss like I'd burned them. "Watch yourself, human."

"I'm not the one who's put a price on your head. You must know what he's saying about you."

Grumbling, their shoulders sank and they slid the dagger back in its sheath. A plain dagger this time—the one with a bronze hilt that matched their sword had been left in Cyrus's gut. The vital evidence pointing to them.

Their eyes narrowed as they watched me for several seconds. Eventually, they snorted. "And you're just going to help me out of the goodness of your heart? You'll prove my innocence, just because?"

"No. I'll do it because you're going to help me. And you'll do that because I'll help you." This felt like a safe path, one they could follow me along. "I know you didn't do it, but I can't work out what really happened. I need the full story."

They made a sound of derision and turned away, starting off down the corridor.

I had to give something before they would. It was risky, but letting them get away without helping was riskier. I steeled myself. "I know you didn't betray Cyrus. That he's the one behind the attack."

Just on the edge of the light, they stopped. The silence rang on, thick with tension as I willed them to stay and talk rather than slipping away into the shadows again.

"He killed the king," they said at last. "The plan was that I would stab him to cover it up, and he'd blame me initially. With that injury and me in the frame, he'd be above suspicion. Then it would 'emerge' that it wasn't me but a changeling all along. I'd be pardoned and come out of hiding and receive my reward." Their shoulders rose and fell. "He could safely say something like 'a changeling was involved in the royal plot' since it was technically true."

I shuddered. UnCavendish. Cyrus had used him.

"But." I could hear their teeth in that word, a crisp, sharp sentence in its own right. They turned, eyes dark beneath their frown. "That was supposed to happen *weeks* ago. He killed his own father; I was a fool to think family ties would keep me safe."

Family ties. I blinked at them, replaying that casual phrase. "You're part of the royal family." Sepher was a shapechanger. Someone had mentioned the first Day King had been one, too. "Shapechanging runs in the bloodline, doesn't it?"

They grunted with dark amusement. "Why do you think Cyrus hates me and Sepher so much? We're a reminder of that blot on our family line."

"A secret... *prinze*?" I supposed that was the ungendered version.

Another chuckle made their face as sharp as when they were a fox. "Hardly. A bastard half-sibling. Lucius enjoyed taking all sorts of lovers, but didn't like to deal with the consequences. He was trying for a child with his queen, and so Sepher exists, but he didn't count on getting one on his plaything, too. Though I think he felt like a stud for having two fae pregnant at once."

"Who knows?"

"Lucius did, of course. He sent my mother away while she was pregnant so no one else at Court would find out. A bastard makes the line of succession messy. But I came back as soon as I was old enough to choose for myself." They lifted their chin, daring me to judge them. "I wanted to meet my father. Turned out he wasn't interested. But city life suited me, and I was a useful kind of person. Do you know how many bargains you can rack up in a city compared to a sleepy little village?

"One of those bargains took me back into the palace and through a wrong turning, I found myself face-to-face with my brother. Cyrus knew who and what I was at once. I think he'd found our father's papers a long time ago and I had the right scent."

Cyrus had complained he could smell shapechangers—he had a stronger sense of smell than most fae. "He recognised you."

"In more ways than one. He knew our father had rejected me, and he confided that he hadn't fared much better. I'm sure you've heard how Lucius treated Sepher, exiling him from the city for his gift. But Lucius was cruel to Cyrus too, only in more subtle ways. Mocking his interests as frivolous, but locking him out of any diplomatic discussions. He sent away any lovers he grew attached to, and the ones who refused to leave mysteriously disappeared. So, we worked together."

My stomach twisted for Krae. They thought they were on even ground with Cyrus, but no way would the prince see his bastard half-sibling as an equal. He looked down on everyone.

"Cyrus *owed* him that death," they bit out. "And I did too. But how do I deserve this? Living behind walls in the dark. I'm starting to forget what the sun looks like."

"You don't. All you did was trust the wrong person. But now you have a chance to trust the right person."

They laughed outright at that, something of the fox's sharpness in the sound. "And, don't tell me, that's you."

"Maybe you can't trust a human who lies. But you can trust me to want Cyrus brought to justice. He's arrested someone I care about, blaming them for the assassination. You know the truth. If we can prove it, you'll be free and so will they."

"Hmm." They ran a hand through their long hair and twiddled the ends. "I help you. You help me."

"Exactly. A deal. Nothing more, nothing less."

"Deals I understand."

It was progress, but I couldn't shake off the sadness of that sentence and all the things lingering behind it. They didn't understand trust, friendship, family, only the cold, hard transaction of a deal and debt and owing.

I cleared my throat of the sudden tightness. "So you'll come forward and speak against Cyrus? Dusk Court will protect you."

"Ha! You're joking right?" Their lopsided grin showed off sharp canines, making them handsome in an odd way. "No one will trust a shapechanger. Cyrus has made sure of it. No, I'll gather my evidence and bring it to you. I've heard my treacherous big brother has a masked ball coming up to celebrate, of all things, *himself*. It will keep him occupied and the palace will be busy—I'll be able to blend into the crowd more easily. You'll be there and so will your Shadow."

"We can meet at—"

"You want me to come to a place and time you set, so you or anyone who intercepts your plans can set up an ambush?" They rolled their eyes. "I'll name the place. You'll receive a message at the party with that information. No nasty surprises for me, that way."

"You have a deal, Krae." I held out my hand, poison smothered. "Give us that evidence, and you'll get your life back."

28

KAT

With that deal under my belt, I felt like I was getting the hang of Elfhame. Maybe I was even winning at its games, as Sepher had called them.

I still had time before dinner, so I headed to the secret entrance to Cyrus's rooms, checking a couple of spyholes first to ensure he wasn't there.

Just because I'd made a deal with Krae, didn't mean I could be complacent. They might betray us or not come through with the evidence. Any proof I could gather myself could still be vital. Maybe I could read more of the notes, work out how exactly Sura was tied to Cyrus's plans.

And that mirror. Sura had told me Nyx had used it to contact her unseelie lover—Bastian's *father*. It made sense he would still have whatever the mirror linked to. Nyx might be gone, but I could help Bastian speak to the man she'd loved and who'd sired him.

But things didn't always run so smoothly, did they? When I

pushed the door, it only opened a crack before stopping with a thud. Cyrus must've placed something on the other side.

Which left me with only one other way to get into his rooms. One that made my stomach turn.

So, after an early dinner, timed to avoid the setting sun, I accepted Cyrus's invitation to walk around the gardens with him. He kept to my right side, always away from the iron bracelet, and I held his elbow, leaning in close so the side of my breast touched his arm.

He harped on about tomorrow's play—another part of his month of celebrations. I fought to keep a straight face, despite Krae's mocking comments coming back to me.

I needed to make him *think* I was trying to seduce him... or at least that I was ripe for seducing. But I also couldn't seem too easy a conquest. Then, I might need to follow through.

I couldn't keep slipping out of his veiled invites and insinuations. I was sure the only reason he hadn't asked me to come to bed outright was because he'd heard about Albionic sensibilities when it came to sex and didn't want to scare me off.

He guided me to an arbour beneath a weeping willow that overlooked a pond. Lily pads blanketed the water at the edges, muffling the sound of a fountain at the pool's centre. A hundred shades of green surrounded us, from the silvery colour of the willow's leaves to the dark shadows rippling under the water's surface.

"Of course," he went on, "not everyone can go to the play or the balls, but for the common folk, we'll have public events in the square later this week." He dipped his chin and leant close. "Don't tell anyone, but the plan is for me to pardon a whole swathe of prisoners. It's going to be a surprise."

It was like he'd reached into my chest and grabbed my

heart. Did that swathe of prisoners include Kaliban? It seemed like a foolish hope, but I'd hoped for sillier things than that.

I tried to hide my reaction, but he was sitting so close, he had to notice how still and tight I'd suddenly become. "What a delightful surprise."

He matched my stillness, a glint in his eyes as he watched me all the more intently. "You have a *friend* in the dungeons currently, don't you?"

I lowered my head as though ashamed. "I confess I am friends with Kaliban. I didn't know he was the Bastard of Tenebris's father until very recently though. They're estranged, after all. I'm not even sure the Bastard cares that he's been arrested, but *I* do." I lifted my gaze to Cyrus's, making sure I kept my chin dipped so I was looking up at him.

Small and weak, that was me.

"Please, Cyrus"—I touched my chest—"I would take it as a personal favour if you could include him amongst those you free. I'm sure he regrets anything he may have done, and I can't believe he had any part in your father's tragic death."

This could be pushing too far, but if it saved Kaliban, it would be worth it.

Cyrus didn't say no right away. In fact, he tilted his head to one side as though weighing it.

Perhaps I could add weight to my side of the scales.

I slid my hand onto his knee as though it was a perfectly natural part of me leaning in to him. His warmth paired with a sharp, citrus scent jarred me, not what I was used to. But I had to withstand him to get what I needed. I swallowed slowly as if overcome by being this close to him, my mouth only inches from his. "I would be terribly grateful."

A dark smile crept over his lips. "Oh, *would* you?"

Not taking his eyes from mine, he grabbed my hand and slid it up to his dick.

I gasped—not faked. But the way he watched so intently—I knew this was a test. What could he get if he did me this favour? How far was I *really* willing to go?

The fucking fool.

I had flirted with a man more dangerous than him. I'd placed myself at the mercy of unCavendish. I had taken poison, for gods' sakes. Did he really think he was *anything*?

Chest heaving, I bit my lip as though hesitant, then squeezed.

He let out a sound that was part pleased, part pleasured, and slipped one hand behind my head. He gripped my hair too tight, yanking my head back so I was practically beneath him as he came closer.

For all I'd felt cocky moments ago, it was the battle of my life not to freeze up. *Remember Kaliban. Remember Bastian. They need this from you. All of Elfhame needs this from you.*

So I let my lashes flutter and lips part as that small distance between us closed.

"Your Majesty." The voice of his new assistant cut through the quiet space under the willow, making him freeze with his breath fanning my mouth. "Forgive the interruption, but sunset approaches."

"What?" He reared back, staring around as if only just taking in that the gloom around us wasn't entirely down to the willow's hanging branches. "How close?" he snapped, standing over me. He came a step closer, feet either side of mine, and lifted my chin.

The way he watched my lips reminded me of unCavendish—he'd had a fascination with my mouth and stood over me like this once. Back then, I'd been too naïve, but now I understood how being seated placed my mouth level with his cock.

My stomach twisted again, knots tying themselves over others.

Remember.

So I moistened my lips, slowly.

"Five minutes, sire. It took a while to find you. If you recall, you said to always ensure you weren't caught in public in case—"

"I know what I said." His chest rose and fell, once, twice, as he swiped his thumb over my mouth. "Shit." He lurched backwards as though having to physically tear himself away. "Good night, my pretty little thing. Such an intriguing creature. I have a feeling I'm going to enjoy you immensely."

He stalked out of the willow's shade, and it was only once he was out of sight, I sank back in my seat.

But his voice, sharp with irritation, still reached me. "I swear to the gods, I will be free of this fucking Sleep before the year is out."

There was only one way to escape Sleep. The Crown of Ashes.

It didn't sound like an idle threat. He knew, and he was after it. We'd had suspicions, but now...

Groaning, I put my head in my hands.

"That bad?"

I snapped upright. "Ella?"

She emerged from the willow's trailing branches, grinning.

I launched myself at her and she returned my hug just as fiercely. Being with the king meant Amandine had been dismissed, so I was safe to drop the act.

"Were you listening in?"

"Once a spy, always a spy."

I scoffed and sank into the seat with her. "Well, hopefully I'm doing a better job at it this time."

"By the sounds of that conversation, you are." The apologetic quirk of her mouth told me she understood what had been happening. She'd gone further.

I had to do the same.

I told her how I'd found Krae and about the meeting we'd arranged, so she could let Bastian know. I didn't trust such information to a written report.

But after, my gloomy thoughts were still there.

"What's wrong? You're wrinkling that beautiful face." She tilted her head, cupping my cheek as though ready to catch the tears that burned at the back of my eyes.

"This is hard. Being away from you. What I... The things I must do."

Her head lowered as she sighed. "I know. And harder because you dislike the person you've got to do it with. At least I've always been paired with people I enjoyed... And I never needed to fight with my heart while it lay elsewhere."

I gritted my teeth and looked up at the arching branches that shut out the sky, smothering the sight of whether it was Dusk or Dawn's time to rule. "I'll do whatever needs to be done."

"Maybe you don't have to." She pulled something out of her pocket and held out her closed fist. "I hope you don't mind, but I went through your things. Thought there might be something useful in there—something less noticeable than a pistol or dagger. I found this." She opened her fingers.

A small bottle glinted in the scant light.

"What is it?"

"Look closer." She held it up.

Clear liquid sloshed around inside the cut glass vial. The

one unCavendish had given me. He'd told me a few drops would knock Bastian out... "Long enough for me to search his rooms."

She grinned. "Exactly."

I kissed her, heart burning with gratitude.

After the start of our marriage, on the rare occasion Robin had been at home, I'd made sure he was drunk. That way, when he shoved me into his room, I could make him *think* we'd fucked, when actually he'd just spilled on my thighs. It was a dangerous game to play with Cyrus, but...

"Thank you," I whispered. "You've saved me."

She pressed the vial into my hand and closed my fingers around it, hard. "You may be stuck in Dawn, Kat, but you still have a few tricks up your sleeve."

29

KAT

From that moment on, I carried the vial in my bodice, ready for my opportunity to search his rooms again.

I didn't have to wait long.

The next afternoon, Cyrus kept us all in the dining hall after lunch, ordering our glasses refilled with a deep berry coloured fae wine.

Strong and dangerous.

I dodged refills and surreptitiously spilt a little here and there. When he wasn't looking, I even poured some of mine into his glass so he would think I'd taken more than a sip.

For a heart-stopping moment, I found the younger of the rose-gold-haired sisters watching me as I poured. Shit. She already disliked me, but had been less outwardly hostile since I'd arrived in Dawn.

I winked at her as though this was a fun prank to play on the king and not part of a larger plan.

She didn't look particularly amused, but she slid her attention away without raising the alarm.

As we drank and laughed, the chatter grew more raucous, and they shared stories of hunting trips. Or at least, that was what I thought they meant when they spoke about "chasing him through the forest." That had to be a stag, right?

"I had him take his clothes off and dance for me," the fae continued. Glass in hand, she pointed at the rest of the table. "And the best thing was? He was tiny—tiny!" She held up her little finger and dissolved into peals of laughter.

Most of the others joined in, but I froze.

A human. She was talking about hunting *a human*. She'd used charm to make him strip and perform for her, and now she was telling it as an amusing dinner party tale.

"Ah, now, look." Cyrus recovered from his laughter, turning to me. "You've upset my human. Come here, little thing." He patted his lap.

This was it. I took a gulp of the sweet-sharp wine, taking courage from the warm haze it spread through me.

Standing up and taking two steps to him felt like it took a century. My stomach protested, curdling around lunch and the small amount of wine I'd actually consumed.

Get on with it.

I sank onto his lap, letting him slide an arm around my waist.

"There, that's better isn't it? *Some* of us don't need charm, do we?" He squeezed me against him, breathing sour-sweetness over my skin as his gaze wavered like he was struggling to stay focused.

Nearly there. I needed to get him drunk enough that his lack of memory and passing out would seem a result of that. But I didn't want him so drunk that we didn't make it to his room.

He jerked his head up to the rest of the table. "We'll have

no more talk of charming the inferior species. No." A wicked smirk lit his face. "Instead, look at my pretty little thing." He jiggled his knee up and down, bouncing me.

With the intent of false seduction, I'd worn the lowest cut dress I had in Dawn, and the bouncing motion threatened to make me spill out.

There was nothing false about my gasp as I covered my chest, desperately trying to keep it inside my bodice... together with the little bottle.

The fae laughed.

Face burning, I caught Caelus's gaze as he frowned and looked away. It was one thing *choosing* to be watched, commanding him to take in my naked body, but this?

Old shame flooded me. I was a girl once more, Father's voice harsh in my mind, reminding me of the need to be demure, chaste, pure, otherwise I would be worth nothing.

In the hot springs, I had been the one in charge, but here, I was a plaything to be humiliated.

Cyrus's hot breath brushed my neck as he gave a dark laugh. "I would say I was sorry, darling little creature," he murmured, "but you know I cannot lie. I'm going to have you today, and once I'm done, I think I'll share you. I've seen how Caelus looks at you—I'm sure he'd love the chance." He squeezed my thigh. "Word will get back to Bastian, and I know you want to see him humiliated after he's hurt you so much."

Not helping the spilling situation was my heaving chest. This would be my chance. Much as his words disgusted me, I needed to smother all that I felt, all that I thought, the indignation that he hadn't *asked* if I wanted to fuck him or be shared.

I stamped it down and made myself turn into the touch of his lips on my throat. "I don't think the Bastard gives a damn what's done to me."

230

Another dark laugh wafted my hair. "I don't believe that for a second. When he hears that I've had you, it will eat at him. When word spreads that half the fae in Dawn Court have had what was his, he'll look a fool."

Half the fae in Dawn Court. Fuck. *Fuck.* That vial wasn't going to work on all of them. I was in over my head. So far over. I was drowning.

But fear wasn't going to help.

So I stamped that down too and slipped an arm around his neck, letting my body press against his, even though it screeched at me to run and never look back.

He pulled away and gripped my chin. "Don't worry, I'll make sure you enjoy it. That's half the fun, letting them see me make you come undone, knowing that your body is mine to play with." His nose wrinkled as he grinned, making it almost a snarl. "That snake will hear you all the way in Dusk."

My pulse thundered. He had to see it leaping in my throat. My face had to be red. I managed to swallow and touched my chest, breathing out his name as though my reaction was one of excitement and not horror.

He leant in for a kiss and horror won out. I turned my head.

No. No. No. I needed to do whatever it took to get another look at the information in his room of collections.

Think fast, Kat. I looked down, playing coy, making myself small. "Not in front of everyone, Cyrus. Not our first time."

"Hmm." He pressed a hard kiss on my cheek instead. "Silly humans and their silly ideas. I thought the Bastard might've trained you out of them, but it seems you need a firmer hand. Very well, Katherine." He pinched my chin and forced me to look him in the eye. "To my rooms, then."

"At last," I breathed.

I weaved through the corridors alongside him, like I was

drunk too, giggling when I tripped up a step. At one point, he pulled me against him and nuzzled against my throat, squeezing my arms so hard I knew there would be bruises.

It made me sick to pretend to enjoy it, sighing and writhing. I dared to grip the vial hidden in my bodice, a reminder that I had a plan, and it was only because of that I maintained control.

He tried to kiss me again, but head down, I reminded him of my need for privacy. I prayed to the gods it would make him forget any ideas of sharing me, but I had a feeling this was one of those many times they wouldn't hear.

With each step, dread filled me. What if the potion didn't work? What if I didn't get a chance to give it to him? What if I had to go through with this?

We continued on our way, but he pressed on faster now, hand wrapped around mine.

He threw the doors open, and I peered around like I'd never seen the place before. I made the sounds a fae king would expect from a mere human upon seeing his grand royal suite, my *ooh*s and *aah*s deliberately suggestive.

Watching me, he smirked and sauntered in. Or, at least, I think he meant to saunter, but the alcohol was catching up to him, making his course through the room crooked.

Nearly there.

I spotted an ornate side table set up with a decanter and glasses and made a beeline for it. "Shall I fetch Your Majesty a drink?"

"I have to say, Katherine"—he plopped into a seat, head swinging back without control—"I had so many plans for you... showing you off, sharing you, making you cry and beg... but maybe I like you more than I expected, because I find myself wanting to keep you to myself... for a little while at least."

Midway through pouring a drink, I glanced over my shoulder at him like he was paying me a compliment.

Arrogant prick.

Unlike when I'd poisoned Bastian's drink at the wedding ceremony, my hands didn't shake as I dripped the concoction into one of the glasses. A quick swirl and all traces of it disappeared.

I dropped into the seat beside him, careful not to spill his drink, and looked up at him, like I was *so* small and he was *so* big and powerful.

"Yes." He smiled slowly, pupils growing wide as he looked down at me. "I find myself liking you very much, my pretty little thing."

"*Oh.*" I let my mouth drop open as though I was a girl from a fairy story, chosen by a fae king and not a woman with only terrible options.

He didn't like me. He didn't even *know* me. Whenever I was around him, I made sure I reflected nothing of myself, only what he wanted. *That* was what he liked.

But if I could keep fooling him into thinking he liked me, I just might buy myself time.

I offered his drink, watching intently as he took it and swirled it.

As I clinked my glass to his, I had to bite back a smile.

Because the high pitched ring of the glasses broke through the sickness swirling in my stomach and the tightness of my chest.

I wasn't the victim here.

I was the snake in the grass, ready to strike, and he was *my* victim.

I wasn't small, just hidden—a threat he didn't see because he underestimated it. With my poison blocked, he thought I'd been declawed.

But it was a different poison in the glass he lifted to his lips. Maybe even one he'd supplied unCavendish with to use on Bastian.

Such beautiful symmetry.

I let myself smile.

He frowned as he gulped down his drink, one hand already wandering to my bodice, as though he planned to get the drinks out of the way and get to business.

I didn't so much as flinch when he touched my breast, because his eyes blinked slowly once, twice, three times, and his grip weakened.

"Oh, Cyrus," I cooed, catching his glass as I swung over and straddled him. It needed to be clear where this was heading, so when he couldn't remember the rest, he'd fill in the gaps for himself.

"That's it." He slurred the words into one sound, head rolling as he fought to keep it upright. He was still aware enough to grab my arse.

Come on. Pass out, you vile toad. I pressed against him, getting closer like I was going to kiss him. Any second now would be perfect.

When I was half an inch from his lips, his grip dropped from my backside and his eyes rolled. I caught his head as it fell and slipped a cushion under it. He needed to think this had all gone perfectly, and a bump on the back of his head would ruin that.

I stayed there a long moment, hands braced on the back of the settee, checking his chest rose and fell steadily. I prodded him and clapped by his ear—no reaction. "Cyrus," I shouted in his face.

Nothing. His whole body was slack like someone in a deep sleep.

Perfect.

Still, I found myself lingering. If I had a knife, I could end this all now. I had poison, yes, but there was something more satisfying about the idea that I could cut his throat and he'd be powerless to stop me.

The fantasy of blood filled my vision, and the part of me that had been made cruel salivated at the thought.

But I would just be a human from Dusk Court murdering Dawn's king. I had no proof of what he'd done. It might satisfy my vicious streak, but it would only make things between the courts worse and get me executed.

I allowed myself one indulgence. My hand rang against his cheek in a gratifying slap. I relished the way my palm stung.

But I couldn't stay here and pummel him. So, with a sigh, I crawled off the unconscious king.

First, I went to his bedroom to see what was blocking the secret entrance and whether I could move it.

I stopped in the doorway, eyes wide.

An enormous mirror stood at the foot of his bed, covering most of the wall. I had never seen one so huge.

It was the most Cyrus thing he could've done.

Laughing to myself, I made my way to his room of collections and picked the lock.

But while one mirror had appeared, the other had disappeared. There was no sign of the scrying mirror where I'd left it or in the display cabinets or any of the remaining boxes (most of which had been unpacked and cleared now).

The letters from Sura sat in a stack on the desk at the far end of the room. They'd been tied neatly with a ribbon, like he'd recently sorted through them. In fact, now I examined them again, I realised the worn edges suggested they'd been handled a great deal. I clenched and unclenched my hands. If I took one, it would be missed.

"Shit."

No scrying mirror. No letters.

I couldn't have risked so much for nothing.

I charged through the rest of his suite looking for something—*anything* that might prove useful. I searched through bookshelves and drawers, down the back of the armchair, up the inside of the fireplace. Eventually I found myself back in his bedroom, rattling through the armoire.

Gold and scarlet glistened as I rifled through the embroidered suits and shirts. Blinking, I flicked back.

The jacket he'd worn in the throne room during the eclipse. The thread that matched the fake Hydra Ascendant insignias the attackers had worn that day and at the Winter Solstice. I sighed with my whole body.

As evidence went, this was as flimsy as the thread itself. Huffing, I continued working my way through the room. A book on the bedside table caught my eye—I didn't have Cyrus down as much of a reader.

When I saw the title, I gasped. This was the book I'd found reference to in the library—the one that spoke of the gauntlet but that I hadn't been able to find a copy of. Feverishly, I skimmed through it, searching for anything to do with the

Crown. At last, I came across the passage that had been translated in the other book. But here, in the original older form of High Valens, it read slightly differently.

"The gauntlet leads to the Underworld. The anointed one must call and the way will open."

I read it three times, checking I hadn't mistranslated. Not the "world beneath" but the Underworld. To get the Crown of Ashes, you had to travel to to the unseelie realm.

I gave a frustrated growl. What an idiot. How hadn't I realised sooner?

And *the mirror*. If I had it, I could speak to someone in the Underworld. Bastian's father or someone else—whoever it was, they might know more.

But there was no sign of the damn thing, and I found nothing else useful in Cyrus's suite.

So, with a sigh, I returned to the lounge. There was one more thing I had to do before I could leave.

Grimacing, I peeled off Cyrus's shirt and unbuttoned his trousers. I grunted as I tried to pull them off and almost fell over in the attempt, but eventually I had him naked and sprawled on the settee. To add to the effect, I knocked a few cushions on the floor.

He looked like he'd had a good evening, but the tableau wasn't quite complete. It didn't say that *I'd* been here.

Before I could overthink it, I wriggled out of my underwear and tucked the flimsy lace under him. That had to be enough to persuade him that we'd fucked, right?

Right?

I scrubbed my face and stole away from his suite, pulling up the shoulder of my gown as an extra show for the guards waiting at the doors.

Their whispers followed me through the halls.

The sun had set by the time I slipped into my room, head hanging, heart sore. I needed this to be over before I had to give any more of myself.

30

BASTIAN

Night's chill still clung to the morning air, misting my breath as I waited in the city's central square with hundreds of others. Arms folded, scowl in place, I played the part of the Bastard of Tenebris, distant and disinterested in the event, only here because it was expected of the Night Queen's representative.

But the hand that had gripped my throat since Kaliban's arrest loosened with every minute. This day would see him freed.

The prisoners waited in a guarded enclosure behind the platform where Cyrus sat upon a sunstone throne. The prisoners blinked at the clear sky above and the clouds blowing in from the nearby sea. How long since some of them had seen the outside world? It had been a week for my *athair*. I tried not to look at him, check if he was all right, but the tug on me was all the stronger now. *I never stopped loving you. My boy.*

Lucan was long minutes into a speech about forgiveness and benevolence, and the importance of justice.

239

From my position on a lower dais off to one side with the rest of the Convocation, I managed not to glare at Mored as he sidled up to me, but my shadows swirled in discontent.

I'd finally managed to catch up with Elthea. However, she'd been ordered not to discuss the topic of hair dye with anyone and had been threatened with a geas if she couldn't comply.

She hadn't said *who* exactly had threatened her with one, but my money was on Mored—as the Master of Magic, he ultimately oversaw everything at the Hall of Healing. If he had a whiff of the hair dye and wanted to keep that information suppressed, he was in the prime position and had the power to do so.

"You'll be pleased about the prisoners, won't you?" he said, just loud enough that the other Convocation members would hear. "Isn't your father amongst them?"

I clamped my teeth around my tongue. He was trying to undermine my position by reminding the others that I'd been raised by traitors and couldn't be trusted to make sound decisions now.

I tasted copper before I dared release my jaw. I lifted one shoulder. "We've barely spoken since my other father's death." My gaze shot to him and I let my shadows seethe. "You remember, the one I killed."

Mored went pale and backed away.

Sometimes, being the Bastard of Tenebris was useful.

Free of that irritant, I was keenly aware of Katherine's presence in the crowd. Her red hair was a beacon, but I kept my gaze away. Instead I caught Ella's eye and gave her a faint smile. She blew me a kiss in return.

She was better at this game than me.

Lucan's voice rose as he reached the crescendo of his speech. "... And to that end, His Majesty—"

"Has decided to *personally* see justice is done." Cyrus flowed to his feet with a thin smile.

At my side, Asher stiffened and glanced at me, no doubt wondering if this was part of the plan.

This was very much *not* part of the plan—at least not the Convocation's version of it.

Cyrus was meant to smile and wave and be seen presiding over the freeing of all the prisoners, giving them another chance at life with the stern reminder that should they fall foul of the law again, punishment would be swift and harsh.

I squeezed the buckle that usually attached my scabbard to my belt—no swords allowed in the king's presence. Probably just as well. Too much temptation when I'd already come too close to harming him—and by extension, endangering Kat.

"For what justice can there be if the very worst are simply let free?" He raised his eyebrows and spread his hands. The crowd nodded, muttering agreement. "Bring forth Justice."

My blood ran cold. The world slowed as if it too was freezing.

Two green-haired members of the Kingsguard brought forward the greatsword. Two serpents, one black, one silver, made up its hilt and crossguard, tiny stars glittering in constellations upon them.

Flashing a cruel smirk, Cyrus drew the sword, letting it glint in the cool sunlight.

Ancient text gleamed along its huge blade, spelling out the only purpose it could be wielded for and its name: justice.

"Bring the first prisoner. Give me a murderer. They deserve to pay, don't they?"

Some in the crowd looked at each other as if wondering whether this was a joke or a trick. Others nodded. A few cheered. The guards between them and Cyrus squared their shoulders.

Public executions were barbaric. We hadn't done them in centuries. It was part of why rolling what I'd thought was Sura's head across the throne room had been so shocking. Such uncivilised behaviour proved the taint of my unseelie blood.

But that didn't stop Cyrus as he had the woman brought before him.

"Your Majesty," Galiene lurched forward, "this isn't—"

Cyrus swung Justice in her direction, pointing. An instant later, its blade clanged to the floor. "Guards, ensure I'm not interrupted."

They leapt to obey, surrounding Galiene until she backed off. She was the head of the City Watch, but Dawn's palace guards had just shown they were loyal to their king.

Once the square was quiet again, Cyrus seized the prisoner's shoulder and lifted Justice—it moved easily despite its great size. In one movement, he sliced.

Blood spattered the front row of the crowd as the woman's throat opened up. Gurgling, she slumped to the ground.

Cyrus hadn't stopped. For a moment, I'd clung onto the idea that this was some stupid joke of his, designed to scare the prisoners and shock the rest of us. I'd expected him to stop with the blade against her throat.

At my side, Asher muttered something.

"It's all right." I nodded as much for myself as him. "The sword will only lift for a just death. As soon as he reaches an innocent, it will be too heavy for him to wield."

Someone like Kaliban. I prayed to every god that his past crimes didn't make his death right in the eyes of Justice.

Because Cyrus wasn't stopping at one. He called for the next prisoner.

A short man was brought forward. He'd violated others. Another death Justice deemed worthy of its bite. I couldn't blame it. This time Cyrus stabbed him through the heart, smiling as the man slid from Justice's blade.

As the guards bundled more fae to the platform and Cyrus cut through them, I weighed my options. But only the Night Queen herself could stop this, and we were far from sunset and almost a month past the eclipse.

The bodies piled up and the crowd grew ashen. Even those who had cheered at first had grown quiet. Convocation members kept swapping covert glances, not wanting to risk revealing that this hadn't been planned and their king was unpredictable and uncontrolled.

At last, the grandmother of a shapechanger family who'd been part of the mass arrests came to the platform. She pulled away from the guard and approached Cyrus with her shoulders back. "We are guilty of what we are, nothing more. My nature cannot be a crime. There has been no trial, and I do not recognise your laws against my kind."

Faolán stood behind me in a bodyguard position, and I could feel the need to move simmering in him before he reached my side.

I grabbed his shoulder. "Do you believe her or Cyrus?"

Gaze locked on the grisly show, he wrinkled his nose in a snarl. "Are you gambling that family's lives on the whims of an ancient sword?"

"This isn't just. The sword knows."

But as Cyrus laughed at the shapechanger and tightened his grip on the serpent hilt, I held my breath.

Justice didn't move.

Nostrils flaring, he flashed a quick, disbelieving smile and heaved. But try as he might, he could not lift the blade.

I exhaled, shakily and released Faolán. "Justice is on our side."

"I hope you'll bring this to the Convocation." Asher inclined his head, determination in the set of his jaw as he glowered at Cyrus. "It's a clear sign this rubbish is entirely made up and it needs to end."

"It's past time," Faolán growled.

"Long past." I squeezed his shoulder before releasing him. "And this will help us argue that."

At last, Cyrus laughed, but it was strained and high-pitched. "Won't you look at that? Justice has spoken." He spread his hands with a tight smile. "The elder must speak *some* truth. Clearly the City Watch wasn't on the side of justice when they arrested these good folk. But *I* shall free them."

They were only arrested because of you. I gritted my teeth, jaw aching as I battled to keep the words in.

"In fact"—Cyrus shoved the sword's hilt into a guard's hand—"free them all. Let my forgiveness be a lesson to you all. Do not stray onto the wrong side of Justice again."

Guards opened the enclosure and unshackled prisoners as they filed out. It roused a few desultory cheers from the crowd, but they still looked pale. I met Kat's gaze for a moment. She looked away quickly, too close to Cyrus's eye line to avoid his attention for long, but she held her hand over her heart, an unspoken message.

As my *athair* reached the front of the line, the grip around my throat eased and my shadows sank to the ground, still for once.

"But." Cyrus's voice cut through the square like a single strike on a great drum. "A king cannot forgive everyone."

I started forward before I even realised what I was doing. Guards closed in, not grabbing me, but blocking the way. Their fingers twitched, ready to draw weapons. I mastered myself, hand squeezing the buckle again.

"Bring Kaliban here."

Folk murmured in recognition of the name.

Cyrus lifted his chin, lips thin and flat as he watched my *athair* approach. "The turncoat who married an even greater turncoat. You chose a false queen, then changed your allegiances in the middle of the war, did you not? And your husband joined Princess Sura's ill-fated coup. By my reckoning, that makes you a traitor twice—perhaps even thrice over, and now..." He held up his hands as though the truth was self-evident.

He'd already plotted against one monarch, of course he'd orchestrated the murder of another.

"Bastian?" Faolán's voice was low and urgent. "What do we do?"

I'd held him back. And now, although my muscles roared at me to get my *athair* away from Cyrus, I had to hold myself back, too. The prong of the buckle pierced my palm, a sharp counter to my pulse, which begged me to step in. "He isn't guilty. Trust in Justice."

At the foot of the platform, Kat lurched forward. "But..." Her strained voice barely reached me before the guards turned their attention to her.

"Kneel," Cyrus said with a sneering smile. He peered down at my *athair* and Kat. "There are those who have pressed me for leniency. There are those who have petitioned for it and offered *all sorts* of favours in exchange for your life. How it must feel to be so popular! Yet, I am the King of Elfhame, and what kind of king would I be if I set such an example? Any fae may murder their ruler and walk free? No. That is not the message I would give my subjects.

"I'm sure the Night Queen would agree." He turned that mocking smile upon me, and I thought my chest would explode from the wild surge of my heart as it demanded his blood.

"He isn't guilty," I whispered, staring at Justice, which waited in a guard's hands, tip resting upon the floor.

Still, it was the most painful gamble of my life. My *athair* had atoned for his sins. He'd turned coat to support Braea because the other side had summoned the Horrors and used them on soldiers and civilians indiscriminately. He'd tried to make that nightmare right. It was their defection at the final battle that ended the war. Without that, we might have wiped ourselves out.

If those things weren't enough, he'd been punished plenty, too.

He'd had his titles and position stripped for backing the wrong side in the first place. He'd lost the man he loved and his son in one fell swoop. He'd lived in miserable isolation ever since, with Kat as the only bright spark in all those years.

"*He isn't guilty.*" This time I said it with a dip of my chin. Justice was on our side.

"It is my right, as the son of the murdered man, to take the life of the one responsible." Cyrus spread his arms wide, presenting himself as the wronged party before kicking my *athair's* back, so he bowed forward. "It's only right that I should use my family blade."

He drew the Brightblade, which swallowed up the thin sunlight remaining as clouds closed in. The sword flared to life.

I'd barely registered his words as I burst forward, body and shadows as one.

But there were so many guards. I dodged them, but they

slowed me. Even the darkness I sent ahead hadn't reached my *athair* yet.

Cyrus's sword rose above his neck. I was still ten feet away.

I leapt, shadows helping me up the platform as I drew my dagger, ready to block the strike.

My lungs heaved. My muscles burned. My arm stretched. I could make it. I could—

The Brightblade fell, scorching the air, searing my eyes.

"I've got you," I whispered as I caught my *athair* and braced.

31
BASTIAN

The strike could hit me instead. My shadows might slow it.

But it never came.

And as I blinked away the terrible burning light of the Brightblade, I understood why.

I had him, yes. But only his lifeless body, still warm, still bleeding as his head rolled away.

All the world pressed on my ears as I stared. All the world and the things beyond it. Space and the Stars above and the great forces that moved such things. The Celestial Serpent and the Tellurian Serpent's ghost. Their love. Their hate. Their wonder and disappointment.

"He plotted against the throne." There was a note of surprise in Cyrus's voice. "So good to know you wanted him to survive to do it again."

Too slow. I had been too slow.

It didn't seem possible. Real. Right.

There were other voices out in the crowd. Witnesses. Most of the city.

Remember who you are. I needed to drag myself up. I needed to function. To salvage something. I needed to be the Bastard, not the son.

People surging. I lost sight of Kat amongst them.

Somehow I released his warm body, shadows setting him down gently as I stood. "You should have used Justice." My voice sounded hollow but hard, like an empty well. "It's protocol and you broke it."

Cyrus bared his teeth, hot pleasure in his eyes. "Like you did when you beheaded Princess Sura, you mean?"

I couldn't reply. He didn't realise she was still alive. Had he held a grudge all these years? Was that why he'd done this? Why he'd demanded Kat as his hostage? They'd been lovers, and I assumed that meant as little to him as sex usually did, but if he'd actually been in love with her...

Lucan cleared his throat. "Bastian is correct, Your Majesty. We have our laws for a reason."

"*Our* laws?" The Brightblade gleamed as Cyrus stepped forward, standing over him. "They are *my* laws. If they displease me, they are gone." He flicked blood off his sword, and it brought my gaze back to the lifeless form lying on the stone platform.

My father. *My athair.*

My vision blurred, and it was all I could do to offer a curt nod before I turned and strode out of the square, barging through the crowd.

I made for the nearest dark place, able to make out that much through the unshed tears.

Shadowed alleyways rose around me, cradling, shielding. I

wound through them as quickly as I could until I hit a dead end and found myself alone.

As the clouds released a misty drizzle, I sank to the ground. I'd failed him.

I'd counted on Justice but Cyrus had circumvented its whims to get exactly what he wanted.

I hadn't just failed him. I'd failed all my parents. Kaliban. Sylen. Nyx. Even the nameless unseelie whose blood flowed through my veins. I had no idea what kind of man he was, but I knew I wasn't someone Sylen would be proud of, nor Nyx.

I had trusted that the system would work. I had trusted my own judgement. I had trusted that Cyrus would play by the rules.

And Justice really wasn't presiding over this day, because it hadn't cost *me*—the one who'd fucked up. No. It had cost my *athair*.

Warm arms wrapped around me. The same warmth I'd felt as I'd caught him, and for a moment I thought he was here. Alive.

But when I gasped, the breath tasted of snowmelt and spring showers.

"Kat," I choked out. "You shouldn't be here. It isn't safe. Your guard will—"

"I gave my guard the slip in the madness after... after... Your shadows found me... brought me here." Her voice was thick, and when I pulled back, I found her eyes red-rimmed and swollen.

It was the sight of her, hair wild like she'd run here on the wind, face crumpled with grief, that unlocked something in me.

"It's my fault." With that, I doubled over, trying to curl up and hide from her, from all those things that had pressed on my ears... from myself.

"No. *No.*" She caught me. Held me. Squeezed so tight, it was like she was trying to stop me falling apart.

But I slid through the gaps, pieces of me fracturing, breaths broken by sobs, heart shattering and shattering until there was only dust left.

"I thought we had time. I thought... after the dungeons..." The words came out jumbled, fragments of half formed thoughts. "I thought we'd get another chance. A fresh start. But he's gone."

"I know. I'm sorry."

She held me. I didn't know for how long, just that I needed it.

"Katherine?" someone called. "Kat?"

"Shit," she whispered and pulled me tighter. "It's my guard."

"You go." Faolán's voice reached through my dark haze. "We've got him."

I looked up, dashing the tears from my eyes. He and Rose hovered nearby, faces crumpled in concern.

Kat shook her head. "But—"

"Go." I pulled away, giving her a reassuring nod. "She can't find you with me. It'll ruin all your hard work."

She knelt there, torn. Her brow creased as though she could figure out a way to stay with me *and* not break her cover, if she could only have a moment longer to think.

"Katherine?" The call sounded more desperate this time. Louder, too.

Eyes shut, she sighed, shoulders sinking. "I'm sorry. I have to—"

"I know."

She cupped my cheeks and kissed me. It tasted of salt and regret. Then she was gone.

Stiffly, I dragged myself to my feet. The world seemed off, like the ground had tilted by just a few degrees. But Kat had given me the strength to find my balance on the uneven ground.

Rose and Faolán accompanied me back to the palace, her at my side, him terrifying people out of our way so we could pass through quickly. It was all I could do to put one foot in front of the other until we finally reached my rooms. It seemed like a voyage and yet no time at all. Time had lost its meaning.

Everything had.

32

KAT

I hurried through the streets and alleyways of Luminis, breaking a little more with each step. I didn't follow Amandine's voice calling my name. If she found me anywhere near Bastian, she would know I'd been with him and report it to Cyrus. All my work would be undone.

Instead, I rushed back to the palace. I could get to my rooms and make it seem like I'd been innocently separated from her in the crowd and came straight back here to safety and definitely didn't sneak off to Bastian after...

After...

A sob choked me, and I had to cover my mouth to hold it in. If I let it take me, there would be no stopping.

It wasn't real. It didn't happen. That was a changeling.

It would all be revealed eventually, and we'd laugh about this with Kaliban.

Deep down, I knew none of that was true. But I could pretend until I was back in my suite.

The image of Cyrus with his sword held high dogged every step. Had he changed his mind about helping Kaliban now he thought we'd fucked? Or had he always intended this?

And Braea. She could have freed him, if she wanted to.

I gritted my teeth as I turned onto the corridor leading to my suite. But it gave no relief to the sob knotting in my throat. I just needed to hold it down a little longer. My eyes burned as I stared at the double doors I'd be able to close behind myself and hide from the world.

A little longer. Nearly—

A hand clamped around my arm. I stumbled, gasped, choked on the tears I was trying to hold down, and found myself face-to-face with Uncle Rufus.

No. Just *no.*

I yanked from his grasp. "Not today, Uncle Rufus."

He scoffed, red face looming over me. "I've tried a dozen other days, but you're always so damn elusive. I've wasted my entire morning here waiting for you. So, yes, Katherine, *today.*"

Inwardly, I groaned as I rubbed my face and took in the dimly lit place he'd dragged me into. A bathroom. Cramped. Enclosed. Normally he cornered me in a larger space like a corridor. I'd never been in a small space like this with him. But now he stood with his back against the door, glowering at me.

My skin crawled, part old fear, part something that burned.

I forced a smile to my lips. "Forgive me. I've been rather busy with His Majesty. You know he likes to keep me close." Let him remember that, as far as he was concerned, I had the protection of a king. "But how can I help you?"

He smiled slowly like I'd stepped into a trap. A shiver fled down my spine. "Originally, I wanted to discuss this deal with your husband. I have paperwork ready for you to sign over the estate. But you..."

He gave a satisfied sigh and that was more frightening than anything he could've said. I fought to keep my breaths even, but my heart raced, priming my muscles to run. Except, he blocked the door.

"You found your way to a king's bed and showed me the way to a much, *much* better prize."

What could he want more than the estate? My mind circled, but I found no answers. "I—I don't understand."

In the half light, his teeth gleamed as he gave a too-wide smile. "Why settle for an estate when I can have *a kingdom*?"

I blinked again.

"Poor, silly little girl." He shook his head and clicked his tongue. "Still doesn't understand. Let me explain it simply for your little mind. I've done some digging, and His Majesty has no illegitimate children hidden in the city. That means no heirs. And if a fae breeds with a human, they're more likely to produce children. That's where you come in. Give him a child and he'll marry you. You'll birth the heir to Elfhame. I'll be great uncle to a future king."

For a horrible, wild moment, I almost laughed.

The worst idea. Uncle Rufus didn't like laughter at the best of times, but when it was at him? Even worse.

I scrubbed a hand over my mouth. "I see. But I fear I may be the wrong woman for this task. You pointed out yourself that I'd failed to give Robin an heir." It was a reasonable response that didn't require me to tell him no. Not when mother nature had already made the decision for us. Thank her and all the gods.

"Ah, that's where this comes in." He fished a bottle out of his pocket. Smoked glass hid the contents as he tilted it in front of my face like a prize. "A fertility potion."

Right. Of course he'd managed to get his hands on something like that.

"What an excellent idea. Fingers crossed it works." Not that I was going to drink the stuff. I went to take it from him, but he snatched it away.

"No. You have to drink it now."

My stomach dropped. Much as I didn't think I could get pregnant, it *might* be possible. I hadn't tried particularly hard with Robin.

I'd been unable to get hold of the preventative since arriving in Dawn. Although Bastian took the fae tincture that prevented him siring children, Cyrus had referenced having a child during his speech on the royal balcony. He wasn't taking any tincture.

"I don't want—"

The side of my face exploded as my head snapped to one side. The world spun. Rufus hit a lot harder than Robin.

"How many times do I have to tell you?" His face contorted, more animal than human, as he shoved into my space. "You always seem to need just one more reminder."

I rubbed my cheek, soaking up the pain that throbbed with my pulse, trying to keep the world still for a second.

"I thought you understood," he went on. "I *thought* you knew what was good for you. But it seems living here has planted foolish ideas in your head. Maybe once the king's put a baby in you, it'll push those out."

"No," I managed to mumble past my pain. "Please. I don't—"

He pinched my nose and flipped the lid off the bottle. "Take your medicine and we'll make a real woman of you."

I clamped my mouth shut before he could tip the contents

in. But it was only a matter of time before I needed to breathe. Seconds and he'd be able to make me drink it down.

I tried to push him away, but he was as immoveable as bedrock.

This was it. Like my breath, the vial of knock-out drops would only last so long. Eventually I would have to take the potion. Eventually I would have to fuck Cyrus. And then…

No. I couldn't let my mind go there. Better to go away. Even though I knew the right herbs to take, the thought of having that unwanted part of him growing inside me for even a moment was something I could not live with.

I gave in and screwed my eyes shut.

But behind my eyelids was burned the image of Kaliban, kneeling before Cyrus.

The fire started there. It spread to the back of my eyes, making tears spill down my cheeks.

But they weren't sad tears.

They were salted with my rage.

I was sick of living in an unjust world. Kaliban shouldn't have died. Lara. The people killed by the Horrors and by Cyrus's false Hydra Ascendant. Dia. Fantôme.

It was an abomination that they were all dead and this man was alive. *This man*. It was some sick joke that Kaliban had been killed today and yet he—*he* got to walk through the palace and lurk in corridors waiting to grab me.

The world was unjust. And maybe in the past I hadn't been able to do much about it, but right now? Unlike when he'd cornered me in Riverton Palace, I could still move.

Striking up and out, I twisted out of his grip. Air burned in my starved lungs as I dragged it in. I darted next to the sink. If I could tempt him away from the door, I could—

I flew backwards, shoes scraping across the floor. Something smashed. Agony burst at the back of my head. The room grew even darker for a second. He squeezed my throat.

It was instinct to go away. To close my eyes or close my mind and pretend I wasn't here, that this wasn't real, that what happened to me didn't matter.

Branches snake overhead, stars blooming between them.

But I didn't want to go back there. I thrashed in his grip, grabbed his arm, dug my nails in.

I sucked in what little breath I could. The taste of his sickly aftershave, too strong.

Mud creeps between my toes, cold and damp.

I didn't want to be a slave to that memory. "I refuse," I choked out.

"You think I need your consent?" He bared his teeth, pushing my chin up, lifting the potion bottle once more.

Leaf mulch and old death clog up my nostrils.

I clung to the wall, a drowning woman gripping the side of a boat, heedless of where it was going, desperate to just keep her head above water. Desperate to stay in her body and fight.

I needed to climb aboard and take charge. If not for me, for Dia... for Fantôme.

My head exploded again as he smacked me into the wall. "Are you listening to me, Katherine? You will take this potion and you will *finally* give this family a child."

Warm liquid tricked down the back of my neck, and I held that sensation close. I even cradled the pain.

I was here. I was now. I could act.

I reached for the lump on the back of my head. The sticky blood was another anchor against the way his hand around my throat tried to tug me away.

I had been here before. I had gone away before. I had fawned and fled and let him win.

It would be easy to slip away. Pretend. Escape. It was a well worn path I could tread with my eyes shut.

But I'd had enough of easy.

I pulled the lock picks from my hair.

33

KAT

I could survive while he was still alive in the world, yes. But I couldn't truly live. Not with him dogging my steps. And I was done with only surviving.

As it grew harder to breathe, the image of Kaliban grew stronger, overlaid on the contorted features of my uncle. It was an outrage that burned under my skin that Kaliban should die and Rufus should live. Who had decided such a thing? How was it allowed to happen?

I'd had enough of other people making the decisions.

I reached down and slid my tools into the tiny keyhole of the bracelet.

"Looking for a weapon?" Rufus sneered, squeezing tighter. "Good luck. I know you're not armed. The king told me."

I could barely breathe now, only gasping in thin snatches, and I dug the picks into my fingertips, reminding myself of what was real. But I returned a smile of my own. "Not with steel, no."

The creases between his eyebrows scored deeper. His sneer faltered. "What do you mean?"

"You buried me. But do you know what seeds do when they're buried?" I wheezed out. "They grow."

He frowned and shrank back as though my strength frightened him.

Just you wait, dear uncle.

"I was in the dark for a long time. I almost rotted there. But not anymore."

The clink of the bracelet landing on the tiled floor was the most beautiful sound I'd ever heard.

And the feeling—gods, the feeling of power buzzing through me was intoxicating. I almost swooned as it instantly peaked to match my fury.

His eyes went so wide, I could see the whites all the way around. He tried to release my throat, but I grabbed his wrist and held him there.

My bottled up poison came to the surface, strong enough to kill, but not so strong that it would be quick. He didn't deserve quick.

His breaths sped, flicking his lips with spittle. Again, he tried to pull away, but darkness crept up the veins of his arm, carrying weakness with it.

I clicked my tongue. "Now, now, Uncle Rufus. You always insisted on touching me, even though I never wanted it. But let me *help* you. Let it be the last thing you ever do."

"No. You can't..." He shook his head, desperation and terror making his face slack. "You *can't*..."

I just smiled. And for once, it wasn't forced.

Clutching his stomach, he grunted in pain and whispered, "Please."

I was beyond mercy.

When he sucked in one last breath and fell, I wasn't horrified. I wasn't sad. Or guilty.

It felt right. If the sword Justice had been here, it would've lifted for me. I had merely chosen a *woman's weapon* instead.

I stood over his body a long while, drinking in the relief that he had no power to change things in the world anymore. I would never walk down a corridor and find him lurking. He would never grab me and try to make me do his bidding ever again.

But...

I did have a body to explain away. He was too large for me to hide.

Running wouldn't help. He'd clearly been poisoned by touch—the dark stain began at his hand—and we were mere feet from my rooms.

I spun in place, searching for anything that might help. Blood smeared a cracked mirror where he'd smacked my head into it. A glass vase lay smashed on the floor. Obvious signs of a struggle. I peered into the mirror's shattered surface, lifting my chin. My hair was a mess and his finger marks were still around my neck.

The victim. Self-defence. It wasn't a lie.

I gasped in again and again, working up my breathing until it was panicked and tight, then I staggered into the corridor. "Help! Help me!"

A pair of guards came running, taking in my appearance before exchanging frowns.

"He wanted me to..." I shook my head like it was too much to speak and pointed towards the bathroom.

One poked her head in. "Good gods." When she turned around, she'd gone ashen. "Looks like he attacked her."

They eased me into a chair and withdrew to have a hushed conversation. I was too relieved at getting away with killing Rufus to manoeuvre into overhearing.

I'd done it. I was free. He would never bother me again. I covered my face, hiding how close I was to laughing.

More guards appeared, securing the corridor. They all took turns peering into the bathroom.

"Where is she?" Cyrus swept around the corner a moment after his demanding voice. "Is she—Katherine!" He picked me up by my arms and took me in from head to toe. "What the hells happened here?"

"My uncle, he wanted me to poison... *someone* for him, so he picked the lock on my bracelet." I shook my head and gulped. "But when I refused, he attacked me. And—and I panicked, so my poison came, and... Please, Cyrus, I need that bracelet back on. *Please*." I hid my face in my hands like I was ashamed.

If I could make him believe it had been removed against my will...

Please, gods. I know I've said a lot of shit about you, but please.

"Who did he ask you to kill?"

Not too obvious. Remember you're afraid.

I lifted my head and gave him a wide-eyed look that said "*you*." Sniffling, I threw myself against his chest. "I don't know what I would've done if he'd managed to hurt you."

He stiffened. "You killed him... for me?"

Seemed my silence was enough of an answer for him, because his arms slowly came around me. "There, there." He patted my back awkwardly, then extricated himself from my hold. "I just need to see..." He smiled with an odd glint in his eyes.

"Your Majesty, are you sure you want to—?"

He waved the guard out of the way and, one arm around my shoulders, entered the bathroom.

He stared down at Rufus's body, at his outstretched hand, black with poison.

"You *touched* him." He clenched and unclenched his hand, attention falling to my fingers.

I could still feel Rufus's grip on my throat. He'd deserved every moment of that slow death. He'd deserved so much more.

Dia's bones against dark earth. Fantôme's soft fur. The girl I'd once been. He'd taken them all.

"He touched me," I bit out. "And that was his last mistake."

Slowly, Cyrus looked up, his face couldn't have been more transformed. Pale, pinched. It was like something pulled down on him, sucking out the colour and the cruel pleasure.

He was afraid. Of *me*.

That sense of power suffused me, but below it ran dread, cold and deep. He wasn't meant to fear me. He was only meant to see something weak and frail. No threat here.

I shook my head as though I was as shocked as him. "I don't even remember what I did. I—I panicked, and my magic just appeared. I didn't mean to kill him, I just... I was so afraid."

He made a thoughtful little sound and pulled his arm from around my shoulders. With a handkerchief protecting his fingers, he scooped up the iron bracelet and examined it for a long while before holding it out.

Obedient, I offered my wrist. I didn't dare to search for the lock picks. I'd dropped them in the struggle, and in the narrative I'd spun, they had belonged to Rufus. If I asked for them, it would blow my story apart.

Cyrus was careful not to touch me as he snapped the

bracelet in place. Only once it was locked did he give the faintest smile.

He insisted on escorting me to my suite, but there was no hand on the small of my back guiding me along.

All the while he fiddled with the tiny key that was meant to be the only way to unlock the bracelet that held my power in check.

34

BASTIAN

Word reached me of Cyrus's latest order just before I was due to report to the queen. I sent my assistant Brynan instead. She would understand.

I charged through the palace corridors and out into the city beyond as it completed its transformation into Tenebris. The dark stone and gathering gloom reflected my mood. Though there should be more fire.

It wasn't enough for Cyrus to kill my athair—he had ordered his head displayed at the city gates.

Anger didn't factor in to it. I was past simple anger.

Fae scattered from my path as I stomped towards the walls.

Technically only Braea could countermand Cyrus's direct order, but I dared anyone to try and stop me on a technicality. My muscles sang, ready to rip apart anything and anyone who got in my way. Shadows swept along with me in a bow wave, harbinger of my arrival.

As I turned onto the road leading to the gates, I couldn't

even speak. My jaw had fused shut from being clenched so hard.

A crowd waited ahead, here to witness Cyrus's show. They'd better get out of my way. They'd better—

I stopped in my tracks.

Spikes had been erected above the gates. The murderer's head was up there alongside the rapist's. Blood coated another spike, but otherwise it was empty.

Someone glanced over their shoulder, eyebrows rising when they spotted me. They whispered to their neighbour, and one by one, word spread of my arrival.

"Where is he?" I managed through gritted teeth. "*Where?*"

The crowd turned. Each person placed one hand over their heart as they had after the Winter Solstice attack. A traditional sign of respect. They weren't here to mock my *athair's* desecrated remains. Then what?

As I glowered, about to demand they tell me what they'd come for, the group parted, and through the centre came a guard wearing Dawn's pale grey. He carried a shroud-wrapped bundle.

"Ser," he said, bowing his head as he reached me. "We're taking the others down, too. We..." He swallowed. "It isn't right. And—"

His gaze skipped past me, and when I turned, I found a retinue of Queensguard arriving. They brought wooden caskets, one marked with my serpent.

They were head-sized, as was the bundle.

Throat tight, I turned to the guard, and he offered me my *athair's* head. There was movement up on the walls as Dawn guards worked to remove the rest of the grisly display.

It was past sunset. They were no longer ruled by their king. And they'd used that to...

267

I blinked at him and took the carefully wrapped load. It was the second time today I'd held my *athair*, felt his dead weight. It dragged on everything, making the world seem slow and distant, making my feet and thoughts sluggish.

"Her Majesty ordered these be sent," the head of the Queensguard, Cavall, announced gruffly.

Braea had seen to this personally. The intensity of my gratitude was staggering.

Cavall's face pinched as they gave me a solemn nod. "These will be buried with the rest of their remains, under the moon, so they may return to the earth with no further interference."

With numb hands, I lowered my precious load into the serpent-marked box.

Behind me, a woman's voice rose in a soft lament that called spirits on to the next place.

Cross into the darkness. Let it cradle you.

A deeper voice joined her in haunting harmony.

Cross into the night. Let it be a comfort.

The whole crowd sang now, filling the night streets.

Cross into eternity where we will meet again.

I clutched the casket to my chest, unable to trust my voice to join theirs. If I sang or spoke, I would break, and that wasn't a luxury the Serpent of Tenebris had—not in public.

I'd come here indignant, ready to rage against anyone who got in my way. I hadn't expected this.

I made it through hearing the first two verses before I lurched forward and gave the casket to Cavall. With a brisk nod, I left.

There were no plans. No direction or destination. There was only one foot in front of the other over and over. The streets I'd walked my entire life.

The Hall of Healing transformed into black marble now it

stood in Tenebris. Narrow alleys with endless steps leading towards the palace. Squares with fountains and wells and little cafés with tables under the stars.

Those tables would normally be full, but tonight I only saw one woman hurrying away, head ducked, a drink in her hand. No families gathered by the fountain sharing the day's news as a child splashed in the water. The well's bucket hung empty.

It was as though the city had died today and I walked through its lifeless remains.

The spires were ribs spearing the night. The streets were veins and arteries, now empty of its lifeblood. The palace's great dome sat above all else—its skull.

I wasn't sure it had a heart. Or was it just that I'd lost mine?

Eventually, I found myself at his door.

I pressed my hand to it and waited a long while, letting the night air nip at my fingers and nose.

Standing here, I could pretend he was just inside. Hating me or not—I'd take either.

If I knocked, he'd tell me to piss off... or open the door and take me in his arms. I didn't care. I just needed him to be the other side of this door.

I stood there until my lip trembled and I could hold it in no longer. The house let me in, no key needed, and soft golden lights sprang up, blurring through my tears.

His teapot sat on the side. The same deep blue one he'd always used, despite its chipped lid. A cup waited next to it, as though he'd come back any moment.

Two pairs of slippers and two arm chairs. Like he'd always expected Sylen to join him by the fire.

The only sign anything was wrong was the bloodstain on the rug. Katherine's, from her nosebleed. Evidence of who I was had been there the whole time.

I had so many questions and no one else could give me answers. But more than that, there were things I needed to tell him. That I still loved him. That I'd stayed away to respect his need to distance, to give him space to hate me. I wanted to talk to him about Kat. He knew and loved her. He would understand why I'd chosen her, and he would smile when I let myself babble on about all the little things I adored about her.

There was so much we'd missed.

With a wordless sound, I sank into the less worn of the two armchairs. "I'm sorry. I'm so sorry."

The stags my father Sylen had carved stood over me, sentinels on the bookshelves, as I buried my face in my hands and lost myself in still and silent grief.

There was no time until I sensed a presence and finally looked up. Faolán stood in the doorway, blocking the night outside. "You all right?"

I nodded. I even smiled. "I'm fine." But my voice cracked, and the next thing I knew, I was sobbing in his arms.

"I've got you." His voice rumbled through me. "I've always got you."

35

KAT

Being away from Bastian had been hard before, but now I knew he was in such pain, it was a physical presence —a fist lodged in my chest.

But I had to accompany Cyrus to yet more stupid festivities. These were in the palace grounds again, since Dawn hesitated to invite Dusk to their side of the palace after what had happened at the wedding. The fools didn't understand the enemy lay within.

Even worse, Cyrus had insisted events start at ten o'clock in the morning so he could have a full day before Sleep claimed him.

The only thing keeping me going was that I'd arranged through my drop point to meet Bastian in the hothouse while everyone was distracted. But as I circulated with a drink, I noted Amandine mere paces behind.

She'd never stuck to me this closely, certainly not since I'd been given a longer rein, but after Uncle Rufus's *tragic* passing,

I'd heard the head of Cyrus's personal guard giving her a brutal reprimand.

Even worse, Cyrus looked at me differently now. From the other side of the fountain, he met my gaze, smiled, raised his glass with a nod, but a wariness lingered in his eyes as they darted down to the iron bracelet.

It was one thing to hear I had magic that could kill with a touch; it was another to see its aftermath.

I would have to keep myself especially small and weak for the foreseeable future—anything to overpaint the image of my dead uncle and his agonised expression.

As I continued around the gardens, I noted the gathering's different tone compared to the last time I'd been here. People seemed quieter, more sober, even though the drink had been flowing for a few hours already. Even the fae guests, who always looked so perfect, had dark shadows beneath their eyes. The atmosphere felt thinner, somehow, like it was ready to snap.

It set me on edge, so when I spotted Rose and Ari, heads bent together, away from the crowds, I aimed straight for them.

As I slipped in beside them, Amandine appeared and gave me a pointed look.

I returned it. "This is nothing to do with Dusk or Dawn. They are my friends—my *human* friends."

Her mouth skewed to one side and she glanced back towards the fountain, but the king was out of sight now. With a sigh, she took a single step back.

Ari smiled at me, expression tight as her gaze skipped to the guard. "It's good to see you, Kat."

Rose, on the other hand, seemed unbothered by Amandine's presence and wrapped me in a hug. "It's been too long."

The feel of her choked me, where normally it would be so —well, *normal.* "You're telling me."

As though reassured by Rose's actions, Ari gave me a quick hug too. "Are you all right? I heard your uncle..."

I shrugged. "Tragic accident."

"Good riddance," she replied with surprising viciousness.

Rose grunted in agreement.

Out of nowhere a streak of white and crimson appeared. "Fluffy," I laughed, almost falling over as the hellhound ran around my feet in greeting.

A full minute later, once she'd finished, I scratched her behind her flaming ears, and she eventually settled at my side, leaning into my leg.

Ari cocked her head at us. "Even though she hasn't seen you in ages, she's still all over you. It's so strange."

"She's the same with Bastian. I probably smell of him."

Rose laughed. "You two are lucky. She steers clear of me and Faolán. It must be the wolfy smell."

We talked about the shop and a show they'd gone to a few weeks ago—safe topics that didn't touch on the politics of the courts, but which filled the well that had emptied over my time in Dawn.

Past them, I caught Amandine craning in. She cocked her head, not quite her usual watchful look, but more... curious?

Another huddle of tired guests passed in silence, one rubbing his head.

I frowned as I sipped my drink. "You two have been around fae longer than I have. Can they get hangovers?"

Rose snorted and tilted her glass so it caught the light. "When they're celebrating this many days in a row, *yes.*"

That explained the low energy.

"Not to mention the executions," Ari muttered with a scowl.

Amandine's attention shot to me, and I opened my mouth to steer the topic away, when I spotted Bastian on the other side of a group.

That fist that had been lodged in my chest since yesterday's executions dropped to the ground.

If the other fae looked pale, he looked positively ill. Purple circles ghosted under his eyes. His usually rich brown skin seemed dull like all the colour had been desaturated from it.

I ached to go to him, to hold him, to grieve with him. Kaliban's absence hit me all over again. The fact it was permanent stole my breath.

And much as I knew he needed me now, I needed him too. Although I'd survived Uncle Rufus, there was still the echo of his hold around my throat. I needed the erasing solace of Bastian's touch.

Ari and Rose had continued talking. They must've picked up on Amandine's reaction because they'd changed topic and were discussing Ari's work and a recent order of spidersilk fabric she'd recently received.

I tried to engage. Being with them was a comfort—truly. But my attention kept skipping over Ari's shoulder to Bastian.

Ella was on his arm, and we made eye contact. Her eyebrows flashed up in a silent question, asking if I was all right.

I inclined my head, disguising the motion with another sip of my drink.

Still holding my gaze, Ella tiptoed to Bastian's ear and whispered something. He laughed, though no amusement reached his eyes and its insincerity hurt my heart. But it made him turn to Ella and he used that excuse to look past her to me.

Over my glass, we held eye contact. A hundred things unsaid passed between us in the smallest expressions. He was not all right. Grief weighed on him and concern wore lines where there had been none a few months ago. He must've heard about my uncle's death by now, and he would have questions. He cocked his head ever so slightly, the only sign he could give of them.

Then someone passed between us, and the moment was broken. Once they'd gone, he was looking away. Sensible.

I tore myself away, just in time for Cyrus to join us. "There she is, my pretty little thing. And with yet more humans. I swear you're trying to take over Elfhame." Despite his winning smile, there was an edge to his tone. "You'll excuse us."

With that, he held out his arm and ushered me into a room in Dawn's side of the palace overlooking the gardens. Floral decorations adorned with fae lights cascaded from the ceiling and corners, giving the illusion that we were still outdoors. The sombre mood was amplified in here. With so few people, every little sound echoed off the walls.

I still had time before I was due to meet Bastian. Gods willing, Cyrus would lose interest in me and I'd be able to slip away outside.

"The Wild Hunt will be abroad tonight," he said as though it was an explanation for why he'd brought me indoors.

They were undeniably dangerous—the reason every inhabitant of Albion, Elfhame, and Cestyll Caradoc made sure to be indoors before sunset on the new moon. If they caught sight of you, they would hunt you to the ends of the earth until they had your soul. The stories differed on what exactly they would do with it, but on one thing they all agreed—it was a fate worse than death.

However, the sun wouldn't set for hours—otherwise,

275

Cyrus would be readying himself for Sleep. The Wild Hunt were nothing more than an excuse.

I hid my sinking feeling behind a deferential sound as I realised he just wanted me away from my friends.

"How are you faring?" He pinched my chin and raised it, peering at my throat.

I noted he only risked that skin-to-skin contact *after* checking the iron bracelet was in place.

Finger-shaped bruises lingered on my neck. I had chosen not to hide them with make-up to remind him that I'd been the victim acting out of self-defence.

Yet, he hadn't summoned me to his suite since.

"Still a little shaken. I wake up from nightmares thinking he's found me again." Not a lie.

Cyrus made a thoughtful sound. "And have you forgiven me for the traitor's execution?"

I stilled, chin still raised though it was no longer in his grip. Lies coated my tongue, ready to appease him, but I couldn't voice a single one.

"Do you at least understand *why* I couldn't let him live?"

I swallowed down the unspoken lies and chose truth instead. "I can't say I do."

"Perhaps that's the difference between humans and fae." But he gave me an odd smile—more a twist of the mouth.

As he steered me towards some seating near the floor to ceiling windows, a number of his inner circle gravitated around us. He took the chaise longue, making me perch at the end with his feet in my lap. Talk soon turned to the finale of his month of celebrations—tomorrow's masquerade ball. Thank the gods it was almost over.

"But why does it have to be a masquerade?" one asked with a sigh.

"Because, all the most *interesting* things happen at masquerades," he said with a smirk, throwing me a sidelong look that made my stomach dip.

He couldn't know that was when we'd planned to meet with Krae. I had to fight to keep from fidgeting as the conversation went on, but that look had me on edge. He had something else planned, no doubt something to aggrandise himself even further. The unveiling of a gold statue, perhaps.

A while later, he left me, searching for something interesting to smoke with a group of friends. The rest of them drifted away once he'd gone, leaving me alone.

Checking the time, I realised I could still make my meeting with Bastian only a little late. I plotted an indirect route outside, as though I was merely wandering and the doors happened to be right there.

Just as my grip closed on the handle, Cyrus's voice came from right behind me. "And where would you be going in such a rush?"

"A rush?" I chuckled. "I just wanted some fresh air, that's all."

Like clockwork, Sepher and Zita appeared with an invitation to play cards. "Or are you afraid I'll beat you?" Sepher asked with challenge in his eyes.

Of course, Cyrus took the bait, and as they sauntered away, Zita winked over her shoulder at me.

Allies. I mouthed a "thank you" before she turned away.

But when I turned for the door, Amandine blocked my way. "His Majesty's orders." For once, she looked apologetic about it, sucking in her lips, but I could've screamed with frustration.

I tried again later, but I couldn't escape. Instead I had to stay inside and watch the minutes tick by as I missed my rendezvous with Bastian. After that, the hours dragged on.

Outside, I could see Dusk fae mingle with Dawn. My friends were right there. Bastian had reappeared, realising I wasn't going to show. They were all so close, just the other side of the glass.

By that time, Cyrus had disappeared and I was past keeping up appearances, so I left even though it was long before sunset.

Amandine shadowed as I stomped through the corridors, nursing my frustration. A trio of guards joined us and took up station either side of the entrance to my suite. Four guards. Twice as many as before.

"I must be important to require *so much* security." I scoffed as I opened the door. "Next you'll be in my bloody bed."

Their laughter followed me into the darkened suite, and I slammed the door on it.

As the movement from that settled, I still sensed something in the windowless antechamber. Not quite movement. Not quite a foot shuffling—no, fae were too silent for that. But a presence that was not my own.

I turned, ready to flee, and a shadow loomed over me.

36

KAT

But shadows weren't something I feared anymore. They fell away, and I surged into them.

"Bas—"

He clamped a hand over my mouth and an arm around my waist and carried me into the sitting room. "Not so near the door," he whispered before lowering his hand.

Fae hearing. The guards.

In silence, I led him to my bedroom. There were no locks on the door, but we'd hear if anyone entered the suite, and that would give Bastian a chance to hide.

Once we were there, I held him, relieved, grateful, aching to finally have the chance when I thought I'd missed it. "How did you get in here? Why risk it?"

"I heard about your uncle, so I needed to speak to you. Then you missed our meeting, and..." He made a low, growly sound that reverberated into my chest. "There were no guards, so I could just walk in and wait."

It was his double outside, keeping up appearances. No one

would suspect he was with me when he could be clearly seen playing the gracious guest.

"And what about getting out?"

He raised one shoulder and one side of his mouth. "That's future Bastian's problem. Right now I just want to make sure you're all right. Your uncle, he didn't hurt you, did he?"

I ducked my chin, not wanting him to see the marks. Much as I'd played the part for Cyrus and the rest of Dawn, I didn't want to be a victim, not with Bastian. Instead I gave him a vicious smile that was all me, no act. "Not as much as I hurt him."

"That's my Kat."

It felt good to hear him say that, like it scrubbed away a little of the lie I was living. It gave me the reassurance to slip from his hold and go to the dressing table. He followed as if drawn in my wake.

He watched me pull pins from my hair. "We're together now. You can tell me what happened."

I cringed away from that idea. "What if I don't want to?"

He came up behind me, gathering the thick fall of my hair and pushing it over my shoulder. "I thought you'd want to." I turned in the tight space between him and the dressing table as he went on. "Process your feelings. Spill the truth. Explain what happened and wh—"

It was my turn to clamp my hand over his mouth. "If it's all right with you, I'd prefer we go with you shutting up and fucking me." I lowered my hand and fisted it in his black shirt, enjoying the way the little serpent buttons bit into my palms. "I've had too many people's hands on my body without my choice, and now I need what *I* choose."

He furrowed his brow, mouth opening like he wasn't sure what to say, whether I really wanted this.

"I need you to help me erase all that. If... if you can. If you want to, that is. I know you've just had—"

This time he silenced me. His kiss said he could. It said he needed to erase some things, too. While he occupied my mouth with a kiss that needed, that consumed, that sent shivers racing across my body, I started on unfastening those little buttons.

He caught my fingers and pulled away an inch, and I felt like the most inconsiderate person in the world, because the shadows under his eyes were even worse close-up—practically bruises. And I'd thought only of myself.

My heart cracked as I cupped his cheek and smoothed my thumb over the dark marks. "And you? How are you—really?"

"How am I? *How am I?*" He blasted out a bitter laugh. "I'm this close to losing my damn mind." He held up his hand. Several small puncture wounds pitted his palm, some healed, some fresh.

He'd done this to master himself. I'd cut half moon nail marks into my palms enough times to understand the cost of self-control.

"I know we have a plan..." His voice was rough, not the smooth spymaster, but someone who fought for each word. "But every time I'm near him, I want to..." His hand fisted, knuckles turning white. "I want to rip him apart. I want to wring his neck. Pound him into the floor. I want to let my shadows crush him until he's nothing but pulp. I've imagined so many ways I can destroy him, Katherine. *So many.*"

I'd never seen him so raw, so on the edge, so... desperate.

It was almost frightening... would be terrifying, if it was turned on me. But I was inside the space of his arms—I was *with* him—and his rage was turned outward. Maybe I was sick, but it made me feel safe.

Yet it took a toll on him to hold it all inside. To keep control. To not act on those fantasies.

Perhaps there was a way I could help him as he'd once helped me.

"Then let me take care of you."

He blinked like he didn't understand.

"You've taken control enough times to allow me to let go. Let me do the same for you."

"You don't need to do that for me. I can't ask—"

"It's for me too. I—I need…" I didn't know how to say it, exactly, but I needed control of something.

Although I'd killed my uncle, which unlike stabbing Robin in a terrified thrashing moment had been a deliberate choice, it was still a choice that had been forced upon me.

There would be no forcing here. I would have a moment of control where every decision was mine taken as and when I wished.

If Bastian would let me.

My chest heaved, the need strong and the fear it would be denied stronger.

He searched my gaze for a long moment, then lowered his hands. "I am yours to command."

Five words had never stolen my breath quite like that.

I placed his hands on my cheeks first, soaking up his warmth, the familiar presence. I kissed each of those cuts on his palm, silently saying I understood.

He watched me, a kind of stillness radiating from him that I'd never seen before. Only his chest moved, steady, deep.

Finally, it crossed my mind that this might scare him. Control was a matter of safety for him. If he was in charge, nothing bad could happen. At least that was what he told himself.

What I was asking of him... and the fact he'd accepted. The responsibility was overwhelming.

I held his face, making him meet my gaze in case he had used that careful breathing to go away and find false safety. "Bastian? Any time you want me to stop, you say. Any time you want this to change—to go back to normal, tell me. I'll do whatever you need. I'm only in charge for as long as you agree to it. Do you understand?"

He slid his hands to my wrists, pressing my palms into his cheeks. "I do. And in case you doubted—I consent to this. Freely. Willingly. Wholeheartedly. I trust you, Katherine."

His words filled me, not with the drunken power I had felt over Cyrus, but something sweeter, something saner. Something that sustained rather than paring me back to sharp edges.

I finished unbuttoning his shirt and slid it over his shoulders, then moved on to his trousers, enjoying the view as I went. His smooth skin, the hard planes of his chest, the shadows that carved out every muscle. They were more defined than before I'd gone to Dawn—I realised now, it was the hours spent training with Faolán. "You have a beautiful body, you know that?"

His eyes widened and a warm flush crept over his face, bringing back some colour where earlier he'd been so ashen.

Hmm, so he enjoyed praise too. I smirked to myself as I hooked his trousers over his hips and let them fall to the floor. I wasn't sure there had ever been a time where he was naked and I was fully clothed. "But you haven't let me explore it properly before, have you?"

He frowned, actually looking contrite. "No, love. I haven't."

I couldn't help giving him a quick kiss, not when he looked like that. "I forgive you. And I intend to make up for it now."

Taking my time, I caressed his shoulders, letting my thumbs follow the line of his collarbone. I held his biceps, amused by how my hand didn't even reach halfway around. I noted the prominent veins so unlike my own and how the slight movements of his fingers rippled along his forearms. Gods, it was fascinating.

His chest was next. I'd buried my face in it so many times, taken shelter and solace there, but I'd never had time to simply appreciate it. The way my fingers looked splayed over it, ever so slightly indenting his skin when I pressed. The way it spread when he pulled his shoulders back and stood tall. The way I could hear the solid *ba-dum* of his heart when I pressed my ear to it.

I stayed there, listening to his rhythm, the reassurance that he was alive and here, when so many things had worked against that. Including the scar that cut through his torso, pale against his rich toned skin. I traced it, thanking everything in the universe that it had not taken him.

Then there was that nipple piercing. Unlike the first time I'd seen him without a shirt back in my rooms in Lunden, I could indulge my curiosity.

I smoothed the pad of my thumb over it, first, glancing up in time to catch him lift his chin. He watched me, eyelids heavy, pupils wide. Holding his gaze, I tiptoed and ran my tongue over his nipple, enjoying the feel of it stiffening. When I closed my mouth around it and flicked my tongue, he sucked in a harsh breath, pressing into my touch.

As I pulled away, I grinned and nipped him before circling to his back.

Good gods, it was a work of art. The Celestial Serpent enhanced his muscles, adding to their shadows. I ran my hand down the cleft over his spine and placed my thumbs in the dimples above his backside.

His back was a shield. When he held me, this was what took the brunt of whatever the world threw at us. He gave me space in his arms so I could find respite.

It made my heart at once full and sore.

Where was his respite?

I was smaller than him, of course, but I slipped my arms around his waist and squeezed. "I'm not a very good shield," I whispered, "but I'm strong. I can share your burdens."

"Where did that come from?" He quickly covered my hands, reassuring.

"I was thinking about how much you protect others. How many times you've shielded me so I can have a moment. But you need that kind of care, too."

In silence, he pulled my arms tighter.

After a long while, I planted a kiss between his shoulder blades (I had to tiptoe, of course), and took a step back.

His backside. That, I simply appreciated.

"Are you just staring at my arse?"

"Staring is such a blunt word for it, but... yes. Yes, I am. It's perfect, really. *And...*" I grabbed it, loving how it filled my hand before I skimmed down to his legs. "You talk about my thighs, Bastian, but yours are..." There were no words to end that sentence; I could only make an appreciative sound.

He chuckled as I moved around to his front, his angry tension gone.

One hand on his chest, I backed him to the bed. Such a novelty to be the one manoeuvring him around. And the fact he obeyed? It was everything I needed.

He sat there, half hard, waiting for me, but I paused, touching his thigh, and raised my eyebrows in question. Was he sure? Caressing his body was one thing, but letting me take charge of actual sex was a step further.

"I *want* you to touch me, Kat. Burn me, my beloved flame."

His submission warmed me, filled me. He chose me, chose this... chose *us*.

So I bent and licked his length, base to tip, letting my tongue curl around his piercing. He shivered for me. I closed my mouth around him and sank down as far as I could, trying to ease my throat to take more, and his shiver became a shudder punctuated with a soft moan.

Mine. That sound was mine. That shudder. The throb of him on the roof of my mouth.

As I lifted, I caught my breath and rolled my tongue over his piercing and the blunt head.

"Fuck!" He jolted, hand plunging into my hair.

Never mind half hard, he strained to attention now, and I lapped up the salty bead I wrung from him.

I went on, swallowing him down as best I could, swirling my tongue, desperate now to taste more of him and know I was the one who'd caused it.

"Please, love," he huffed out, raw and ragged. "I need to—"

When I squeezed his balls, he bucked into me with a cry, cutting off my breath. His thighs grew tight, and when I shoved him back, to lie down and enjoy my attention, he obeyed. I let him thrust into my mouth harder, faster, until my eyes watered, because I could feel the way it built in him—the trembling loss of control. The thing he needed.

I triumphed when he bellowed and spilled across my tongue, sweet and salty and thick. I swallowed him down and licked up the last drops as his length twitched and pulsed. And when I sat up, I grinned.

He lay there, panting, eyes screwed shut. "That was..." He groaned, running a hand over his face.

"It was, wasn't it."

He peered at me out the corner of his eye. "I'm not sure I've ever seen you smug before."

I preened, very much enjoying it, though my body throbbed with its own need.

As he got his breath back, I slid my gown off my shoulders and let it drop to the floor. He sat up, gaze flowing over me, slow as honey. "Then again, I'm sure I'd be smug if I looked like that." I stepped into the space between his knees as he went on. "Still, I'm the one who gets to enjoy you. Be near you. Love you." Arms looping around my hips, he kissed my soft belly. "Do I get to worship you yet?"

I ran my fingers through his hair and along the edge of his ear. "Do you think you're ready?"

His groan reverberated through me, adding to that throbbing need. "If you keep doing that, I soon will be."

I climbed up on the bed, straddling him. In this position, the memory of Cyrus tugged on me, intrusive and unwanted. I screwed my eyes shut, shoving it away. "Bastian." His name was a reminder, a truth, the salve that would get rid of my wound. "I need you to..."

He held my hips, held me here and now, so I could open my eyes. He looked up at me, eyebrows pinched together in painful understanding. "Erase other places, other times... other people."

"Yes." The word ended on a hiss as he slid his middle finger between my legs. Back and forth, he glided, rubbing away one uninvited fingerprint after another, the times I'd been grabbed, the dark nights with Robin, being tugged onto Cyrus's lap.

My hips rolled, caught in his rhythm, as pleasure kindled in me, embers spreading. And they helped, too. They caught aflame and burned away each intrusion, until the violators were nothing but ash on the breeze of my heaving breaths.

"There she is," he whispered, every word fanning the flames as he dipped a finger in me.

I whimpered, trying to ride him more deeply, but he only let me have that moment and instead used the slickness to circle my apex. The smooth friction of it rubbed away the world until there was only him looking up at me as he kissed and sucked my breasts, and me, rocking over his hand, chasing, chasing, chasing.

Then I was exploding. The world ended in white-hot flame. It consumed my shuddering body, scorched my cries, took everything base and human and broken and transformed it into a creature of flame that soared.

When I sank back to earth, he caught me. Our kisses rewrote new stories over all we'd burned away. Under me, he was hard again, and I slid along his length, winning a deep groan that rumbled from him into my mouth. I felt it in my bones, my heart, my essence.

I pulled away just far enough to hold his gaze as I guided him to my entrance. I waited there for throbbing seconds, and he seemed to understand he was still mine to command, because he held still.

Slowly, slowly, I lowered myself, groaning at the familiar fullness, the sweetly aching stretch.

"Katherine," he breathed, hands fisting in the sheets. He had a way of making my name more than its syllables. A prayer to gods who actually listened. An incantation. A purpose and intent.

I rolled my hips, urging him to say it again. It was a hit I needed. A drug whose addiction I'd never even try to break.

He obliged, whispering against my lips again and again as he rose to meet me, driving deeper, until we were both shuddering and slick with sweat and sex, one body with one mind.

But I still had one touch I needed to wipe from my flesh.

Pulse thundering, I eased his back to the bed and took his hand. With a shaky breath, I placed it on my throat.

His fingers stiffened, not gripping. "Are you—?"

"My body is mine. I won't be defined by what someone else has done to it. Not anymore. This life is mine. *I* am mine."

Hesitation evaporating, he took hold of me.

As his fingers tightened, there were no memories. Nothing unwanted crowding in. Only us.

I took up my rhythm, riding him, a new beat drowning out what went before. Relief flooded me, mingling with my pleasure. This was my body. My choice.

Hands on his chest, I let it drown me, riding the surge of his hips rising to meet mine, the rough cries I wrung from him, the flex of his fingers that were capable of killing but that I trusted to hold rather than destroy.

I lost myself in our mingled pleasure as it peaked together, and only rediscovered myself as I collapsed on his chest. We caught our breath, wrapped in our own satiation. Eventually he lifted my chin, kissed me, and we found each other in that quiet time, slowly emerging to remember the rest of the world existed.

Outside, the sun had set, and when I got up to head to the bathroom, I peeked outside. The palace grounds were quiet and dark. The party had dissolved.

He welcomed me back to bed, pulling me under the covers, and we lay there talking. He spoke about Kaliban, his regrets, how convinced he'd been of his hatred. He asked how we'd met, and I told him the full story of our friendship.

We wiped tears from each others cheeks in the glittering dark.

I told him what had happened to Uncle Rufus. I didn't cry. My heart didn't crowd my chest, too loud or too fast. The monster was slain. I was safe.

I didn't need heroes—I'd saved myself. And now my perfect villain had helped me reclaim the last marks that evil had left.

We discussed the revelations about his family. The questions spilled from him, but I had no answers, not even hiding in the corners where Sura had planted the truth. "She's the only one left who might know more. We could find her—travel under a flag of truce. I'm sure she'll speak to you about a personal matter like this." I caught his cheek when he frowned and tried to look away. "She wanted you to know, eventually, that's why she told me."

The muscles under my hand went hard. "And I still owe her for that. You haven't had more headaches since then, have you?" His thumb traced over my brow, gentle, concerned.

"She can tell you more about your mother, you know. Something that isn't coloured by whatever Braea feels about what she did." Much as it pained him, Bastian had stood by his decision to kill Sylen. He carried that guilt but had thought it best for his country. Yet I wondered if Braea felt the same.

He made a noncommittal sound and fell quiet.

Softly, the orrery in the sitting room chimed midnight. I felt every strike. "So many nights I've lain here, thinking about the fact you were just the other side of something thinner than a piece of paper, wondering if I could tear through."

He pulled me closer, brow pressed to mine. "I've done the same. Sleeping on my side of the bed, wondering if you're here at that exact moment." He took my fingertips and kissed them.

"Every morning, I wake with my hand still in the space between us, and for a moment, I swear I can feel you."

I bit back a sob, eyes burning with tears. The cruel parts of the world were creeping back in.

"This is only temporary, love. I swear it." He held me and let me cry out my mixture of sorrow and frustration and impotent rage. "We will—oh *shit*."

I sat up at the same moment he did. "What is it?"

"Fuck. *Fuck*." His gaze had gone distant as he shook his head. "Outside. My double."

Stomach coiling in dread, I rolled to my feet and gathered his clothes. After so long, practicality came easily. "Nothing good, I'm guessing."

"It's Sura's daughter. She's in the gardens."

37

BASTIAN

I had drawn the short straw, staying outside at the party while my other half was with Kat, and then I'd lingered after to avoid any risk of us being seen together. I could escape inside if the Wild Hunt came. Besides, what were the chances of them coming to the palace twice so close together? Then, as the sun had set, an unnatural fog had rolled in—not something usually associated with the Wild Hunt.

I'd been half dozing, focusing on what my luckier self was doing with Kat when I heard someone barrelling through the gardens and crept out from my hiding place.

Eyes wide, she ran headlong into me. Something in the air made my skin itch, like angry wasps crawled over me.

I caught her by the shoulders as she stared up at me, gasping for breath. "You need to help. Please. *Please.*"

Her presence alone was enough to tell me Sura had to be nearby. People were drunk and tired. Dawn was unstable. The rift between the courts had never been bigger.

It was the perfect time for her to attack.

But on a new moon?

"Is your mother an idiot? Are *you* an idiot to follow her into this madness?" I gave her a little shake, unsure if I was more angry at her because I knew she was my cousin. *My cousin*, and she'd put herself at risk like this. "You know it's a new moon, right? You must know what happens if they find you."

And just like me as a teenager, she couldn't resist snapping back and rolling her eyes. "I don't need to worry about the Wild Hunt because I have *this*." From her pocket she pulled a smooth stone, etched with symbols no one in this world understood but that kept the Horrors at bay.

A wardstone.

I'd never heard of them working on the Wild Hunt too, and this one looked a little different from the ones surrounding Horror territory. Had Sura discovered a new use for old magic?

"But..." She looked back the way she'd come. "My mother... she told me to run. I hid. I thought I could help, but..."

Sometimes I hated being right. "Wait here." I urged her into my hiding place and slipped into the darkness.

KAT DRESSED and put together a hasty plan to leave her rooms and draw away her guards, so I could get outside and deal with whatever the fuck this was.

But Kat found the corridor empty. The guards must've figured she was safe in her suite for the night and clocked off early.

When I kissed her and went to leave, she shook her head. "This is *our* work now. I know Sura, too. You need me to help with this."

We didn't have time to argue, and the gods knew I could do with the help. So, we pulled up our cloaks and crept through the palace. I strained, listening for other fae.

"Shit," I breathed, grabbing Kat before she rounded a corner. "Guards. And that's the quickest route." Any other would take us out of the way, slowing us down.

She nodded, mouth flat, and took my hand.

"This is the wrong way," I whispered once we were away from the fae I'd heard.

"Trust me." She strode ahead, confident, and I had no choice but to follow.

A few minutes later, we reached a dead end, and I bit back my frustration.

Glancing back, she raised an eyebrow, no doubt able to see my feelings. "I said *trust me*." She pressed her fingertip against a leaf in the wall decoration, and with the softest click, it slotted into the wall, which swung open.

A secret passage. Of course.

I huffed a relieved breath and gave her a rueful smile as she led me inside. "Sorry for doubting you."

"There's an exit near one of the doors the servants use. I haven't found it guarded... yet."

"Then let's hope your luck holds out."

We worked together, me guiding her through the darkness and her murmuring directions.

After a minute, she asked, "What do you think is going on?"

"Sura must be planning to take the throne." It was the only possible reason for her to be here.

"Then why is she fucking around in the gardens?"

That was a question I had no answer for. "I'm not sure. But

she knows who I am. I just hope that means she'll listen to me."

"You think you can talk her down?"

I gritted my teeth, not at all sure. "She wants the throne, but there has to be a way. Either I'll negotiate with her to keep Braea alive, or I'll persuade Braea to let her and her daughter live."

I couldn't lose anyone else. I didn't know Sura well, but she was the only relative I had left who knew the truth. All those questions I had about my mother...

"Maybe Braea will accept the daughter as her heir," I went on, thinking out loud. "She might be the only way to keep them all alive. A bargaining chip."

Kat's hand went stiff in mine. "She's only a girl. Barely fifteen."

"She's old enough." Court life didn't care about age, gender, frailty, or *anything*. It sucked everyone in.

"Was I 'old enough' when my uncle threw me in that grave? Because I was her age when that happened."

It was a kick in the gut. I'd had my fathers—they'd helped me, guided me, encouraged and protected me. No one had protected Kat.

I stroked her knuckles. "I'm sorry. You're right. I'm just... We need to fix this."

She made a sound of understanding and pointed us left at the next passageway.

But I couldn't keep my thoughts on track.

If Sura was killed, who would protect her daughter? If she was to be believed, Braea had tried to prevent me from ever existing. Would she erase her granddaughter's existence, too?

"I need to reach Sura. Quickly."

Kat touched my arm. "We're here. Are you all right?"

I shook off my troubles—we didn't know what we were dealing with yet. I couldn't make any decisions until I had more information. So, I flashed Kat a reassuring grin. "I like sneaking around in the dark with you. Reminds me of the maze."

But my joke and rakish grin only roused a half smile from her. She squeezed my arm, then led the way out of the passages.

The gods were on our side tonight and the servant's entrance wasn't guarded. After all, no one was foolish enough to go outside on the new moon.

No one but us and Sura and whoever else she'd dragged along.

We slipped outside, Kat holding my arm, since she couldn't see in the darkness. Once the night swallowed us up, she whispered, "You know... we could work with Sura."

I huffed, breath steaming in the cold air. "You want to kill everyone?"

"You once said I was treading water and no one could do that forever. Eventually I would drown. You and the courts are treading water, barely keeping your heads above the surface. Yes, you've found flotsam to drag yourselves onto. As long as you all stay still, it will keep you alive. But what if a wave comes?"

I stared ahead, jaw clenched. She didn't understand. She didn't know what it was like. How could she? She'd only been here a matter of months.

"Because I see a wave coming, Bastian. A big fucking wave. If you think this piece of driftwood is going to save you, you'll doom your people to a slow death."

Whether she meant to or not, her words cut me. A thousand little cuts that stole any reply. Was this what she really thought? That *I* would do such a thing to my people?

"Dusk and Dawn must work together, and that's never going to happen when the Night Queen and Day King can't look each other in the eye and learn to trust each other. There will *always* be mistrust and scheming."

The air burst from my lungs, and I had to catch myself against the wall we skirted as we aimed for my cousin's hiding place. "You want to use the Crown?"

"The fact your mind jumped straight there tells me you know as well as I do it's the only way."

I shook my head and forged ahead. "Dawn can't be trusted to have power without enforced boundaries. *Especially* not Cyrus of all people."

Can Braea be trusted, though?

I didn't want to ask the question. And I really didn't want to think too hard about the answer.

Little doubts like this had bubbled up since my *athair* had revealed my identity. I'd managed to fight them, but the voice had grown louder since his death, like his shade was the one whispering in my ear.

Glowering, I smothered it and pushed through a shrub's low branches. I held them out of the way for Kat to pass. "It's better for everyone if that thing remains hidden forever."

"But—"

"We're here."

My cousin was a small shadow, curled up at the foot of the statue. She peered up at us, eyes wide. Confusion flickered across her face—probably at seeing me again.

"It's all right. Someone has gone for your mother." Vagueness meant I didn't need to explain my ability to split.

Kat helped her up. "Are you going to tell us what's going on? And what your...?" She cleared her throat, no doubt remembering our etiquette around names. "I'm Kat and this is Bastian."

Slowly, the girl nodded. She really was as young as Kat had pointed out, and now, the way she looked at us, fearful, made her look even more like a child. "Amaya." She swallowed and drew a long breath. "My mother came here to get this crown she's been going on about for months. She wants to unite the courts. Said I'd be the perfect candidate—that I would help lead them. I'm not sure why she thinks Dawn would listen to me."

Kat and I exchanged glances. Amaya didn't know her father's identity. Looking at her now, it was so obvious she was of Dusk and Dawn, and specifically Cyrus's child. She had the same shaped eyes as him and the way she'd rolled them when she'd insisted to my other self that she was safe from the Wild Hunt—that was entirely him.

"I thought you'd gone to help her. Please—go after her. She said something about 'the anointed one' but I don't really know what it means. After I hid, I heard a woman with her, and... I was so scared, I ran." She hung her head. "I left her, even though I knew something bad was going to happen."

A woman? Who had Sura met in the gardens? "What did you hear, Amaya?"

"She said... 'I'll do it myself, and you can be sure I'll use iron.'" She covered her mouth, eyes bright in the darkness. "'This time there'll be no escape.'"

38

BASTIAN

Amaya's words reached me as I found the first body. Clad in black, grey, and darkest green, with soft leather boots and a hood, she was dressed for stealth rather than battle. I pulled back the fitted jacket, revealing the Hydra Ascendant insignia over her chest. Crimson and gold. Not scarlet. The differences in the two designs were stark, now I'd studied them. This was the real thing.

Who was "the anointed one" and what were they meant to do? How did Sura mean to find the Crown of Ashes here of all places? There had to be one final piece she needed in order to reach it—something that had been under our noses the whole time.

Drawing my dagger, I summoned darkness to shroud me and hurried towards the trees. More of the dead, all dressed the same, wounds bloody and steaming in the night air. Who had killed them? The Wild Hunt took souls rather than cutting down mortal bodies, so it didn't seem their wardstones had failed.

The trail led to the Great Trees and a figure emerging from their ancient shade.

Braea rubbed a bloody smear from her cheek, scowling.

A sickly sensation stole over me—the cold presence of iron. Metal gleamed in her hand, partially covered by her sleeve. An iron blade?

She looked up and stopped dead. "*You*. You've come for me. At last."

As my shadows abated, I swallowed down the bitter taste at the back of my throat. "I came as soon as I realised something was wrong."

"Bastian." She exhaled, eyes easing shut. "I was just about to send for you. You always know my needs—sometimes before I do." She glanced over her shoulder and turned back with a stern set to her jaw. "The sacred ground of the trees has been sullied. It needs clearing up."

The bodies. It would cause an outrage if it was discovered, and Dusk would be blamed, since it had happened during her rule, and, judging by the blood, at her hand. "Of course." I nodded, biting down on all the questions. What had happened? What had she done? Where was Sura?

"Thank you, Bastian. Sometimes I think you're the only one I can trust." She approached, stopping when she drew level with me. With a deep sigh, she cupped my cheek. "You're the grandson I should've had. It may sound foolish, but sometimes I see my daughter in you."

I held very still. Had she guessed? The emotion in her voice felt real, calling to my yearning to know more of my mother.

She smiled sadly. "If you weren't half unseelie, I would've made you my heir. But some things aren't meant to be." She shook her head, gaze shifting to the palace beyond as she patted my cheek and let her hand fall. "This has to be done quickly and quietly. Tell no one what you find."

I bowed my head as though this was a completely normal request and my chest wasn't a storm of feelings I couldn't master or understand. She disappeared behind hedges leading away.

I wanted to go back with her, back to the palace, back to this morning, when I'd met with her before sunrise, back before that to a time when I didn't know she was my grand-mother and might have killed my mother.

Whatever I would discover beneath the trees—it could be nothing good.

As I approached the Great Yew and the Great Oak, the darkness pressed in, deeper than my shadows. A form lay on the ground face-down, silent and still.

Before I turned her over, I knew.

It was Sura. Dead.

I would get no answers to my questions. There would be no negotiation.

I scrubbed my face, pushing away what this meant for me. Bastian had to squash his needs and let the Serpent do his work.

What did the scene tell me? They were the only answers I'd get now.

Her blood soaked into the soil from a single stab-wound. Efficient and precise. A red mark darkened her temple.

They'd fought. Braea had managed to hit Sura in the head,

stunning her long enough for the finishing blow. But it was so neat. A perfect kill.

As I frowned down at her, I realised she held something, and for a moment, it was like Lara lay before me.

Not me. The Serpent. The Bastard. Whatever I needed to be to get through this.

As Kat and I had with Lara, I opened her still-warm hand. Not a pendant this time, but the bright red smear of something crushed.

Berries? I was missing something. Something I should see, some link that would make perfect sense. I dipped my finger in the smear and touched it to the tip of my tongue. Sweet. Overly so. Not something I'd eat for pleasure. And why bring them to a fucking coup?

There was something else caught in the redness—a light, grainy substance. I couldn't risk consuming more of this mysterious mixture, not when it might've contributed to her death. Sura wouldn't have taken anything Braea had given her, but she might've been eating the stuff when Braea found her, and that had affected her ability to fight. Not necessarily a deadly poison, but something that slowed her, granting Braea the advantage.

As carefully as I could, I placed her arms across her body. Her sleeves pulled back, revealing angry marks on her wrists.

Burns.

From iron.

That wasn't an iron blade Braea had carried gingerly in her sleeve, but cuffs. What magic had she inhibited?

I rewrote the confrontation in my mind.

Fight. Hit on the head. Cuff. Kill.

This was no death in battle. Sura was already a prisoner

and subdued. Braea could've let her live. We could've questioned her.

Instead, Braea had executed her with ruthless efficiency.

I always thought I'd saved Braea the horror of killing her own daughter. I'd killed my father that day. It had been messy and horrific. I was already damned by that action. The guilt and self-loathing had seized me at once. I wanted to save my queen that same torture.

But the wound in Sura's chest was clean. No marks of hesitation.

Killing in self-defence or to protect the realm, I could understand. This was the ruthless killing of a helpless captive —her *daughter*. She'd left her face down in the dirt.

We found her on the banks of the river, a tiny baby in her arms. The river had washed the blood from her clothes and snapped the arrows.

I had been able to turn my back on the accusations against Braea when it came to my mother. Sura was far from unbiased. She could *believe* the queen was responsible for her sister's death enough to say it, even if she was mistaken.

I'd been clinging on to that idea, because it meant Braea was the person I'd always believed in. The person I'd fought for. And I didn't want to think ill of her.

But kneeling over Sura's body, covering her face, so I could carry her away and bury her in secret, I could turn my back no longer.

The truth hadn't been twisted. Braea had killed my mother.

39

KAT

I knew from the look Bastian gave me that Sura was dead. His double must've found her and the information passed between them in silence. I rubbed Amaya's back and tried to smile brightly. "We should get you out of here, hmm? Somewhere warm." I shot Bastian a meaningful look. "And *safe*."

His mouth flattened. He was going to argue.

Before he could, I dragged him to one side. "Aside from Asher, the last two relatives Braea knowingly met, she killed," I hissed as quietly as I could. "I'm not taking any chances."

"How do you know she killed Sura? I didn't say—"

"Not with your words, no, but your face shouted it. I know you, Bastian."

He looked back at Amaya, brow crumpled. He was torn. Shocked. Hurt. He'd lost so much with Sura—not only an aunt, but a chance to know more about his mother.

I took a deep breath and touched his arm. "Take some time to think about it, and if you're sure Braea should know about her, fine, tell her. But this is not knowledge that can be taken away. Once she knows, she knows."

I bit my tongue against saying the most brutal version of the truth.

Braea was currently two for two when it came to killing her heirs. He and Amaya were only alive because she didn't know of their existence.

That bitter pill could wait for another night.

"You're right." He sounded relieved. "This isn't a decision to rush. Let's get her to Faolán and Rose."

We slipped back into the palace. Kaliban would've called my thoughts loud.

Even if Braea didn't kill Amaya and embraced her as her last surviving heir—another chance—I didn't trust the queen as far as I could throw her. She'd been a terrible mother, trying to control Nyx, just as my father had tried to control Avice and me. She wouldn't hesitate to manipulate and control her granddaughter.

Amaya deserved whatever chance I could give her to be a girl.

My eyes burned as I shepherded her into the secret passage. In silence, we passed through the courtyard lodestone and out into Dusk's part of the palace. Amaya watched everything, but didn't say a word. Her earlier panic had retreated, leaving a resigned stillness in its place.

We would break that with the news of her mother's death, but not until we had her somewhere safe.

The thought weighed heavily all the way out into the city streets and to our friends' front door.

Rose answered quickly, despite the hour. Her braid was messy from sleep, but she seemed remarkably awake as she took us in and immediately stepped back so we could enter.

As she closed the door behind us, Faolán padded down the stairs, yawning and rubbing his eyes, shirtless. "What?" He blinked at Bastian, me, Amaya and shook his head. "Just... *what?*"

"He doesn't do well with being woken up. But I think he's trying to ask what the hells is going on?" Rose pulled out one of the chairs around the kitchen table, gesturing for Amaya to take it.

But she was busy staring at Faolán, eyes ready to pop, despite the fact she swayed on her feet. I couldn't blame her, he was rather... massive, even amongst fae.

With a reassuring smile, I steered her to the seat while Bastian gave a calm, condensed version of the night's events, leaving out the part where Braea had killed another daughter.

"Sura's alive?" Faolán suddenly didn't look so sleepy as he joined us at the table, rubbing Rose's back.

"And knows about the Crown." Rose eased into a seat. "How was she planning to get hold of it?"

We turned to Amaya.

"I don't know the plan in detail. Just bits and pieces. Someone in the palace was bribed to collect an acorn from the Great Oak and—"

"A berry from the Great Yew," Bastian finished.

"Right. She made new wardstones—infernal magic, she called it. She had pages copied from an old book. And there was talk of an 'anointed one,' whatever that's supposed to mean."

Infernal magic. An anointed one. I tried to keep track of all the elements and slot them in amongst everything else we know about the Crown of Ashes.

"Mother would get the Crown for me. She said she put in the work a long time ago to ensure both courts would agree.

She was talking about me, wasn't she?" Amaya grimaced, gaze dropping to the table. "She once said she'd seduced the heir to Dawn, how he thought himself in love with her, but she only wanted one thing from him. And eventually, around the time of her coup, she got it. I never understood why she told me that. But... it's because he's my father, isn't it? *I'm* what she got from him." She searched our faces, finishing on mine.

"I believe so. I found some letters she sent him. They were lovers. And in you, both courts have an heir."

"But I don't want to be a queen, anyway. Especially not after..." She searched my gaze, jaw ratcheting tight as though she was steeling herself. "My mother... she's dead, isn't she? That's why she isn't here."

Everyone else sank back, sharing silent glances. Bastian stared at me. He wasn't prepared to deal with this. Telling his cousin, who had no idea they were related, that her mother was dead—killed by her grandmother. What a fucking mess.

So I held her shoulder. "I'm sorry. But I'm afraid you're right."

Slowly, she nodded, pursing her lips. "I had a feeling. The way she said goodbye, it was like she knew it would be the last time. And Kaliban..." She looked up at Bastian. "She always respected him and was sorry to hear of his passing. We're in the same boat now, aren't we?" She gave him a tremulous smile, which he returned.

One side of his mouth quirked, reminding me of the bored fae I'd danced with in Albion. I recognised the distance in him —he had shut down all feeling. I'd done it enough to know the signs.

Half shrugging, he said, "As boats go, it's a pretty shitty one."

He got a laugh from her, which soon turned into a sob, as she bent over the table and cried into her arms.

The grieving girl Rose put an arm around was a far cry from the slightly arrogant young woman I'd met at Sura's base all those months ago. She was a child—*a child*—and Sura had planned to use her as a piece in her plans to take the board. I bit the inside of my cheek and nodded for Faolán and Bastian to follow me to one side.

"We need to get her out of the city," I murmured while Rose comforted her. "I know it's a lot to ask, but—"

"I've got it." Faolán nodded like I was asking for nothing more than a cup of flour. "Where am I taking her?"

This was the part I didn't yet have a plan for—not entirely. "Do you think Ari and Ly will help? Just while we get something else arranged?"

Bastian answered with stillness. He had to be remembering our earlier debate. But the longer I thought about Amaya left in Braea's hands, the more certain I was that it would end only with her death.

I would not let that happen.

"I do," Bastian said at last. "Ari will do anything to help, and Ly... he's shown he can put our differences aside for the sake of the realm."

With that settled, we dispersed. Rose helped Amaya get settled on their settee, and soon she was curled up on it, asleep. Bastian and Faolán left to secure mounts to get her out of Tenebris before the sun rose.

And I stepped out into the cool night, turning my feet back towards the palace and my imprisonment in Dawn.

40

BASTIAN

oth parts of me came together to bury Sura. I chose that same hilltop where I'd burned myself a month ago. She'd loved her city, and this spot gave her a view of it with the sunset beyond.

By the time I got back to the palace, it was a perfect midpoint between Braea leaving me in the gardens and the coming sunrise. I forced myself to her quarters. There were too many questions that needed answers and I wasn't sure I could function until I got them.

Her assistant, Ennet, showed me into the bathing chamber with its sunken bath. Pink tinged the foamy water and the washcloths hanging over the side.

"You have a report for me?" She glanced up from pulling a wide-toothed comb through her tight curls, distributing a thick cream.

Like this was any other night and not whatever the fuck this had been.

"You killed Sura."

"And *you* didn't." She arched one eyebrow. "I have to wonder if that was deliberate."

I took a half step forward, the movement a burst I didn't intend. *Pull yourself together.* The Serpent didn't lose balance, didn't react. He was calm, even when Bastian Marwood was hurting.

"You saw me that night. You know I gave everything, *did everything* I could to save you. I *thought* I'd killed her, and I was proud to do so—*for you.*"

She held my gaze a long time, comb falling still. "You did. And I am grateful for it every day. I suppose a changeling could explain her survival."

"And what about tonight? What happened?"

"Hmph." It was a dark sound that rippled across the bath's surface. "She came here to set in motion her plan to get rid of me. Thankfully, I was able to defend myself."

"Braea." Her name echoed around the chamber, blunt. "I know she was cuffed in iron. Powerless."

"Does it matter what she was in that moment? She'd come here to take my throne. She'd already tried once before and apparently dying wasn't enough to deter her, so here she came, back again. I simply did what needed to be done."

Was that how she thought of my mother's death too?

She showed no remorse. She didn't even seem remotely distressed by the fact Sura was dead or that she'd been forced to take her life.

Kat was right about Amaya. If Braea found out about her...

Braea cleared her throat. "No one can know."

My head snapped up. "What?"

She frowned like it was obvious. "About Sura. What happened tonight or that she was still alive in the first place. I worry what they might think of... of *you.* People will make all sorts of parallels between one death and another. After Kaliban's arrest, they might wonder if you were part of the coup all along."

All sorts of parallels.

What she really meant was, if they knew she'd killed Sura tonight, they'd start to wonder about Nyx's death, too. And Nyx had been beloved by Dusk Court and a sizeable portion of Dawn. She had no coup to count against her. The mourning had lasted months, with little shrines popping up all over the city.

Or so my fathers had told me. I'd thought it odd that they should share that story all of a sudden, but now it made perfect sense.

There were other things they'd said over the years that now hit differently. They'd told me about Nyx, how wonderful a queen she would've made, how clever she was, how determined. Sharp with a retort, but kind as well.

What parts of her did Braea see in me? How much did she see the daughter she'd loved so much, right up until the moment love hadn't been enough and keeping her had become more important?

"Bastian?"

I yanked myself back from the drowning thoughts and inclined my head, calm like the Bastard who was only here because he had a job to do. "We will keep this information close to our chests."

But one other thing my *athair* had said pricked my thoughts like a burr. *That infernal book of hers.* Kaliban's words, then tonight Amaya had mentioned infernal magic.

"There was one more thing. Something my—*Kaliban* said before the end. He mentioned a book you had. It sounded like it contained powerful magic." I trod carefully. "I thought it might help us, especially since I saw the Wild Hunt on the palace's island."

Her eyes widened for a second, just like they had when she'd seen me tonight shrouded in shadows. "A book? Really?" She scoffed and raked the comb through her hair viciously. "You know his mind wasn't what it once was. Did you hear he was found on the street shouting nonsense at people? No wonder his neighbours reported him."

She made it sound like he'd lost his mind, but he'd been entirely rational.

Hitting a knot, she scowled and attacked it, ripping out as much hair as she untangled. "You know, I always wondered why he didn't leave after Sylen's death. Now I suppose I have my answer. He stayed so he could help with another coup attempt. I would not pay any attention to anything he might have said."

"I see." Taking a stiff step back, I excused myself.

"Pay him no mind at all," she called after me.

I did see. Too well.

Braea could not be trusted.

41

KAT

I had a troubled sleep and woke later than I'd planned. This was the day of Cyrus's masquerade ball, and judging by everyone's low mood at yesterday's party, it wasn't going to be the exuberant affair he'd planned.

A king who didn't get what he wanted meant trouble for everyone else.

As I hurried to get ready, Zita appeared at my door with a box. "I..." She glanced at the guards. "Can I come in?"

"You'll need to—I'm running late." Letting her in, I flashed a grin, but she didn't return it.

In fact, an uncharacteristic crease scoured the skin between her eyebrows, and the muscles of her compact figure were tight rather than loose and limber. The pale grey dress she wore was uncharacteristically sombre, too.

"What's wrong?"

She touched a finger to her lips and waited until the door was shut and we'd reached my bedroom before answering.

"I'm worried for you. Cyrus has been acting strange this morning. Paranoid. Sepher said he's never seen him like this."

"Hmm." I twisted a section of hair and pinned it, missing my lock picks. "Paranoia seems like *exactly* the sort of behaviour I'd expect from him. There's something else."

In the mirror, she lowered her gaze and placed the box on the bed, busying herself with opening it. "This morning... Two of his servants 'slipped' in his bathroom and cracked their heads on the floor. He didn't bother to send for a healer in time and now they're dead."

My hands lowered. He'd killed Adra, of that I was sure. Not to mention those who'd died in his fake Hydra Ascendant attacks. But those deaths had a purpose in his eyes. Adra needed to be silenced before she revealed his secrets. The attack victims were collateral damage on his campaign for the throne.

But these two servants? Random. Senseless.

"He was angry, and they were in his reach."

Zita met my gaze in the mirror. "With how close he keeps you, I fear you may be the next person in his reach."

I took three deep breaths, letting the next hairpin dig into my fingertip. We were so close to being able to prove his guilt. Krae had agreed to meet us with evidence *today*. Once we had that proof, we would have to move quickly. I just needed to keep this up a little longer.

"I'll be fine." I got on with pinning up my hair. "Is that box from Ari?"

"That's it? You're not worried?"

I shrugged. "Does it make a difference if I am?"

"No. I suppose it doesn't." She smoothed her dress—faint lines blended with the folds, looking like pale grey marble.

"Ariadne had this delivered to me, since you're not supposed to be wearing anything that hasn't been provided by *His Majesty*."

I'd managed to get a message to Ari via Ella, and she'd worked based on that and the measurements she already had.

Thousands of crystals winked back at me from inside the box, shading from a deep starry night to dusky violet to sunrise yellow to, finally, hot coral pink. I'd asked for something that united Dusk and Dawn, and she'd executed that to perfection in the colours. She even knew me well enough to choose one of the only shades of pink that suited me.

Ariadne, less threadwitch, more thread*genius*.

"Well, that's..." Zita widened her eyes as she pulled the outfit from the box. "Wow. *Bold*."

I swallowed at the design. Less revealing than the gold dress from her wedding, yet more daring. "I hope I can carry this off."

42

KAT

I entered the masquerade a little late, which by fashionable fae standards was the perfect moment. Sepher escorted me on one arm and Zita on the other, and he *absolutely* looked smug about the fact. He'd arranged for Celestine to walk on my other side, bracketing me from view.

"It seems a shame to keep such a gem hidden, but I think it best we keep you away from my brother as much as possible today." Yet the look he gave me was more sharp than protective, like he also saw me as prey.

I shifted, the iron bracelet settling against his sleeve.

Almost imperceptibly, he flinched and the way he looked at me changed.

I wasn't a hapless victim. Not anymore.

And the outfit I wore wasn't easily hidden, especially contrasted with Zita's grey gown and matching mask.

Ari had taken my brief and made a skin-tight body suit that covered me from ankle to wrist and throat. The colours blended to the brighter sunrise tones from my waist upwards. Cupping every curve, it fitted so seamlessly, it looked as though the glittering crystals were attached directly to my skin. Over my arms and bust, the top edge of the crystals mimicked an off-the-shoulder neckline, fading into a sheer fabric that blended into my tan skin, and that in turn ended with a gold collar.

Unlike the gold dress, I was in no danger of spilling out if, for some reason, I needed to run.

I never could shake practicality.

She had even encrusted a pair of shoes in midnight toned crystals to match, so they flowed into the bodysuit. My mask was a copper sunburst with glittering strands that blended into my hair.

I had to give it to Ari, she was an absolute master of her art, and even though the fabric clung to me in every place possible, it allowed me to move like a second skin. I walked with my head high.

Sepher glanced at me and made an approving sound. He wore a leafy green mask and matching shirt, which hung open even wider than usual as if to make up for the fact his face was hidden.

I wasn't sure of his motivations. He was no hero, but at least he didn't pretend to be one like Cyrus did, and he seemed to have some level of respect for me. I would take him over his brother.

Just like I would take Bastian on the Moon Throne over Braea. But that was a problem for another day. One monarch at a time.

At my side, Celestine craned, searching the crowd with a little bounce in her step.

What had her so excited? But I couldn't tell who or what

she was searching for, and instead I used her as cover to scan the glittering ballroom.

I spotted Bastian's hair quickly—a single point of utter blackness that made all other colours seem washed out. His back was to me, though, but I met Ella's gaze through her peacock mask. We exchanged subtle nods. All was well for our plans. We just needed to wait for Krae's message to give us the exact place and time for the meeting.

Bastian looked down at her and seemed about to turn, but Ella placed a hand on his arm and whispered something. I was sure she warned him not to turn and look at me.

Play the game.

After all, it was coming to a close, pieces making their final manoeuvres, ready to declare checkmate.

I turned my back on them and accompanied Sepher, Zita, and Celestine through the crowd. We managed to avoid Cyrus as we smiled and chatted, accepting drinks whenever they were offered. If I was seen avoiding alcohol, people would question why I needed my wits about me. Every so often, Sepher and Celestine swapped glasses with me, so I only drank the occasional sip.

My heart pounded in anticipation of meeting Krae and finally ending this ordeal. I couldn't keep my eyes off the ornate orrery that stood at one end of the ballroom. Even the music's beat seemed to count down.

Soon. *Soon.*

I dared a glance at Bastian. I'd kept track of him on the periphery of my vision. The darkness, I longed for.

"Ah, *there* she is." Cyrus's voice rang out over the music and the crowd. "Come here, my pretty little thing."

The music stopped. The crowd parted.

I turned and smiled.

He wore gold. *Of course* he wore fucking gold. Cyrus was about as predictable as a winter cold and even more unwelcome.

No mask. I would bet a lot of money he didn't want to cover his face. Legs and arms spread, he was sprawled on his throne, apparently relaxed. But as I obeyed his summons, I caught a glimpse of the tension edging his smirk.

Danger. My heart whispered it with each beat.

Yet, I had to walk into that danger.

The crowd formed a corridor leading to him. Their eyes were on me. Their murmurs were about my outfit.

When I reached the foot of the dais, I bowed, slow and deep, and the king preened, clearly happy to have a public display of my obedience.

"Leave us." He sent away the cronies gathered around him, then beckoned me. "Closer."

I sauntered up the steps.

"Closer," he repeated, patting his leg when I reached the top.

Run. Danger. Run!

But instincts didn't play by the rules of this game. They were wild things and thought we could do whatever we wanted. That wasn't true.

It had never been true.

We had to skirt their rules and *seem* to believe in them. We had to wear the smiling mask, while inside we nursed our poison and vitriol until we could use them as tools for our hidden rage.

So I sat on his lap and let him lift my chin as the music resumed.

"My naughty little thing." A dark flicker entered his eyes as he said it, setting my teeth on edge. "You are only *mine*, aren't you?"

I frowned like it was a strange question. "Of course, my king. *Of course*. Who else would I belong to?"

He made a low sound, snatching his hand and attention away. There was a cut on his knuckles.

The ill feeling iron left in my stomach doubled. Zita was right. Something was very wrong. He'd never questioned me like this before. And that cut... he'd hit somebody. One of the servants he'd killed? But he wouldn't think I had cheated on him with one of them.

Draping myself over him, I surreptitiously scanned the crowd, not for Bastian this time, but for who *wasn't* here.

Ella, Rose, Ari, and Perry. Asher, Lysander, Faolán. Sepher and Zita and their friends. Brynan and his partner, Gael. I counted the Convocation members, though I didn't know them well.

Caelus. There was no sign of Caelus. Guards had seen me entering the hot springs with him. Had word reached the king?

"Not searching for him, are you?" Cyrus's voice, soft yet sharp in my ear.

I blinked, innocent and confused. "I was merely enjoying the outfits."

He made a dismissive sound and ran a hand up my thigh. "I'm enjoying the thought of tearing this one off you later, particularly as I can't remember much about the last time I had you. I'll be sure not to drink so much today."

My throat closed. Shit. Not today. We would act quickly, but I wasn't sure we could get a king dethroned in an afternoon. I needed an excuse.

I caught his hand, stopping its path. "But... I'm not sure

how I feel after you killed Kaliban. Whatever he might have done, he helped me."

His nose wrinkled, somewhere between a sneer and a snarl. He pulled his hand free and caught me by the throat, sliding his palm up it so I had to meet his gaze.

Mine. Mine. My body is mine. I had to remind myself, but it worked. I didn't try to go away or get dragged into that memory.

"Don't you adore me anymore, Katherine?" He said my name slowly, dragging out the syllables until it became a threat. "Or is it that you're afraid of your *beloved* Bastian seeing us? Perhaps your allegiances lie elsewhere after all."

"No." I leant into his touch to prove my point. "Not at all. I just..." I fluttered my lashes, looking away. "You look so strong up here and... I confess I'm a little afraid." I said it on a shaky breath, like it excited me a little, too.

"*Good.*" He kissed the corner of my jaw, squeezing my cheeks so my teeth dug in.

Despite the pain, I let out a little breath of relief and forced myself to run my fingers through his hair and caress his pointed ear. I was his lover. He was happy with me. All was well. *All was well.*

"After all," he whispered right in my ear, grip growing harder, "you were heard enjoying yourself yesterday."

Blood flooded my mouth. I clung to its coppery taste instead of letting fear drag me away.

"A man might wonder what his lover was up to without him... or *who* she was up to it with."

Shit. All was *not* well.

Someone had heard me with Bastian. We hadn't been careful enough.

"That's right. The guards heard you," he went on. "They

assumed it was me, that I was waiting in your rooms. But we both know that wasn't the case, don't we?"

I could barely swallow.

"I didn't set them straight. I can't have everyone knowing my little fuck creature has fucked someone else. Not when I'm the king, and you didn't have my permission."

"Your Majesty, I—I didn't have anyone else," I managed to whisper around his grip. More cuts opened up inside my mouth, strengthening the metallic taste. "We haven't... *you know*... in so long, and I needed relief, so I... I touched myself and thought of you."

My jaw sagged with relief when he released me. As he threw his head back and laughed, the jagged little cuts throbbed.

I forced my mouth shut, despite fresh pain lighting up with every movement. His laughter was unreadable. He could believe me and be pleased with my answer. He could be about to erupt. I had to believe in my lie if I was going to make him believe it, too.

So I shifted further up his lap like I wanted—*needed* to be close to him, and he squeezed me in, catching me in his trap.

His gaze landed somewhere out in the crowd as his laughter died to a smirk. "My poor little thing, so starved of attention." He kissed my throat and worked his way down, hand clamping on my hip.

I couldn't squirm. I couldn't pull away. Instead, I held still, pretending my tension was a result of focus on his touch.

When he reached my cleavage, right at the top edge of the crystal neckline, he bit down. Hard.

I flinched, but caught my pain between my teeth, making no sound. What the fuck was he doing? Was this...?

But I realised as he pulled away, my blood on his lips,

322

teethmarks on my skin—his eyes were still fixed out on the crowd.

I followed his gaze.

Bastian stood there, staring at me, at the marks Cyrus had left. From twenty feet, I could feel how tightly he held himself, thrumming like a bowstring.

Calm down and look away, Bastian. Look away. I shouted it in my thoughts. If he didn't, Cyrus would realise we'd been playing him all this time, and we were so nearly done.

We had almost won.

43

BASTIAN

He'd spilled her blood. It was on his lips.

On. His. Fucking. Lips.

I didn't just need to kill him. I needed to *destroy* him.

I was about to charge forward, when I felt it. The look boring into me. Kat's green eyes. They burned with intensity and reminded me of what I should've been able to remind myself.

Play the fucking game.

I dragged in a breath and grabbed Ella. Pulling her close, I cupped her cheeks, and her eyes flashed wide for an instant as she must've thought I was about to really kiss her. I stopped an inch away, but my grip either side of her face hid the fact our lips weren't quite touching.

"Ella," I bit out, "I am going to fucking murder him. He's marked her. He's *hurt* her."

She huffed out a breath and looped her arms around my

neck, helping with our deception. "He has. But you need to calm down. I promise you will get to rip Cyrus apart, but not if you lose control." She pulled away as though our kiss had ended, and tiptoed to my ear, clinging to me as though overcome. "Don't fall apart now. Get a fucking grip."

I nodded and squeezed her in a hug. "Thank you."

When we pulled apart, Rose, Faolán, Asher, and Perry returned. With Krae calling the shots on our meeting, I was concerned this could be a trap, so they'd snuck into the nearby corridors, watching for unusual guard movements or anything else that could signal a setup. Faolán shook his head.

"All good," Rose confirmed.

We resumed our mingling, with Ella doing an incredible job of chatting and flirting her way into every corner of the ballroom while we waited for a message from Krae. I kept an arm slung around her shoulders and let her talk, taking the opportunity to watch the exits and look for any sign of Krae or their messenger. I couldn't help checking the grand orrery at one end of the room, impatient for this to be over—fearful for Kat if it didn't. Cyrus's behaviour was escalating. I needed him out of the way before it went further.

But the minutes ticked on—thirty minutes, an hour, an hour and a half...

Much as I loathed Cyrus, at least this whole scheme kept my mind occupied. As soon as things grew quiet for even an instant, my mind pinged back to last night's realisations. Braea had killed my mother. Braea could not be trusted. What did those things mean for me? Who did they make me?

I didn't have time to dwell on such questions. And no matter what, I still owed Braea. I worked for her. I served her and our realm. That was the only thing that mattered.

If I kept busy, I didn't have to prod at it.

Out in the crowd, I caught a glimpse of Orpha. She'd been out checking parts of the palace the others couldn't afford to be seen in. Another head shake.

As I continued my search for Lysander, Asher, and Perry, I spotted Celestine craning over the crowd like she was searching for someone.

Before I could work out who, a body crashed into me. Their drunken dancing had sent them flying, and I barely pushed Ella out of the way before catching them. They laughed right up until the moment they looked up and saw it was me they'd fallen into. Their eyes widened and they stammered out an apology. I set them back on their feet and gave them a little shove back onto the dance floor.

At least, it had been a dance floor earlier. Now it was split roughly fifty-fifty between those dancing and those in various states of fucking.

"Oh, we've reached that stage of the party, have we?" Ella tilted her head, watching the nearest couple.

But I was looking down at the note in my hand.

Dining room. Five minutes. No sooner. No later.

I marked the time and slid the note into my inside pocket. Out the corner of my eye, I caught Faolán's gaze and gave him the nod that said we'd made contact.

He subtly shifted, ready in case of any traps we'd missed, and touched Rose's shoulder. Understanding passed between them as I turned my attention back to Ella.

"Yes, it is that time," I sighed. "And if we stay here, folk will wonder why we're not joining in." I steered the group deeper into the crowd where we'd be lost in the heave of bodies, and only then did I finally dare to look back at Kat and Cyrus.

Except his throne stood empty.

I swallowed, searching left and right for a glimpse of golden crown or crimson hair.

"Don't you need to go?" Faolán eyed the gilded orrery at this end of the room.

"Where's Kat? Do you have eyes on her?"

He turned to the throne. "Shit. No, not since..." He touched his chest in the same place Cyrus had bitten her. "He pushed her away not long after—I'd guess to clean up."

Rose appeared at my side. "I can't find Kat or the king. I heard he disappeared a little while ago and she's just been summoned to him."

Right as the ball turned. In front of so many people, she wouldn't be able to slip him drugs to knock him out or find some other clever way out of the situation. "I need to find her."

Ella's nails dug into my hand. "That's the last thing she would want. You need to meet with Krae."

"But what if he—?"

"Ella's right." Perry set her jaw. "We'll look for Kat, and it will be less suspicious if we're the ones who *just happen* to stumble across them."

For a moment, my throat felt thick. "*Thank you.*"

Ella squeezed my hand, rubbing the place she'd just clawed. Our friends crowded me, each one offering a nod or a touch of reassurance. I wasn't alone and neither was Kat.

"We'll find her." Perry jerked her chin towards the corridor leading to the grand dining room. "Now get in there and make sure we can end this."

Steadied by their faith, I turned and shouldered through the crowd. My shadows gathered close. They could sense the moment had come and they were as ready as I was for this to be over.

Gripping the door handles, I paused and checked the time. Get in there. Get Krae's evidence against Cyrus. Present it to the Convocation and the queen. Get rid of Cyrus. No more need for hostages. Get Kat home.

I set my shoulders and opened the doors.

44

BASTIAN

The room sat ready for dinner to be served, cutlery gleaming in the light spilling through the glazed balcony doors. With one long table at the far end and three others perpendicular to it, everyone would be able to see the raised top table. At its centre was an empty space with a silk cloth and no place setting.

A lone figure sat there, silhouetted against the windows overlooking a balcony.

"Krae?"

No answer.

I stilled. Something was off. A trap.

But there was no sign of anyone else, so cautiously, I approached.

Coppery hair hid their face, but it was Krae.

They could have sold us out to Cyrus in exchange for a pardon. And Cyrus had a history of staging attacks during events. He had a flare for the dramatic.

It certainly *felt* like a trap.

I circled the table, every sense on high alert. A burnt scent in the air made my nose wrinkle—scorched meat and hair.

Past the table, I could see dark bands tying Krae's wrists to the chair.

"Shit," I whispered and edged closer, shadows ready in case this was an ambush.

Handprint shapes had been seared through their clothing, leaving charred holes and raw red marks on their arms. That burning smell—it was *them*. If this was a trap, it was one they'd fully committed to.

I pushed back their hair. A snare dug into their throat, the other end secured to the back of the chair, keeping them upright.

Their eyelids fluttered as they stirred. "I'm sorry... I didn't want to tell him, but..."

Cyrus had tortured them. The realisation swept in on a wave of nausea.

"Doesn't look like he left you much choice. Let's get you out of here." As gently as I could, I untied their wrists while my shadows eased under the snare and loosened it enough to slip it over their head.

"He burned it." They gestured towards a pile of smoking ash.

Before I could work out what "it" was, I felt eyes on me and a voice rang out from the balcony.

"Here he is, right on time. The queen's loyal dog."

45

KAT

As soon as Cyrus spoke, Bastian jerked upright, placing himself between us and Krae. I'd seen them move at last—unconscious, not dead. Thank the gods.

Cyrus had summoned me here to enjoy the view. Pale marble faces looked out from amongst the wisteria clinging to the palace walls and around the balcony's edge. Many of the carvings smiled or laughed, while a handful scowled as though the plant's incursion was more welcome in some quarters than others.

With such a picturesque setting, I'd assumed it was the view of Luminis he wanted me to see, but as soon as I'd spotted Krae in the chair, it became clear our plan was fucked. And seeing Bastian arrive, I realised the view I'd been brought here to witness was his capture.

So long as Cyrus thought I was on his side and had nothing to do with the Krae and Bastian's meeting, I had a chance to stop this. I just needed to gain the upper hand. *Somehow.*

I smiled as though catching Bastian unawares was exactly

what I wanted, because I only desired what the king beside me did.

From our position at the wisteria-knotted balustrade, Cyrus squeezed me closer, his smirk sharper and more cruel than I'd ever seen. Somehow he'd found out about Bastian's meeting with Krae, but didn't seem to know about my involvement.

At least, I hoped not. Though I feared my body would give me away.

"My pretty little thing, your heart sounds ready to explode. Are you afraid of the Bastard of Tenebris... or perhaps *for* him?"

I scoffed, leaning in to him. "Not afraid, my king—I'm *excited*. You've foiled his little plot and now we're going to find out what treachery he had planned for you."

He made a pleased sound as Bastian glowered at us. "What *treason*. Because that's what this is. *Treason*. I am the king, and that wretch had a hand in my father's murder." He pointed at Krae, who'd managed to stand, but sagged over the table. "Now, here is the Night Queen's Shadow, son of *two* traitors, meeting with a fellow traitor. Undoubtedly to plot *another* regicide."

So that was his plan—have Bastian arrested for treason. How to get out of this? I had no weapon, nothing to hand. Bastian could run, but the Kingsguard waited outside—I'd heard Cyrus give the order to keep their swords ready and stay out of sight until "the right time." They wouldn't hesitate to cut Bastian down.

I needed to let him know. "Ah, and your guards outside are witnesses. So clever." I spread my hand over Cyrus's chest. A little higher and I could strangle him, but he had the advantage. Quicker and stronger, he would stop me before I stood a chance. No. I had to be smarter than that. More patient.

An opportunity would come my way. And if it didn't, I would make one.

Bastian nodded slowly—message received and understood. "If you have evidence against me, I suppose that means you can kill me now and it won't cause any issues with Dusk." He seemed to be speaking to Cyrus, but his gaze was on me the whole time.

He thought we had Krae's evidence. Meaning, if Cyrus died in this confrontation, we'd be able to present Krae's evidence and, in the eyes of the law, it would go from murder to lawful execution. But Cyrus had burned it. Maybe we could salvage something from the ash.

"The problem is, Cyrus, *you* killed your father, didn't you?" Bastian spread his arms with a bitter smile, coming a little closer. "Hey, I'm not one to judge. I can understand—I was protecting a throne; you wanted one."

Cyrus dug his fingers into my hip but remained silent.

"It's a shame you don't have evidence to back up your wild accusations." I stared at Bastian, hoping he would understand.

Bastian's eyes widened the slightest amount before turning back to Cyrus. "Nothing? No confession speech? Normally we can't stop you making overblown speeches." He frowned "The thing I can't wrap my head around is the Winter Solstice attack. Why drive Horrors to attack your own city?"

"They needed a hero." Cyrus indicated himself, a wide smile spreading across his face as he lifted his chin, looking like the statue sketches I'd found in his desk.

He'd positioned himself as a heroic figure, taking action, looking bold and dashing. Whereas his father was nowhere to be seen that day.

He wanted the people to cheer when he took the throne. *A man of action.*

Although it wasn't a direct confession, the fact he'd said this much meant he didn't intend for Bastian to survive this confrontation, and he trusted me enough to keep his secret.

I could really do with that opportunity right about now.

"Perhaps today, they need a villain." Eyebrows pinched together, Bastian said it thoughtfully, and something in his tone sent a chill through me. "Fine. You can take me, but I need to tell her something first."

"How touching." Cyrus waved for him to go on.

"Katherine, I love you."

I froze.

He shook his head, eyes soft, expression pained, showing all the feelings he'd kept hidden. "It's been torture to see you in his arms, a poison straight to my heart."

Why the hells was he saying this? He'd warned me to never —*never* reveal my heart, but here he was, spilling it in front of his enemy.

My thoughts could race to only one destination that explained it: he was really handing himself over and expected to die. This was his last chance.

Head hanging, he turned from me to Cyrus. "But I see you have her now."

The king leered, lifting my chin. "You love her, still? Then I'm sure you'd hate to see this." He bent and kissed my shoulder, gaze on Bastian, while I stared, silently asking what the fuck he was doing.

With his eyes, Bastian begged for this to stop. His jaw flexed as though he was barely keeping himself from charging at us and ripping Cyrus off me.

"Or this…" Cyrus kissed my neck. "And I can't imagine how much you'd hate to see her kiss me, especially as she'd do so willingly." He lifted my left arm, showing off the iron bracelet for a moment before pinching my chin and making me look up at him. He smirked all the while. "This little trinket means she's immune to magic. You see, *some* of us don't need to charm humans into our beds."

My skin crawled with every word. The way this was escalating, I knew he'd kiss me on the mouth next, and I would have to kiss back, playing along. I felt along the balustrade, searching for anything I could use as a weapon. If I caught him while he kissed me, I just might have the advantage.

My fingertips brushed something cold like the stone balustrade, but smooth. Feeling along further, I realised it was several somethings, and I recognised the shape. Lock picks.

It couldn't be. *How?* I dared a glance down, just as a shadow slipped out of sight. Bastian's picks delivered by his shadows.

"But *Cyrus*," Bastian said, pulling the king's attention back to him, "isn't that iron uncomfortable for you?"

"It's worth it to see the look on your face."

Of course. Not a surrender, but an opportunity.

Hands behind my back, I started on the lock just as Cyrus slid his hand into my hair. I needed to be quick, but I also needed to make my cooperation believable. "Let's show him how a king gets exactly what he deserves," I murmured, eyes half closed.

"And let's make sure he has a good view." He yanked my head back, and for a heart-pounding second, the picks slipped in my grip. I jolted, catching them and arching into Cyrus, drawing a pleased sound from him as he pressed his lips to mine.

A different shaped mouth. Hot, wet lips. The savage grip on my hair right where I still had a lump from Rufus smashing my head against the wall.

It was all wrong. But I couldn't flinch away. I battled to stay pliant, focusing on the delicate twist and push of the lock picks without alerting him. I needed to get this bracelet unlocked before he deepened the kiss—I didn't trust myself to hide my disgust when he pushed my mouth open.

At last, there was a soft clink of the bracelet hitting the balustrade.

I moaned my relief as the iron sickness ebbed away and magic swept over me in an angry buzz.

Cyrus had his hands on me, his lips on me, his vile stink. His callous, murdering being was all over me.

No longer.

I drew upon my power, calling every scrap of it together and pushing it to my lips.

It tingled, stronger than when I'd killed Rufus. It would take him quickly—more painlessly than he deserved, but I just wanted him dead. I needed this to be over.

His grip tightened, pulling me taut. The poison taking hold, making him lose control. The picks fell from my grasp, but it didn't matter. Just a moment longer, then he would slip away.

Softly—so softly, Cyrus laughed against my mouth. I dared to open my eyes, braced for the sight of blackened tendrils spreading over his face.

But he looked down at me, skin perfect, and breathed, "Oh, you treacherous little thing."

46

KAT

I couldn't move. Couldn't breathe. Couldn't think.

Just one question screeched its way through my mind over and over.

Why isn't he dead?

Cyrus narrowed his eyes at me like he was trying to figure me out. "I wondered if you would go through with kissing me in front of him. That's why I made Elthea give me a supply of the antidote. This felt like a good time to take it, especially after seeing the state you left your poor uncle in."

The antidote. To my poison. I couldn't hurt him.

On the balustrade, my groping hands found something that turned my stomach. I flinched away from the sudden silence.

Iron. The bracelet.

I forced myself to grab it and rammed the open end upward, aiming for his throat.

He caught my wrist and squeezed until my grip spasmed

337

and the bracelet clinked to the tiled floor. "Now, now, pretty, *naughty* little thing." He shook his head like he was scolding a pet. "Even when you fucked me, you were doing it just to get close to me, weren't you?"

"I didn't fuck you," I spat out. If I was about to die, at least I'd disabuse him of that notion. I'd screwed him in as many ways as I could, but never like that.

"Ah. I suppose I should've known." He laughed, holding up a warning hand as Bastian started towards us. "I still have hold of her, Bastard. Any closer and she dies."

Sighing, Cyrus shook his head. "The little disappearances. The way you refused your uncle's gift of a fertility potion—I assume he wanted you to use it, then kill me off once the heir was assured. So many little signs. I had an inkling you might not be all you portrayed, but I didn't want to believe it... not until I had that report from the guards. Don't you think fae know the difference between the sounds someone makes when they're touching themselves and the ones they make when they're being fucked?"

My chest was going to explode. There wasn't enough space for my lungs to gasp in this much air and for my heart to flutter so erratically. He'd found us out. He knew.

"I *thought* your little indiscretion was with Caelus—after all, they told me you'd also gone to the hot springs with him. But the poor fellow got all the blame with none of the pleasure, didn't he? I wondered when I saw the way this one looked at you when I marked your precious little body. So I took the antidote, just in case you were still holding a place in your heart for the Bastard of Tenebris. And thank the Sun and Stars I did."

His head snapped around to Bastian. "You. *You.*" He spat it out like a curse. "You killed the woman I loved, and now I have the woman *you* love. Such poetry. It will soon become a tragedy if I make *her* past tense, won't it?"

"Sura," Bastian breathed. "All this is about *Sura*."

I understood now. His hatred of Bastian was rooted in vengeance. Kaliban—that was why Cyrus had beheaded him, giving him the same death as Sura.

On the edge of my vision, Bastian lunged, shadows surging with him.

With a jerk of Cyrus's chin, light blazed between us, burning even in my periphery. Bastian's cry lanced through me, and I yanked against Cyrus.

"You don't get to say her name." He finally released my wrist now my hand had gone tingly and weak. Instead he held me by the throat. "And *you* don't get to escape. She tried to kill me, Bastian. You saw her and you can't deny it."

I managed to glance over, braced to find Bastian burnt, but his skin was fine. On hands and knees, he felt his way closer, blinking as his gaze shifted, never quite resting on us. Cyrus had blinded him. I choked in his hold, reaching out for the shadows rippling across the floor, like they might see for him.

"You should be worrying about yourself, naughty little thing." He bent me back over the balustrade until I couldn't bend any further and my feet lifted from the ground.

I sucked in a breath and tried to hook my heels around the decorative stone. "Please, Your Majesty, I didn't mean to. It was charm." I held up my wrist, no iron clamped around it. "Without the bracelet, I—"

"You really are a devious little bitch, aren't you?" He laughed right in my face, blocking out the sky above. "It's a pity you weren't born fae—you'd have been perfect."

"Let her go," Bastian bellowed, working his way closer.

"Oh, I will." Cyrus smiled, pushing me further, further.

He was going to push me over the edge. He'd watch me fall and see if I was going to disintegrate or if only *bits* of me would disintegrate.

47

KAT

I reached out for something—*anything*. Stone. Stone. More stone. A tightly curled branch of wisteria. Then I found the smooth edge of one of the discarded lock picks.

Muscles coiling, I pretended I was too absorbed in Bastian's plight to be a threat. "Bastian? Bastian?"

He blinked, squinting in our direction, and managed to stand.

When Cyrus sneered at him, I swung.

The pick arced through the air, a glinting point. Almost at his eye. Almost there.

The metal flared, bright cherry red. It burned. Oh, gods, it burned.

I cried out with the effort of keeping my fist closed around it and that path towards his eye, but—I couldn't.

It fell from my grasp.

The acrid stink of burning surrounded us as Cyrus's hair

and mine singed. He scowled and pushed further. "Look what you made me do." Further.

I was horizontal now, feet barely touching the balustrade's carved stone. All he had to do was let go and I would fall. Even without the veil, this height would kill. No question.

Tears hot in my eyes, I grabbed the stone. It was the only thing left.

Something nudged my fingers. I opened my hand. Cold steel pressed into it. The hilt of a weapon.

How?

But as my head tilted back, dipping below my hips, letting gravity pull me down, I didn't have time to even guess an answer to that question.

Backside slipping off the balustrade, I swung.

It came into view. A massive sword. Too huge for me to wield.

But it sang through the air, and the serpents on its hilt nestled against my fingers, welcoming.

There was a moment of resistance as I hit Cyrus, then the blade bit into him.

Hot and red, blood spilled over my thighs and splashed my face as his eyes widened. His jaw went slack, more blood trickling out. The grip on my neck eased.

For a horrible instant, I fell.

Every muscle and organ in me jolted, and in that moment of panic, I grabbed his wrist. He slumped to the floor, and, pulse pounding, I used his weight to balance myself onto the right side of the balustrade.

Catching my breath, I stared down.

At my feet lay the Day King, eyelids fluttering as he looked up at me. The blood was so bright against his golden hair and golden outfit and the golden crown that had fallen from his head. It kept seeping from the deep gouge under his arm. I'd cleaved almost to the centre of his chest.

"No," he choked out, dimming eyes on the sword.

I blinked at the sword. The black and silver serpents on its hilt fell still, and it grew heavy, forcing me to rest its tip on the floor. Justice.

I'd done this. With help from the sword. But how the hells did it get up here?

But I had one more thing to do before I worried about that.

Cyrus's final breaths bubbled in his ruined chest, and I needed him to know something before he died.

I stood over him, shaking not with fear or shock, but with all the outrages he'd committed in his short time as king. "That was for Kaliban and for all the lives you destroyed, and I hope it's as painful as it looks."

Footsteps sounded behind me and, before I could turn, Zita stepped into view. A vicious smile split her face, which had been painted a pale marble grey to match her mask. She looked down at him and inclined her head. "May you always have the justice you deserve."

"No. You can't. It's... not fair... I'm king." He wheezed, gaze passing slowly from me to her and back again before it slid away. There was no more wheezing.

Bastian rubbed his eyes, blinking, but his gaze was able to go to my face and trail down until it hit the dead king.

Dead. Very, very dead.

It was done.

He couldn't touch me anymore. Hurt anyone else. Scheme or kill.

His time affecting the world was over.

Only after long seconds of breathing in that knowledge and living with it could I rouse myself and frown at Zita. "Where... How... What?"

Sepher emerged from inside. "If you'll settle on exactly what question it is you're asking, my wife and I will be only too happy to answer."

Bastian stepped between us, shadows roiling around his knees. "What is this?"

The prince spread his hands. "The grand reveal, of course. You've seen plays, haven't you?"

Zita eased into place at his side, and he stroked the back of her head as though reassuring himself she'd made it through whatever the fuck had just happened.

I stepped around Bastian, refusing to have this conversation peering around him. Beside, I had Justice, and if we were in danger from Zita and Sepher, I suspected the sword would be on my side. I hoped. "You..." I glanced back. Zita had appeared from nowhere, or... "You were hiding amongst the wisteria and carvings."

She spread her painted arms and bowed. The grey dress suddenly made sense. Not drab, but camouflage. She must've gone somewhere to paint her arms and face to match before coming out here. When, though? How long had she known? *How* had she known?

"See, Bastian, I knew she was the clever one. Let us fill in the rest of the gaps. We found out about your little meeting with Cyrus's former lackey. I had hoped Katherine would've kept us informed of such things, since we're friends now, but seems she's slow to trust."

"I wonder why." I glowered at the couple, getting the distinct impression I'd played a part in someone else's game. "But how did you find out?"

"Don't you think Dawn has spies of its own? And some of them might not like the direction their new king was steering things in."

Dawn's spies had listened in on us, intercepted our messages, found out gods knew what. How deep did they have their claws in our plans?

He gave a knowing smirk. "It's good to know you enjoyed the hot springs so thoroughly."

I gasped as Bastian stiffened. "Caelus?"

Oh, gods, what a fool I'd been. I thought he liked me, so he could be trusted, but... "He was passing you information all along."

"Not the *whole* time." Zita winced. "Just once he saw what kind of king Cyrus was."

"Luckily," Sepher added, "we managed to get him to the healers before he succumbed to the beating my brother gave him."

"At least he's alive," I muttered, my guilt over getting him in trouble with Cyrus easing.

Bastian crossed his arms. "Perfect timing for me to wring his neck."

Sepher held up his hands. "If it's any consolation, your plan would never have worked. Whatever evidence they had" —he jerked his chin back towards the grand dining room—"it would never have been enough to convict a king. Not when Cyrus could worm his way out of it."

"You don't know that," Bastian gritted out.

Zita sighed and cocked her head. "But we do. If their evidence was that strong, they'd have brought it forward a month ago."

Bastian's jaw twitched, but he didn't argue.

Grimacing, I nodded slowly. "And even if it was enough,

Cyrus would've found a way to get his hands on it and destroy it at once."

Sepher gestured behind him. "Which is exactly what he did as soon as he found Krae. Sometimes, Bastian, you're too noble. Certainly too noble to outmanoeuvre my brother. For all he likes—*liked*"—he smiled with a satisfied little huff, as though speaking about Cyrus in past tense was the greatest pleasure in the world—"for all he liked to play the hero, there was not a scrap of nobility in him. He killed Adra to silence her. Did you really think a few pieces of paper would be safe?"

Bastian made a low sound of begrudging agreement. "And that would've left Krae's word against his."

I glowered. "A shapeshifter against a king. No prizes for guessing how that would've gone."

"Exactly." Sepher's tail swished in time with the syllables of the word. "So, I told him."

"*What?*" Bastian and I blurted in unison, both taking a step forward.

Again, the prince raised his hands. "Now, now, before you do anything rash. I had a plan."

"Oh, *a plan*. Bastian, don't worry, he had *a plan*."

"What a relief," he bit out, scowling at Sepher. "He'd better be about to explain that fucking plan or else we're going to have to explain why there are *two* members of Dawn's royal family dead on this balcony."

"I'm sure he will, if you would let him speak for five seconds," Zita snapped.

Bastian drew a long breath, rubbing the bridge of his nose. I clamped my jaw shut. The blood on my body suit was growing cold, but there was still too much energy surging through me to really feel the chill.

Sepher cupped the back of her head with a soothing touch.

"I needed him out of the way. He was a danger to me and the people I care about." He waved his hand vaguely. "And to the rest of society, I suppose. I knew the evidence wouldn't work so long as Cyrus could argue against it, so I needed to goad him into doing something foolish, giving you the chance to kill him in self-defence."

My stomach dipped in horrible understanding. "You used us."

Tension radiated off Bastian. His fists shook at his sides, and his shadows had gone very still.

Sepher's gaze twitched to Bastian, and his stance shifted. "'Used' is such an ugly word."

"It's the right one, though, isn't it?"

Bastian shook his head, the muscles in his jaw rippling. "How did you find out about the meeting location?"

"When the messenger came looking for Kat, I told them no one was being allowed close to her other than her friends. After what he did on the throne, they found that believable." At least Zita had the good grace to hang her head as she admitted her deceit. "So I offered to take her the message, and instead I delivered it straight to Sepher... and Cyrus. We had Justice ready, so I brought it here and hid amongst the wisteria. It took me a while to climb along the balcony and get it to you."

Sepher nodded. "We couldn't risk him seeing her."

She must've clung to the balustrade, keeping inside the safe area, so she didn't get disintegrated by the unstable sections of the veil.

Bastian surged forward and grabbed Sepher's shirt. "Couldn't risk him seeing her? You could've got Kat killed."

Sepher's tail twitched, but otherwise he stayed remarkably still. "Do you really think he would've let Kat live once he found out she'd been playing him all along? He already thought she was fucking Caelus. I had to pull him out of the dungeons half dead. *I helped you.*" His teeth flashed as he spoke in a low tone of warning. "Now she can return home to Dusk. All the guests can."

"And what about the part where I murdered a king? Did you forget about that?" I squeezed Justice's hilt, wondering if it would help me fight off the guards when they came to arrest me. Somehow, I doubted it.

"Did you?" Sepher arched one eyebrow. "You see, I thought you had a witness who could verify that Cyrus murdered our father, and then my brother lashed out, attacking the poor, defenceless human."

All true, if not the full truth.

"Luckily," Zita went on, "Sepher arrived just in time and executed him, preventing conflict with Dusk over him killing one of their hostages, *and* enacting justice. As the son of the murdered man, Sepher is well within his rights to claim the life of his killer."

"Efficient, really." Sepher smirked at Bastian, who made a low sound.

He released Sepher's shirt. "Next time you come up with such an 'efficient' plan, you can do your own dirty work."

"Except, don't you see? I couldn't." Sepher scowled at his brother's body, which lay just behind my feet. "I pledged fealty to him—it would've raised suspicion if I hadn't. It bound me so I couldn't directly harm him. I had to go to these lengths to manipulate the situation."

"And us." The adrenaline pumping around my body ebbed, leaving a deep weariness. I leant on the sword, but it had grown cold as well as still, and it seemed to sap my energy more than grant it.

He brushed the front of his shirt where Bastian's fists had

creased it. "I won't apologise for doing what needed to be done."

Bastian slipped a hand around my waist, helping steady me. "What will we say to the public?"

The question drew a smug smile from Sepher. "I have a plan for that."

48
BASTIAN

After, we found Krae clinging to the dining table.

"You've met your sibling, right?"

Sepher blinked at me.

"*Half*-sibling." Krae folded their arms. "He knows. He just doesn't care."

But Sepher's mouth hung open in a way that said he really *didn't* know. "You're... our father's..." Slowly, he approached Krae. "I thought you were just Cyrus's lackey, but you're..." He took them in, finishing on their red hair, so similar to his own. "I have a sibling... who isn't a dick... and who's also a shapechanger." Laughing, he shook his head. "I should've known as soon as I saw that hair."

Krae's brow furrowed. "I thought Cyrus told you and you just didn't... He told me, 'Sepher doesn't care for his siblings.'"

"I didn't, when I thought I only had him. Can you blame me?"

No one could.

Later, as the day inched towards sunset, we all stood on the royal balcony, with a space for Krae. They looked uncomfortable being in the limelight and had asked for their royal status to remain a secret.

Dowager Queen Meredine also joined us, freed from the tight leash Cyrus had placed upon her.

I placed a hand on the small of Kat's back. It was such a tiny gesture, and yet it felt like the entire world turning right. She was back home in Dusk, standing at my side, safe, wearing the deep, emerald green that suited her.

Everything was as it should be.

Or almost everything.

Below, the crowd stood in silence. They stared up at us, no doubt wondering when their king was going to make his dashing entrance. Would they accept their hero wasn't what he'd seemed?

I pressed my lips together to keep the wince off my face. I didn't envy Sepher the task of taking Cyrus's place when he was a shapechanger.

"People of Tenebris-Luminis, I have news. This afternoon, Elfhame shifted." He didn't smile, though I was sure he intended the pun—a reminder of what he was. "You know of my father's murder, and you have heard the accusations following it. None of that is news. But what had been hidden until today was the truth. We have all been deceived. Dusk included."

The silence slowly cracked as heads bowed together and glances were exchanged. No doubt, they wondered why Prince Sepher addressed them—he'd never done so before.

I joined him at the front of the balcony, giving a thin smile. I couldn't decide if I was furious at him for using us or if I admired his manoeuvring. We'd agreed certain parts of this would be better coming from me and other parts from Dawn.

"Krae was falsely accused, framed by the use of their dagger. They did not assassinate King Lucius." Technically true, though they'd played a part in the plot.

"And from Dusk," Sepher continued, "Kaliban was put forward as another scapegoat. But my brother took advantage of reputation and prejudice to present these two as guilty. A hero who ended a war by changing his allegiance to the right side, despite the damage it did to himself, and a shapechanger."

Hero. Not traitor. Not turncoat. Not any of the words I'd heard my fathers described as throughout my entire life.

A hero.

I couldn't speak. My throat was too thick, my chest at once too empty and too full. He was gone, but the new Day King stood here declaring him a hero.

"Get on with it, then," Sepher whispered out the corner of his mouth.

I swallowed and pulled myself together. "The deception ran deep. The attackers dyed their hair so suspicion would fall upon Dusk."

Sepher threw me a glance, brow furrowing. He hadn't known that piece of the puzzle.

"However," I went on, "the true killer stood in plain sight all the while, pointing fingers so he would avoid detection."

The noise below rose, a wave rushing in.

Nodding, Sepher took up the explanation. "Your king was murdered by his own son—my brother, Cyrus."

The wave broke. Hundreds of questions added up to a roar below.

If this went wrong, I would take Katherine and flee. Albion would be safer for her than Elfhame. Though further would be better—I was sure her sister would grant us sanctuary.

Gradually the noise died down enough for Sepher to continue, but some still shouted out, demanding answers. "As Lucius's son, I had the right and duty to execute Cyrus. The sword Justice confirmed the righteousness of his death—it allowed itself to be wielded to take his life."

The shouts petered out. Perhaps even more so with the fresh reminder of the recent public executions. The people trusted in Justice. When our own judgement failed us, blinded by rumour and reputation or simply by a lack of evidence, the threads of magic and fate that moved Justice bent towards the truth.

Behind us, there were whispers. "I heard the only one seen with him on the balcony was the human." That sounded like Mored.

"Even if it was her, she used the sword." Lucan's tones were unmistakable. "It was a just death."

"I'm just glad that paranoid fool is out of the way," Deema muttered. "He saw enemies everywhere—how long before he looked at you and saw one?"

With relief, I lifted my chin and my voice, "Therefore, I present to you King Sepher."

Below, quiet reigned once more, shot through with questioning glances.

"Long live King Sepher," someone shouted.

"King Sepher," another voice rose. Bit by bit, the cry spread.

The cheers were perhaps less enthusiastic compared to the ones that had welcomed Cyrus as king, but I would give them time. With a little luck, they would realise the same thing the Convocation members had. Cyrus had looked and acted the part of the heroic kings of old, but it was merely a gloss for aspirations to paranoid tyranny.

Sepher's first order as king was to announce an end to

several of his brother's laws, particularly those against shapechangers, and his second was to formally return the guests to their respective courts. Once all but Kat had crossed the balcony and left through the doors to their home courts, Sepher dismissed everyone.

There was a collective exhale on the balcony. I suspected the same thing happened in the crowd below.

Kat and I caught Sepher and Zita near the door to Dawn.

"Bastian." Sepher nodded, stiff in a way that didn't suit him. "That went better than I expected. I was waiting for someone to throw rotten cabbages at their shapechanger king."

Kat raised one shoulder. "They weren't forewarned—throwing cabbages requires planning."

His brow and shoulders sank as he made a low sound.

I cleared my throat, interrupting their snark before it could escalate. "There was mention of Kat being seen with him on the balcony," I murmured.

She swallowed, paling.

"Someone in the city could have spotted her." Sepher waved a hand. "But they won't question our version of events too closely—they'll be too glad of the outcome."

"That's easy for you to say," she hissed at him.

But I had to admit, the faces filing out of the doors to Dusk and Dawn seemed more relaxed than I'd seen them in weeks, and the mood in the square seemed far less tense than it had after he'd presented his laws.

I stroked Kat's back and nodded towards the guards chatting and laughing. "What do you see? Do any of them look like they're angling to arrest you?"

Her scowl shifted from Sepher to them, then to Tor and Galiene as they filed past us with smiles, wishing us goodbye.

Her ability to understand people had allowed her to see too much of me sometimes, but I hoped she'd use it for her own good now.

The tight muscles under my hand softened as she exhaled. "Not right this second, no."

Zita returned from speaking with the king's new assistant, and pointed over her shoulder. "The sun's about to set."

Sepher stared at her for a long moment before he groaned. "And I care about this now because I'm the idiot who made himself king." He looped an arm around her shoulder. "I'll see you later. Try not to have too much fun while I'm forced into Sleep." As he walked away, he grumbled to Zita, "I suppose this is my life now."

Once they were gone, Kat elbowed me, eyes wide. "Did you hear that? He sounds... *resigned* to the Sleep."

Steering her towards Dusk and beyond grateful for it, I shook my head. "Why do I feel like I'm missing something?"

We stepped through the lodestone, and I let out a breath. I'd been using lodestones all my life, but part of me had feared she was going to disappear as we went through this one or that I'd wake up and find out getting her back had all been a wishful dream.

But she was still here and looking up at me with a sly smile. "It means Sepher doesn't realise he has a choice. He doesn't know about the Crown."

49

KAT

When I walked into our suite—the real one where we lived together in Dusk, not Dawn's not-quite-copy—I burst into tears.

It was silly. There was no practical purpose. It was only a place.

And yet it was *our* place. The only one where I'd felt at home, save for his arms, which came around me now. Without a word, he picked me up and carried me to the armchair by the fire, letting me nestle into his lap.

All the weeks of staying strong and hiding what I really felt fell away as he stroked my hair and kissed the top of my head. I wasn't a spy or the king's "pretty little thing" or a hostage. For a moment, a blessed moment, I was just Kat.

He held that space around me, silent and still and warm, until I stopped shaking and my tears ran dry.

"I'm sorry. I'm so silly. I'm not sad, I just..." My apology faltered when faced with his raised eyebrows.

Once he had my attention, he swept my cheek dry with the

pad of his thumb. "You know there's no need to apologise, don't you?"

Slowly, I inclined my head. He'd never wanted me to make myself smaller, easier to consume. That included my feelings.

He kissed away the tears on my other cheek. "And you know your feelings aren't silly, right?"

I frowned. "Aren't they? I'm finally home and the first thing I do is cry."

"Is that a reaction to being home? Or is it the response to everything you've had to do and live through in the past month?"

Eyes burning all over again, I looked up at him. "It's just... now I'm safe to finally show that response."

"You are," he whispered as fresh tears spilled. "*You are.*"

I took my time in that quiet space. He didn't rush off to report to the queen, but when I'd calmed and spotted it was past sunset, I sent him to report to the queen. He hesitated until I insisted I was fine and had plans of my own.

"Tired of me already? Oh dear," he teased as I shoved him towards the door.

I hurried to change for an appointment that was long overdue.

THE STABLE YARD was lit by lanterns—the fae lights here were prone to hiding amongst the straw if left free, so they had to be contained.

I tugged at my sleeves. My old highwaywoman clothes were comfortable and practical, though something about them didn't fit right anymore. They weren't exactly tight or too loose, just... not right in a way I couldn't put my finger on.

But that didn't matter, because a black head reached over the stable door of the large stall in the corner. Vespera huffed the air and I ran to her.

I tripped over myself to get the stable door open and fling my arms around her neck. "My beauty. My darling girl."

She made a chuffing sound of greeting that blew my hair and almost knocked me over in her excitement.

"Yes, I'm here. I'm sorry. I never wanted to leave you." I would've cried, but there was nothing left in me, just sore eyes and an ache at the back of my throat.

But I needn't have worried she'd be grumpy about me abandoning her. A quick scratch behind her ear and I had her rumbling in a contented purr.

I settled into my old routine of grooming her. Brushes for her fur. A damp cloth for her eyes and nose, which she wriggled away from as if to tell me, "I *like* having sleep in the corner of my eye, *thankyouverymuch!*" But I prevailed and even managed to get her to let me clean her claws and check her ears.

For a long while, just the business of grooming and being in her quiet presence was enough to occupy me, but my mind eventually turned to this new world I found myself in tonight.

As the new king, Sepher *seemed* more interested in living his life than gathering power or searching for the Crown of Ashes. But seeming wasn't always truth. He'd manipulated us into killing his brother. Was that really for justice and the safety of those he held dear, like Zita and Celestine? Or was it so he could take the throne?

Had we traded in one would-be tyrant for another?

Vespera butted her great head into me—a reminder the

chin scratches had stopped. "I'm so sorry, mistress. How neglectful of me." As I worked my nails through her thick fur, she watched me, eyes half shut. Her purring deepened as her eyes closed, the picture of contentment.

Whatever Sepher's plans and motivations, we'd won ourselves a moment of peace. It might last an evening or a year.

However long, I intended to make the most of it.

When I returned to our suite, pinching myself at the fact I could just walk into Dusk's side of the palace without guards stopping me, I found Bastian already there. He had the fire lit and the lights low, and as soon as I walked in the door, he was on me with an engulfing hug.

Maybe he expected me to cry again. I almost did when he produced the orrery and the moth-hilted dagger, both of which had been taken when I'd arrived in Dawn. "How did you—?"

"My spy retrieved them. I need to give her a raise."

"You do." I slid the dagger into my belt and squeezed the orrery. "I thought I'd lost it."

"You can't lose it, just like you can't lose me." He buried his face in the crook between my neck and shoulder and took a long breath. "My gods, you smell so good."

"You're joking, right?" I pushed his chest and wriggled out of his grasp. "I'm all sweaty from grooming Vespera. I need a shower."

"No, no." He advanced as I backed away. "It's good. You smell of *you*."

When my back hit the wall, I could've twisted out of reach, but I found I didn't want to escape anymore. Not when he'd just said something so delightfully foolish. "And you... like that?"

His hands landed on the wall either side of my head as he entered my space. "I've missed it. And this." He cupped my cheeks, wiping away the smear of dust I'd spotted in the antechamber mirror and intended to clean off in the shower.

His touch trailed down over me, firm, unhurried, making me forget my exhaustion, replacing it with stirring desire that made my back arch. "And this, I missed *this*." He pressed against me, crushing me against the wall.

I couldn't help the little sound of want I made as I looped my thighs around him, letting him take my weight.

He answered with a groan as his growing hardness made contact with my centre through the infuriating thickness of our clothing. "And, Stars above did I miss these." He gripped my thighs and pulled into them, wrenching a soft cry from me as the pressure hit exactly the right spot.

"You do remember," I panted, rocking against him, "we fucked twice while I was in Dawn, don't you?"

"Yes," he breathed against my ear before pulling back to look me in the eye. "But it isn't just making love to you that I missed. It's knowing you're here... you're safe. Getting to do this and not having to rush or keep half my focus on listening for anyone approaching." He planted a languorous kiss on my mouth.

His lips toyed with mine, a back and forth where he led, then I did. I could feel his focus on it, the stroke of his hands on my thighs, the press of his body slotted perfectly against me. His attention was entirely mine.

I was breathless when he pulled back, just far enough to

rest the bridge of his nose against mine. Eyes screwed shut, he went on. "The fact that tonight I'll be able to reach out when I wake up and find you instead of the empty space where you are meant to be. I can't wait to go to bed just to be able to do that." He opened his eyes and locked his gaze with mine. "I swear for the rest of my days, I will never take that for granted."

"The rest of your days?" Hearing him say that did strange things to my stomach. Good things. The kind of things the old Kat had given up believing in. But that maybe...

No. Not maybe. *Definitely* the kind of things that I had here with him.

"Every single one of them, if you'll keep me that long."

"I will keep you, Bastian. *Always.*"

He laughed into the thin air between us and fell upon me again.

This kiss started languid and unhurried, but somewhere between my hips grinding into his and his tongue teasing mine, it built into something faster, hotter, needier. A desperation to prove that we were reunited. We tugged at each other's clothing, hearts racing together, breaths merging.

Someone cleared their throat.

"I told you we should give them some space." Ella's voice filled the room.

I jumped, thwacking my head on the wall. Bastian kept me upright, but he stared at the doorway.

There stood Ella, Rose, Faolán, Perry, Asher, Ariadne, and Lysander, all wearing expressions in varying states of shock, awkwardness, or amusement.

"Let's leave them to it," Rose said with a chuckle, turning.

I held up my hand. "No, stay, we'll... uh..." Rubbing the back of my head, I let Bastian put me down and straighten my shirt.

"Right," he said as he worked. "Of course. You haven't seen Kat properly in a long while, either."

I refastened the buttons I'd managed to get undone. We gave each other a once over to check we were both decent and nodded before stepping apart.

There were some awkward laughs as I hugged Ari, Lysander, and Asher, but I squeezed my friends close. Faolán's hug almost suffocated me. "Well done," he muttered gruffly.

For a moment, my eyes burned at what was high praise coming from him. It was too much like Kaliban saying he was proud of me, and that was something he'd never say again. I cleared my throat and nodded as we pulled apart. "Thank *you* for keeping him sane." There was no doubt in my mind that the extra sparring with Faolán had stopped Bastian doing something truly foolish.

"He's not so bad... once you know how to manage him." He flashed a grin before Rose elbowed him out the way and threw her arms around me.

"Stop hogging her!" She squeezed, almost as strong as Faolán, and I huffed out the breath I'd only just caught. "You were fucking fantastic. At the ball—I don't know how you let him..." She clasped my cheeks, checking me over, then shook her head. The shadows under her eyes seemed at odds with the pretty flush of her cheeks.

"Are you all right? You look tired."

She laughed and swatted off my concern. "Have you gone to the Cyrus school of compliments?"

"Oh, gods, sorry, no I didn't mean—"

"You're taking too long. It's my turn." Ella swept in.

I held her close. "Thank you. *Thank you.*"

Her chuckle shook into me as she refused to let go. "For what, exactly?"

"*Everything.*" I arched back enough to look her in the face. "You played your part to perfection. In Dawn, they were still talking about our fight just yesterday. And that vial of whatever it was..." I exhaled shakily. "It saved me."

"No. *You* saved yourself. Without quick thinking, the tools don't matter. You held your nerve and used everything you could get your hands on. I'm just relieved you're home."

"Me too." I eased from her embrace and found Perry waiting patiently.

She opened her arms and let me walk into them. There was a strong stillness to her hug. She didn't squash me, she just held on. "And how are you?" she murmured into that stillness, while the others chattered, high on excitement.

"I'm fine." It came out without thought, but it wasn't true.

"Hmm?" It was a doubting sound. A fishing sound, like she knew there was more.

"Or... well... I'm not sure I know."

She nodded and stroked my back. "It might take you a while to process and work that out. Days, weeks, maybe even months. Especially as you probably need to convince yourself that you really are safely home again." Pulling back, she gave me a comforting smile. "Just know that's all normal. And if you need to speak to anyone about it, you have us."

I did.

We spent some time in the living room, catching up, drinking tea and brandy, enjoying that we were back together at last. Ari reassured us Amaya and shapechangers who'd fled the city during Cyrus's rule were getting on well at their estate, and Lysander grumbled that the place was getting crowded with so many refugees. But he grinned at Bastian after he said it.

I noted all the decor in the room had changed and got the

full story of how Bastian had destroyed it, complete with dramatic reenactment from Rose. Here, now, with this distance from it all, we laughed until we had to rub our aching cheeks and stomachs.

And once we were done with laughter, we fell quiet and raised our glasses to Kaliban and the others taken by Cyrus. I caught Bastian's eye and we both mouthed Sura's name, too.

It was approaching midnight by the time everyone left, and when I turned from waving them off down the corridor, I found Bastian watching me, a half smile on his face. "Now, where were we?" He stalked closer, backing me up against the wall. "Hmm, yes, this feels familiar."

"I think it was more like this." Planting a kiss on his lips, I looped my arms around his neck and my legs around his waist.

Just as we were rediscovering the breathless place we'd been when the others had arrived there was a rap at the door. "Ignore it," he muttered against my lips.

I obeyed and tugged on his hair so there was no room left to talk.

Another rap. "Summons from Her Majesty."

He groaned, and I sighed. "I don't think you can ignore that."

"Good fucking gods," he growled into my hair, making me shiver. "Do I need to murder everyone else in the world just so we can have some time alone?"

"Now *there's* an idea." But instead of shedding blood, I released him and waved him away before finally getting that shower.

50

BASTIAN

A week flew by, lost in meetings. *Yet another* new king to liaise with meant more Convocation meetings and more of Braea's summons. Shapechangers who'd left the city returned, and some found other fae had simply taken over their homes, so I got dragged into that as well as a public burning of Cyrus's register.

My days disappeared in work, when really I wanted to lose them with Kat now she was home.

But in the background, I worked on another problem, weighing up information, digging up a little more here and there, until I was sure. Next, I had to calculate the best approach—this matter required a delicate hand—and wait for the perfect opportunity to arise.

On a sunny afternoon, a message arrived, alerting me to just that.

I strolled up behind him, like this was nothing more than a relaxed walk. "Caelus."

He blinked up at me, slapping shut the book he'd been

drawing in. There were no signs of injury from Cyrus's beating —Elthea had healed him well. His hair glistened in the sun as he ran a hand through it. "I didn't think the Night Queen's Shadow had time for walks in the gardens."

I bit back a laugh, not wanting to show my hand too soon. "Join me." I gestured ahead like this was a request rather than a barely veiled order.

He cocked his head, a faint frown creasing his brow, but he fell into step beside me. In silence I steered us towards a pair of gushing fountains in the form of a stag and a rearing hind. The noise would cover our words.

He watched with a bemused smile as I leant against the fountain's edge. "Is something wrong? Is it Kat? Do you need—?"

"I always wondered who Dawn's spymaster was."

He fell stone still for a beat, then slowly, he straightened, eyes narrowing, sharpening, shoulders pulling back like he was ready and not the relaxed man he'd been a moment before. Just those few changes made him look like a different person—the kind of person who could be a spymaster, rather than merely a member of court known for being good-looking and... *nice.*

The man who stood before me was keen like a knife, calculating, and far more clever than I'd given him credit for.

He watched me for a beat longer, then sighed and took the spot next to me. "What gave me away?"

"You know how it is—it's never just one thing." I shrugged, watching as a wren bobbed past, disturbed by our presence. "Sepher named you as his source for uncovering our plot with Krae."

"*Hmph.* He never could resist boasting."

"You know what his vanity is like. And after hearing that, other things clicked into place." I eyed him sidelong. "You were sent to Albion not to marry their queen, but just as I was—to spy on them... and me."

He cracked a smile and met my gaze out the corner of his eye. "Just as you spied on me."

In some ways it was like looking in a mirror, but one that reversed things. He wore a friendly exterior and hid in its shadows. While I wore shadows and hid the gentler parts of myself behind them.

"I *did* break into your rooms," I conceded.

"Oh." His gaze went distant. "*Ooh.* So that's why Katherine intercepted me in the corridor and flirted so damn well when I thought she only had eyes for you." He chuckled, shaking his head. "Well played, Marwood."

"Then *you* kept hanging around her to get information about me."

"I knew she would be a way to get to you. The way you looked at her in Albion, I'm shocked it took you so long to realise how you felt. But it wasn't only that." He pressed his lips together. "There is something intoxicating about her. Maybe it's as simple as the red hair... maybe it's the idea of seeing her unleashed at last. I know that's an appeal you understand."

I huffed at the fact I'd been so transparent even back then. "So that's why you went to her as soon as she arrived in Dawn —you do care about her. She feels bad about using you, you know. And about Cyrus hurting you."

"I know. She came to visit and see if I was all right... as well as giving me a few choice words about telling Sepher your secrets." He shrugged, mouth twisting. "That's exactly why she needn't feel bad. It was mutual gain, like in the hot springs. I enjoyed watching you two, just as you enjoyed being watched."

For a long while, there was only the splash of the fountains as I let my thoughts drift back to that evening. I suspected Caelus's went in the same direction. "What I can't work out is... why help Sepher and not your king?"

Caelus made a dark sound, a glower darkening his face. "For the same reasons you wouldn't have served him in my position. He was a prick."

I chuckled and nodded. "Entirely fair assessment."

"His goals and methods"—he shook his head—"no. I couldn't. And when I saw the way he treated Katherine, I was afraid for her. I care about my court. But I also care about her. Helping Sepher work against Cyrus worked for both agendas."

Like it was straightforward. Then again, Cyrus hadn't lifted him from nothing. Caelus hadn't sacrificed too much of himself, of his time, of those he cared for in service of King Cyrus.

"I knew the risks," he went on, "and thankfully I avoided the worst of them."

I let out a long breath, shoulders sinking. "Well, I'm grateful for it, and she is too."

"And, for what it's worth..." He faced me fully, eyebrows pinched. "I didn't know there was a changeling in Lunden. I've heard how things escalated with him, and I would never have allowed that."

He seemed annoyed it had been allowed without his knowledge. I couldn't blame him.

"I know Cyrus sent him."

"Exactly why I couldn't trust him to rule."

We both sighed in shared relief that we were free of him. The fountains soothed me as a blackbird started its song.

"So, what now?" Caelus gripped the fountain's edge. "Has the Shadow come to kill off his rival?"

"Do you think you'd see me if I was trying to kill you?"

He smirked. "Do you think you could catch me?"

"You can relax. There's been enough killing lately. Besides, another spymaster would only come along and replace you. You've served your court well. I like to think I serve mine. How about we keep doing that? And maybe once in a while we can use that shared drop point for the good of all Elfhame." I rose and held out my hand.

He looked at it for a moment, then stood. "And for those we care about."

On that, we shook hands.

51

KAT

As I returned to our suite and found no sign of Bastian for the tenth day in a row, I had to wonder if Braea was deliberately keeping him away from me. There had been more summons from her in the hours of darkness, and during the day, he seemed to be constantly busy. Maybe I was just being paranoid.

Maybe.

I didn't escape the queen's demands, either. After Cyrus's death, I had written a report of my time in Dawn and had a full debriefing that lasted a couple of days. Faolán joined Bastian and me for that, so it didn't end up in a different kind of debriefing. (Ella would be so proud of that one.)

It hadn't ended there, though. In the weeks since, I'd been ordered to re-write my report and add to it more times than I could recall. I was sick of the sight of the damn thing.

Then there were the more pleasant demands. We had a lot of social invitations, including a trip to Ari and Lysander's estate.

It was a special kind of privilege to know I'd been missed, but all together, it felt like we barely found five minutes to be alone.

I, however, found myself alone in our suite, without Bastian, when there was a knock at the door. I looked up from the report I was adding an addendum to—gaps weren't allowed, according to Her Majesty's feedback after my fifth version. A guard brought in a parcel from Zita.

In their takeover, they hadn't yet found the mirror, but she had come across Ella's lock picks. I hadn't seen them since I'd killed Uncle Rufus, and for a long while I just stared at them.

These little pieces of metal had saved my life.

I ran my thumb along the edges, finding a sharp area of damage on the handle of one. Must've been from our confrontation in the bathroom. I'd lost track of the picks in the chaos, but now I had them back, I could repair and return them to Ella. Remembering Bastian had files in his workroom, I headed inside to search.

The place had been tidied since I'd last been in here. Most of the projects had disappeared. But at the centre of the table sat a flat, bark covered block. The wooden tablet Sepher had given Bastian. He'd told me about it, but I'd been so busy since returning to Dusk, it had slipped my mind.

The bark definitely formed the shape of a flaming crown. I turned it over, searching every side, but that was the only symbol I could pick out. It had to relate to the Crown of Ashes, but how, exactly?

"What secrets are you hiding?"

The gauntlet sounded like a place, perhaps in or leading to the Underworld—"the world beneath"—certainly not an object. What if it was a map showing the location? I squinted at the craggy bark. Nothing but organic shapes.

Then there was "the anointed one"—whoever that was. "We'll need them to enter the gauntlet," I sighed. "And 'It can only be found after shedding skin.'"

I straightened. "Wait. Bark is a tree's skin, right?" I ran my hand over the rough surface. "Is there something underneath this?"

It was a piece of wood, of course it didn't answer, but...

I reached for Bastian's tools.

Minutes later I was hunched over the workbench, surrounded by the resinous scent of raw wood and little heaps of bark that I'd painstakingly peeled away. The piles grew as I worked, and my breath caught as it revealed lines. Not rings like a tree normally had, but—

"What the hells are you doing?" Bastian stood in the doorway, eyes bulging. "We'll never be able to fix—"

"Look." I held it up. "There's writing underneath."

His mouth hung open mid-word as he covered the space between us in two strides and stared at the few letters I'd uncovered. "Stars above, there is." He pushed it back into my hands and grabbed another knife like the narrow one I was using. Together, we chipped away from the edges, finally meeting in the middle.

"'The way is through the trees,'" I read out. "The gauntlet. Has to be. That's a route somewhere, right?"

"So, a forest? Lucky we don't have a country that's covered in them. Oh, wait." He flashed a sardonic grin. "Let's see if there's anything on the back."

"Or the sides," I added.

But there were no more words, just the mingled wood of two trees—one a light brown, the other a darker, warmer colour.

I huffed my frustration. "I thought there'd be more of a clue than that. Maybe if we speak to the others, they'll have some ideas. There has to be something we're missing." I held up the tablet, tilting it in the light. "A hidden code or secret text or *something*."

"No, I think it is only the message. We have to work out what it means. It's not just any old tree." He frowned at the writing, brow crinkling in this way that made me want to kiss it. He took a sharp breath, bolting upright. "What if it's the Great Trees? This is yew and oak wood that's grown together."

My mouth dropped open. If that was true—

"It's just a theory, but what if Sura came here not for some last piece of information but to enter the gauntlet itself?" He gave a short laugh of disbelief.

I squeezed the wood. "That would mean the path to the Crown has been here all along."

As soon as I mentioned the Crown, he blanched. "No. Kat. Wait." He caught my hands and lowered the tablet to the workbench. "What are we doing? We're not meant to be searching for the Crown. The longer that thing stays hidden, the better. I just need the queen to *think* I'm looking for it."

I squeezed it tighter. "So you're lying to her."

"I can't—"

"I know. Not a lie, but you *are* deceiving her. You don't trust her anymore, do you?"

He went still. He didn't even breathe. Slowly, he swallowed and straightened, a wall growing higher. "The Crown is too dangerous for anyone to wield. No one can be trusted with it, so no one should have it."

"I would trust you with it."

He laughed, a bitter, spiked thing. "Me? Who is going to follow me? I may be Nyx's child, but I still killed my father and I'm the son of traitors. Not to mention half unseelie."

"The people look to you already. When Cyrus put forward his register, they *all* turned to you for guidance—for leadership."

"That was just a matter of practicality. I was the only person who could do anything to soften his foolishness."

"And when they saw what Cyrus had done to your *athair*— was that practical? Who did they want to serve? Who inspired them to act against the king? You. All of it was for *you*."

He opened his mouth, undoubtedly to argue, but I charged on.

"They love you. Perhaps not in the way they've loved Braea or Cyrus, but they see parts of you and they love you for it. They see that you've sacrificed for them, risked for them, acted for them, *always*, and they love you for it. If you let them see more, then I know they'll love you even more."

He pressed his lips together, glaring at the wooden tablet. "They don't love me. They fear and respect the Serpent of Tenebris. There's a difference."

"Perhaps that was true, before, but since Cyrus took the throne, you've shown yourself as the voice of reason. They know everything that tempered his harshness was down to you. *Now*, I think they love and respect you."

"Kat, it's you they love. The flame-haired woman who had the courage to kill her abusive husband... and who's rumoured to have killed a villainous king. They love *you*, and I just happen to be the lucky bastard at your side."

"Then I will help them learn to love you."

He turned away, shaking his head with a heavy exhale.

A thick silence opened between us, but I couldn't help turning over the fact his objections had all related to his own suitability. Nothing about Braea.

"So you won't reveal who you are. What if the queen dies? What happens then?"

"A fucking disaster, that's what. She has no heir, only distant cousins, of which Asher is the closest. Without a clear line of descent, it would be... messy. A civil war we can't afford."

"No, what you can't afford is for her to remain in power."

He whirled on his heels. "What are you saying?"

"You ask her. Whose arrows killed your mother? What's the 'infernal book' Kaliban hated so much? Why did she keep insisting you prioritise the Crown of Ashes when people were dying? She's left a lot of unanswered questions, but I will tell you one thing with certainty. She let Cyrus abuse his position just so she could look reasonable in comparison. She let people die under the pretext of not rocking the boat. Bastian, these two courts are not a fucking boat—they're a cobbled together raft that's going to sink before it finds dry land."

Eyes round, jaw slack, he looked stricken. "You want to get rid of Braea." He whispered it like he barely dared say the words out loud.

"Don't you?"

His hands raked through his hair like he couldn't stay still. "That isn't... *No.* I don't. Kat, I don't think you understand. You've only seen me since..." He huffed and shook his head. "I grew up in the stable quarters with a name marred by two turncoat fathers. Braea saw something in me. She gave me a chance in her Queensguard—a chance many said I'd *never* get because I was destined to only ever be another Marwood traitor. *She* lifted me to that honour—one I hadn't dared to dream of. And then after Sura… she elevated me even higher. Now, I have money and a much more comfortable life, yes, but, more importantly, I have the power to act, to keep my people safe and the courts at peace. All thanks to her. Everything I am is because of her."

"No, it's because of *you*." My chest ached as I stared at him, desperate to make him understand. "It's your actions that put you here. She only gave you what you always deserved."

His jaw worked side to side before he yanked a drawer open and tossed the tools in, ignoring their allocated sections. "You don't understand how Elfhame works. Even *if* what you're saying about Braea is right, we do not need more instability right now. We need peace and calm and a moment without a throne changing hands for *five fucking minutes*."

I clenched my jaw like that would help me stay together when all I wanted to do was burst. He was wrong. Absolutely fucking wrong. And yet I couldn't persuade him.

It was too soon. We were still too close to Cyrus's death and Lucius's before that. I would try again in a couple of months. He would listen then.

He glanced at the window, harsh lines carved between his eyebrows as though they'd been gouged with the knives we'd used on the tablet. "The sun's setting. I need to go and brief the queen."

He strode for the door, and I'd never seen him in such a hurry to leave my presence. Almost outside, he pulled up short and gripped the doorframe. He didn't quite look over his shoulder, just to the side, casting his face in profile against the darkened hallway beyond. "I love you," he murmured as though unwilling to leave on harsh words.

It eased my heart a little, but the deeper ache was still

there. My eyes burned as I looked at the one I loved so dearly. "And I love you. I just... I wish you saw yourself as I do."

He made a soft sound, then disappeared, leaving me alone.

What if he didn't just need time? What if he never let go of Braea and all he'd done in her service? Could we live around that wrong or would we just be surviving?

Outside, the sky darkened.

BASTIAN CAME to bed late that night, slipping between the sheets without calling for the lights to come on. "Are you awake?" he asked softly.

I'd been lying there awake for hours, unable to shake off my fears after our argument. "Mm-hmm."

"About earlier. I hated leaving you on that note. I... I hated almost everything about that conversation, in fact."

I reached out, placing my hand on his chest. The warm point of contact soothed a little of my anxiety, and when he covered my hand with his, it helped even more.

"I... I can see why you might think... *that* about Braea." He spoke haltingly, rather than with his usual smooth confidence.

It made me keep quiet where I might've spoken to comfort him or joked to ease the tension, but I didn't want to interrupt whatever battle he was working through in order to say these words.

"I admit, I've found myself questioning her since she let Cyrus take you and finding out about my mother. I don't trust her... not with Amaya or with my identity. And I've noticed she turns questions back on me. Whenever I confront her, somehow she manages to deflect blame elsewhere."

I could picture it. He'd question her about me going to Dawn or Kaliban being arrested, and she'd make it his fault. It sickened me.

"She killed my mother. I accept it now. Sura wasn't twisting things to justify her actions. Braea really did it."

My eyes burned as I looked up into the darkness. The pain in his voice pierced my heart. This was all so hard on him. Yet he'd started to see through Braea's manipulations.

"But," he went on, "what I think or feel doesn't matter. I have no choice. It would be selfish of me to pick anything or anyone else. I must think of my people. She is queen and I've committed too much to that and to her to turn my back now. She isn't perfect, but she's what we have."

My mouth dropped open, but I couldn't speak—there was too much inside me and no one thing could get out. Was that what he really thought? She was the only option? He mattered so little?

"She's made the hard decisions and become the Night Queen rather than the mother, the person... Braea. Your own feelings and desires don't matter when you're running a country. It's the same as me killing my father for something bigger than myself."

I hated the way it sounded like he was trying to convince himself—and succeeding.

He stroked the back of my hand. "What I have to remember and you need to understand is, she's always done it all to keep stability for Elfhame."

To keep stability or to keep power? With Nyx and Sura dead, no one could challenge her. Kaliban had lost Bastian as a son rather than risk her uncovering the truth. He had believed Nyx's fears that Braea would kill him if she knew. Even Bastian admitted he didn't trust her with Amaya.

Her lack of heir kept her safe.

"I admit, she's a hard person, sometimes. But I hope that as you get to know her, you'll understand why she is the way she is."

In the darkness, I waited, but he said nothing more.

He'd come so close to admitting Braea was a danger to anyone who got in her way—him, me, and every single person in Elfhame included. Yet he'd walked himself back from that precipice and had tried to talk me away from the edge too.

I'd been wrong. Elfhame wasn't clinging to a raft, desperate to survive.

Bastian was. He'd piled everything on it, his soul included, torn up into little pieces, one given for each life he'd taken, every person he'd tortured, the countless ways he'd used others in service of Braea.

After all, hadn't he used me in an attempt to flush out Dawn's spy in Albion? I was not the first. In Bastian's list of betrayals, I probably wasn't even the worst.

The problem was, the raft Bastian had been clinging onto for the past fifteen years was his queen.

How on earth could I compete with that?

52

BASTIAN

I barely slept. Kat's accusations were thunder in my thoughts, and I hated arguing with her, so I argued in my mind instead. All night long.

No surprise, we were subdued the next morning, both dragging ourselves from bed before dawn. I suspected she did it for the same reason as me—she couldn't sleep, so lying there felt pointless.

I was mentally pulling together some of my arguments from the night so I could explain them to Kat and make her understand, when a messenger arrived with a note from Braea.

She wanted to meet me early for our handover. I groaned, too tired to bite it back.

"What's wrong?" Kat was at my side at once, so concerned, it gripped my heart.

What had I done in life to deserve the care of such a person?

"Just an earlier summons than I was expecting. Which

means a longer meeting." I flashed her the note along with a reassuring smile. "No one's died."

But Kat's face dropped like someone had.

"What—?"

She snatched the edge of the paper, taking another look at it. "This... is this Braea's writing? Or her assistant's?"

"Braea wrote it."

"This... I think it's the same writing as the letter Cyrus had —the one encouraging him to take the throne."

I flinched. "What? *No.*"

No. Because if that was true...

I snapped, "Why would she want Cyrus to act against his father?"

"I don't know. To make herself look good in comparison? Or maybe she thought he'd be easier to overthrow once she got hold of the Crown?"

My heart thumped, loud and hard like it was preparing for battle. Everything around me was crumbling. "No. That's..."

If that was true, then I'd been living a lie. If that was true, then what had I killed my father for?

It couldn't be.

I clad myself in the cool, calm exterior of the Serpent of Tenebris.

I wasn't going to fight with Kat. Not again. "It's an interesting idea, and I appreciate you looking out for Elfhame, but a silly little note proves nothing, especially as we can't compare it to the letter to Cyrus." I tossed the message on the fire— something Cyrus should've done with anything he wanted to keep secret—and left for my meeting with Braea.

It felt a lot like running away.

I LISTENED to Braea's updates and orders. A lot of busy work and nothing truly important. But in my head I only heard Kat's voice.

All night it had needled me, and as we approached dawn, I still couldn't bloody well escape it. Even reminding myself of my job, my persona, Bastian's personal concerns still gnawed on me.

Finally, Braea handed over a list of books from Dawn Court that might relate to the Crown and asked me to request them, since Kat and I were on good terms with Sepher—his manipulations aside.

I looked at the list. It was long, and many of the volumes seemed, at best, tangentially related to the Crown of Ashes. She was grasping at straws.

"Why do you want the Crown?"

She blinked at me, eyebrows raising.

"I thought you just wanted to keep it out of Cyrus's hands, since he was pursuing it. As best we can tell, Sepher doesn't even know of its existence. So why are you still after it?"

She opened and closed her mouth three times.

I'd never seen her speechless before. It felt like the world was tipping over so slowly I almost didn't notice until I started falling with it.

"And Sura. What happened? Because she wasn't fighting when you killed her—she was cuffed in iron. Helpless." The words spilled out, a glass toppling over as everything else fell. More questions came, so quickly I could barely keep up. "And Nyx? How did she die, exactly? Whose arrows shot her off that bridge? You always made it sound like the unseelie attacker was guilty, but I heard it was you."

If she admitted the truth, would that make it better?

"Why did you finally agree to try and help the shapechangers? For their sake as your people? Or to appease me? And why *didn't* you help my *athair*? Even though I practically begged you to free him. How many times have I asked you for something personal like that? Yet still you insisted on conceding to Cyrus. *Why*? And what geas did you place on Kaliban to stop him talking?"

Leaving him to Cyrus's mercy, I could understand if she truly thought he was guilty.

But there was one thing I couldn't shake off or explain away. One question she had never really answered.

"Did Cyrus request Kat as a guest, or did you offer her?"

Her eyelids fluttered as she pulled back.

"Because the way I see it, if Cyrus asked for her, you could've negotiated. You could've offered someone else. *Me.* Think of what I could've done in Dawn—the information I might've been able to pry out. But instead you let a human who barely knows our ways walk in there—a fucking lamb to slaughter."

"She's hardly an innocent."

My blood boiled. "Braea." I'd never said her name in warning before, and it stilled her.

Slowly, she approached, brow furrowed. "What has got into you?" She reached for my shoulder, but I twisted from reach.

"No. I need you to answer me." I hated that it was a need. I hated that I trembled and had to clench my fists to stop it. I hated that my world felt like it was cracking and I had no power to hold it together. "Just one answer. Pick any of those questions and give me a proper fucking answer."

With a sigh, she turned and paced away. "Your father. I did place a geas upon him. Something he couldn't speak of."

Not the question I thought she would choose.

At one of the high windows that looked out over Tenebris, she stood with her back to me and leant against the frame as though she was too tired to hold herself upright a moment longer. "Back when he was fighting for the other side and some called me a pretender to the throne. Those days feel like a dream, they're so long ago."

I knew she was millennia old, but it had always been an abstract idea I couldn't quite grasp. Yet now, she looked and sounded every one of those years.

"The war had been raging for so long and so many were dead. I wanted the throne, yes, but most of all, I was desperate for it to end. You know"—she half turned—"I was the first person to suggest it might end us. Not sure I ever told you that."

She hadn't, though it was an idea that troubled me more days than I cared to admit.

"A book was brought to me. Some old, old fae—old enough to call me 'child'—appeared in our camp one evening, just as the sun was setting. I took the timing as a good omen. But then I saw what he carried. A book of infernal magic—rituals from the time before the unseelie were banished, when magic was wilder and needed to be tamed with spells and incantations."

One thing my *athair* had been able to say was "her infernal book"—I'd assumed it was his way of cursing the thing, not an actual text from the age of myth.

"There was a spell inside that allowed the caster to create huge beasts that could be set upon their foes. Creatures that wouldn't question orders and could be controlled with the right words."

The simmering of my blood had calmed, and now it ran cold. I had the horrible sensation I knew where this was going. *Please, gods, say I'm wrong.*

"He whispered in my ear, told me I should use the spell, create an army that would win me the throne." She hung her head and crossed her arms. "I admit, I considered it for longer than I should've. An end to the war. I was desperate. Yet not so desperate that I would kill every fae who opposed me. So I sent him away. But I kept the book."

The palace suddenly seemed very quiet, like every fae in Tenebris held their breath and waited for her to go on.

"It was almost a year before I had a different idea. A better idea, or so I believed at the time." She exhaled, shoulders sinking. "I need you to understand, Bastian. I really did believe it would be for the best. Or better than the alternative, at least."

"You used the book," I whispered. "You made them." I couldn't bring myself to name them, but the iridescent black gloss of their carapaces skittered on the edge of my vision.

"*I* didn't. I had a spy plant it in their camp. Somewhere I knew it would find its way to their would-be queens. I knew it would turn folk against them—it would cost them support and soldiers. They would come to me and Lucius *en masse*, horrified at what their leaders had done. And the war would be over."

Just as my fathers had. The great General Sylen Marwood's defection at the eleventh hour had handed her and Lucius their thrones.

My shadows clung to me, still and tight, like they knew there was a greater darkness coming.

I didn't want to hear her next words. I didn't want to believe it.

But they came anyway.

"I gave them the means to create the Horrors."

The world that had tipped before, upended. My body felt as though it had been stuffed, leaving me little space to breathe, muffling all sound.

I'd known the Horrors had been made. But I thought they'd been an accidental side effect of so much magic being blasted across battlefields, one the other side had harnessed. Not something that had been created *deliberately*.

"You gave them just enough rope to hang themselves." I didn't even sound like myself—it was like someone else spoke and I just paid witness.

"After the war, I tried to control the creatures using other rituals in the book. Nothing worked for long, except for the wardstones. We had to ensure the magic users who'd carried out the rituals were executed so they wouldn't be able to tell *anyone* about that book and the secrets of how to raise the Horrors. I couldn't have anyone else using them like that again."

She turned to me, a bitter smile on her face. "I regret what happened. I didn't know they would be unleashed upon the country—I thought they could be made and then *un*made. Hells, I expected their ranks to defect before the creatures were ever deployed. I can only thank the Stars above that book also contained instructions for the wardstones, or else, I dread to think..." She shivered, pulling her arms tighter around herself, hip leaning into the table at her side. "But, I promise you, Bastian, I didn't expect them to use them on civilians so much."

I shuddered away from the image of Innesol's families lined up, and the husks that remained after. "*So much?* Then you knew they would be used on civilians and that wasn't enough to stay your hand?"

"Is it not better this way?" she snapped. "Better that I have ruled over peace for a thousand years than let war rage on and on? Don't look at me like that. I didn't create the Horrors, I merely gave them the means to, if they so chose. And they *chose*." She drove her finger into the table, jabbing out those three words. "They chose their fates. Their decision lost them the war and won us a thousand years of peace. Is that not worth any cost?"

I pressed the heels of my hands into my eyes, but I couldn't obliterate the little shoes lying in the wreckage of the town. "Children, Braea. They used them on *children*."

"They did. *Them*, not me. You know there is always a price. *Always*. And now you understand the first one I paid for my throne." Her voice trembled—something I'd never heard from her. It made my hands fall away. "Sometimes I think I also paid with my daughters' lives—my punishment for allowing the Horrors to be made."

Did she really believe the ends justified the means? Even now, knowing all she did?

I didn't have the energy to process this. I didn't have the ability to feel when a mountain had just been dropped on me. There was one practical thought in my brain. "Where is the book now?"

"Safe."

That was something. There had to be answers in its pages —she might have missed something that would banish the Horrors for good. But that could wait. The Horrors weren't going anywhere.

"Well." I swallowed, nodded, not quite feeling connected to my body. "You certainly answered my question."

"I owed you that much. Your father knew about the book—he was one of the few with knowledge of it who wasn't executed. Hence the geas."

I was still nodding. "I need to..." I started towards the door, needing to escape to somewhere quiet to make sense of all this. Because it was starting to feel like I'd been working for a monster. That couldn't be, and yet...

"I'm afraid there's something else I need from you." She actually sounded apologetic. "But perhaps the trip will give you a chance to clear your head. I know I just piled a lot on you. It's natural that you should need a little time."

I forced my back straight and inclined my head. I was the Night Queen's Shadow. I didn't get to be Bastian Marwood. "What does my queen need of me?"

53

KAT

When Bastian returned to our suite, his face was ashen. I supposed he didn't want to resume our argument. I couldn't blame him. At least I was about to go and meet Ari and Rose in the atelier—that would give us both some space.

Then Bastian walked out of our bedroom with a bag, and my stomach lurched. "What's that for? Are you... leaving?"

Me? Forever? I bit my tongue on those pathetic additions.

"Braea needs me to attend to some business outside of the city. Faolán's coming too. We'll be gone overnight, since it's the new moon and we won't make it back before the Wild Hunt ride, but there's an inn we can stay in. We'll be safe." His stiff smile didn't meet his eyes. Not even remotely.

They were haunted.

Something was very wrong. I crossed the carpet to him, but it still felt like a vast distance separated us. "Bastian? What's the matter? Tell me. *Please.*" I went to cup his cheek, needing to

389

reach out and let him know whatever was troubling him, I was here to face it with him.

He caught my wrist, grip unyielding. "Don't."

"Don't what?" I couldn't keep the frustration from my tone at being treated like the stranger I'd been to him last year. "I just wanted—"

"Don't ask me to choose between you and my queen." His chest heaved and this wild look entered his eyes, like the Wild Hunt's hellhounds were on his heels.

"I didn't..." But then the meaning behind his words hit me with all the blunt force of a battering ram. "Because you'll choose her."

"I *must* choose her." The words burst from him as he threw my wrist from his grasp. "The Night Queen's Shadow should have no doubts. I have done awful things at her command. I have commanded others to do awful things in service of her. Tell me, Kat, who is meant to choose? The Bastard of Tenebris who killed his father for her? Or Bastian Marwood, who loves you beyond reason?"

I couldn't answer. Seeing him like this tore at me. Even when his being split in two, he was not this divided.

He raked his hands through his hair. "If you'd asked me a year ago, I'd have told you I couldn't even entertain any other option when weighed against her. But now... Now, answering terrifies me more than I can describe."

I managed to breathe out my question: "Why?"

"Because if I choose you, it will mean the past fifteen years of my life, killing my father, becoming this... it will all have been for nothing. Choosing would destroy everything." His eyes widened and he clamped his mouth shut as though he'd made a terrible confession, then charged out of our suite.

"Bastian, wait! It's..." But the door slammed behind him.

He had wavered. His voice had cracked.

I'd broken him.

He'd poured so much into Braea and her rule. Fissures in her were fissures in the bedrock of his very existence. He'd always paved over them, no doubt helped by smooth words from her—maybe even reminders of all she'd done for him.

But I'd picked and picked and she'd done *something*, and now we'd torn him in two.

When I got to Ariadne's atelier, Rose knew right away that something was wrong, even though I didn't say a word. With Faolán and Bastian both gone, she suggested she could stay over and keep me company. I could've cried with gratitude.

Just as we were getting her settled into what had once been my bedroom, a message arrived from Sepher asking me to meet him in the gardens.

Nerves fluttered through me. When Bastian had thrown the queen's note on the fire, I might have... rescued it. It sat in my pocket now, edges singed, the ash a guilty secret that I was sure marked me.

I'd asked Sepher to give me his brother's letters. If the queen's writing didn't match the one I'd found in Cyrus's drawer, I would drop it. After seeing the state Bastian was in this morning, it felt cruel to raise it even if the writing was the same.

That was a problem for future Kat.

I had a king to meet in the gardens, and this time the thought of it didn't fill me with dread.

Sepher sat on the bench near the Great Trees, scenting the late afternoon air. A box waited on the seat next to him, and I had to force myself not to hurry over. It looked a lot like the boxes that had been in Cyrus's room of curiosities.

"You're cutting it close to sunset, aren't you?" I gestured at the darkening sky. "You've got, what? Half an hour?"

"Forty-five minutes," he grumbled. "I've learned to be a very precise timekeeper, thanks to my new affliction."

"Most wouldn't call kinghood an affliction."

Chin raised, he smirked. "I'm not most."

I didn't bother to hide my eye roll.

"This is for you." He placed his hand on the box. "Don't open it. At least, not around me." He shuddered, tail swishing. The whole movement put me in mind of a sabrecat shaking off flies.

I narrowed my eyes. "Why? Is it trapped?"

"*No.* Just letters and... that mirror."

I contained my reaction, but it spiked in my veins. A pulse of energy. I had mentioned it to them like it was merely a pretty trinket. I didn't want to raise questions of its importance. They would lead too close to Bastian's true identity. "A mirror? Such a generous gift, *Your Majesty*."

"The damn thing gave me the creeps. Normally I like mirrors, but this one doesn't show me myself." He wrinkled his nose as though that was the worst betrayal. "It feels like I'm being watched. Besides, there are ravens and moths on the frame—more suited to Dusk than Dawn, so here you go." He slid the box towards me. "Now, I have forty-two minutes left of my day, and I intend to spend them with my wife. Enjoy your evening." With that, he sauntered off.

Once he was gone, I hurried to my suite with the box. Rose emerged from the bathroom as I arrived, panting. "What's this?" She eased into one of the armchairs as I placed the box on the table and threw it open.

"You remember the letter I found in Cyrus's office?" As one of Bastian's most trusted operatives and friends, she knew the contents of many of my reports, including that one. Besides, Faolán wasn't the best at keeping secrets from his wife. "I *think* it should be in here."

Sure enough, inside was the bundle of letters from Sura, the mirror, a handful of other notes and messages, and, right at the bottom, the letter that had been caught in his desk drawer.

First, I opened that and one of the letters from Sura.

Seeing them side-by-side, it was clear right away they hadn't been written by the same hand. The loops and sizing were similar, like they'd learned to write in the same place, but the co-conspirator's writing was free and relaxed and Sura's had a stiff formality to it. And the lower case *E*s were completely different—Sura wrote hers in a single loop, whereas the co-conspirator created a *C*, then cut through it with a horizontal line, creating something that looked like a curved upper case *E*.

Sura wasn't the one who'd planted the idea of killing his way to the throne.

"Is that the one?"

I smoothed the letter on the table so she could see and pointed out the differences in the handwriting. "And this is from the queen." Swallowing, I pulled the message from my pocket and set it down.

Smooth, relaxed writing. That same unusual *E*.

"It matches," I breathed, almost afraid to speak any louder. "Doesn't it?" I pushed it towards her with a wide-eyed look. "Tell me I'm wrong, because I'm not sure I want to be right."

It was one thing having suspicions that the queen disliked me and didn't always act in her people's best interests, but this? Actively encouraging Cyrus to stage the attack on the palace that had killed so many? Bastian was already broken. What would evidence of his queen's treachery do to him?

Brow furrowed, lips flat, Rose looked from the mystery letter to the queen's scorched message and back again. She gulped and nodded. "That's it then, isn't it? Evidence that she hasn't been working for the good of the realm but... against it?"

"*For* herself."

She looked away, rubbing her stomach like the idea made her feel sick. "You think that's why she didn't do more for shapechangers when Cyrus was targeting them? So he would look worse and worse, and she would look reasonable and benevolent in comparison?"

"Let people get desperate enough that they're begging her to do something—*anything*—and she could pull out the Crown of Ashes, place it atop her head, rule day and night, and she would look like she'd done it all to save Elfhame."

Between the freckles, Rose's usually pale skin went pure white. "We need to tell Bastian. As soon as they get back."

I winced and sagged against the chair. "I'm not sure what good that will do. I've already tried to talk to him about Braea. He has a lot of excuses for her."

She fidgeted in the silence, poking through the box and pulling out the mirror. "Sepher gave you this? Does he think a gift will make up for manipulating you into killing his brother for him?"

I snorted. "He's going to owe me for that for a long, long

time. The mirror was Nyx's. I think it's the one she used to contact—"

Shit. I almost said "Bastian's father." Rose didn't know about his parentage. I cleared my throat. "To contact her unseelie lover. If we can work out how to use it, he could be an ally against Braea, and even if he can't, maybe he knows something about the Crown's location. That book I took from Dawn suggests it's in the Underworld."

Rose snatched her hands away, leaving the mirror on the table. "So not only do we have to worry about a Crown that could end the Sleep and mustn't fall into the wrong hands, but there's also a mirror that gives a direct link to the Underworld? Great. That's just great. Let's *not* use it."

I understood her concerns. During my time in Elfhame, I'd learned the reason the unseelie were so feared. They blamed the seelie and anyone allied with them for their banishment to the Underworld.

"What if it's our only option?" I peered at it, trying different angles, but there was only darkness within its silvery surface. Even if it didn't help with the Crown, I might be able to introduce Bastian to his father. That alone was worth the risk.

"Hello?" I called into it.

"I thought you didn't want the queen to have the Crown. We can just leave it where it is."

I leant over the mirror, eyes straining for any change in its surface. "Nyx's child has need of your help."

Was that a ripple or were my eyes playing tricks on me? I didn't dare blink even though my eyes burned.

"What do you mean, Nyx's—?"

A thundering knock shook the door, making us jump.

I clutched my chest. There was nothing in the mirror. "Did you invite Ari?"

Frowning, she shook her head. "And she wouldn't knock like that."

An unpleasant sensation prickled between my shoulder blades. Something was wrong. Most of the knocks at our door were messages for Bastian, usually from the queen. But she'd sent him away.

I made contact with my magic, letting it tingle over my skin without quite raising any poison, then opened the door.

The head of the Queensguard, Cavall, stood there at attention, black armour gleaming, face pale and strained. "Her Majesty wishes to speak to you."

Her Majesty? Had the sun set already? I glanced into the living room, but the only thing visible out the windows was a thick fog. "I hadn't realised the time." My stomach clenched though, almost as sickening as when I wore iron. She was the last person I wanted to be around.

"Come on then." Rose stepped forward, as if to leave with me, but they raised their hand.

"Everyone else in the palace is to stay in their rooms on pain of death."

"On pain of death?" I chuckled. "That's a bit dramatic."

Their expression grew even tighter. "*On pain of death.* Even guards have been ordered to return to their barracks."

Beyond them, the hall was empty. Usually Bastian had at least one guard on the door—someone he trusted personally. That sensation of wrongness grew, a dagger's tip between my shoulder blades now.

"Well," I said brightly, like everything was fine, "I'll be back soon."

Rose caught my arm as I went to leave and bent to my ear.

"I don't like this. There's a ill scent on the air, Kat. Something dank. And that fog... it's unnatural."

I nodded, but there was nothing I could do about it. With the Wild Hunt abroad, we couldn't get a message to Bastian and Faolán—or anyone else outside the palace. We were on our own. "I'll be careful."

With that, I followed Cavall into the empty corridors. The quiet pressed on me, making my footsteps too loud. We rounded corners and went down a staircase—not towards the queen's suite. "Where are we—?"

That was when I saw it.

Crowded into an alcove at the bottom of the stairs—a spot that usually housed a guard. Black and shiny and huge.

A Horror.

54

BASTIAN

Squeezing the reins, I bent my head into the rush of wind, letting it blast my face and tug on my hair. I wanted it to drive every thought from my head. I wanted to be empty. That would be easier. If I didn't think, I could keep being the Night Queen's Shadow, the Serpent of Tenebris, its Bastard.

It felt like Bastian Marwood was falling apart, leaving pieces of himself on the road behind us.

Because I could not reconcile their choices. The Serpent was supposed to choose the queen. But Bastian wanted to choose *his* queen.

It was impossible.

So I ran away. The task Braea had set me didn't really require my personal attention and there were quicker methods of travel, but I needed this. Plus, I had a feeling Kat would sleep better without me tonight—if I stayed away there could be no arguments.

Yes, I was a coward.

"You in a rush?" Faolán shouted as he caught up.

Below, my stag's chest heaved. I was pushing the creature too hard. Almost as hard as I had the night I'd brought Kat to Elfhame and raced to the Hall of Healing. I called for him to slow to a walk. "Sorry, I just..."

"Looked like you were trying to outpace your thoughts." Faolán glanced back—the city was a distant smear, reflecting the morning sun. "Never managed it myself, but let me know if you do. Or... I hear talking helps."

I gave him a look out the corner of my eye. "You, the person who barely strings more than a dozen words together are advising me to talk about my feelings?"

"I said thoughts, not feelings, but whichever works for you." He shrugged, patting his stag's shoulder as it reached for a low-hanging branch of new growth—beyond the city's magically influenced warmth, spring was only just breaking through the cold. "Rose says I'm a good listener."

"Because you barely talk," I grumbled.

We rode on in silence for a long while. Maybe it was because he didn't try to fill it that I found myself speaking at last. I kept it factual—all the things I'd discovered, the information Kat had found in Dawn, her opinions about the queen, the secrets Kaliban had revealed in the dungeons, and, finally, the truth about Braea and the Horrors.

I finished with, "I don't want to believe any of it."

"Oh?" It was the first sound he'd made since I'd started. Part of me had wondered if he'd fallen asleep in the saddle.

"If it's true, then what and *who* have I been fighting for all this time?"

He rubbed his beard. "Sounds like someone who sees us as

—what are the little ones in chess? Pawns? We're just those to her, not people who want peace, stability, long lives... families."

"I always thought... I thought she felt the same way I did."

I weighed my actions and decisions against what was for the good of the people, their protection and safety. Had I just *assumed* she did the same?

"Hmm." It was a pregnant sound that pulled me from my spine-crumbling misery.

"What?"

"Haven't you been acting against her for a while? Keeping secrets, like Cyrus's guilt, Kat's spying, clues about the Crown."

I laughed, throat tight. "That isn't acting against her! It's just... holding back some information."

Eyebrow raised, he gave me a look that cut through my excuses.

I had been playing a game behind her back, convincing myself that it didn't count because it wasn't direct action against her.

"She still didn't answer me about Kat, you know."

"I noticed that. She'd rather tell you about the Horrors than admit what happened in that room with Cyrus. There's your answer."

"So not only are people pawns to her, but *my person* is just another expendable piece on the board. I thought she cared about me. I thought..."

"Hmm. Even though Sepher played us all, he did it to keep the people he cared about safe."

The idea that Sepher treated people better than Braea did was a sobering one. It kept us quiet for a long while.

Eventually, I shook my head. "You haven't said anything about my mother."

"Makes no difference to me. Though I was wondering—do you think the queen knows? Subconsciously, maybe? She's always favoured you."

"No. Kat thinks I'd be dead if she did."

"*Well...*"

Head falling back, I sighed. "Don't tell me you do too."

"She had two daughters." He held up two fingers. "Both are dead by her hand. I'm not the best at maths, but..." He folded down those two fingers and showed me his fist.

"But you work for her. Don't you—?"

"No. I work *for you*. My loyalty lies *with you*. Rose is the same. And I'd bet good money Orpha, Brynan, and all your other operatives feel the same."

That deflated me and I found myself frowning at the road ahead. "You sound like Kat. She said others don't see me as I see myself. They look to me in a crisis."

"We do. And gods know we've had enough of those recently. Even if no one knows who you are, you're already a good prince." His gaze slid to me along with a sly smile. "As long as you don't expect me to bow to you now."

I laughed, something that had seemed impossible when we'd left Tenebris-Luminis. "Thank you, Faolán."

WE ARRIVED at the estate of a reclusive older fae who read the queen's message with pursed lips. Despite her obvious irritation, she let us take the books Braea had requested—enough to require both our stags.

She offered us shelter from the new moon, but we still had some hours before nightfall, and I wanted to get back to the city, if possible. We'd be cutting it fine, but it was worth a try, and there was a last inn we could stay at if we didn't make it in time. Now I'd had a chance to talk to Faolán, I wanted nothing more than to speak to Kat. The sooner, the better.

But the weather had different ideas, and rain muddied the way for much of the afternoon. Despite our efforts, we were still a couple of hours away as the sun dipped lower and lower and the sky darkened. We would have to stop at the last inn before Tenebris, over an hour from the city gates. There was no sign of it yet, though, and Faolán's shoulders grew tighter and tighter as we raced the sunset.

The Wild Hunt would ride soon, and no one wanted to lose their soul to such creatures.

Only when we entered a gloomy green valley did Faolán speak. "There it is." Ahead, the inn nestled in the vale, cosy and safe from the night's threats. "I'm not giving you the bed if they only have one, *Your Highness*." He flashed a grin and galloped ahead.

"No respect," I muttered, urging my stag after him.

Thankfully, I didn't need to sleep on the floor—they had space. We soon had our stags settled in the stables before hurrying along the path lined with white narcissi and into the inn. A warm common room welcomed us, and we set ourselves up at a table near the door, with full plates and tankards that refilled the moment they got in danger of emptying. They were scant comfort to my frustration at being so close to the city and yet not able to make it before nightfall.

I was starting on my second ale and Faolán on his second plate of food, when he suddenly cocked his head. "There's someone out there."

I straightened, putting down my tankard, one hand going to my sword. "The Hunt?"

"No, it's..." He paused, listening. "A human. On foot. Alone."

"If the Wild Hunt catch them, they're dead... or worse."

"Well, they can stay out there," the innkeeper snapped. "Not opening my doors on a new moon."

"No, it's—*shit*." Faolán was on his feet, throwing the bar up on the door.

Without thought, I blocked the swearing innkeeper from reaching him.

In burst Rose, panting.

Faolán slammed the door behind her, making the whole building quiver. "What the bloody hells are you doing out in this?" He was cantankerous at the best of times, but I'd never seen him look so utterly furious. I almost didn't recognise him. "You do know it's the new moon, don't you? You do know their hounds will scent you? You do—?"

"She knows." I smoothed a hand onto his shoulder, but he shook me off and stood glaring at her, as, hands on knees, she caught her breath. "I thought you had more faith in Rose than that."

He paced into the centre of the room, grumbling that I didn't understand.

"I made it, didn't I?" She straightened, tugging her coat tighter. It was only then I took in her bare legs and feet poking out the bottom. She'd shifted to her wolf form to come here, carrying her coat in the bag now slung over her shoulder. "This couldn't wait until morning. In fact, I think the new moon is important."

I frowned at her in question as Faolán turned and asked, "What is it?"

"The queen has Kat. There are Horrors in the palace. And I don't know what the hells the queen's doing, but Sura's infiltration was on a new moon. If she was going for the gauntlet..."

All warmth left me. I wasn't sure how Kat or the Horrors fitted into Braea's plans and I dreaded finding out, but I knew one thing. "She's going after the Crown."

Faolán growled. "And we're stranded here."

55

KAT

The Horror didn't attack. It just... stood there. A silent sentinel.

I wondered if it was a statue, but its void black eyes followed us. Good gods, no wonder Cavall looked so fucking pale.

Once it was out of sight, I whispered to them. "What is that thing doing in the palace?"

Their lips flattened, and we went on in silence for several paces. "I don't know. Only that there are more and Her Majesty has the guards confined to their barracks—the palace is theirs." They gestured at another pair of Horrors flanking the doors ahead. "I'm only here on her direct orders to bring you to her."

It was bad enough passing those monsters, but when I realised the doors led outside, I balked. "It's a new moon."

"Her Majesty has reassured me the Wild Hunt won't be a problem."

My skin crawled under the gaze of the two Horrors.

Outside, grey mist shrouded everything, only broken by hazy lights of pure, cold white.

Cavall squared their shoulders and went first.

My pulse pounded with the wrongness of this. You didn't go outside on a new moon. Every child in Albion knew that. Dozens of fairy stories warned us about it, and before we could read, we sang nursery rhymes to remind us.

But, what the Night Queen wanted, the Night Queen got. And, for now, I was her subject. I needed to at least pretend to be a loyal one.

So I followed, each step carefully placed to be as quiet as possible.

We met her in the grove, the Great Oak and Great Yew looming up into a fog so thick, I couldn't see their tops.

"Leave us." With a twitch of her fingers, she dismissed Cavall. "The Horrors will protect us from the Wild Hunt."

"Protecting?" I eyed the dim shapes of the four creatures surrounding us, just inside the blanketing mist. "Is that what they did at the Winter Solstice?"

"They can be trusted. They can't be turned against me. Bribed. Tricked. No one can appeal to their better natures, because they have none. So long as they are appropriately tethered, they are perfectly loyal." A small frown flickered on her smooth face. "For a time, at least."

That addition did nothing for the cold sweat coating my skin. How long did we have? I didn't trust her not to gamble with my life. Maybe that was why she'd brought me here—the canary who would die once her luck with the Horrors ran out, buying her time to flee.

"Then, let's be quick." I managed a tight smile. "What is it you want from me?"

"Practical. That's one thing I like about you, Katherine."

She smiled, as cold as the fae lights drifting through the fog. "You've been helping Bastian with his search for the Crown of Ashes. But I get the impression my Shadow isn't keen on seeing it put to use. You, on the other hand... he's made it sound like you think we should use the thing. And that puts us in alignment."

"Who'd have thought it?"

She chuckled, lifting her chin. "We're actually more alike than you may think. You seduced Bastian to keep yourself safe —a powerful man like that. I can see the appeal. Then, trapped in Dawn, you... well, you went for the seduction route again, didn't you? No judgement. We have to use whatever tools we're given." Nodding slowly, she scrutinised me. "No, if anything, I can't help admiring you."

"Such a compliment. I still fail to see how your life has *anything* to do with mine." I gritted my teeth. She hadn't been forced to stab her husband with a shard of glass to stop him from killing her. She hadn't risked herself to get close to an enemy. She knew nothing of the price I'd paid for safety.

She was a queen. She always paid with other people's lives.

"I see that judgemental look in your eye. You don't understand how precarious it is to be a ruler. How close you have to keep your enemies."

"Close enough to send them letters encouraging them to take the throne for themselves?"

Her eyes flashed wide before she huffed out a little laugh. "A sleuth, too. Aren't you just multi-talented? I suppose he didn't burn the letters, did he? Silly little boy, always collecting things."

I thought I'd get a reaction that I could read the truth in. Not a confession.

"You understand, then, that I do whatever is required.

Which brings us here." She gestured and the mist parted, revealing the spreading branches of the Great Yew and the soaring ones of the Great Oak. "This is how we reach the Crown of Ashes."

"'The way is through the trees'—the Great Trees." Bastian's theory was right. I stared up at them—the markers of the covenant that gave fae their magic. They'd grown the tablet, their woods merging to leave a clue about where to find the Crown in case part of that covenant ever needed to be broken to allow a Night Queen to rule by day.

"Once I have the Crown, I can keep you, as my subject, safe. I can keep your darling Bastian safe. None will rise against me once I am free of the Sleep. No more foolish Day Kings with their paranoid ideas or wild plans with so much unnecessary bloodshed."

"A plan you put him up to."

"That plan was his own. I merely gave him the nudge. The fact he didn't give a damn about the collateral damage—that was all on him." Her jaw tightened, reminding me so much of Bastian, I felt foolish for not noticing it sooner. "Enough about Cyrus. We're here for the Crown. This is the way, but I just can't get it to open." She blasted a sigh and paced, expression pinched. "Right time. Right place."

The new moon. That was why Sura had risked the Wild Hunt—the gauntlet would only open on the night of the new moon.

I bit back a curse. Yes, we'd kept information from Braea, but she'd found clues of her own and we had no idea.

"I anointed a servant with royal blood and nothing!" She spun on her heel, spreading her hands. "What am I missing?"

I rubbed my mouth as if deep in thought, but actually it

was to hide the flickering smile of relief. She thought the anointed one meant anointed with royal blood.

I was sure it referred to an acorn and a berry from the Great Trees, after all, Bastian had found Sura with those crushed in her hand.

But she did have royal blood too. Maybe it required all three combined.

Shit. If Braea realised, all she had to do was reach out and take an old acorn from the ground and pluck a shrivelled berry from the yew. She could eat them and then the gauntlet would open.

It was no longer a case of *if* the Crown was discovered, but when... and by whom.

It couldn't be her. But Sura was dead. Amaya and Bastian were too far away. Braea was going to work out this last piece of the puzzle tonight.

I needed to get into the gauntlet before her. Somehow.

I just needed royal blood.

Shit. *Shit.*

The queen went still. "What is it? You've just realised something."

Bastian had royal blood, and he'd given it to me. *Technically*, I had royal blood. And, thanks to my poison and Elthea's medicine that had stabilised it, the yew and the oak's power ran through my body.

I only hoped it counted for the gods or trees or whoever the hells determined how the gauntlet worked.

No time for hope though.

I shoved past the queen and stepped into the shadows between the trees. "I come here for the Crown of Ashes. I am the anointed one and I call for the gauntlet to open."

The air split with a ground-shaking creak.

I planted my feet, but Stars above did I want to run from the sound of something whistling through the air.

I needed to face this. I needed to be first through the gauntlet. That Crown was Bastian's. Not hers.

Braea stumbled backwards, eyes round and fixed on something behind me.

A doorway. It had to be.

I let out a little laugh of relief. She wouldn't be able to follow me—not without the trees' fruit.

Something slammed into my back. Air whooshed from my lungs, hot and metallic. I reached out, ready to catch myself on hands and knees, but I didn't fall.

I blinked down.

I blinked again, trying to make sense of... of...

Red. Bright, bright red.

Bark. Sticky and dark.

Pain. Just starting. Radiating now, from my shoulder... where a branch had pierced my body.

56

BASTIAN

Rose and Faolán tried to stop me leaving, but I pushed past them. Wild Hunt be damned. I would give my soul if I had to. For Kat, I would give anything.

I needed to get to her. I needed to stop whatever Braea was doing. This whole fucking trip... it was to get me out of the way. And like a damned fool, I'd gone along with it. I cursed my earlier cowardice—the reason I was here, too far from the city.

I hurried past the little white narcissi that smelled just like Kat, saddled my stag, and rode into the night.

Sensing my urgency, he galloped hard, cutting corners, leaping rocks and logs. The darkness of the new moon had swallowed up the countryside and it consumed us too. Over my shoulder, there was no sign of the inn's lights. We passed a huddle of houses locked and shuttered without so much as a curtain cracked open.

At this pace, it was three quarters of an hour to the city, an hour at most. What were the chances of the Wild Hunt being at this exact location at this exact moment?

I'd just given a fierce smile at the thought when I heard the howls. Not quite hunting dogs. Not quite wolves. I'd heard Fluffy make the sound once, the day the Horrors attacked.

The hair at the back of my neck rose.

"Fuck."

The Wild Hunt's hellhounds had caught my scent.

Their riders would be close behind.

The stories said there was no escaping them, but Ari had told us how they'd chased her once, and she'd managed to flee to safety. I would do the same. I would beat them to the city. If that meant they came for me again at the next new moon, so be it. As long as Kat was safe.

I bent to my stag's neck and whispered in that old tongue my father had always used to train them. All I said was, "Please."

Head lowered, he put on a burst of speed, and I placed my hand on his shoulder in thanks.

But the keening howls grew louder and strange hoofbeats joined my stag's. I searched the darkness for some sort of shelter—if I holed up in a stable, perhaps they'd get bored and leave, then I'd be able to continue on my way.

There was nothing.

They thundered closer. The air shook with their presence. The magic around me screeched and scraped, discordant and agitated.

I clung to the reins, ducking lower, urging my stag faster. Anything. I would do *anything*. The Wild Hunt might make a bargain. They could have my soul if I could go to the palace first and do this one thing.

My shadows spread, licking over the ground in a lake of darkness. They didn't slow the riders or their hellhounds.

The white hounds sprinted through my shadows, crimson

flames marking their ears and eyes, streaking behind their paws and tails. Just like Fluffy in theory, and yet there was a sharpness in their eyes, a lean hunger in their bodies, like they would never be satisfied, no matter how much they fed or how many nights they hunted. No, that sweet girl had never belonged with them.

Finally, I looked back. The riders were shockingly close—only ten feet away. Thirteen of them on stag and horseback, shrouded in scuffed armour and shadow. Death clung to their steeds, some skeletal, some not quite solid. Their eyes burned with silvery fire, just as Kat and I had seen when they almost caught us in the stable yard. Except this time, instead of searching, they fixed on me.

They would have me. There was no escape.

Still I leant and urged and begged my stag, desperation stinging my eyes. "Please. *Please.*"

But they surged around us, thunder made flesh and bone.

My stag bellowed in terror, but there was nothing we could do.

They forced us to a stop, blocking the way forward, back—anywhere. I swallowed, calculating the best wording for my bargain to ensure they couldn't take me until I'd made sure Kat was all right.

Before I could utter a word, the Wild Hunt bowed.

57

KAT

I was still gaping at the branch when a root speared my stomach. Breaths coming short and sharp, I looked over my shoulder to see the face of my attacker.

There was no face in the darkness. There was only the trees.

That was why I didn't fall. The Yew held me up with its branch lodged into my shoulder, the Oak with its root in my gut. Their magic burned.

I sucked in sharp little breaths, struggling to inhale around the pain. What had I missed? Where had I made the mistake?

It wasn't meant to—

Another branch burst from my side, soon followed by another and another. I jolted with each one, unable to cry out.

Braea stared, backing away, the colour leaching from her face in the cold light.

When the trees lifted me, I sagged in their cruel hold. I didn't even twitch when they tore away my necklace. Blood spilled from my mouth, slicked my hands, soaked into my tattered dress. Agony laced every breath.

I could only wheeze as my bones creaked and cracked.

This was a punishment. I was not the anointed one and so the trees, the guardians of the gauntlet, were tearing me apart.

My blood wasn't truly royal. Or it was too long since I'd consumed the acorn and berry. Or I'd made some other error that meant the way wouldn't open for me.

The ground fell away. Branches and leaves surrounded me under the endless night with no stars and no moon.

I lost count of the holes in my body but I knew one thing.

I was dying.

And deeper than my flesh—that searing magic? It was like they were trying to scour my soul, burn it from my body—from existence.

My very being tore.

I tried to clench my fists, like that would allow me to hold on. *No. I don't want to. I need to stay here. I need to...*

There were so many things I needed to do. Get the Crown. Tell Bastian about Braea. Tell him how much I loved him. Hug my friends. Ride Vespera one last time. The estate...

The world went dark. Pain became a distant concept, like breath and gravity. I was somewhere else, barely holding on to the precipice of my physical self.

"*Let go,*" a whisper crept into my ear. Dark, comforting, like a mother soothing in the night.

"*Let go or your soul will be destroyed,*" came a second voice. Deeper, with a resonance that lulled.

But wasn't letting go dying?

Hadn't I spent my entire life clinging on, again and again? Survival had been my religion and creed. The one idol on my altar.

And now? I'd sought out the gauntlet so I could create a life that was truly worth living.

The edges of my self, my soul singed to flakes of ash, streaming away.

"*Let go,*" the first voice repeated, pressing urgency in their tone.

I threw a thought out into the void. "*What about my body?*"

"*That will die anyway. This is the challenge of the gauntlet— hold on and be utterly destroyed. Let go and your soul will be carried down—*"

"*We shouldn't be telling her this,*" the deeper voice hissed. "*You never told the others.*"

"*She isn't just anointed. She is* of *us. Can't you feel it in her magic? Like me. Like you. Like calling to like.*"

The burning magic intensified as though it was the voices' attention and everything left in me shrieked. I had no idea if my physical body still existed, but if it did, it was screaming.

"*I see.*" The lower voice paused. "*She is our creature.*"

"*This is the risk,*" they whispered as one. "*This is the challenge. Do you dare to die?*"

So I hadn't erred. This was the gauntlet. Dying was... the point.

The Crown was in the Underworld. To make a place that was better, to let the people I care about truly live, I had to go there. Maybe there would be some way back. Maybe not.

"*Such hope is holding on. You must give yourself entirely.*"

If I went forward, there would be no way back.

Sura. She'd said goodbye to Amaya because she intended to sacrifice herself to retrieve the Crown of Ashes for her.

Braea had anointed that servant, willing to use them to gain it.

And when that had failed, she'd brought me to the Trees as her next sacrifice.

I'd always clung to survival, and slowly I'd begun to build a life. But here I was with a chance to not merely survive the world but *change* it.

Death was the risk. But I could leave something better for the ones I cared about.

I could stop others suffering as I had, caught in the politics of Dusk and Dawn. I could ensure Bastian had the throne and ruled by day and night, not confined to the Sleep. My death would be enough to push him to stand up to Braea and rule. He would make a good king. Our friends would help.

It wasn't an easy decision, but it was the right one.

"*This is the risk,*" I sent my thoughts into the whispering dark. "*This is the challenge. And it is worth it.*"

I let go.

58

BASTIAN

When the Wild Hunt straightened from their bow, they spoke. Not any language I'd ever heard or could attempt to mimic or transcribe. It scraped over my bones, whispering that I should understand.

But I understood none of this. Did they bow before they took your soul? Some sort of twisted honour.

I pointed my sword at the leader. I didn't remember having drawn it, but its dark blade was a comfort. "You must wait your turn. I have work to do tonight, but after that, you may have my soul. I'll come willingly. Do we have a bargain?"

The hood twitched as though taken aback, and a low, rasping sound came from within. They spoke the oldest tongue, but their voice was broken like it had never been made for speaking any language of this world.

I had to replay the sounds in my head to make sense of the strange intonation, the cracked sounds.

"Our prince misunderstands our presence. Our prince requires no bargain with us."

The rider at their side lowered their head, a tattered veil covering the opening of their hood. It wafted as a feminine voice came out. "What would our prince bid us do?"

I searched their shadowed faces. "Send this prince forward, then. If he won't entertain a bargain, I will fight him for my soul."

They watched me with an air of expectation.

"Our prince would... fight himself?"

"What?" My sword lowered. "Are you calling *me* your prince?" My stag spun on the spot, letting me take them all in. "You're of Dusk Court and you... know who I am."

"No. Yes." The leader spread their gauntleted hands and it was only then I realised they hadn't drawn any weapons.

"Neither and both," the veiled one added.

"A prince twice over." Thirteen voices rose, their discordant sound a pressure on my ears, a caress on my bones. "Here on the surface. And in the world beneath."

"Speak some damn sense. I don't have time for this."

"He does not know who he is," the leader said.

"Nor who we are." The veiled one shook her head.

"We were the guard of the first unseelie king who ruled the Underworld. We stood with him when he and his people were banished many ages ago. We... transgressed on our hunt one night, choosing the wrong quarry, and for that we were cursed."

"Never to live," their voices rose in a shared chant. "Never to die. To serve our king and hunt evermore."

"Just as we still hunt," she went on, "we still serve the descendant of that king who rules in the Underworld. And we serve you, his son."

Everything went still. Every part of my body. Every thought in my mind.

Long moments passed. I wasn't sure my heart even beat in that time.

Eventually, I choked in air as though my lungs had only just remembered how to work.

Nyx's lover. My birth father. He wasn't just any unseelie lord, but one of the Kings of Death.

I raked my hand through my hair, trying to wake up the rest of my body. "And what is it you want from me?"

"That is not the question. Our prince should ask what it is he wants from us."

The leader bowed his head. "We are his to command."

It wasn't an army. But it might just help.

"I need to get to the palace as quickly as possible."

"It will be done." The leader and the veiled one flanked me, while the others fanned out behind. Their steeds pawed the ground but left no hoof prints.

I gave my stag a reassuring pat before urging him on. His eyes rolled as though he was trying to keep the strangers in sight, but he surged forward at my command, muscle and sinew as focused as an arrow.

"I always thought you were unseelie so you couldn't cross the river's enchantments, but I saw you in the palace's stable yard. Are you... something else, then?"

The veiled one made a noise that made my teeth ache. I thought it was the Wild Hunt's version of a laugh, but it was as though a dead creature had forgotten how to laugh and someone had described it to them. "We are unseelie. However your queen did not seek to block our kind. She warded the river against our king, specifically. He may only enter your palace along a path paved in blood and death, as is his power."

I huffed, breath steaming in the night air. "No wonder I've always found it so uncomfortable to cross." His blood ran in my veins, so some shade of Braea's enchantment acted upon me.

The shadows behind her veil tightened as she bent lower over her steed. "She killed your mother, and for that our king seeks her death. A life for a life. I would gladly deliver her, given the chance."

Braea's first words to me the night of Sura's death suddenly made sense. *You've come for me. At last.* With shadows cloaking me, she'd thought I was my father come to kill her.

The reins creaked in my grasp, audible despite the thunderous hoofbeats. So many things made more sense now. "She wasn't trying to protect her people, only herself."

"Such is the way of tyrants. She could not be seen to lose control of her daughter, but she also refused to bear the consequences."

Braea really had killed her own daughter for that—what might she do to Katherine?

I urged my stag faster.

I only hoped it would be enough.

59

BASTIAN

Tenebris was quiet and dark, locked up for the new moon. We passed through the city with ease and clattered across the bridge to the palace in single file. My heart was in my throat. Where was Kat?

But I could see nothing through the fog.

"The queen hides what she does," the Wild Hunt's leader intoned as we dismounted.

We left the stags and horses at the main entrance, and I ordered the Wild Hunt to stay their hands against any fae we might encounter. If guards tried to block our way, I wouldn't have them killed. I would find a way to explain and get them to stand down.

But inside, there were no guards. There was... no one.

The Wild Hunt followed me into Dusk's side of the palace, as a shriek pierced my ears.

Scything claws cut through the air from both sides. I barely rolled out of the way as the spot where I'd been standing was assaulted by a pair of Horrors.

Shit. Two together. If I could evade them, the Wild Hunt might buy me time to pass.

But a low sound of anguish came from both the Wild Hunt and the Horrors, the noises almost identical.

Ears ringing, I blocked strike after strike from the Horrors. Yet something wrong clawed at my spine, and not only because they were inside the palace, standing in place of guards.

It took long moments of me ducking and searching for an opening before I realised. Their movements. They were always scuttling and strange, but this was different. They twitched and strained as though trying to fight every action.

The Wild Hunt blocked them easily but didn't coun-terattack.

"What's wrong? Why don't you fight back?"

The veiled woman drew the attention of one, while her leader closed in. The perfect opening.

But instead of driving their blade between the joints of the monster's shell, they placed their hand upon its chest. "*Ivunhalem.*"

It was a language I didn't understand, but at once, the Horror stilled. Its scything limbs lowered, a warrior relieved to set down their weapon.

Too distracted, I barely blocked the other Horror. It jarred my arm and rattled my teeth.

The veiled woman darted in, touching the creature's chest. "*Ivunhalem.*"

Again, it stilled, and this one lowered its head, pressing into her touch, so like a stag with its rider, it stole my breath.

"They are ours," she said, stroking the black carapace.

"Your... pets?"

"*Our people.*"

My mouth dropped open and stayed that way for a beat before any sound would come out. "Your... *what?*"

"What you call Horrors were once unseelie fae. Dark rituals dragged them from the Underworld and turned them into... this." Her voice broke.

"The wards surface dwellers use to contain them—they are based on our language." The leader bowed their head. "Your queen has dug up spells that use our words to control them tonight. And they understand. We hope this means they are still there inside."

"No." Her voice shook as her hood snapped in his direction. "That would be a worse torture. Knowing they had been through all this and were inside, aware all that time."

"We might be able to get them back."

My mind reeled. Not monsters. People. *People.* Stolen away from their homes. Bodies turned against their will. *Used* to wage a war they had no part in.

I could think of no violation more complete.

Did Braea know?

"Come, my prince, you said time was short. I saw an image in this one's mind"—they gestured to the creature that had once been a fae—"your flame-haired one is with the Great Trees." They motioned for one of their followers to remain.

The darkened corridors flew past me, dizzying, horrible, haunted by the terrible truth. The Wild Hunt subdued more of their kin with a touch and a word, one staying each time to keep them soothed. How many had I killed without knowing what they really were?

It was all I could do to keep moving. One foot in front of the other. One parry after another. I had to get to Kat. Had to.

The cool night air was a relief to my burning thoughts when I burst outside with the last remaining member of the

Wild Hunt—their leader. "There are more of my kin out here. I will subdue them."

I needed no more encouragement and sprinted for the Great Trees, knowing the path well despite the fog.

Braea spun as I emerged from the mist, her eyes round. "What are you doing here?"

I panted out the only question I gave a damn about: "Where's Kat?"

Her gaze dropped, but her back straightened, like she was trying to block the way to the centre of the Great Trees. "I can explain. Just give me a moment to—"

I pushed past.

Red hair merged into red blood. Tree limbs and human limbs. Bark and skin.

The world fractured.

I fractured.

There was nothing, because everything lay at my feet, destroyed.

I was on my knees, veins, heart, mind frozen as I gathered into my arms the only thing that mattered.

Kat's broken body.

60

BASTIAN

There was no breath in her. No pulse. No warmth. No nothing.

She'd... gone.

I shook my head again and again. I could accept anything else but not this. Not a world without her.

"Kat?" I smeared blood from her face. Hoping, searching, needing. "Katherine? Love?"

I whispered to her, called for her, kissed her eyelids, her lips, tasting her copper and my salt, asking the gods for some true love's kiss miracle.

None came.

"I couldn't stop her," Braea said behind me.

"Shut up." I hunched over Kat, keeping her to myself, keeping up my hunt for something to cling onto. Because if she was gone...

No. I refused it. Absolutely. Utterly.

No.

"She went after the Crown of Ashes. She tried—"

"*Shut up!*" It was a roar, as broken and raging as everything inside me. The ground shook. The trees creaked.

They had betrayed me. The source of our power. The core of our bargain with the land. And they'd betrayed me by taking her.

"She tried to enter the gauntlet," Braea whispered, like she couldn't speak past her grief. "I'm so sorry for your—"

"Say another word and I will cut out your fucking tongue."

Her shocked silence was a palpable thing, thick like the fog.

I placed Kat upon the ground. It didn't matter that the soil was cold and damp. She was gone. Nothing mattered.

"You." I turned to Braea, voice not my own, but something as alien and cold as the Wild Hunt's voices. "You made her go after the Crown. You knew she thought we should retrieve it. *You* did this."

From the mist, a Horror emerged—an unseelie created, shackled, and controlled by her.

A wave of rage burst from me, shadows racing out to it as I roared, "*Ivunhalem.*"

When she saw the creature fall still, her face paled. "How did you do that?"

"It's their language," I bit out.

"But they're monsters, they don't have—"

"They weren't always monsters, though, were they?"

She flinched and shook her head. "I didn't do it." That was all the answer I needed. "*They* chose to use the book."

"And you knew they would. Just like you knew it would turn innocent fae into *this.* Just like you knew Kat would go after the Crown and die."

I stared at her—my queen, my grandmother. And as I

stared, the thing I'd worked for all these years, the thing I'd killed for, tortured for, deceived for, placed Kat in danger for broke apart, as thoroughly and irrevocably as the body at my feet.

She was nothing, and I owed her nothing.

61
KAT

The instant I let go, everything became easier. That burning tear at my soul stopped. Instead I flowed down a narrow path that converged and grew wider, like a stream winding ever downwards, gravity its friend.

Then I passed into something darker—not an unwelcome darkness, but an enclosing, safe one. Damp and rich. I didn't even feel the seizing terror that my uncle was burying me again.

This was right.

"*That's it,*" the voices whispered, like leaves in a breeze. "*You are with us.*"

Like a comforting embrace, the tunnels around me tightened as other pathways branched off.

No, not pathways, I realised. *Roots.*

Those voices. They were the trees. I'd started in their branches, travelled down their thick trunks, and now I quested deeper, under the earth.

"To the Underworld."

I seeped into the soil.

I was nothing.

It was free. Easy. No thought. No action. Just being.

Until a great breath tore through me. I lay on cold, damp soil. A grey sky soared overhead, marked by a black sun.

Ghostly white flowers surrounded me, their skull-like heads nodding in an almost imperceptible breeze. Their straight, green-black leaves whispered wordlessly, as magic stirred, restless and strong.

I sat up, checking my body over. No blood. No injuries. I felt physical, normal, not a spirit or ghost. Though my necklace was gone, the ring Bastian had given me remained on my finger. I twisted it, heart sore.

A short distance away, a sleek black plinth rose from the flowers, and beyond that a tangled forest blotted out all else, thorny and impenetrable.

But I held my breath and rose, because I was sure that plinth held what I sought.

A circlet of charcoal and ash sat upon its shiny surface.

"The Crown of Ashes," I whispered, a little afraid I might blow it away. But even the breeze that stirred the tangled branches and bone white flowers didn't disturb so much as a speck of ash on the plinth.

Frowning, I circled it. It was a perfect crown, faceted and intricate, yet lifeless and matte like the remains of a fire long burnt out.

I'd found it, but how was I meant to get it back?

Unless that had all been a test of my resolve. I could imagine that kind of deception from the Great Trees so closely tied to the fae.

430

But all that blood. All that pain. The holes in my body. There was no coming back from that.

Still, I'd come for the Crown, and here it was at last. I would find a way to get it to Bastian. I reached for it when a shape unfolded from the forest's shadows.

Feathers and darkness, smoke and sharp shards of cloth and obsidian, and from it all rose a man, tall and pale and laughing.

His unearthly beauty and the glow of his eyes told me exactly who he was at once—one of the unseelie Kings of Death.

Pale, pale skin stood out in stark contrast with his hair, so black, so dark, I'd only ever seen its like on one other person. Unlike Bastian's, though, his hair fell around his shoulders in smooth lengths.

"You've passed the challenge. Your soul survived." He smirked, eyeing me. The smirk faded, replaced by a sharp, raised eyebrow. "Not many make it to the gauntlet with everything that's required, and the few who have were ripped apart by it. Intriguing that a *human* would be the first one to embrace death."

"How do I take the Crown back if I'm dead?" It was foolish, but a tiny ember kindled in me, whispering that he might say he would return me to life so I could emerge triumphant, Crown in hand.

"So much hope. Such a human affliction. Are your lives too short for you to learn that it's a fruitless sentimentality to cling to?" Sighing, he shook his head and peered upward. "Still, you burn brightly, and such a life force has its uses."

Overhead, a greenish white streak rose into the grey sky, like a single lightning bolt. Strangest of all, though, was the fact it seemed to end at me.

"That thread is the tether to your body. Or what's left of it. Things may travel along it, but only for a while after death." He reached up and plucked it, like a string upon a harp, letting out a cold chuckle as the note resonated through me. "And yours shines so brightly, as though you believe it might save you."

Like that, he extinguished the ember of hope in my heart.

This was it. Death, with all its permanence.

For so long, I'd believed I couldn't change my circumstances, only survive them. So I'd focused on that one thing. Survival at any cost.

Tonight I had tried to change everything, for me, for Cristian, for our friends and the people of Elfhame.

And that was what had killed me.

Such bittersweet irony.

All that time, I'd been wrong. I had changed my circumstances, and I had changed myself.

But now I knew something beyond all doubt.

I lifted my chin and smiled in the face of this king's cold cynicism. "Dying for something important is better than surviving for nothing."

The corner of his mouth quirked. "Such pretty words. But I suppose you are standing here in my realm, so you must truly believe it. Touching. I've seen the world up there, there is nothing worth dying for."

Arrogant prick. He knew nothing of the price I'd paid or why I'd paid it, and the sting of that cost was still too fresh for me to keep quiet, accept the Crown, and send it back to earth like a good little girl.

"There are people I care about and who care about me," I snapped. "But I'm starting to see why that may be an experience you can't possibly understand."

"You mean *love*?" He laughed, properly this time, head thrown back. It was short-lived and switched to icy calm so quickly, it was dizzying. "There is no such thing. Or if there is, the world hates love. It's a waste of time. It offers a hand and then claws you." He bared his teeth, so like Bastian it made my heart sore. "It's a splintered handhold that stabs rather than saves."

"That sounds like the voice of bitter experience."

"I thought myself in love once. I was the fool you are now. And all it got me was a dead lover, killed by her own mother." He came closer, looming over me, cold fury in his voice. "All I could do was watch. And neither she nor our unborn child came here, so the world denied us reunion even in death. *That* is how I know love is a waste of time."

I stared up at him. Pale gold eyes, but they glowed like Bastian's. The hair. The way his teeth bared when he practically snarled his sentences.

And that story. Truncated, but...

"It isn't a waste. Your son... he isn't here because he's *alive*." A shocked laugh burst from me. "He's the one I love. The reason that tether burns so bright."

But instead of wonder lighting up his face, he sneered. "How pathetic. I knew humans could lie, but I didn't expect such a desperate attempt to return. Do you think this story will make me give you back your sorry little life? Then again, should I be surprised a surface dweller would be so foolish?"

"My life is *not* sorry." It wasn't just my tether that burned now, but my whole body. "It is full and rich and all the more so because of your son. I can take you to him. I know who he is, where he lives. You can meet him—know him." Now my eyes burned too. "Believe me, he is someone worth knowing."

I tried to hold them in, but the tears escaped.

I cried for the family I'd left behind. For Faolán with his grumbling love. For Rose's cheerful strength that never faded. For quiet Ariadne who had her moments of shocking ferocity. For Perry's inner calm, no matter the shit that was flying at her. For Ella's outrageousness and love, both of which lit up the world around her.

I cried for Bastian. For the one who'd shown me there was a world beyond survival. And whose father stood before me now, the last parent he had left, but who refused to believe he lived.

But most of all, I cried for myself. For the fact I finally had a life worth living. And yet I'd lost it.

Yet there might be one more thing I could do beyond getting the Crown.

Hand over heart, I lifted my chin and squared my shoulders, meeting the king's scepticism with every scrap of belief I held. "I swear on everything I am, everything I was, and everything I ever had in the world above—I'm telling you the truth about your son."

As he glowered down at me, light bathed the clearing and finally drew his gaze upwards. "*Interesting.*"

Above, my tether shone brighter than the black sun of this place, brighter than lightning, brighter than an inferno.

I held my breath, ready for him to take my hand and ask me to take him to Bastian.

"Perfect." He smiled slowly. "Bright enough for me to travel along and pay a little visit to the Night Queen."

"What about your son?"

"The invention you hoped might buy you back your life?" He scoffed. "No."

Fine. If he wouldn't accept my help, he could have my gift instead.

"Then I'm to remain dead." I nodded as though accepting my fate. "Will you at least grant me one final boon? It's only small."

His attention returned from my tether, eyes narrowing. "How small?"

"Your beauty reminds me of your son, for whom I hold such great love. I cannot say goodbye to him, but might I kiss your cheek in his place, so I may at least pretend?"

There was a moment where he puffed up, so subtly he probably didn't realise. But I'd gambled on his beauty being a source of vanity and that look confirmed I'd gambled well. "Humans are so susceptible to us. I will grant your desire." He chuckled as he bent lower, presenting his cheek. "Your commitment to this lie is both amusing and commendable."

I smiled sweetly, steadied myself on his arm, and tiptoeing up, I called upon my magic.

It leapt to me, alive in a way this world wasn't, stronger than it felt in the world above. A dark symphony.

Like he felt it, his eyes went wide, but my lips were already upon his cool cheek.

He jerked away, hand going to the purple mark I'd left upon him. "What have you done?"

"Aconite. Not concentrated enough to kill you right away. I'd say you have about five minutes. Maybe ten."

"*What?*" The word boomed around the clearing. "Are you trying to make me *like* surface dwellers? Because this is *not* how you ingratiate yourself with someone."

"No, I'm making you take me back. It's the new moon, so the veil is at its thinnest, right? And you said my tether was strong enough to take you back. If you can take yourself and the crown up there, you can take me, too."

"Why would I do anything for you now?" Beneath his fingertips, tendrils of poison crept over his cheek.

"The antidote is with my body. Take me back and I'll give it to you." I snatched the Crown. At my touch, it flared to life, cherry red embers glowing amongst the ashes.

He made a faint sound and I whirled on my heel. "Will you take me back and live? Or will you die for your own stubbornness?"

Sweat glistened on his brow, and his handsome features strained. The effects of my poison. "Idiot surface-dweller. If you're telling the truth and the antidote is with your body, I can just go back up there and take it. I don't need you alive."

Shit. I barely stopped my face from falling. If I acted like I still had the upper hand, he might believe it.

"But, since you spun such a pretty story, I'll give you a chance. The way back is open, but it is hard. You need to travel along the link back to your body, forged by your soul coming here. The way up just as painful as the way down. And you know the struggle of living. The pain of loss. The constant spectre of uncertainty. If you go back, it will always haunt you." He stepped aside and the shadows amongst the trees yawned. "Or, you can go forward to the next place. There will be no pain. No struggle. No loss. Ever. You felt how easy it was to let go. It will be that easy for eternity."

Easy.

So little in my life had ever been easy.

"It's natural to move on. Your body is broken. You can feel this is the natural next step. You know this is right. It is the way of things."

The darkness beckoned.

He bent closer, breath fanning my cheek as he whispered in my ear, "No more danger. You'll be safe. Forever."

Wasn't that all I'd ever wanted? To be safe.

I'd found moments of safety. Instants where I could let go. Little pockets of life where I didn't have to plan ahead or check over my shoulder or fear walking around a corner and headlong into some new danger.

I was rid of Robin and Rufus and even Cyrus. But there would always be a new predator who wanted something I didn't wish to give. Braea waited above. There would be more after her.

Safety was only ever fleeting.

"I will take the Crown to whoever you choose. You can just walk into the night, forget everything."

Bastian would have the Crown, and I wouldn't need to cling to anything for survival.

I could forget about courts and palaces and magic. Kings and queens and their cruelties.

The easiness of being nothing had been peaceful. As lulling and alluring as the escape of drink.

And yet...

I didn't want to walk into the night.

I wanted to watch another dawn, another dusk. I wanted to breed more roses and see if I could achieve that rich purple I'd dreamed of. I wanted to lie in the sun sated with cake and sex.

I wanted to live.

And I wanted to do that with Bastian.

I wanted to win another smile from him, another laugh—hells, a hundred more. I wanted to hear him say my name a thousand times. I wanted the touch of his skin on mine, the little gestures that said he was there and he wanted to touch me just because—just because it was pleasing, just because that warmth was a reminder, just because he loved me.

The next place might be safe, but it didn't have any of those things.

And I wouldn't settle for that.

I'd settled for too long.

I would live. And this time, I'd do it properly.

62

KAT

The world tore at me, cold air on raw nerves, shattered bones crunching back together. I tried to scream but my lungs weren't yet whole. Everything was agony.

But in my hands, I had the Crown of Ashes.

Even with broken fingers, I cradled it against myself. I'd risked so much, I couldn't lose it now. My muscles shrieked as I demanded they work while still knitting together.

My heart leapt to life, dragging a first, gasping breath into my new lungs. Oxygen was like fire in my chest, burning but also bright, and I sucked it in, greedy for air, greedy for the sweet agony of living.

When I rose, it was dark. Not a crack of light. Not a sign of the unseelie king.

I reached out. Rough bark, sticky with sap.

It split open as though it had been waiting for my touch, and cool light crept in.

Another fathomless breath. Glorious, fresh air. Every place it touched in my nose, my throat, the corners of my lungs—I was hyper aware of it. Each beat of my heart was a thunderous drumming that pulsed through my entire being.

I was alive.

Alive.

The trees unfurled around me, and I emerged from the strange cocoon I'd woken up in. The ground was twenty feet away, but as I peered out, a yew branch swept into place before me. When I stepped onto that, an oak branch provided my next foothold. Another step, another branch. There was even one at my side, like a gentleman offering an arm for support.

Below stood Bastian, his back to me, shoulders squared as he faced his queen. Speech was a strange sound, like my new ears hadn't quite adjusted, but the volume told me they argued. The soil beneath their feet glistened red with my blood. It was saturated.

She craned around him, eyes going round when they landed on me.

Slowly, Bastian turned. He went still, staring like I was a ghost.

In a way, I supposed I was.

"How...?" The queen's expression creased in confusion. "How did you get in there? And how did you *get back*?"

I smiled and paused in my descent, conscious of the fact I stood above her. "You weren't counting on me coming back, were you?"

A fleeting look crossed her face. Guilt she tried to hide. "Give me my Crown."

My smile became sharper, harder, and I took my time on the last few steps down to earth. It hummed beneath me, so heady that for a moment I had to grip the yew branch at my side. The Great Trees were the centre of the bond with the land that gave fae their power, and through them, I was connected to it all.

The sensation faded, and once I was steady, I lifted my chin. "No. You already have one."

Her nostrils flared, and something dangerous flashed in her eyes.

Lips parted, Bastian watched me, breaths shallow and fast.

Braea sidled up to him, hand raising, shaking with barely suppressed rage. "*Of course.* That's how you got through the gauntlet. It all makes sense. And now you have a crown of your own. Clever little human, except... you aren't, are you?"

I had no idea what she was insinuating. Some last ditch attempt to save herself from the truth.

She took his shoulder, squeezing until her knuckles went white. "She's been lying to you, Bastian. She made you bring her here so she could take my throne. That's why you've been turning him against me, isn't it? You planned this all along." Her teeth flashed in a bitter, cold smile. "What are you? A changeling? Fae blooded?"

Bastian blinked and turned to her, yanking out of her grip. "What are you—?"

"She has *royal blood*. That's how she was able to travel through the gauntlet." An edge of fear mingled with desperation shook through her voice. "Take the Crown from her. Quickly now. It's the only way. Otherwise she'll use it to steal the throne. You know how many died last time—we can't have another war of succession."

I couldn't help laughing. Her head snapped towards me.

"You truly can't see beyond what you want, can you? You're the only one here obsessed with keeping your claws in that throne. You're the one who killed your own children for it. I have no interest in your precious throne. I took the Crown because I couldn't allow you to have it. You are not worthy. Unlike your grandson."

As I stepped before Bastian, her eyelids fluttered. The rage on her face turned to dawning disbelief.

"He gave me his blood. *That* is how I was able to open the gauntlet. I'm not here to take your throne, Braea. At least, not for myself."

Bastian's chest rose and fell in a deep, deep breath, and he swayed towards me, hand rising in the space between us, then pausing as if he didn't dare touch me. Perhaps he was afraid he'd find I was just a ghost after all. With an imperceptible nod, he turned to his queen. "You killed my mother."

Her face dropped, the tightness of confusion giving way to slack shock.

"All she wanted was to be with the one she loved and raise their child together—to raise *me*. And you killed her. You thought you'd killed me, too."

She shook her head, breaths uneven. "It can't be. The child wasn't even born yet. It couldn't have—"

"Survived?" he bit out. His shadows gathered, a tight, seething mass that spelled out his rage. The hum I'd felt since awakening grew stronger—the tremble of distant thunder. "'It' did. 'It' is *me*."

She stumbled back from the spreading shadows, unblinking gaze never leaving Bastian. "You wouldn't hurt me. You wouldn't—"

The ground shook. The world was breaking. There was no other way to describe the sound or the violence. I stumbled and hugged the Crown to my chest, in danger of dropping it in the quake.

Braea was attacking... or Bastian was defending us.

Then the blood-soaked earth between us exploded. Darkness, feathers, the flap of great wings—something burst from the ground.

Or, some*things*, I realised, as I picked out the form of a raven amongst the maelstrom, its glittering eyes fixed ahead.

Its talons tore the air. Its wings cut through the night. It was huge and surrounded by so many of its kind I couldn't count.

This had to be the King of Death's doing.

The raven screeched. And its call was answered throughout the flock, as with one mind, they burst through Braea's chest.

Her bloody shriek pierced the night, cut short an instant later.

Bastian grabbed me as the air became thick with beaks and feathers, tearing talons and buffeting wings.

"You're... real." He gasped against my shoulder, arms tightening as he shielded me. "I thought..." He had to shout to be heard above the ravens' deafening cries, and the howling gale of their flight. "I was afraid... My gods, Katherine, I was so afraid." He drew a shaky breath as he buried his face in my hair.

"I'm here." I clutched his jacket, the Crown caught between us. "I'm alive."

He pulled back just enough to meet my gaze, hand warming the chilled skin of my cheek. His hair blasted in every direction and mine whipped against our faces.

"Since it looks like we're about to get torn apart by ravens, I need to say this now. I'm sorry. I made a mistake. I've been making the same mistake for the past fifteen years, in fact. You've been trying to show me, help me, steer me out of this doomed course... but I couldn't accept it. I shut my eyes and refused to see. But I see now." Nodding, he drew me tighter against himself as the ravens grew wilder. His smile was the first light of the day and the last. "*I see now*. Thank you for being my beacon."

He pressed a last desperate kiss to my lips. There was no art to it, no seduction, only pure emotion. A thank you. A goodbye. A final stand that we made together.

Locked together, we waited. It wouldn't be the worst way to go. Again.

We waited. And waited.

The ground's shaking eased to a tremble.

No cracks had opened up to swallow us whole. No ravens had torn us to shreds.

We peered up in time to see the ravens coalesce into a single, dark shape. From the blue-black feathers emerged the unseelie king. His pale face remained impassive as he looked down at the blood and gore and scattered bones that was all that remained of Braea.

Slowly, his mouth curled. "I've been waiting thirty five years to do that."

63

BASTIAN

The fog was dissipating, and in the distance the faint light before dawn painted the horizon.

But I stared at the fae before us. The sharp angles of his face could've cut diamonds as effectively as his ravens had cut through Braea. His only visible flaw was the purple stain marking his cheek.

He brushed off his sleeves, raising an eyebrow at Kat, then me. "We never did get to introductions. Drystan, King of Death... amongst other things."

At my side, Kat stiffened and disentangled herself from my grasp. "It's a night for finally doing things that are long overdue. Meet your son, Bastian."

The cool stiffness of his face dropped for an instant. It had to mirror the shock registering on my own.

Your son. This was... *He* was...

"You... weren't lying. I thought you were just trying to save your life." He blinked, then his glowing eyes locked on me. "My Hunt—they told me they'd scented you in the world above... I

445

thought they were mistaken." He huffed and shook his head. "I should've known their hounds wouldn't get such a thing wrong. Bastian?" He made a thoughtful sound. "She told me she'd always liked that name and wanted it for our child. Of course, I agreed. She could get me to agree to anything."

My father. Nyx's lover. The one she'd died trying to reach. The man who'd sired me.

I could barely breathe. This was too much. For one night. For one lifetime.

"I thought there was nothing left of the woman I loved, but your smile is hers—I saw the one you gave your beloved as you apologised. And your frown—your frown is hers." Eyes softening, he touched his thumb to my brow.

"And there is a lot of you in him, too." Kat squeezed my hand, waking me from my stupor.

"I see it." I studied him, marking all the ways my own features suddenly made sense—not strange and unseelie, but his. "The eyes, the shadows, the ability to split in two."

His head cocked as he frowned. "In two? Many ravens, yes, but that I can't do. At least not that I'm aware."

"Then where—?"

He doubled over with a grunt, clutching his stomach. "Unfortunately, it looks like our acquaintance will be brief. Your beloved has poisoned me."

"Katherine!"

She winced. "I can explain. One moment." She picked across the ground between the Great Trees, then ducked to scoop something up. "Here." She returned with her necklace, the chain broken, and held it out to... my father. "The antidote."

Still bent over, he peered up. An unpleasant flush marked his face, the strain of agony unmistakeable. He eyed the little bottle gleaming under the cold light, mistrust in the flat line of his mouth.

"She speaks the truth," I offered.

With a huff, he snatched the vial. "I thought it was all a lie. I wasn't expecting to survive, but at least I'd get to kill *her*. And you..." He pursed his lips at Kat. "I had to admire your cunning, so I gave you a chance."

"So, let me get this straight." I raised an eyebrow at Kat. "You poisoned my father?"

"I had to. He wasn't going to let me come back from the Underworld."

I rounded on him as he flipped open the bottle and downed its contents. "You were going to keep the woman I love?"

He spread his hands as the creeping poison faded. "It's a long story. But the sun's coming up and I can't stay past dawn."

"How are you even here at all?" I glanced back towards the gorge surrounding the palace. "I thought you couldn't cross the river."

"I didn't have to. I followed the tether between her soul and body. I intended to bring the Crown up here and ensure the person of her choosing received it, but a certain tiny human had other ideas." He narrowed his eyes at her sidelong. "Keep an eye on this one."

The fading mist swirled as the Wild Hunt emerged. Kat gasped, her magic humming as she instinctively called upon it. I caught her hand and gave a reassuring squeeze.

"My liege." Their leader bowed his head. "We served your son this night, but our people..." A dozen Horrors followed from the mist.

Drystan's brow wrinkled, the pain so sharp *I* could feel it. "What has been done to them? I thought they were missing not... *this*." He swallowed and dragged himself straight, shoulders back. "The veil is thin enough to get them home. Retribution can wait another moon."

I recognised that desire, and I suspected the feral smile that accompanied my reassurance was one he'd recognise. "The ones who did this are dead. You just took the last of them."

Sure enough, his expression mirrored mine. *My father*. I felt a little less alien, a little less like I didn't belong in this land of seelie folk.

"Then I wish I could do it twice over. Come"—he motioned to the Wild Hunt—"let us take these wanderers home."

"Wait." Kat stepped forward. "The Crown—how do we use it? Otherwise as soon as the sun rises, Bastian will be forced to Sleep. Does he just... wear it?"

"Him? No. You retrieved it and survived. By rights, I suppose it's yours." He took it from her grasp and raised it as if about to crown her. "Hmm. There should be a little grandeur to the event—after all, this hasn't been worn in millennia." He raised his chin, drawing a long breath as energy pulsed from him, a deep reverberation beneath the earth. "Come to us. Witness us."

The last of the fog melted away, revealing faint shapes that rose and consolidated into forms. Fae, humans, even a young sabrecat and a stag.

I squinted at the stag. The same one who'd fallen in the city streets after carrying me and a poisoned Kat here from Faolán's camp.

"Fantôme," Kat breathed, fingers pressing to her lips as she reached for the sabrecat cub.

And there were others I recognised. Fae who'd fallen in the Solstice attack. Others I'd helped Elthea shroud beneath the Hall of Healing. Lara, her blond hair pale and luminous in this ghostly form. Another blond human I didn't recognise stood between her and Fantôme.

Drystan surveyed the audience as he led Kat to the central point between the Great Trees. "Those you've known and those who've known this place."

The next familiar faces stole my breath. My fathers. Together again after so long. Sylen wore his armour, but it bore no sign of the terrible wound I'd inflicted upon him. And Kaliban was whole, his smile wide as he whispered to his beloved and pointed Kat out to him.

My eyes burned. There were so many things I needed to say to them both, but nothing would come out.

They inclined their heads, though, like they knew, and nodded over towards another figure.

I'd never seen her face, not in person, but I'd seen portraits in Braea's personal quarters. So like Sura in a lot of ways, but softer. In fact, Sura stood at her side, an unreadable look on her face.

"You're here." Drystan's cool, regal façade cracked along with his voice. As though he didn't realise he was doing it, he pulled the crown closer to his chest as he stalked towards her. "Where have you been? I searched my realm for your soul passing through, and I had my Hunt search this one in case you were stuck."

"I was right here. With our son." She came to me, steps floating half a foot in the air, gown flowing in a breeze even though the night was still. "I was so determined to keep you safe from *her*, my strength became bound to yours in that tiny little body. I am so sorry I couldn't stay alive for you or tell you I was here. It seems wrong that I could only give you a name."

I stared. In battle, I'd heard grown fae cry out for their mothers when they fell. I'd never understood it.

But here I was now, face-to-face with *my* mother. The one who'd carried me as long as she could and had fallen in her attempt to save me. Who'd kept on carrying me, even in death. Who'd given me a name—the start of an identity.

Her voice was every soothing sound I'd ever heard. Every caress of the cheek. Every time someone had mopped my feverish brow. Every flip of a too-hot pillow at night.

My chest filled with so many words I could never speak them all, but I managed to get out a handful of them. "You have nothing to apologise for. It's because of you, I had a chance."

She reached for me, but her hand clasped as though she realised even though I saw her now, we still could not touch, just as her feet didn't touch the ground. "My boy." She glanced up at Drystan. "*Our* boy."

Tears glimmered in his eyes as he searched her gaze with a longing I understood. "Will you pass over now?"

"My mother is gone, so he is safe and I may go. I will leave with you, but you know it's only temporary—I will continue on to the beyond."

He clenched his jaw and bowed his head.

"Now"—she flashed a grin that I'd seen in the mirror a hundred times—"weren't you about to do something?" She nudged him before coming to my side. Apparently ghosts could touch the King of Death.

"You always could distract me." Shoulders pulling back, he became regal once more, cold like marble, even though he carried a crown made of ashes.

And there, before an audience of the dead, the Wild Hunt, the bound Horrors, and me, Drystan crowned Katherine.

64
BASTIAN

Nyx... No, *my mother* squeezed my hand. Although I couldn't touch her, I felt the cool whisper of her drifting through my fingers.

The blackened coals of the crown stirred to embers as soon as it touched Katherine, blazing to life, the fire blending with her hair, casting a warm glow on her face where minutes ago she had lain here seized by the pallor of death.

A crown didn't make her a queen, but she was *my* queen. I would honour, worship, obey, kneel before her and beg, if I had to. Anything she asked.

The light to the east was brighter by the time it was done and I felt every single one of the hours I'd been awake as well as several more.

I scowled at the threatening sun, not ready to say goodbye, and found Drystan scowling at it too.

"As bad as each other," Nyx muttered.

He made a low grumbling sound, pulling her hand into the crook of his arm as he turned to Kat. "You have my mirror.

451

Even though I had packed mine away, I heard you calling through it. You were rather loud. Take it and cast it into the sea."

"Won't it break?"

He scoffed. "You think a mirror belonging to the King of Death can be broken? Bastian, you have been neglecting her education if she believes fae artefacts are so easily destroyed." But the way he shook his head was goodnatured, so like Kaliban, it hurt but a good kind of hurt.

The kind that said I'd been loved. Always.

"Throw my mirror into the sea. It will end up where it needs to be."

Her brow furrowed and I could feel her hesitation where she held my hand. I couldn't blame her, "where it needs to be" sounded ominous.

But she agreed, and Drystan stepped back, ready to return to his realm. "The sun comes."

In that moment, I hated it for doing what it always did. This one night, I'd have welcomed an extra hour—even just an extra ten minutes.

"Goodbye. And... thank you." I didn't know what else to say. There wasn't enough time to work that out.

Nyx peeled herself from Drystan and bent close to me. "I needed you to survive," she whispered, "but I always wanted you to be happy. And now I see you are, I can rest easy."

With that, she rejoined Drystan and around them, the whole host, including the Horrors herded by the Wild Hunt, became thinner as the sky grew brighter.

She was right. I *was* happy. Bastian Marwood, not the Bastard or the Serpent or the Shadow. *Me.*

Kaliban flashed a grin at Kat. "I told you you were loud." He and Sylen raised their hands in farewell and faded from sight.

With an approving nod, Drystan gathered a smiling Nyx close, and they disappeared into a burst of ravens who scattered to nothingness, leaving us alone with the rising sun.

"The Sleep," Kat muttered suddenly, as though a spell had broken. "He said I'd know how to use this thing when the time came." She touched the Crown atop her head as if checking it was still there. "Let's see if that's true." She tiptoed, steadying herself on my chest, and kissed my cheek.

There was the faint sensation of something snapping—a distant thread that whiplashed back to me, driving the breath from my lungs.

Kat flinched, staring up at me. "Are you—?"

"Yes." I caught her hand and held it to my chest as the sun broke the horizon and no Sleep came for me. "All is well."

65

KAT

We had a lot of explaining to do. A dead queen. A crown that had suddenly appeared and was, of all places, on *my* head. A new Night King who was not subject to Sleep.

First, we had to explain to the guards who'd been drawn by the shaking ground of Drystan's appearance and had seen the host of the dead and me being crowned by an unseelie king. One of them found Braea's crown amongst the... bits and, unsure what else to do, handed it to Bastian.

I thanked the gods Drystan had killed her. I couldn't have asked it of Bastian, not after seeing him so torn before. And after Cyrus outmanoeuvred me by taking the antidote, I wasn't sure I could've taken her myself. Braea had already mistrusted me, and she was fast and strong enough to evade my touch with ease. It had taken a month of groundwork to get my opening with Cyrus.

Then there was an emergency Convocation meeting, where Sepher and Zita could not stop staring at Bastian and the fact he now carried the Crown of Night and yet was awake during daylight hours. It took a long time to go through the whole story of all that happened since sunset and Bastian's true identity. Then there were the questions, particularly from Mored.

"I still don't understand how *she* has one of our ancient Crowns on her head. Why should she be the one to bear it? She's only had the gift of magic for five minutes."

At my side, Bastian gritted his teeth, jaw going solid, but before he could speak, I lent forward. "Oh, sorry. Did I miss the moment *you* died to retrieve it?" I wrinkled my nose at him. "You didn't even know of its existence until five minutes ago."

He turned wide eyes upon Sepher. "Are you going to let her speak to me like that? She's a human, what is she even doing here?"

Sepher cleaned his claws. "Yes, I am, actually." His eyes flicked up, the slitted pupils narrow. "I'm also going to remind you that my wife is a human."

Mored blanched. "Well, uh... yes, of course, but that's different. She's just his—"

"*Just his what?*" Bastian's low voice cut through the room, leaving silence in its wake.

As though he'd forgotten Bastian was no longer the queen's representative but king in his own right, Mored slowly turned, face frozen in panic. It was a delicious sight. "Dear... friend?"

"Be clear, all of you"—Bastian surveyed the table with a look that could've turned fire to ice—"I love this woman. If our fates were different, I would marry her a million times over. But regardless of contracts, you will treat her as though I am her husband and she is my wife. You will listen to her. Obey her orders. Treat her like the fucking queen she is. Do you understand?"

My chest grew tight, filled with something warm and bright. He was more than revealing his heart—he'd declared it and ordered others to act according to its wishes.

Everyone at the table nodded and murmured their agreement, only Mored kept quiet... right up until the moment Bastian's gaze snapped to him. "Y-yes, Your Majesty."

Zita sat back, smirking as she observed it all. She knew what life amongst the fae was like.

"Now that's settled." Sepher arched an eyebrow and slid his gaze to me and Bastian. "How is it you're awake while the sun is up?"

Zita leant forward, hand on his. "And can he have the same?"

"I can grant that power." I shared a glance with Bastian. "But we need something in return."

Sepher's eyes narrowed even as a smirk tugged at one corner of his mouth. "A bargain?"

"We *are* in Elfhame."

Lucan cleared his throat. "Well, of course, there needs to be discussion of—"

"This isn't a matter for debate—at least not with *you*," Zita said, gaze not leaving me. "The Sleep is part of Sepher's *life*, not a political bargaining chip. Get out and let us discuss this."

Lucan opened his mouth to argue, but Deema stood. "You heard the woman. Out." She clapped once and hustled the rest of the Convocation from the chamber.

Once quiet had settled, Sepher turned his hand, entwining his fingers with Zita's. "And your terms?"

"We work together. Not you manipulating us like you did to get Cyrus out of the way. No plotting behind each other's backs. *Together*. For one nation. For the good of all—or as many as we can as best we can. Agree to that, and I will free you from the Sleep."

At my side Bastian straightened, but he didn't argue. What one nation would look like, exactly, I wasn't sure. But if Elfhame was to have two monarchs who weren't separated by sunset and sunrise, this was the only way it could work.

Beneath the table, he slid his hand on my thigh and squeezed in silent praise. It warmed me, giving the confidence to raise my eyebrows at Sepher, prompting.

He sat there in quiet thought for a long while, fingertips tracing his lower lip over and over. Zita whispered in his ear.

Eventually, he took a long breath. "I can do that." A slow smile spread over his face as he leant forward, planting his hands on the table. "Now, how are we going to rule this country of ours?"

66

KAT

It turned out, negotiating with Sepher and Zita was the easy part. Next came the aftermath, which was... complicated. There was dealing with the Convocation and various other officials, as well as planning for the new government with Sepher and Zita.

But Bastian had them agree to delay the public announcement of his ascension to the throne. "Just for a few days," he said, "while the dust settles."

He claimed it was to give him a chance to get used to the idea, to make preparations for the announcement, for stability. There had already been two new kings in as many months and Elfhame needed a moment's peace, he said.

But when he caught me in a corridor and kissed me silly because we hadn't seen each other all day, I noticed he didn't wear his crown.

"You're king now," I reminded him, "isn't it scandalous to be caught kissing a human where anyone might see?"

There was a momentary scowl at my reminder, but he soon

smothered it with a grin. "I thought my Wicked Lady liked a little scandal?"

Before we had a chance to get any more scandalous, Ennet came around the corner and pointed a pen at us. "Ah, there you are, Your Majesty. I've been looking everywhere for you. Brynan said you weren't to be interrupted, but there's a matter that needs your attention."

With a deep sigh and a quick kiss on my cheek, Bastian disappeared with her.

Still, speculation of a different kind ran rife through the palace, and from there it seeped into the city beyond. Word spread that Braea had died. That I'd killed her. That she'd secretly named Bastian as her heir. That he was really her grandson or that Asher was or that they were waiting for some other secret heir to return from overseas before crowning them.

Of course, some held on to the idea she was still alive. After all, she hadn't left the palace in the past thirty-five years, afraid Drystan would kill her if she left the protection of the River Velos. Her people only saw her on the royal balcony.

I heard the whispers when I went to visit Rose and Ariadne (not wearing the Crown of Ashes—I didn't want to add to the rumours yet). Dutifully, I reported them to Bastian.

He cursed, then went off in search of Orpha, muttering something about "damage limitation."

The next afternoon, he strode into the suite carrying a hamper. He grabbed a coat from the hooks in the antechamber and donned it.

I looked up from my book. "It's not that cold in here, is it?"

"Come on," he said simply, continuing into the bedroom.

I followed, calling after him, "Is something wrong?"

"No, but we need to be quick. He's there."

"Who's where? Quick to do what?"

He tossed a satchel on the bed. "The first part will become clear shortly. And quick to pack a bag."

"For?" I drew out the word. "I need some more clues if I'm going to know what to pack."

"Too slow." He grabbed a couple of items from the drawers and shoved them into the bag.

"Are we in trouble? Are we going on the run?" I glanced back towards the entrance to the suite. He hadn't barricaded it, but part of me expected guards to burst in. A horrible thought made my stomach dip. Those rumours... "Are they arresting me for killing Braea?"

He blinked up from buckling the satchel. "What? No. *No.* Nothing bad, just... I want to be gone long before Ennet grabs me. Brynan is running interference, but I'm not sure how long he can keep her away."

Brynan was still his assistant as he'd always been, but there seemed to be a minor rivalry developing between him and Ennet, since she was officially the Night King's assistant. Bastian was still clinging on to the Shadow's offices, due to their convenient entrance to the secret passages. Ennet seemed to have accepted that, but she kept on at us to move into the royal suite.

Bastian took my hand and pulled me into the living room. "Here."

With a whispered word, he made the air before us shimmer, then four dark lines formed, connecting to form a tall rectangle. It swung open, revealing utter darkness.

With anyone else, I might've found that absence of light frightening, but not him. I held his hand and trusted myself to his shadow door.

We stepped through onto a rocky clifftop, face-to-face with

Faolán. The wind pierced my clothes at once, stealing my breath and blowing clouds along at speed. "What's going on?" I called over its bluster.

"Faolán very kindly spent the afternoon riding out here, so we could jump to his location." Bastian clapped him on the shoulder.

Faolán flashed the bracelet I'd spotted him wearing before. "It's an anchor point. He can reach me anywhere. Rare magic." He slid Bastian a wry look. "Lucky me, eh?"

"How else do you think we stay in touch when he's in the field? Thank you."

The shapechanger grumbled, pausing by the shadow door. "Just give me a warning when you come back. I don't want you appearing while I'm... *busy*."

"Hey, you interrupted *us* while we were trying to get *busy*. Fair's fair." Bastian gave him a wide grin.

Shaking his head, Faolán disappeared and the door shut behind him. A moment later there was no sign it had ever been there, save for the faint ripple of Bastian's magic dissipating.

"So, why are we...?" Before I could finish the question, he turned me around to face a small house built of pale silvery stone. Two storeys, with a small tower at the end closest to the sea. A ramshackle garden of wild, windswept plants surrounded us, all of them crooked, bending inland. The smooth stone and miniature spire reminded me of Tenebris, but this was simpler, more humble than any building in the city.

"Come on, you're not dressed for this weather and it's about to rain." He pulled me into the shelter of his coat, my back to his chest, and slid an arm around my belly as he walked me inside, stealing a kiss as he shut the door.

461

We left our shoes and his coat in the small porch just as thick, drenching rain started.

"It's Asher's, but he rarely gets a chance to come here," he half explained as we moved further inside.

Rich, dark wood clad the walls and covered the floor and ceiling, sweeping upward in a staircase at the far end of the room. The embroidered wall hangings and velvet upholstered seating covered in oversized cushions and thick, plaid blankets made the room feel enclosed. Safe. Cozy.

Bastian called for the fire to light, and I understood how my ancient ancestors must've felt in their caves on a wintry night.

"We have a stocked larder, and I think you'll like what's in there." He nodded towards a door I hadn't noticed amongst the panelled walls.

I poked my head in while he busied himself in the sitting room. Dark tiles like smoked glass covered every surface, and at the centre of the room was a large, sunken bath. I let out a little moan at the sight. It was similar to the one in Bastian's rooms back in Lunden, big enough for me to float in, starfished without touching the sides. A bath I very much hadn't taken full advantage of—I'd been too lost in those days.

When I returned to the living room, Bastian was grinning. "Told you, you'd like it."

"Right, but..." I spread my hands. "What are we doing here? It's a long way to come for a bath."

"Well, first of all, we're having dinner." He stepped aside revealing plates and bowls of food on the small table by the window, a cluster of candles—a real candles, not fae lights—at its centre. "Don't worry, it's all from the palace kitchens. I didn't cook. No one needs that. Though I did try, for you, it just..." He winced and pulled out a chair for me.

As I took it, he went on, "Then we can take a bath, sit by the fire... go to bed. Whatever you want. We have a few nights here. That's why I wanted to get away before... anyone could summon me."

"You've arranged all this so we can have some time alone together." I couldn't help how wide my smile went. I didn't want to hide how pleased I was. Didn't need to. Not here. Not with him.

"I'm sorry it's been so hectic since you got back from Dawn." He sighed as he took the seat opposite. "It feels like I saw you more when you were there."

I made a low sound of agreement. The month since I'd returned from Dawn felt more like a year.

Bastian offered me the choice of wine or a sweet elder-flower drink. I chose the elderflower and he followed suit, pouring glasses for us both. Drinking less alcohol had made me realise how much it dampened everything, good and bad. And now I·was where I wanted to be, I had no wish to water down my existence.

We loaded our plates with steamed beans, roasted carrots and potatoes, and a savoury cheese and spinach pie whose lid was an intricate latticework of pastry. "So what is this place, exactly?" I asked as I eyed the two jugs on the table—there was a choice of a creamy sauce or thick gravy. I went for the gravy, careful to avoid the lid of the pie. No one wanted soggy pastry.

"It's a holiday home of sorts. Dusk's royal family has had it for centuries as an escape from the city and political life. It passed to him when Sura died, since he was Braea's closest relative and she didn't leave the palace." His brow creased as he cut into his slice of pie. "I suppose, technically, it should be mine. Don't worry, I'm not going to take it from Asher."

"You are king now. You could just order him to give it to you."

He made an amused sound, though there was no glint in his eye. "To be honest... I don't really feel like the king."

"You don't say."

"I know it's idiotic. Just like... mourning Braea is." The pained look on his face made me put down my forkful of food instead of eating it. "I accept it's better that she's gone, it's just... I suppose I mourn who she once was. All she did for me. Even as I'm horrified at what she did to my mother and to you." A deep frown scored his brow. "It's like she was two people and I can't reconcile these two sides in my mind. And I feel so foolish for not seeing it. Am I truly that stupid?"

"You're not stupid at all," I murmured. "Or idiotic. People have different facets that can surprise us. You saw there was another side to me beneath the terribly proper Lady Katherine."

"That's because I met the Wicked Lady first. You showed your hand and I couldn't unsee who you really were—brave and vibrant and wicked clever. I could never reconcile that with the folded hands and shame of Lady Katherine."

"Then what about you? You're the Bastard of Tenebris, but also Bastian Marwood."

"Bastian and the Bastard." He grimaced, a battle written on his face. "Sometimes I'm not sure who's more real."

My heart clenched at his confession and the fact he trusted me with it. How could I help him?

"But"—he raised his eyebrows at me, expression easing into a crooked smile—"I know this dinner is real, and it's growing cold."

I chuckled, though it turned into a moan as I took a mouthful of food. Damn, the palace chefs knew how to cook.

Subtle spices had been baked into the pie—nutmeg and something else I couldn't identify—and they'd sprinkled nigella seeds on top. Honey glazed the carrots, creating a sticky sweetness. And the potatoes.

Good gods, *the potatoes.*

Their corners were crisp, their insides perfectly fluffy, and they mopped up the gravy like they were made for that one purpose.

Somewhere along the way, I'd closed my eyes, and now I opened them, I found Bastian watching me with a faint smile. "I love it when you lose yourself like that."

My face grew warm, not with embarrassment but with pleasure. Would it ever grow old having him look at me like this? It didn't feel possible.

We ate in pregnant silence for a little while, save for the odd sound of enjoyment. It was that kind of food—you couldn't help showing your appreciation.

Eventually, I looked up and found him staring at me over the rim of his glass.

"What's wrong?" I dabbed my mouth with the napkin. Did I have gravy on my chin?

"Not wrong. Right." He gulped his drink, throat bobbing like it was an effort. "Kat. That night. When I found you by the trees, I thought..." He shook his head, eyes bright. "My world was over. I couldn't fathom existing in it without you. Are you sure you're all right? Nothing since—no pain or—?"

"I'm fine. Good. *Great.*" I took his hand and squeezed. "I'm here. I'm healthy. And my only complaint is that we have to run away to a remote clifftop to get a moment to ourselves."

He sighed and took a more sensible sip. "Good."

"Though I have to ask you the same, my king in denial." I

raised an eyebrow as he stilled. "A lot has happened lately. Are *you* all right?"

Exhaling, he looked away. "My mind has been very... full. Meeting my mother... my father... losing *Athair*... Braea's death... The throne. It feels like everything has changed but I haven't had time to wrap my head around any of it. None of it feels real." He took a sip and shook his head. "I'm sorry. We're not here to think about anyone else. Just us."

"This *is* about you. Especially if it's on your mind."

"It is. I keep trying to push it aside and get on with work or making sure you're all right... and plotting this little trip..." He flashed a grin. "But somehow it muscles in, like it's too big to keep contained."

"Bastian." I set down my knife and fork. "You discovered the woman you thought was your mother for your entire life was not. Your queen and employer was your grandmother. Your mother was a princess and next in line to the throne, and she was killed by that grandmother to prevent her going to your father and giving birth to *you*. Then, your father, who happens to be an unseelie King of Death killed her with a flock of ravens. I would say that's allowed to take up a lot of space in your head."

"When you put it like that... Though, there is another matter." He winced and went to the bag he'd hastily packed. "I found this." He pulled out a book.

Cracked oxblood red leather decorated with the moon's phases in gold. A gate stood below the arcing moons, foreboding, like only death lay beyond.

"It's the one they used to make the Horrors," he went on. "I've kept it with me ever since I found it in Braea's things. I can't risk it getting into the wrong hands."

None of this shocked me. It explained the uneasy feeling

the book gave me. "No. We can't. Especially not now we know what—*who* the Horrors really are. Have you tried destroying it?"

"Of course. It doesn't burn, won't cut, and the ink didn't run in water."

We discussed it as we ate, deciding to try contacting his father at the next new moon and see if he had any ideas. Maybe the book that was used to turn unseelie fae into Horrors could be used to return them to themselves.

With nothing more to say about the terrible book, our conversation turned to how people would react to his announcement as king. The way he spoke about it, I knew he just meant it as a thought exercise, but it was a truth he would have to face. I wanted to help, and yet forcing it on him wouldn't make the change any easier to handle. He needed time to process and heal from Braea's manipulations.

Outside, dark clouds gathered over the sea, and it was hard to tell where day ended and night began. There was no orrery on the mantlepiece, either.

This was a place to escape time as well as court politics.

67

KAT

We had dessert (of course), and curled up on the settee, reading while we let our food go down. He disappeared into the bathroom and the splash of a bath running drifted back into the living area.

If there were three things in life I couldn't resist, they were cake, hot baths, and him. And I already had two of those. So I padded in, undressing as I went.

His eyes alighted upon me, taking in every inch of my bare skin. He'd lit dozens of real candles in here, and their flickering light caught in the dark, silvery tiles as well as in my hair.

We sank into the bath and took our time watching the view out the window to the east—a dim sliver of gold faded over the mountains, signalling that the sun had set. As I leant back against his chest, I felt the relief easing through him.

"Is it silly that I still get to sunset and expect a summons from her?"

I took his hands and kissed one palm, then the other. "It was your routine for fifteen years. I don't think it's silly at all."

He made a soft sound as though reassured and idly played with my breasts, teasing my nipples in this way that had me pushing into his touch.

I twisted to face him, sliding over his wet body with ease. "You've taken your sweet time to touch me."

"I intend to take my time with you tonight, love." His hands slid up my back. "I wouldn't want to break you."

That phrase. The same as when we'd danced and he'd promised to make love to me with his other self. "You mean...?"

"If you still want—"

"Yes. *Yes*, I do." The thought alone made my blood stir.

"*Good.* I can't wait to see you taking us both." He stood and led me from the bath.

He disappeared behind me to get towels, stepping back into view with one wrapped around his waist. From behind, another towel came around my shoulders, and I gasped, finding his double behind me. He dried me off while the other Bastian towelled his hair and watched.

Together, they led me through the sitting room and upstairs, a thick towel wrapped around me. Every muscle and mole was identical, right down to the intricate shading and stars of his tattoo. Even the way they walked with easy confidence. I finally understood what he'd tried to explain before. This wasn't Bastian and a copy—they were the same person, consciousness split.

The bedroom occupied half of the upper floor. A large, arched window took up most of one wall, overlooking the sea, which had become darkness capped with white waves. Rain pelted the panes, leaving droplets that studded the black clouds beyond. The bed had no canopy, but sat at the foot of the window, facing the sea.

He called the fire to life, its pinkish light bathing the room in warmth as his other self pressed against my chest, warming me. We kissed, slow and deep, every point of connection flaring to life.

At my back, more warmth as they caught me between them and the other one gathered my hair, pulling it to one side as he kissed the back of my neck. Two pairs of lips upon me and one of those at that sensitive spot at the nape of my neck —it was too much. I shivered, clinging to the fae before me.

Caught between them, I should've felt trapped. But it was as if some strange alchemy took place in the space of their arms, turning the press of their bodies either side of me into something precious, somewhere safe, a kingdom where I was cherished twofold.

They eased my towel undone and let it fall, so there was only skin upon skin, hot and soft from the bath. One stopped kissing me as the other caught my cheek and turned my head, capturing my mouth with his.

It soon became confusing as hands smoothed over my skin, massaging out every hint of tightness, squeezing my breasts, lightly caressing my thighs and backside, and I lost track of which hand belonged to which Bastian. They shared me, kisses blurring together, a grip tightening in my hair to tilt my head back so the other could kiss me deeper, wring me out harder, overwhelm me all the more.

I didn't realise they were walking me to the bed until one knelt upon it and the other sat me before him.

Anticipation burned in every fibre of my being. Both Bastians. At last. Curiosity had nibbled me ever since I'd read about three people enjoying each other in that book Queen Elizabeth had made us read. And since Bastian's promise, the nibble had become a gnawing want in my bones.

From behind, he slid his hands along my thighs, nudging them apart.

The Bastian before me took his time, gaze drinking me up from head to breasts to parted legs. He shook his head when his gaze reached my aching centre. "So fucking exquisite. You deserve to be worshipped, you know."

"We should do that," he murmured behind me, chest rumbling into my back.

As one knelt before me, the other squeezed my thighs, fingers dimpling my skin as he lifted and spread them as wide as they would go.

My breath caught in that place of sweet anticipation, waiting, wanting. Needing.

With slow reverence, Bastian bent and swept his tongue along me. The breath I'd held burst from me with a soft moan.

"I *think* she likes that." He chuckled behind me, letting his shadows take over holding my thighs.

Between my legs, he pulled back and looked up at me, eyes dark. "If we only *think* it, we aren't trying hard enough. I want to *know*." With the flash of a wicked grin, he lowered his head and devoured me, as his double massaged a sweet-smelling oil between his hands and slicked it over my breasts.

They kissed my thighs, the sensitive spot at the back of my neck. Their fingers glided across my nipples and into my centre. Their tongues delved inside me, over my skin, between my lips.

I couldn't keep track. Certainly couldn't keep sanity.

They held me arched, open, at their mercy, around and inside me, playing every part of my body until I cried out, lost in shuddering, all-consuming pleasure.

When I caught my breath, he pulled away with a self-satisfied smirk. "*There.* Now we know." Gaze never leaving me, he backed away and took a seat at a small side table.

I frowned. "What are you—?"

"Shh." From behind, his thumb skimmed over my lips. "We have plans for you, love. Don't you worry. You'll get every filthy thing you want."

I swallowed, heat flushing my skin, torn between the thrill of his promise and shame that he knew the places my mind went.

Yet it wasn't the old shame that had once plagued me. Part of me still believed I shouldn't want this, I should endure it for the sake of someone else's needs. Yet here, in Bastian's arms, I was able to claim it, take it, transform it.

I wanted this so much, it burned my veins, and the echo of shame only fanned those flames higher, hotter. I lifted my chin.

"*There.*" At the table, he poured himself a whisky, sat back with his ankle crossed over his knee, and nodded. "Fuck her."

The rawness of his words seized me and the casualness of his manner made my shame hotter, as his other self lifted my backside and slid under me.

He sipped the amber whisky, gaze intent as his other self paused at my entrance. A wicked smile curled his mouth as he pulled me down onto him.

I whimpered, head falling back onto his shoulder as my eyelids fluttered at the slow fullness.

"Keep your eyes on him, love," he whispered in my ear as the pressure of his piercing hit the spot that had me arching in his hold. "Show us how well you obey us. Show us how good you are only for us." With that he drew from me, his other self's silver gaze upon me all the while.

It felt illicit, being fucked and being watched. Where

Caelus had watched me before, though, this was Bastian, and although I knew it was also him filling me so sweetly, it felt like it was someone else. It should've horrified me. Should've disgusted me. But the knowledge that it was him made this safe.

I wasn't breaking any rules—I was being *good*, earning his praise... *their* praise. Gods, I couldn't keep the world straight with two of him.

"Are you going to come for us again, my dear ember?" he murmured in my ear, words reverberating into my back as he guided my hips to meet his and slipped his middle finger over my apex with just enough pressure to make me buck.

"I think she needs more if she's going to take us both," the one watching said, placing his glass on the table.

"We wouldn't want to break her." The one behind me circled his finger in a steady, maddening rhythm.

"That's it," he murmured from the table. "You're perfection, love. This view is..." He shook his head, gaze locked on me, drink forgotten. His chest heaved as though our exertions were his.

"You feel so good," he rasped in my ear. "So slick. So tight. I could fuck you for the rest of my life and it wouldn't be enough."

I arched, whimpered, terrible tension stretching me out, pushing against his unyielding hold.

The Bastian who sat opposite, leant forward with a predatory half smile, running his thumb over the point of his canine tooth. "Look at her. *Look at her.*"

The sight of him transfixed by me, the feel of him inside me, upon me, touch circling firm and fast—they layered over each other. I stood no chance.

My body came apart, trembling, arching. I cried out, lost in beautiful, bright oblivion that pounded through my entire being.

When I returned, I found myself still grinding back onto him, body running on instinct. He gave a deep groan that thrummed through me, yet his other self still sat, watching.

"Please, Bastian." I reached for him. "I want you."

"So greedy," he said with a dark laugh. "You already have me, *Katherine*. I can see you're enjoying it. Your cheeks have gone that pretty pink colour I love so much."

"But... you promised." I frowned up at him as the Bastian at my back eased me off him and set me on my knees.

The one before me flowed to his feet, and when I went to glance over my shoulder at what the other one was doing, he caught my chin. "Eyes on me, love."

"Yes, Bastian." It was worth saying to see the flush of pleasure spread across his skin.

I obeyed as he slid his thumb up over my lower lip. As I took it into my mouth, his other self placed his blunt tip at my entrance.

With lust-darkened eyes, he watched me suck him in, curling my tongue around his thumb. "Do you want us both at once, love?" His voice had gone gravelly and raw with his own want.

I slid back, fighting a smile as I knew the effect my next word would have on him. "*Please.*"

Both of him groaned, and the one before me bit his lip. "Gods damn you, woman. You know exactly what you're doing when you say that, don't you?"

"Maybe."

He shook his head, stroking his length, though he was already hard. "On your hands and knees, then."

Again, I obeyed. I held his gaze as he slid into my mouth,

though my eyelids fluttered and I made a little sound as his other self slid into me at the same time.

"Is that what you wanted? Both of us in you at once?"

I could only answer with a moan around him as they both took up a long, slow rhythm.

This was beyond illicit. Beyond scandals. This was fantasy made flesh.

I used every trick I knew to suck him in, to roll and flick my tongue over his head, to tease the skin around his piercing, but it grew harder to focus with each thrust from his other self. My breaths grew heavier, my skin burned, and I could barely keep my balance with one hand on the bed and the other fisted around him, trying to make up for the fact I couldn't take him all the way down.

Trying to focus on pleasing him had the unexpected bonus of amplifying every other sensation. His fingers biting into my hips, another hand gripping the hair at the back of my head. The cool air on my skin as rain hammered on the window. The way he glided all the way out before thrusting right back in, taking me from empty to full at dizzying speed.

"Does our flame think she can take this, too?" Slippery from the oil, his thumb slid between my buttocks, teasing that tighter entrance.

I twitched, the touch adding another layer to the sensation threatening to drown me once more. Perhaps I couldn't take it, but I wanted it. Stars above, did I want it. I nodded carefully, pulling my eyebrows together, since I couldn't say *please*.

"She does." The Bastian before me nodded to his other self and watched as he slowly sank his thumb into me.

It was too much. The final thing that broke me apart into shards of bliss. My cries were blocked by his length pumping into my mouth, but I heard his praise. "That's it, love. You can take more. You're doing so well."

The praise continued as he used his shadows to add more fullness alongside his thumb, stretching me gently. Another climax built on the aftershocks of the last one, rising so quickly, I didn't know where one ended and the next began.

He kept whispering sweet filth to me as he caught me when I sagged, breathless, and he eased from my body.

"There, I think you're ready now." He smiled down at me, smoothing hair from my sweat-slicked brow. "Do you think you are?"

Eyes wide, I nodded.

"So eager," he chuckled.

They took it in turns to kiss me, as they manoeuvred me so I was straddling one of them near the edge of the bed, with the other one standing behind me.

"Are you sure about this?" they asked as one. "You don't have to do anything, you know."

"I know. And I know I can call a stop to this whenever I want. *If* I want." I braced one hand on his chest as I guided him to my entrance. "But right now, I want this."

He groaned as I sank all the way down his length. "Hold there." His other self's grip tightened on my hips as he kissed the back of my neck, his chest flush against me. "Now, breathe with me."

I joined him as he drew a slow breath in through his nose and out from his mouth, then another. The last bit of tension left my body, exhaled, and I nodded.

The Bastian behind me placed himself at my back entrance, while the other one took up a lazy circling of my apex with his thumb. Gently, he eased inside.

Oh gods. It was a lot. Too much. I sucked in a shallow breath, and he stopped.

"Stay with me." Beneath me, Bastian squeezed my thigh and inhaled, long and slow. I followed, keeping up that rhythm, and the tightness slackened.

"That's it," he murmured in my ear.

Once I'd relaxed, he continued his slow entrance. It was a battle to keep my breaths even as the pressure built beyond anything I'd ever known.

At last he stopped, fully seated. He paused there, letting me get used to the sensation of being so full. More of those long, slow breaths helped my body ease around him. It didn't hurt, but we were just this side of the line and if he wasn't careful, I knew he could push me across it. I suddenly understood why he'd talked about taking his time and making sure I was ready.

"All you need to do is stay as relaxed as you can, let me take care of everything else. This will be a lot." He held my gaze without any hint of teasing, deadly serious. "If it hurts or you want to stop, tell us or tap twice if you can't speak. Understood?"

I swallowed and nodded slowly, not quite daring to move when my body teetered at such a delicate balance. It was all the more challenging to maintain control like this when pleasure simmered in me, wanting to boil over.

Holding my hips, he lifted me off them. I gasped at the sudden, absolute emptiness and it was as though I could finally take a fuller breath.

"Are you all right?" he murmured in my ear.

"Yes. *Yes*. I'm just... a little overwhelmed."

"Do you want to stop?" the one before me said, serious again, his thumb falling still.

"No. Please, don't."

"That's unfair, love," he said on a groan as they pulled me back onto them. "You know what that word does to me and I have to control myself right now."

"I'm sure you'll manage." My voice came out breathless as I reached the bottom of the stroke.

"You're playing a dangerous game, Katherine," he said beneath me, as he took over holding my hips and the one behind me slid his hands up over my breasts. He gave a merciless squeeze and nipped my ear, making me arch into them both.

I let out a strangled cry, my entire body throbbing.

"Just because I'm not going to ram you while we're like this, doesn't mean I don't have other ways to punish you, love."

I'd always loved his praise, but it seemed I could enjoy his punishment too. "Do your worst."

Both parts of him gave a dark laugh.

"Be careful what you wish for." His grip slid to my throat, the perfect balance of allowing me to breathe and commanding as they both thrust into me. He pulled me back, arching my body so he could claim my mouth and taste the moans they forced from me.

Where other times making love became harder, faster as we both chased a crescendo, they took me slowly, sensuously, as deeply as they could, like we had all the time in the world and they would use every minute. I felt every inch of their steady lengths, aware of each bit of progress in and out, rhythm perfectly matched.

Once, thanks to a piece of paper with our names on it, the law had stated that Robin Fanshawe owned me. Yet, until this moment I had never felt so thoroughly possessed. Bastian

Marwood had every part of me, body, heart, soul, and all the indefinable strands between.

And, in return, he gave me every part of himself.

They held me, cherished me, and I felt twice as precious, twice as loved as ever before. I teetered on the verge of tears, just as I teetered on the edge of obliterating bliss. There was nothing like this and no one like him.

And he was mine.

The world faded with each drive of my hips into theirs. Their breaths surrounded me. Their hands placed me exactly where I was required, using me beautifully. Their mouths praised me, bit me, sucked the point of my leaping pulse, and spoke delicious filth in my ear on a hot breath.

"Fuck, you look incredible. You have no idea how many times I've dreamed of doing this with you." His voice was raw, and I could see the strain on the face of the Bastian below me as his eyebrows drew together.

All I could do was hold on as a languid wave came for me, so huge it seemed to move slowly, so overwhelming, it decimated completely.

There was nothing. Only the wave. Only all-consuming bliss.

His distant voice called me back from senselessness. "My glorious forest fire. You're going to be the death of me."

Beneath and behind me, he tensed, breaths harsh, movements shuddering as he barely kept control, until as one, both parts of him cried out. I could feel his pleasure, hot and consuming as he twitched inside me, hips jerking.

I could barely kiss him back as he held me, barely move as he gently pulled from me.

"Kat?" Sitting up, he stroked my cheek. "Are you—?"

I made a small sound of confirmation, too limp to nod or

speak. It felt like I'd been pulled apart and put back together, but this new form needed a while to become solid, like the wings of a newly emerged butterfly.

Together, they took me into the upstairs bathing room. Even though it was smaller, the bath was still luxuriously large. He ran it hot, the way I liked, and the scented steam tugged at my eyelids as the three of us sank into it.

I must've dozed off, because the next time I blinked, the water was cooler and he was lifting me from it. "There she is. See? She's alive."

"Hmm, good." They surrounded me, words merging together in a warm cocoon. "I was getting worried. That wasn't too much was it, love?"

As another towel came around me, I nodded, smiling at the concerned look they shared. "In the best possible way."

He made a low sound as we returned to the bedroom. In my drowsy state, I tried to walk, but only my toes touched the ground as they carried me between them. This was better than the best part of being drunk—where the world became fuzzy and soft and I wasn't quite sure what was real or not. I might be walking on clouds, I stepped so lightly.

I found myself laughing softly as they laid me in the middle of the bed, though I didn't know what amused me so much. "Bastian," I breathed as they lay on either side of me. "I... I read about love... I dreamed of it... but I never knew it would be like this. I survived without you, but this feels like living."

Arms tangled around me, one of them stroked my hair, they kissed my brow, my cheeks, even my nose as I sank deeper and deeper into the bed and the darkness behind my eyelids.

Before I fell away completely, I caught his soft reply. "It does, doesn't it?"

I woke with a start. Trying to work out what had tugged me from such a deep sleep, I stretched my aching body. There was no Bastian. But there was a silhouette at the window, a darkness deeper than the black clouds.

I slipped from the bed, wincing at the cold, and pulled a blanket around myself before padding over. After all we'd done together, it was silly to feel a thrill when I wrapped my arms and blanket around him and he pressed into me, but apparently I was silly when it came to Bastian Marwood. Being allowed to touch him still hadn't grown old.

I peered around him. Outside, huge white caps carved the sea into rough shapes and pounded into the cliffs of the opposite headland. Lightning cracked the sky in two, soon followed by the crash of thunder. That was what had woken me.

"What's wrong?"

"Nothing." He turned and wrapped an arm around me, gaze on the raging sea. "I was just watching the storm."

Another streak of lightning fractured the night, reflecting in his eyes, and less than a second later thunder rattled the window.

I shivered and tucked against his side as the wind shrieked and clawed at the house and its little garden. "It's coming closer."

He shook his head, squeezing me tighter. "It's already here."

68

KAT

Despite the storm, we had a blissful stay in the little house.

The next day was beautiful and cloudless, so we went down to the cove and enjoyed the beach, splashing in the water and dozing in the sun.

Back at the cottage, I threw Drystan's mirror off the cliff—Bastian had thought ahead and packed it in his haste. Then we cooked together, both equally bad, but we managed to put together something resembling a stew. Not pretty and not gourmet cuisine, but sustaining and simple. That was all we needed.

But, of course, we had to return to Tenebris-Luminis.

And at once, life swooped in.

We'd barely greeted Faolán when Bastian was dragged away for an update from Brynan. I hid my crown in a bag and checked with the shapechanger where his wife was—lunch with Ari and Ella at our favourite restaurant, Moonsong Spire.

I surprised Ari and Rose by making an appearance, and

they pulled up an extra chair, though Ella's still sat empty for now. Part of the appeal was that they allowed Fluffy to accompany us. She took up her spot lying across my feet. Now we knew about Bastian's father, it made sense. I smelled familiar to her—like her one-time master.

Of course, when Ella arrived, she took one glance at me and gave a knowing look. "You seem *very* relaxed... and thoroughly fucked, if I might say so." She raised her eyebrows at me as she took her seat.

"You're one to talk," Rose muttered, covering her glass when the server went to pour her wine.

Ari barely bit back a grin as she elbowed Ella. As we ate, I got the story of how Ella had been having fun with two fae women, but it was clear they were very much in love with each other and she was a novelty for them to enjoy.

"Not that I blame them." Ella widened her eyes. "They're the same for me. Fae bodies are so interesting... the same but different. Still..." Her gaze drifted away.

Dark eyes narrowing, Ari cocked her head. "You sound... wistful. Don't you want to find someone you love?"

Ella snorted into her wine, somehow making such an undignified gesture pretty. "No, thank you! I'm enjoying— what was it my mother once said?—*slutting* my way around the city. Also, it's wonderful fucking all kinds of fae and not needing to worry about getting pregnant. Besides, love blinds you." She blinked around the table at us as though only just realising who she was speaking to. "Not you! *Me*, I mean. It's much simpler this way, and I prefer my sex nice and simple."

I filed that comment away to discuss later when it was just the two of us, and raised my coffee cup. "To sex that's as simple or complicated as we wish."

Once we'd finished, I was full and tired. We hadn't slept

much at the cottage, finding much more interesting things to spend our nights doing.

But, as soon as I got to the palace, I was intercepted by Ennet and ushered into a meeting to discuss the announcement of Dusk's new king. Bastian looked as tired as I felt, and we barely kept our eyes open as we went over the plans.

By the time it finished, we were dead on our feet. But, of course, it didn't end there. When we left the Convocation chamber, both Ennet and Brynan were waiting at the doors, her with her trusty notebook and him with a dozen matters for our attention. It seemed they had decided to team up to tackle their reluctant king.

We wound our weary way through the corridors, with her making notes as she walked backwards at such speed, she must've done this a hundred times before. The Convocation must've warned her of Bastian's words about listening to me, because she was just as attentive to my comments as his, marking them in the book with a thoughtful nod without seeking his approval before Brynan moved us on to the next item.

"Well, here we are. The other matters can wait until you've had some rest." She flipped the book shut as she and Brynan stepped aside.

But the double doors behind them weren't the ones to our rooms.

Bastian frowned, rubbing his eyes. "This is Braea's suite."

"*Actually*, it's the royal suite. We've had it cleaned and your belongings brought through while you were on your trip."

Bastian opened his mouth but just huffed. I knew that look. He was too tired to argue, and I couldn't blame him. My eyes felt like they'd been rolled in sand and roasted.

So I squeezed his hand and smiled at her. "How efficient.

Thank you both for your help." With matching nods, they disappeared down the corridor, leaving us to plod inside.

I fell against the door as I shut it, groaning, "Can I just go to sleep here?"

"I don't think that would work." Though his shoulders sagged, he peeled me off the door and led me inside. "But a nap is an excellent idea."

The quiet was a blessing—the only thing I really noticed as I followed him through the suite into a bedroom with the curtains drawn. We got halfway through undressing before giving up and crawling into the bed, crowns discarded.

"Just an hour." He took my hand, kissed it, then cradled it to his chest. "Love you," he muttered as his eyes closed.

I watched him in the soft daylight creeping around the curtains.

The Night Queen's curtains. The Night Queen's bed. The Night Queen's rooms.

Despite the exhaustion making my bones heavy, discomfort crawled over me.

Bastian had apologised, but I couldn't help wondering how much he truly accepted what Braea had become... and if he ever would. If his father hadn't killed her, would he have been able to?

Yet, I couldn't blame him. It had taken so much before I'd been able to finally act against Uncle Rufus. We all had well-worn paths etched on our minds—beliefs scored into our bones. They were hard to deviate from, even when we wanted nothing more.

He had begged me not to ask him to choose, and thankfully, I hadn't needed to.

That night in Riverton Palace, he would have gladly killed

Rufus for me. I would be that strength for him, if ever he needed it.

I clung to the comfort of that thought, and it was enough to let sleep consume me at last.

IT WAS ALMOST dark when I woke much more than an hour later. I rolled over, hoping a new position would help, but my unease was nothing to do with an uncomfortable mattress. A prod of instinct right between my shoulder blades. Something off.

The only sounds were the distant ones of palace life. Nothing out of the ordinary. Nothing that could've woken me. The Crown of Ashes slumbered on the bedside table where I'd left it, so that wasn't the problem, either. I pressed a finger to it, and it flared to life, deep red amongst the black ashes.

It had been a long day... a long few months. And I'd been moved into the Night Queen's suite. It was natural to feel strange after all that.

Bastian's senses were more acute than mine, but he lay there sound asleep. Better that he stayed that way after putting double the effort into making love to me with both parts of himself, so I slipped out of bed, grabbed my robe, which had been thoughtfully draped over the back of a chair, and padded through the rooms. I didn't want to get a drink from the en suite bathroom, in case the noise woke him, and it took me a little while to find another bathroom and grab a cold glass of water, which I took to the balcony.

The sun kissed the horizon, casting deeper shadows, lighting the sky in pink and purple as a last goodbye to daylight. At least, until tomorrow.

Below, the city was changing from Luminis to Tenebris with the lengthening shadows as it did every evening. Folk hurried to and from work or socialising or chores, some gathering in the streets, since they were once more allowed to do so.

It all seemed so normal, but, like Bastian had said, over the past few weeks everything had changed.

I only hoped I had changed things for the better—for Elfhame and for us.

Then again, we'd been through betrayal, spying, murder, Horrors, the truth, and so much more, but we were still here. I held my hand to my chest, pressing the spot he'd kissed into my heart.

We got through all that. This would be nothing.

Smiling to myself, I drained the rest of the glass and turned to head inside.

A form stood in the doorway.

Not Bastian. Not Ennet or Brynan. Even shadowed, I knew the set of her shoulders and the silhouette of her curly hair.

"Braea." I dropped the glass as her name fell from my lips. Its tinkling shatter barely registered over the roaring pulse in my ears. "How are you...?"

"Alive?" Her teeth gleamed as she stepped out into the last rays of sunlight with a mocking smile. "You mean the clever little human hasn't worked out my family's great secret? You disappoint me."

As she closed in, I backed away. I needed a weapon. No. I couldn't fight her. She had fae speed and strength, and I was no warrior. I needed to escape.

"Great secret?" My chuckle came out strangled. "Well, now I'm intrigued."

That's it, take your time explaining, give me a chance to work out a plan.

"I didn't realise it had passed to Sura until I saw her at the Great Trees, but it's the only way she could've survived being beheaded."

"She said that was a changeling."

"*Did* she? And when did you meet her?"

I clamped my mouth shut. Fuck. I needed to get a grip of myself.

Her eyes narrowed above a thin smile. "Seems I'm not the only one who's been keeping secrets. Still, yours aren't going to matter very soon. Think, though, did Sura really tell you Bastian had executed a changeling? Or did she let you assume that?"

She'd told us a changeling worked for her and that they loved her enough to die for her. No, she'd given us the information and let us make the connection. Wrongly.

"You understand now—or at least you're getting there. It's simply darling that humans think we can't lie just because we can't say words that aren't true." She advanced, and I matched her steps, easing backwards over the broken glass. "Sura must've split herself in two during the coup. A wise move, it turns out. One that's kept my family alive more than once over the generations."

That was where Bastian got it from—not an unseelie trait from his father. But that meant... "What about Nyx? Why didn't she split to escape you?"

Sadness fell over her features, dulling that smirk. "She was too heavily pregnant. Trying to keep that child killed her."

"No, *you* killed her." It burst from me, and I had to grit my teeth against the white hot desire to also remind her who exactly "that child" was.

Sura had been pregnant with Amaya during her coup, yet still early—early enough to split, perhaps. That must've been the reason for her timing—so she could still divide herself safely in case her plan went wrong. If she'd waited any longer, she would've been stuck as her sister was.

She'd seen her sister's fate and refused to share it.

Braea wrinkled her nose as though being reminded of the truth was a distasteful inconvenience. "Thrones require sacrifices."

"Like the people Cyrus killed? Or should I say, the people he killed with *your* encouragement? You never do your own dirty work, do you? I knew you were manipulative, but why did you need him to do those things?"

"Are you still whining about that?" She rolled her eyes and took another step closer.

I took another step back.

"I needed him to make a few mistakes and look like the fool he was."

So I'd guessed right. It should've filled me with triumph but instead there was only the cold certainty that she didn't mean for me to make it off this balcony alive.

"I wasn't expecting his methods to be quite so... unpredictable," she continued. "Still, it was working before you killed him. Even the people of Dawn were looking to me to save them from their own king. Once I had the Crown of Ashes, it would've been the next logical step to grant me more power, since Cyrus clearly wasn't suitable to rule." She sighed, expression sharpening as she closed in.

My back hit the balustrade. I glanced over my shoulder. There were no faces carved into the stone, no wisteria for Zita to hide within. This time, I was on my own.

"For months, I was so focused on Cyrus and the Crown, I didn't see the real problem. *You.*"

I chuckled breathlessly. "How could I possibly be a problem to you? You're a fucking queen."

With nowhere else for me to go, she closed in, sauntering like a sabrecat who'd cornered its prey. "Oh, yes, the poor, defenceless little human act. Very good. Is that how you drew Bastian in? He's so protective, so dedicated to helping those who can't help themselves—it's an easy weakness to manipulate to your advantage."

"You would know," I spat, reaching for my magic so it would be ready the instant she closed in.

"Lucky for me, a poor, defenceless little human is an easy problem to fix. Especially when there's an antidote to neutralise her poisonous touch." Her eyes glinted, as cold as the dread flooding me. "That's what you are, you know—*poisonous.* You've been dripping it in Bastian's ear, turning him against me. He never questioned me before you came. He was mine. *My* Shadow."

She was almost in arm's reach. Another step and she would be.

I peered back over the balustrade. The only way out was to jump, but the ground was far, far below, and Cyrus's description of what would happen kept me fixed to the spot.

"He's king now. What makes you think that with me out of the way, he'll go back to being your Shadow?" I needed time. Time would give me an answer. A way out. *Something.*

"Silly girl. I've been living in these walls since my so-called death waiting for my opportunity. I've seen everything he's done—and all that he hasn't, like taking his place as king. He doesn't want it. Part of him probably knows I'm still here, and he's glad of it."

I swallowed, not wanting her to be right, and yet...

"He's been mine for fifteen years," she went on. "You've been around for all of fifteen minutes. Once you're gone, he'll remember his loyalty. He'll step back in line and everything will go back to how it was before your brief little life interfered with mine. Better, even." Her smile spread, beatific. "He's another chance for me. Another heir. One already moulded in my image. He knows rulership comes with a cost. He knows there are always hard decisions. He is willing to pay."

She closed that final gap. I had to take the chance—she hadn't said outright that she had taken the antidote...

"I wouldn't be so sure." I went for her throat.

She didn't even blink as she caught my wrist with horrible ease. But the sleeve of my robe had ridden up—the bare skin of her hand was on mine.

With every scrap of energy I had, I shoved my power there. The tingle on my nerves was unbearable as blackened purple bloomed over my skin.

Her grip tightened.

Teeth bared, she yanked me closer, nails digging into my flesh as she pressed a dagger to my throat. "He killed his own father for me. What do you think you are compared to that? I could ask him to do anything and he'd obey."

She'd definitely taken the antidote. This concentration of poison—she should be dead already.

And as for Bastian...

Maybe she was right. He didn't wear his crown. It was something I'd forced upon him. And hadn't he begged me not to make him choose between me and Braea? Hadn't he done too much in her service to ever turn his back on her? Wasn't that the thing I'd feared?

"Get your fucking hands off her."

69

KAT

He stood in the doorway, little more than a shadow now the sun had vanished entirely. Darkness pooled around him, snapping, agitated.

"Bastian." Braea's smile was bright as she turned to him and twisted me in her grasp so my back was to her chest. The knife never left my throat. I couldn't even swallow without it digging into my flesh. "My grandson. My blood. How didn't I see it before?"

His gaze fixed on her arm around my waist. "I said, get. Your. Fucking. Hands. Off. Her."

"She went for me. I only drew a blade to protect myself. My darling, it doesn't have to be like this. She's already killed one king. Do we really know she wasn't involved with Lucius's death?" Shaking her head, she walked me towards him. "And what about your life? Do you think she'll stop now?"

She went slowly, voice soft, like he was a wild animal that only she could soothe. "Can't you see what she's done to you? To *us*? To the *realm*?"

492

His eyebrows pulled together as his eyes flicked to me, like he could see the chaos I'd caused with my desire for change.

"We were always a team, weren't we?" she crooned. "Solid. Stable. Always working towards what was best for Dusk Court. And now?" Her face was inches from mine, her eyes gleaming with unshed tears.

She released the arm around my waist, but I was trapped between them, trapped by a sinking feeling that dragged at my bones.

She took his hand. "Now you're looking at me like you want me dead. Stars above, she's done a good job of poisoning us, hasn't she?" She laughed softly, thick with sorrow. "But you can end this, Bastian. We can go back to how we were. Better. You don't have to be king and take on all that heavy responsibility—the attention you don't want. You could be my heir. I can bring you into the light, prepare you gradually to be Dusk's hero rather than my Shadow."

Slowly, his chin dipped.

Was that a nod?

At the edge of my vision, shadows crept in. "No, Bastian. Pl—"

The press of her blade cut me off. Warmth trickled down my neck. Any further and I'd be dead.

I stared at him, willing him to see the lie hiding amongst her words.

Sure, she believed what she was saying. And maybe she would do everything she promised. For a while.

But how long before Bastian put a foot wrong and did something that went against her wishes? How long before she suspected him of lusting for her throne?

How long before she killed another heir?

He gave a firm nod this time, reaching his decision. "So

much has changed. Things I never wanted." In the tight space between us, he squeezed her hand and pulled from her grip. Gently, he wrapped his fingers around the dagger's hilt. "Let me finish this."

She surrendered it to him, and I could feel her smile against my cheek before she shifted back just enough to watch as Bastian took over holding her blade to my throat.

I had room to swallow, staring up at him. He couldn't mean this.

A sad smile flickered on his mouth—already mourning. His other hand pressed against my hip as if to hold me still.

My pulse leapt, pushing against the blade.

"I *am* sorry, you know." His gaze slid to hers. "You say you want to bring me into the light. But you had fifteen years to do that, and you didn't. You kept me in the darkest places, doing your dirty work. Now, someone else has beaten you to it."

Out the corner of my eye, Braea frowned and the push of her chest against my back eased off. "What are you—?"

His hand at my hip snapped out.

She gasped, grabbing my shoulder, but Bastian dropped the dagger at my throat and moved me to one side, out of her reach.

Every part of my being fought to understand the scene before me.

He had her by the arm, a knife in her stomach, angled upwards. "I could take having to make hard choices, the sacrifices made for the greater good, the times I had to torture our enemies to get information that would keep our people safe."

I sagged against the wall, sudden tears burning my eyes as I understood his ploy.

He walked her across the balcony, and she staggered with him. "I, of all people, could understand killing a loved one to protect something you truly believed in. I gave you a chance with the shapechangers, with my *athair*, with Cyrus. Always, I thought I was doing the right thing. Stability above all. And I believed *you* meant stability."

She choked as she hit the balustrade and arched back, like she could get out of his grip. But she stared up at him, face frozen as though the real terror was hearing in stark terms the litany of wrongs she had done to her people.

"Even after I found out you'd provided them with the book that summoned the Horrors." He blasted out a heavy breath, brow drawn low as he shook his head. "I believed that if I'd been there all those years ago, I could've talked you around. Every time, I told myself you didn't realise the full extent of the harm you were causing. I made excuse after excuse for you."

He fell still, holding her gaze a long time, before going on in a voice as soft and final as death. "But what I cannot—*will not* abide is you laying a single fucking finger on Katherine." There was a terrible wet sound of flesh rending as he twisted the knife. "And that is why I cannot suffer you to live a moment longer. You will not poison anything else in my life or in my kingdom. I am your Shadow no more." He took a half step backwards, yanking the blade out, and braced his hand on her shoulder, clearly ready to push her over the balustrade.

But he didn't give her that last shove.

Instead, she smiled up at him, blood on her teeth, and he flinched, grunting. He staggered back and that was when I saw.

The hilt of a knife neither of us had spotted. The blood spilling from just below his ribs.

He stared at it as she pushed him backwards, and the world spun, slowly at first, then faster, faster.

"No. You will not take this from me. You will not have my

throne. My palace. I've worked too hard to secure my power. Traitor. *Traitor*."

Kat. It was my voice in my head, even, sane, commanding. *Move*.

She pushed him off her blade, letting him slump to the ground.

I rushed forwards and slumped alongside him, heart beating so hard it hurt. "Bastian?"

His eyelids fluttered as I pressed on the wound, his blood slicking my hands. There was so much of it, pooling around us.

"Your double. He's safe, right?"

"No time to split... came as soon as I heard you out here. Needed all my focus to make sure you were safe." His mouth curved a little as he slowly reached up and cupped my cheek. The glow in his eyes dimmed. "If I split now, he'll be as injured as I am. Kat, I... I..."

His eyes sank shut. His hand fell.

He moved no more.

"Bastian?"

Nothing.

No. No. No.

He wasn't moving. He wasn't...

I shook my head, this awful, sickening energy flooding me, making me stand. I couldn't stay still like him. If I kept moving, maybe that meant he could...

From the other side of his body, Braea's shoulders heaved as she stared at him, brow low, eyes wide. I swore she had this tiny smile on her face like she was glad.

After all, she'd killed another heir.

And that was when it sank all the way in like she'd pushed the blade between *my* ribs.

He was gone.

She had killed him.

I searched for a weapon.

I had nothing. Only myself. My body. Fat and muscle and bone, nerve and sinew, mortal and frail. The last thing I had left to try and change anything.

I ran at her.

A roar came from me, something deeper than rage, deeper than hurt, an unending vein of primal fury that surged through me. I charged past Bastian's still form and I did not stop.

I didn't stop when I slammed into Braea and dug my fingers into the wound in her stomach.

Her screech of pain was a vicious victory.

It put her off-balance, letting a weak little human like me carry her away from him. I wasn't tall, no, but I had strength in my thighs and for once in my life, my weight was an advantage.

I didn't stop when we hit the balustrade and the world tipped.

The queen fell.

I fell.

This was it. No surviving. But it was worth it. She'd killed Bastian. Nothing else mattered. I would join him in the Underworld.

I let her go and willed my eyes open—I would watch every moment of this finale.

Red mist clouded the air as her feet hit the veil that separated Dusk's part of the palace from Dawn and the outside world.

She screamed.

And then she couldn't.

Because, inches from my face, she disintegrated into a haze of blood that sprayed my skin.

It had been less than a week—too soon for her to split. She was dead. For good, this time.

I would be next. I braced for it. At least it would be quick.

Except, then, everything stopped.

Breathless, I stared at the ground below as what was left of the Night Queen splattered into it. But gravity didn't seem to be working on me.

I blinked down at my body.

Shadows held me.

I was only just level with the bottom of the balustrade, and gently, they pulled me back over it.

They gathered me to Bastian, who sat on the stone floor of the balcony in a pool of his own blood, holding the wound in his side.

I let out a wordless sound, part whimper, part sob.

Because he was looking back at me, expression strained like I had inconvenienced him by flinging myself over the balcony.

And if he was looking at me and pulling a face, then that meant he was alive.

His shadows set me down, and I grabbed him. "I thought you were fucking dead."

He only gave a soft grunt as he wrapped one arm around me. "I've had a chance to gather some strength." The world around us did feel depleted—quieter, like he'd drawn from its magic. "It's all right. Asher's healed worse."

"Can we *please* stop testing Asher's healing abilities?" I squeezed my eyes shut to try and erase the image of him falling off Braea's blade and held him, hating how the metallic, dirty stink of blood tainted his scent. For a long moment, we stayed there, chests heaving together, a mutual reassurance.

We had survived.

I fastened the tie from my robe around him to staunch the bleeding before dragging myself away and calling for the guards to bring a healer. He'd drawn a little strength from Elfhame's magic, but he was still wounded.

When I sank to his side, I buried my face in his shoulder. "For a minute then... I thought you were actually going to kill me. But... you saved me."

He pulled back, shaking his head as he cupped my cheek, palm slick with blood. "Katherine. My beautiful idiot. I would choose you over her—over *anyone*—a thousand times in a thousand lives. *You* have saved *me*."

70

BASTIAN

Stepping out onto the amphitheatre's stage was like walking into a wall of noise. Chatter, cheers, gossip, all mingling with the dull roar of people crowded together, moving. Half the city was here for the announcement and the other half crowded outside.

In our planning, we'd chosen the amphitheatre instead of the royal balcony so we weren't above our people but with them. It hadn't been done before, but then again, neither had the rest of what we'd announce today. Sepher had cracked a joke about Kat having a poor record with monarchs and balconies. He had a point.

In the amphitheatre's front rows were Meredine and the Convocation members. They were in for a surprise with the latter part of our announcement. But some of them had grown complacent—a surprise was just what they needed to shake them up a little.

At the end of a row, Ari and Ly stood with Amaya, bracketed by Rose and Faolán on the other side and Perry and Asher behind. With Braea gone, we'd deemed it safe for my cousin to come to the city, but I felt better knowing our friends had her protected.

I'd overheard her conversation with Kat as she'd helped Amaya get ready. It turned out Sura had split before the coup, one part of her taking refuge in Dawn's side of the palace, since Cyrus believed himself in love with her and would keep her safe. I'd heard the cringe in her voice as she'd admitted, "I think that was when I was... made."

If not for the red hair, I would've missed Krae. Fully healed from Cyrus's torture, they stood near an exit. They'd spent a little time at the palace, but mostly Sepher rode out to meet them. I wasn't sure what they did together, but I got the impression he was getting to know his sibling.

He and Zita waved as they circled the stage, confident and comfortable in their roles. I supposed we should do the same, now I was... king. A face rather than a shadow. *Real.*

I nudged Kat, about to suggest it, but when I looked down, she was already smiling and waving like an expert.

Of course she was. It was probably something that had been drilled into her as a girl. Much as I hated her father's lessons, she did look the part. The Crown of Ashes glowing upon her head. The deepest crimson of her gown. The way she carried herself, shoulders back, head high, taking up space. She belonged here. Even more than I did.

Yet after facing Braea last night, standing here felt... right. I had been serving my realm for years, and now I would do so as king. Kat had helped me realise that.

"You know," I murmured in her ear, "we could rule, you and I. You could be a queen."

Not breaking her stride or missing a beat of her wave, she gave me a sidelong look and replied, "I don't want to be a queen. I've spent my life as a pawn in other people's games. And a queen is still a piece on the board. I don't want to be someone else's toy. I want to be the one influencing the game." She turned to me, resolute. "I want to be a player."

Despite all the people around us and the crown upon my head, I wanted nothing more in that moment than to fall to my knees and kiss her feet.

But before I could do any such thing, we reached the centre of the stage and the cheers died down to a curious hubbub. More than once I heard the question, "Why are they wearing crowns?" We'd tried to suppress the news, but keeping rumours silent was like trying to dam a river with wishes.

"You're up," Sepher whispered.

I clenched and unclenched my hands, finding my palms clammy with sweat. Good gods, was I nervous? I'd talked in front of crowds a hundred times before, and yet this was different, wasn't it? I was speaking for myself rather than as Braea's representative. How would the people react? As far as they were concerned, I was the Serpent, the Bastard, the Shadow. Not someone to stand before them in this bright daylight. Not someone to be accepted.

Remember who you are.

And that was Bastian. The Bastard had been a tool for coping with what had to be done, but I'd come to rely on him too much, almost losing myself in the process.

It had taken Bastian Marwood, together with the woman he loved, to stop Braea from abusing this realm any longer.

Kat squeezed the crook of my elbow before taking a step away, letting me have centre stage.

I wanted to grab her hand and pull her back to my side.

But instead, I drew my shadows close and lifted my chin, surveying our audience. "People of Tenebris-Luminis. I hear the question you're asking, and I can't blame you for asking it. Not so long ago, I would've been as shocked as you are to see me wearing the Crown of Night. But I recently learned a truth that has been hidden for too long."

I swallowed down the strangeness I still felt at announcing what sounded like such a wild claim. "The late Princess Nyx was my mother."

The crowd erupted. Gasps, questions, my words repeated. Refusal. The pointing out of my features—my skintone, the shape of my eyes, the way I frowned.

A new question spread. "How didn't we see it before?"

I held my breath, waiting for quiet, as arguments broke out and merged together. *Just because he's her son, doesn't mean he'll be a good king. He killed the Horrors. He saved my sister when the palace was attacked. He helped my shapechanger uncle.*

Kat gave an encouraging nod. "It's a good start."

Finally, there was the soft quiet of hundreds of folk leaning forward, waiting for more.

If admitting who I was had been hard, this next part was harder. I explained how we'd all been deceived by Braea and it wasn't the unseelie lord who'd killed Nyx but her own mother.

Silence reigned over the amphitheatre.

One benefit of not being able to lie? No one questioned me as I spelled out the bald truth in language that left no space for ambiguity or for twisting it into lies.

Still, I couldn't help the shame. Shame that I'd enabled Braea so long. That I had buried myself in excuses rather than seeing the truth.

I'd dared to voice it all to Kat, and now I kept her reassurances in my heart. I had made a mistake in trusting Braea and what I thought she'd stood for so fully, but mistakes were part of living. It was good and bad. Pleasure and pain. Love and loss.

Just as I loved Sylen and carried the pain of killing him, I had loved Braea and now carried the pain of knowing her love had come at a terrible cost.

As much as I held on to control so often, I knew now—I couldn't control her. I certainly couldn't control *everything*. And, as dangerous as all that felt, the world hadn't ended.

With renewed strength, I spoke into the shocked quiet. "And so, although it wasn't done with the blade of Justice, Braea's death *was* just."

Heads bent together, whispers passing back and forth. I caught snippets—speculation about whether I had killed her or if it had been Kat. The city was already rife with rumour that she was the one who'd killed Cyrus, so they slotted this news into their narrative. I let them speculate. We'd worked together to remove Braea—it didn't matter to me who got the credit.

"However, there was much of the unjust about Queen Braea and King Lucius's reigns," I went on as Sepher stepped forward, lending Dawn's support to my words.

"And too much division," he added. "Between the courts. Between your rulers. Between your leaders and yourselves."

"So we have agreed on a new way. One that will allow Elfhame to move forward from old divisions and fragile peace and into an era of prosperity and safety for *all*." I squared my shoulders, bracing myself for the next part. The Convocation was going to hate this, but they would have a choice—melt into obscurity or take part in the new way. "To that end, rather than ruling *over* you, we will work together with a council— one elected by you."

There was a beat of stunned silence, then another eruption of excited whispers.

It had been a week, but I was still surprised Sepher had agreed to it.

In the Convocation chamber, he'd admitted he had no interest in being king. He had only wanted power in order to keep the people he cared about safe. He knew all too well what Cyrus had been like and that eventually his attention would have turned to Celestine and perhaps even Zita. Especially once he realised Zita really had cursed him the day on the royal balcony. That was his motivation for removing his brother from the board.

It was one I could relate to.

Sepher judged his audience to perfection, only speaking up once the chatter dulled. "This marks a new era of service and of transition."

I could tell by the way he said "service" that he wasn't entirely convinced by that part of our plan, but once I'd explained it was the only way for us to eventually be able to step back, he'd leant in, asking, "You mean we can get our lives back?" As soon as we'd confirmed that, he'd agreed to it all.

"When power is too concentrated, it is too easily abused, so although we will remain as your kings and your queen, while the council is established"—I encompassed him and Zita with a gesture, though I was sure it drew attention to Kat, too —"once power is handed over and new processes established, we will abdicate. No more heirs. No more thrones. And, thanks to the Crown of Ashes, no more monarchs who can't look each other in the eye."

This time, the crowd's reaction was less of an eruption and more of a slow bubbling that rose to a simmer.

I had to admit, Kat's suggestion had shocked me, too, at first, but after everything I'd seen since my return to Elfhame, I viewed my country differently. Perhaps it was the time away. Maybe it was Kat's perspective.

We'd seen power abused too much. We'd lived in too much mistrust. And, personally, I had clung to the old and established, mistaking that for stability and peace, when really it was a monument to wicked gods who deserved to be forgotten.

On the front row, Celestine practically bounced on the balls of her feet, leaning in to the empty space at her side. Her breathless question reached me, "Does this new age of cooperation mean marriages across the courts will be allowed?"

Except, I realised that wasn't an empty space. When I forced my aching eyes to turn to it, I found Orpha, looking up at Celestine with a guarded smile.

I was just wondering what that meant when other whispers crept in. I couldn't catch full sentences, but one word repeated over and over.

And with it, more and more eyes turned to Kat.

They'd put the pieces together and reached their own conclusion. She'd killed Cyrus and Braea. She'd cleared the way for me and Sepher. She bore the Crown of Ashes and all the power that entailed, allowing Day and Night to stand together.

I slipped to her side as the whispers became cheers. "I'd say you are a player now."

Head cocked, she gave me a puzzled look.

"Listen to what they're saying—to what they're calling *you*."

A beat later, her eyes went wide, but I leant in and murmured it in her ear, anyway. "Kingmaker."

71

KAT

Beyond the day to day of working out how the hells to manage elections in a country that had never held them, the first task I had as Kingmaker was to venture south to the border.

There were negotiations before that, of course. Asher and Perry acted as our diplomats, liaising with Queen Elizabeth's representatives. We agreed to open up trade and travel between Albion and Elfhame.

Along with the negotiations had been confirmation that no relatives of Robin Fanshawe had been found. Markyate Cell belonged to me. Though Perry confirmed there was some discomfort on Albion's part. A foreign not-quite-queen owning Albionic land? That wouldn't do. It was a thorn I needed to work out.

Otherwise, all that remained was to meet and sign the agreement.

There was an alarming moment just as we were leaving the city and a host of riders arrived. Bastian braced for a fight, and

I reached for the yew bow hanging from Vespera's saddle as soon as I saw their insignias.

Crimson and gold hydras. The real Hydra Ascendant, this time, not Cyrus's fake version.

Had they come to put Amaya on the throne? Was this an attack to avenge Sura? How many would die today?

But as the tension hummed, stirring my magic, the woman who rode at their head approached and knelt before Bastian, laying down her sword. "We offer our weapons and allegiance to Dusk Court's rightful ruler... if His Majesty is willing to take it."

It delayed our setting off by a day, but it was worth it to see how everyone looked to Bastian for an answer and how he didn't hesitate to pardon and welcome them into service. He commanded shadows, but he was no longer hidden by them.

Understandably, the citizens of Tenebris-Luminis were wary—after all, as far as most of them knew, these people had been their enemies. The Solstice attack and the bloody wedding weren't memories that would fade quickly.

Rose came up with the good idea of them helping round up the remaining Horrors to return them to the Underworld where Drystan might be able to return them to their true selves using the book we'd given him.

With that settled, we set off for the border at last. We arrived as the last stones were being removed from the wall between our realms, creating a gap to allow for easier trade.

A young sycamore tree stood ready for planting, its roots balled up, though soon they would spread between Albion and Elfhame, sealing our bargain. It had been enchanted to block fae monsters but would allow folk to travel between our nations a little more easily.

I paused outside the tent that had been erected to shelter

the queen from the summer sun. A ball of anxiety twisted in my stomach.

A warm hand closed over my shoulder. "You'll be fine. I haven't seen many people able to deny a deal with you—myself included." Bastian flashed me a grin before offering his arm. "Particularly not when you're wearing *those damn boots*."

"I didn't think you'd noticed them."

"That would be impossible."

My pleasure at his reaction didn't erase the nerves, though.

It was probably considered a dirty tactic to introduce an additional item right as we were supposed to sign the papers —something akin to poison being a woman's weapon. But I didn't trust this to cold lines of text in a message. I needed to ask for it—*demand* it—personally.

So I took his arm, adjusted the Crown of Ashes, and together, we entered the tent.

The queen was as regal as ever, sitting with that effortless elegance I'd admired in Lunden. And her crimson hair was as shocking as ever against her pale skin.

Though now I saw her, I realised how much brighter mine had grown in my time in Elfhame—the same impossible colour as hers. I hadn't been born fae-blooded as she had, but I had been changed by living amongst their magic and eating their food.

I'd been changed by more than that.

So I was able to approach her as *I* wanted. Not playing the part of a lady. Not crossing my hands. Not making sure I was just demure enough.

But as myself, with thigh high boots and a gown of night and starlight that showed off too much of my body.

I returned the queen's knowing smile, and I managed to keep it on my face when I met Lord Cavendish's gaze. The real one this time. He stood at her shoulder, a little too close. And there was something about the way his arm brushed hers that revealed a closeness I hadn't noticed in Lunden.

They were lovers.

Good for her. I only hoped he was a better man than unCavendish.

Bastian's hand covered mine with a reassuring squeeze that asked if I was all right seeing the face that had abused me. I gave the barest nod. I was no longer in that place. I had support and resilience and all the joys of a life to help me weather the storms of panic and trauma. And when they failed, I had counted breaths and numbered sensations to keep me in the here and now.

I didn't need to go away anymore.

There were niceties, though I was still getting used to the deference people gave when you wore a crown. Honestly, I was impatient for them to be done.

But finally, we got to the contract.

Sepher had asked me to sign as his proxy, since he remained in the city, helping with the forthcoming elections. I paused with the pen over the paper. "There is one more thing." Unhurried, I set it down, making Cavendish frown. "We can't be allied with anyone who'd treat marriage in such an archaic way, leaving too many stuck in pairings that are unhappy at best... and dangerous at worst."

The queen pressed her lips together. "Yes, I've heard about you *stealing* my subjects the past few months. *We* can't have that."

Damn. I hadn't counted on news spreading so fast.

"These women aren't being 'stolen,'" Bastian cut in smoothly as I hesitated. "They come to Elfhame of their own accord."

"And," I went on, "they wouldn't need to come if they could simply petition for divorce without needing a royal decree."

Her nostrils flared as she speared first Bastian, then me with a sharp look. Cavendish mirrored her, leaning forward, ready to whisper in her ear.

"Shouldn't people be allowed to choose who they marry?" I eyed them both, knowing full well that in such a world, they would be allowed to marry rather than being secret lovers. "Isn't that a fair way to live?"

She made a grumbling sound that hinted at agreement.

"And therefore shouldn't they also be allowed to choose who they divorce?" I held my breath for every woman shackled to a Robin of her own. My own fears caught my voice. I was lucky, they were old, but for too many others they were fresh and current.

"People change... or reveal who they really were all along." Bastian's tone of painful truth made my heart sore. "Keeping women locked in marriage to such men is... it's a cruelty beyond comprehension."

Cavendish's eyebrows pulled together. "But the nation—"

"Divorce is freely allowed in Elfhame. It always has been. Our realm has not fallen apart. The fabric of the world has not shredded away. Albion will be fine."

The queen considered Bastian, and I could see her teetering on the edge of a decision.

I took off my crown. "I'm not asking this of you as a King-maker, I ask it as someone who suffered under those old laws. You didn't put them in place, but you can change them."

Her chin rose as she took a deep breath. "Very well. But once we have new laws in place, you'll stop harbouring women fleeing their husbands."

"Assuming those new laws keep them safe."

With a sigh, she waved for the scribe to come over and I silently celebrated my victory.

ONCE THE DEAL was updated and signed, the queen looked up at me, an amused quirk to her mouth. "There was someone who petitioned most vehemently—"

"Demanded," muttered Cavendish.

"—to join us on this journey north. Someone who wished to see you." She gestured to a guard, who opened the tent flap.

Grey haired and as familiar, rough, and comforting as an old woollen coat, in walked Morag. Horwich leant on her, limping worse than before I'd left.

The sound that escaped me wasn't the Kingmaker's. It was all Kat.

I didn't tell my legs to move, but somehow I was crossing the tent.

Morag hunched over in a bow. "Your Maj—"

"Stop that. Stop that right now." I gathered her into a hug, squeezing as hard as I dared. "You're here... but you never leave the estate!"

"For you, I have." She clapped me on the back, perhaps a little more softly than usual, then pulled back, giving me the same Look she always did. "You look..."

"It's just a dress. And, yes, I brushed my hair." I laughed, though it teetered on the edge of a sob.

"You look... *happy*." She nodded as she said it, as though her body needed to emphasise that word and not just her voice.

I took her hand and Horwich's. "I am." Gods, my eyes burned. Because I truly was. Happiness wasn't something I'd expected—not since I'd grown into a woman and discovered the reality that came with that. It wasn't something I'd dared hope for. And yet, somehow, I'd stumbled into it.

No. That wasn't right. There had been some stumbling, true, but also, I'd grown my happiness, nurtured it along with myself.

I stroked their papery skin, eyes burning at the way Horwich's chin trembled for me. "And I want you to be happy, too—both of you." I angled my head to one side, raising my voice. "Would it please the Queen of Albion to see Markyate Cell in the hands of two of her own subjects rather than someone who wears a foreign crown?"

There was a thoughtful pause. "That would solve the last issue standing between us, yes."

Morag stared past me, the wrinkles in her face deepening.

With a breathy laugh, Horwich shook her shoulder. "Don't scowl like that. She's giving us the estate." He shot me a look, eyes wide. "You are, aren't you?"

I grinned and squeezed their hands. "You two have been running it without me for long enough. Now it isn't in debt, I daresay you'll be able to turn a profit, and knowing you two, you'll have all the tenants on board, too. Or maybe you'll give them all their parcels of land or sell them. I don't know. It's yours to do with as you wish."

Morag touched her chest, sharp eyes bright like she might cry. "My home."

"Your home."

Once that piece of paperwork was drawn up and signed (only after Morag paused, pen hovering, and checked I was sure), Bastian and I emerged into the afternoon sun.

A hole had already been dug for the young sycamore tree, and we witnessed Asher and Cavendish lower its root ball into the rich earth. Queen Elizabeth stepped forward and poured a scoop of earth over it. "Let this tree stand as a marker of our alliance."

"And a guardian of both our people." Bastian accepted the hand trowel from her and added more soil to the hole.

I stood at its edge, able to look down at the tangle of roots and the rich earth without feeling like they were going to drag me down or that the earth would swallow me up and bury me alive. I took a handful from the pile of soil, needing to feel its grainy dampness.

It mingled Albion and Elfhame, the gently humming magic that had grown familiar. Ages merged in this handful, animals and plants that had died, cold minerals that had never been alive.

Between poison and trees, I had died a couple of times. But now?

Now, I lived.

EPILOGUE

KAT

B astian and I decided we'd take our time and walk to Rose and Faolán's for dinner. It had been a busy month since our trip to the border and summer was at its height. Tonight, however, there was a nip in the air, a reminder that autumn would be upon us soon enough, but I didn't have it in me to complain. This was the first night we'd both had free in weeks and nothing could sour my mood.

We chatted as we passed through the palace corridors, catching up on the day. He'd finished rearranging his workroom in readiness to start making new creations in there rather than only fixing broken things. Amongst Braea's belongings we'd found Nyx's sketchbooks—it turned out she had been a sculptor, and that had given him the idea. The plan was to try out clay, like she had used, and wood carving like Sylen, but he was still waiting on some materials to arrive so he could get started. "Not that I have time to use them," he muttered before falling quiet as we crossed the bridge leading to the city.

I held my breath all the way, turning to him with a raised eyebrow once we set foot on the street. "Well?"

"Nothing. I think it worked."

He and Lysander had researched how to lift Braea's enchantment of the river, and now he could cross without it feeling unpleasant.

I tucked against him as we wound through the city to Rose and Faolán's home.

When we reached their door, he gave a low chuckle. "Still a highwaywoman, aren't you?"

I blinked up at him. "In what way?"

"First you stole my orrery, and somewhere along the way you stole the rest of me. Tonight, it's my warmth." He smirked, pulling his light jacket around me. "My Wicked Lady."

I didn't fight the pleased hum that came from my throat. Tiptoeing, I pressed into him and entered my plea a few inches from his lips, turning it into an invitation. "Guilty as charged."

He ducked, ready to accept my surrender, when the door flew open and light and warmth spilled onto us and the street beyond.

"I knew I heard you." Rose took us in and raised an eyebrow, smoothing her hands down her oversized apron. "But if you need a few more minutes...?" She motioned as if to close the door.

"No," I chuckled and entered.

Bastian followed, hands on my shoulders as he murmured, "You'll face your punishment later."

Heat chased through me. I blamed it on the merry fire in the hearth, but that was absolutely a lie.

There were greetings before we sat and Rose continued bustling over the stove.

"So what's all this for?" Bastian eyed the chairs squeezed around the kitchen table.

Faolán jolted straight. "We invited you to dinner," he said a little too quickly. "You know how dinner works, right?"

"Hmm, but also Lysander, Ari, Ella, Perry, and Asher." I pointed at each seat in turn.

Bastian and I shared a look and he nodded as he rested his arm on the back of my chair. "You have *never* hosted us all here at once. If it's that big a gathering, we usually do it at the palace. Might as well make the most of it while we're still there. Though, of course, if you want to make this a regular thing, we can build you a bigger house—you've more than earned it with your service to the realm." He shrugged, lulling them into a false sense of security before he hit with the real question, "So what's going on?"

Faolán leapt up and went to help Rose. "You need a holiday. You're getting paranoid."

"Right," Rose chuckled, stepping back and letting her husband pull a tray of pies from the oven. "Friends can invite friends around for dinner. Even *all* their friends."

"Hmm." As one, Bastian and I perfectly imitated Faolán's signature sound.

But we couldn't get anything out of them, so the conversation moved on to what was for dinner (chicken and leek pies topped with poppyseeds, served with mashed celeriac, peas, and what appeared to be a vat of gravy), while Bastian toyed with my hair.

"My gods," I groaned at Rose's summary of the menu. "You're killing me with just the description."

Laughing, I looked around and found Bastian giving me this look that made me stop. It wasn't sad, but maybe wistful adjacent, with this pinch of his brow that had me suddenly self-conscious. His fingers fell still.

"What?" I touched the top of my head. "Is my hair sticking up?"

He exhaled with a soft shake of his head. "No. Your hair is perfect. This is perfect, in fact. Just like I imagined."

Before I could ask what he meant, there was a knock at the door and in poured the rest of our friends.

"Thank the gods you're here." Rose hustled everyone in. "These two were grilling us and I can't keep it quiet any longer." She joined Faolán as he finished mashing the celeriac and wiped his hands on a towel.

Suddenly solemn, he cleared his throat, an arm coming around Rose's shoulder.

I glanced at Bastian, but he was watching them, a little frown on his face.

"We're having a baby... well... *babies*."

"Babies?" Ella squealed.

The sentiment echoed through the room. I was on my feet, eyes burning as I flung my arms around them both. Rose had spoken about how she wanted a big family one day, like the one she'd come from, but that she was resigned to one, maybe two children if they were lucky, considering how rare fae pregnancies were. "Babies—more than one?" I asked as I let Bastian catch her in a hug.

"Well, Faolán never told me I'd end up with a whole *litter* of children."

"Healers have checked her over. There are three heartbeats as well as Rose's." The giant rubbed his beard in a poor attempt to hide his proud grin. "And I did tell you, my darling flower. Multiple times."

"Fine, but I never *believed* you. Twins, maybe, but triplets? I suppose wolves *do* have litters." She patted Bastian's shoulder as he wrapped his arms around Faolán and tried to out-crush him. "We might need to take you up on that offer of a bigger house."

"Consider it done," he choked as he lost the battle with Faolán.

"You can let him go now, dear, he's agreed. You're all my witnesses." She winked.

So it was, in the warm cosiness of Rose and Faolán's house that we ate, drank, and were merry.

Very, very merry.

As we finished dinner and Faolán presented a cake he'd made under Rose's supervision, I raised my glass. "To the future, and to three children who are going to be very spoilt by their aunts and uncles."

"*So* spoilt." Ari widened her eyes.

"And happy," Perry added.

"To the future, wherever it may take us." Ella wore a tight smile.

Glasses clinked, a few tears were shed.

"To the future... and to cake," Bastian announced over the coffee sponge with its perfectly piped icing. He met my gaze with a private smile.

Everyone received a slice on a dainty little plate—something I particularly enjoyed watching Faolán with his massive fingers handle so delicately—and the group broke into several smaller conversations.

Ella ushered me to one side, near the door. "I didn't want to overshadow the happy couple's announcement, but... I'm leaving."

"So early? Well, don't forget your jacket—it's chilly tonight."

She gave that same odd smile she'd given during her toast. "I don't mean going back to my rooms, I mean... I've been called back to Albion."

Almost spitting out my mouthful of cake, I blinked at her. I must've misheard. Must've.

"I've been putting off telling everyone, because that makes it real, but I'm travelling back with Zita's old performing troupe tomorrow. The queen only let me come here on a temporary basis so I could check you were all right and to aid with diplomacy on Albion's behalf. I made a deal—if I came here, I'd owe her a favour. And technically I do still work for Cavendish."

"Then you can't leave," I blurted out. "You're privy to all sorts of national secrets. I can't let you go." I put down the plate and took her hands.

"Only half eaten? I should've waited until you finished your cake. But I must go. Helping unCavendish was treason. I really do owe them *a lot*."

"*I* didn't have to do anything. I worked for him, too."

"Yes, but you almost died to stop a war." She shook my hands. "I believe Her Majesty considers you even."

"I couldn't have done it without you. And that's... that's not me trying to bargain to make you stay, it's the truth. You saved me. You were the first one to see more than just a tired woman desperate to make money."

"That's because you were never 'just' anything. I'm simply glad you realise it now."

We loitered by the door talking a little longer before I waved her off to break the news to the others. I ate the rest of the cake, along with my feelings, in two bites.

"She's leaving, then?" Bastian's words ruffled my hair as his hands came to rest on my shoulders.

"And I've finished my cake." The sorrow I swallowed down made me sound petulant, I knew. But I also knew I didn't need to hide how I felt. I could be as big, as loud, as emotional and take up as much space as I needed to.

"Now that *is* a tragedy." He kissed the crown of my head and turned me to face him. "We will visit. I'll track down the person who made Faolán's bracelet and see if we can get another one made. Then you can see her all the time."

My chin wobbled as I fought a losing battle with my tears. He just held me and let me give in, until I was ready to come up for air. "I know it means I'm lucky. The fact I'm this sad, I mean."

"It does." He thumbed the tears from my cheeks. "And it means you have a future to worry about. I'm very glad of that, particularly as you seem to enjoy doing things like drinking poison and throwing yourself off balconies."

I couldn't help smiling at that. "Well, you do insist on putting yourself in situations where I need to do these things to save your life."

He huffed, hands planing down my back. "That's fair. But what else is in our future? We have work to do for Elfhame, yes, but one day, maybe next year, that will be done. What then?"

"Next year? You're optimistic." Despite my sarcastic tone, the way he said *our future* filled me, warm and hopeful, like a light left in the window on a dark night.

"Indulge me, Katherine."

"We have to finish the logistics for the nominations and elections—the number of council seats still hasn't been decided. Then we'll need to work out a way to make the campaigns fair so it's not only rich people who get elected because they can afford to promote themselves. *Then* there are the elections themselves and getting the new council in place."

Just thinking about it was enough to give me palpitations. "We've got so much to do, I'm not sure I can think beyond that."

"So that's what's on your mind—I wondered why you've been tossing and turning in bed." He stroked my hair and kissed my brow. "We'll have to wear you out tonight so you can get a proper night's sleep."

He said it so casually, it took me a moment to understand the innuendo. He must've seen the moment of realisation, because he cracked a wicked smirk.

I widened my eyes and nodded sagely. "That's a plan I can get behind."

We stayed there a little while in quiet anticipation, but my unasked question bubbled up. "Earlier you said this was just like you imagined. What did you mean?"

"Oh. That." His smirk turned crooked as he looked away, and I could've sworn there was the faintest hint of pink on his cheeks. "It's silly really... but it means something to me. Back when you were still unconscious in the Hall of Healing, and I was, rightly, convinced you would hate me when you woke up, I..." He sighed and shook his head. "Just for a moment I had this fantasy of coming here and having a relaxed dinner with our friends. You were laughing, smiling, happy, and I had my arm slung over the back of your chair while I played with your hair. It was brief but so vivid. And good gods, I wanted it."

The confession made every hard thing left in me melt. The fact he'd wanted something so simple and pure during such a hopeless time—the fact he'd wanted *me*... him... this. My throat was too thick and aching to speak, so I smoothed his shirt instead, wanting to soothe every old hurt and tell his past self that hope was worth holding on to.

His brow creased as he finally met my gaze. "Sitting there

tonight, I realised... that was the moment, exactly as I'd imagined, and yet so much more. After everything in Lunden, I didn't think it possible, but here we are."

I smiled, finding my voice and nodded once, sure. *"Here we are."*

Maybe Bastian wasn't too optimistic. Almost a year on from that dinner, the elections had been held, the council was in place, and we'd helped them get through their initial challenges. It wasn't perfect. There were arguments. But Elfhame was ruled by its people.

Despite his campaign, Mored wasn't elected to the council. Such a shame. But Deema and Tor were, and I felt content that the realm would be in safe hands.

I only hoped Bastian was as sure *he* was in safe hands. Blindfolded, he let me manoeuvre him in front of the door of the modest house on one of Dusk's streets that looked west towards the setting sun.

We'd chosen it together, just around the corner from Kaliban's old home, which now inhabited by a young shapechanger couple he'd helped escape during Cyrus's rule.

Bastian's shoulders were loose as we stopped before the front door. Over the past couple of months with the council taking up their responsibilities, we weren't as busy, and this was the most relaxed I'd ever seen him. He'd even admitted there was something to be said for sharing his burdens with me, our friends, and the council.

And as for me?

I was... content.

Life wasn't easy, just as Drystan had warned me, but it was pretty close to perfect.

Well, except for the anxiety rolling in my stomach.

Next week, Bastian, Sepher, and Zita would officially abdicate, and we'd all move out from the palace. That in itself wasn't the reason for my apprehension, though.

We would be moving *here*, into this house that Bastian hadn't seen inside since we'd made the purchase... which I had refurbished without any input from him.

I wrung my hands, nibbling on my lip. Shit. What if he hated it?

The plan had been to surprise him, but also, selfishly, it was the first time I'd ever decorated a home. Our childhood house had been entirely under my father's control. Markyate Cell had been Robin's with no money to update it and too many unpleasant memories to make it a home. Then I'd lived in Riverton Palace, then in Bastian's rooms here in Tenebris. And I didn't count my time in Dawn as living—only a temporary prison.

I'd always been in other people's spaces, but this was ours from the start.

I'd had help to do the work, of course—joiners and masons and all kinds of specialists. Ari had sewn curtains that would give us privacy, since we were somewhat known in Elfhame. Rose and Faolán had painted the walls alongside me, working around juggling the triplets.

But Bastian knew nothing of what I'd done inside and yet had trusted me with it all.

He cocked his head. "Are you still there?"

"Yes." I drew the word out and swallowed. Maybe this wasn't ready yet. Maybe I should paint everything white and start again.

"Are we going to head inside?"

I took a deep breath. The spiced scent of the roses climbing over the front door mingled with the sweet honeysuckle that intertwined with its branches. Together, they calmed me.

He trusted me, and I could trust myself. I unlocked the door and ushered him inside. With the fae lights and the fire called into existence, casting the space in a warm glow, there was only one thing left to do.

On tiptoe, I untied the blindfold.

He blinked and turned, taking in the room.

I clasped my hands tightly, breath held. I'd painted the wall behind the fireplace a rich plum, and dark rosewood shelves lined the alcoves either side. Was it too busy? Too dark? I should've gone for white or cream, making the most of the natural light.

"I put your *baba's* carvings on the shelves." I pointed out where the wooden stags and hinds stood in pride of place amongst the books. "My sister's ship is here next to Kaliban's orrery—the one from his mantlepiece." Avice had given us a detailed model of her ship, the *Venatrix*. It sat above the fireplace, safe from burning thanks to the magical nature of fae fires. Underfoot, we had the rug from Kaliban's house, cleaned of my blood.

"Then in the kitchen"—I hurried over to the other end of the room—"I just liked the amethyst." A large, thin slice of it covered the wall above the sink, instead of tiles. "And we have Kaliban's tea pot." My eyes burned when I touched its chipped lid.

Obviously, he could see exactly where the items were, but I'd started babbling and couldn't stop. I needed him to understand that I'd thought of him as well as myself.

"You need to see upstairs, too." Hopefully he'd like that. I led the way to our bedroom, which occupied most of the upper floor. This was the part that worried me the most. Ariadne had sewn sheer drapes around the bed with tiny black gemstones that glimmered as the curtains wafted. The ceiling was midnight blue with gold stars and a silver moon. It was entirely too much. Too over the top.

"The window," I blurted. "I don't know if you noticed, but it's the same shape as the one in Asher's cottage. I loved it so much, and it overlooks the setting sun, so..." I gestured uselessly.

The cottage had inspired my decoration downstairs with the dark wood and plum wall. I wanted to create somewhere just as cosy for us. I'd chosen bathroom tiles in a similar smoky mirror effect, and had chosen the largest copper bath I could fit in the room, with space for three for those occasions when he split in two.

I dared to look at him. His eyes were wide, his brows raised.

Oh, gods, it was too much.

"Don't panic. I didn't forget your workroom." I grabbed his hand and took him back downstairs. A small hallway led to the garden, which I hadn't yet started on, but would be a fun project for the future, while another door led into his work-room. "I left it white," I explained as I took him inside. "I thought you could decorate it however you like—or at least have somewhere to escape the... *bold* colours."

I stood there, wincing as he turned at the centre of the workroom. "Or we can paint it all white or grey or—"

"Is that what you're so worried about?" He turned to me. "That I won't like the colours?"

"Do you?"

"Katherine Ferrers," he sighed as he crossed the room and

took my hands. "This is absolutely, utterly..." He shook his head, eyes a little bright. "It's fucking perfect. So incredible, I've been speechless the whole time. I thought you were going to just give the place a lick of paint, but you've... you've given it touches of the people we love as well as somehow making it uniquely ours." He pressed my hands together and kissed my fingertips. "*Thank you.*"

I huffed out all my anxiety and sank into his embrace. I'd managed to make *us* a home, and next week we would move in and fill it with the richness of our lives. It was somewhere we could grow together and maybe even grow old.

We stayed there a long while, wandering through the rooms, taking in the peaceful quiet of our house. The particular way moonlight shafted through the bathroom window, hitting the dark tiles and the copper bath. The crackle of the fire, which was softer than the roar of the palace fireplaces. The hush like the place was waiting for us to bring it to life.

Eventually, we dragged ourselves outside and started back to the palace. When we reached the bridge and he still hadn't spoken, I tugged on his arm.

"You know, it is all right if you don't love it or want to change any of it."

"Why on earth would I want to do that? Didn't you hear me earlier?"

"Then why are you so quiet?"

"Oh, I see." He chuckled and slid an arm around my waist as we nodded to the guards. Only once we were past them and walking across the bridge, did he bend to my ear and murmur, "I'm wondering how in the world I'm going to pay you back for making us such a perfect home. I may have to put you on the throne."

The hot breath of his words in my ear made me shiver with

pleasure, but I had to frown at that last part. "I told you, I don't want to be a queen."

His laugh was low and dark—seductive in this way that made me completely foolish. "That isn't what I meant. Don't you remember what I said back in Albion?" He pushed the hair back from my neck, tickling the sensitive skin behind my ear. "I asked if you wanted me to fuck you over the throne... and you never said no."

I sucked in a small, sharp breath. I swallowed. I didn't know how to reply and didn't want to interrupt his line of thought.

"Don't think I've forgotten. You may not be a queen, Katherine, but I think you'd look glorious on a throne... naked... completely undone... crying out my name. My ember sparking bright."

I made a small sound of confirmation.

"I'm so glad you agree. Maybe we can fit it in before we do away with thrones completely." And like that, he snapped upright, stepping off the bridge and into the palace grounds like nothing had happened.

Gods, this fae knew how to put me off balance. And I loved him for it.

I cleared my throat and started towards the gardens, though it was a challenge to drag myself away after all the dark promise of his gravelly tone. "I'll see you in our rooms—I just want to check on the hothouse first."

"Then let me accompany you." He changed course and offered me his arm. "You can show me what else you've been working on, besides our new home."

We skirted the palace, and he asked about my work in the hothouse. I'd been given a room in there to use for my rose experiments and would continue to use it once we'd moved. At the moment, I didn't have much time for more than pottering, but I'd managed to hybridise a few promising new varieties to see if I could start on the path towards the deep purple that had always been my dream.

I explained how I'd chosen two flowers for each experiment, how the rose that would bear the seeds had to be stripped of its petals in order to be pollinated, how then I'd waited for the rose hips to form and mature before harvesting. Then they were dried, the seeds extracted and germinated, the seedlings nurtured.

The hothouse gave me a longer growing season and Elfhame's magic made everything grow quicker and larger, but it was still a process that required time.

"And after all that, you still don't know the exact results until they flower. Months of work could all be for nothing. But these buds are looking promising—I've got one that's a dark, raspberry pink. It might help me get to purple in the end."

I looked up when we entered the formal gardens and I realised he'd gone quiet again.

He wore this small smile, pleased and... something else. "I love you, Kat, but I *adore* hearing how passionate you are about your work."

My cheeks flushed hot with the pleasure of being admired and a little of the self-consciousness of being perceived.

He grabbed me. Kissed me. Consuming me in a way that said he wanted to have every part of me. Thorough, like he might be able to drink the passion from my lips.

Just as I was about to suggest we skip the hothouse and go to our suite, the heavens opened, drenching us in cold rain. We pulled apart, laughing and wiping the water from our eyes.

Hand in hand, we ran to the hothouse—our nearest shelter.

Under the light of the glowing plants, we headed to the far end where the smaller rooms with the poisonous plants and my roses were housed. "It probably won't open until tomorrow or the day after, but..."

He teased a lock of wet hair from my cheek and shrugged. "We shall see. And if it hasn't, we'll come back again tomorrow. We have time."

I was just breathing in the truth of that when we arrived in my workspace and ahead—

"Oh!" I ran the last paces to the flower—the *open* flower—calling a fae light to follow so I could see more clearly. A full, round rose, its petals velvety and lush, deep raspberry on the outside and darker at the centre.

I touched the edge of one petal. Soft. Real. I called the light closer, so I could see the middle more clearly.

Darkest berry purple.

I made a little choked sound.

It was *purple*.

"You did it," he murmured, squeezing my shoulder.

"Not exactly as I'd pictured, but... it might be even more beautiful."

"I'm learning that's what life is like."

I laughed and flung my arms around him with a squeal. "I did it." For some foolish reason, I cried a few happy tears into his shirt, which mingled with the rain.

He kissed the top of my head and pulled back. "Now you've bred the most gorgeous roses I've ever seen, what's next? Last time I asked, you replied with a list of things that needed doing. Almost all those things are done. What comes after?"

"Well, we'll be together."

"*Obviously*. Though I like having your confirmation."

I canted my head. "And I foresee you making lots of beautiful things in your new workroom."

"Beautiful?" His eyebrows raised. "Not useful?"

Here in a fae palace's hothouse, full of pretty flowers and luminescent plants, with a purple rose that I'd bred, in the arms of the most gorgeous person I'd ever known, it felt silly that I'd once worshipped usefulness. Thank the gods, that was in the past.

"Yes," I replied with a lilt that acknowledged my past foolishness. "Beautiful. And existing for that sole purpose—giving us a reason to live and fight." Just as he'd said in this very hothouse.

"Mm." The sound rumbled between us, pleased. "Good. What else?"

His praise was warm, safe, something I craved, something I'd earned. "And I will grow beautiful, impractical, useless roses that we can look at while we dine."

"My favourite." His lopsided smile warmed the tone of his voice, and I felt it as he pressed a kiss to my lips. "You've earned a visit to the throne room after this. I'll send everyone else away."

My body drew tighter as I pressed against him, biting my lip at the delicious promise.

"We have sculptures and flowers and an appointment with that throne." His playfulness faded, the look in his eyes growing intense, serious. "What else is in our future, love?"

"I'm..." I blinked and shook my head. "Actually, I'm not sure." I straightened his rain-soaked shirt, recalling how his clothes had also been drenched the first time we'd met.

The set of his shoulders told me that just as on that night, I had his undivided attention and always would.

"I used to think I had only the terrible options I deserved. I was too broken for anything better. Anything more. But now, when I look ahead, I don't just see options. I see a life. I don't know what it will be, but I do know one thing." Fingers splaying over his chest, trusting that I could lean into him, I lifted my chin and held his glowing gaze. "It will be a life lived truly and a life truly lived."

THE END

If you aren't ready to say goodbye to Kat and Bastian, you can get your hands on a cosy short story where they celebrate the Winter Solstice, as well as bonus scenes and other goodies over on my newsletter.

aseria art

AUTHOR NOTE

I keep sitting down to write this author note and not knowing where to start. Maybe because it means the series is over. Maybe because... well... how do I begin?

You see, this series has been an absolute labour of love and one that's changed my life.

We think of the characters in books being changed by their experiences—that's what a story is. Not just stuff happening, but stuff happening to a person and having consequences and remoulding them.

But books also have the power to change the people who write and read them. And Shadows of the Tenebris Court has certainly changed me. I'm utterly humbled that I've had messages telling me it's changed some of you, too.

Thanks to your love of Kat and Bastian's story and other tales in the Sabreverse, I get to keep doing this (making things up and writing them down). Please know that it's appreciated more than I can adequately say.

But enough about me! Kat and Bastian. My beautiful idiots.

Going on this journey with them has been an absolute joy and privilege (and painful at times, of course, but we need the emotional rollercoaster, right?).

About a year ago, I jotted down a note for myself that just read

Kat's journey—from poison to power.

Because no life is without adversity. But sometimes we can take the poison from those moments and turn it into something new. Not something that's the same as before, but something that's broken and yet beautiful. Not something that's stronger, but something that has grown into a new shape, which shows its past and takes our branches in a new direction.

I feel like that's been the core of Kat's story—surviving adversity and finding a way to grow despite the damage that's been done. It was so important to me that Kat didn't magically get rid of her trauma but still managed to not just survive, but *thrive*.

I hope you enjoyed travelling this path with her, even if it was challenging at times. And I really hope you love getting a glimpse of how her life with Bastian will be *after*.

Finishing a series is uniquely bittersweet. You get to share what you hope is a satisfying end to their tale, but also... it's the end. You've carried these people with you for months and years. You've put them through hell (Sorryyy!) and helped them drag themselves back out again. And then it's done.

The full circle moment where Kat is reunited with Morag and Horwich was when it hit me. The return to where it all began (in spirit if not in geographical location), but where everything is different because Kat is different.

It was the first time I got a little misty-eyed about finishing the series, seeing Kat and Bastian back in Albion, grown, together, changed. *Sniffle*

Of course, the joy of books is that we never really have to say goodbye. Kat, Bastian, and their friends are all still there inside the pages—all you have to do is open the book to see them again.

But, if that isn't enough, there is more...

It was a pleasure returning to Sepher and Zita for this book. You can read the story of how they went from "I came here to kill you" to "I would kill for you" in *Slaying the Shifter Prince*.

Fair warning, it is a villain/bully romance on the darker end of the scale (captor/captive, he collars her and comes up with other cruel and unusual punishments for her assassination attempt, their journey to love goes via obsession and hate sex). It has been referred to as "unhinged," which is completely fair! I think of it as if *The Cruel Prince* had claws (literally). As always, you can find content warnings on my website: https://www.claresager.com/a-kiss-of-iron-content-warnings

If you want to learn more about Ariadne and Lysander (and Fluffy!) and Rose and Faolán, I've also told their stories in *Bound by a Fae Bargain*, a duet of interconnected standalones.

Stolen Threadwitch Bride is about Ari being taken to Elfhame by Ly (against her will!) and discovering her power. It's been referred to as a cosy comfort read, which I love.

These Gentle Wolves follows Rose as she tries to rescue Ari and ends up trapped with Faolán in a haunted house. It's *Little Red Riding Hood* meets Crimson Peak, with grumpy x sunshine and a marriage of convenience.

Then, of course, Kat's little sister has a whole series of her own, beginning with *Beneath Black Sails*—enemies-to-lovers, pirate x pirate hunter, I'm sure they definitely couldn't get into any sort of betrayal situation and that things will be entirely angst-free and calm... *Side-eyeing the sarcasm.*

And, finally, if you really just can't say goodbye to Kat and Bastian, I'm working on a short story at the time of writing (29th December 2024), which will come out in the next week. Kat and Bastian get to actually celebrate a Winter Solstice without any Horrors attacking. That will be free for my newsletter subscribers, and you can get your hands on it as soon as its available by signing up here: https://www.claresager.com/polback

As for this book, thank you again for reading. I hope you enjoyed it and found it a satisfying conclusion to Kastian's story!

It would help me so much if you were to leave a review on the store where you bought it—it doesn't have to be an essay, just a sentence is great! The algorithms love to see lots of reviews as they show you're engaging with a book, and your fellow readers put a lot more stock in what you say about a book/series than any marketing I can do.

If you have a bit more time, please consider adding that review to GoodReads, StoryGraph, or whatever other apps and sites you use to track your reading and share your recs.

And finally, thank you. Yes, again. Your reviews, recommendations, fan art, pterodactyl screeching messages to your friends telling them they MUST read this series, and all the other ways you've shared your love for this series have made a huge difference to me, helping more readers find the Sabreverse, and I could not be more grateful.

THANK YOU!

All the very best,

Clare

    x
    December 2024

PS – Make sure you turn the page—you never know what you might find...

ACKNOWLEDGEMENTS

Oof. This was a tough book to write, so I have a lot of thank yous...

First, to Carissa, Lasairiona, and Tracie—my work wives. Thank you for all your support, understanding, and love—and for Tracie's trusty stopwatch!

Alyssa—AKA The Best PA/Right Hand Woman ever. This year, especially, has been a wiiild ride, and I'm so glad you've been here to keep me on the straight and narrow.

Alyssa (again) and Andrew, Andra, Clare, Karolina, Laura, Mariëlle, Michelle, Noah, and Tempest—my amazing beta reading/editorial crew! Thanks so, so much for your time and effort, as well as your patience.

Bibi—my awesome agent! Thank you for championing *Shadows of the Tenebris Court* and helping spread the word for Kat and Bastian's story.

My author friends—your support, understanding, and commiserating is always vital. Special mention to Meg and Sacha—love you guys. <3

Charlie Arpie, Agnieszka Gromulska, Stephanie Hulsebus, and Nate Medeiros—for the stunning artwork included in and on this book. It's been such a joy to work with you and I'm thrilled to share your work.

Maria Spada—for the amazing covers for this series. It has been an absolute pleasure having your designs on these books.

To Catherine and her dear friend Deema—the former for so generously bidding in the Books for Palestine auction to name a character in this book, and the latter for inspiring her, leading to the name of Elfhame's treasurer.

My friends and family—for... y'know... *everything*. I promise I will have a better schedule next year!

Deedee and Dash—my little monsters, for being endlessly entertaining and for all the purring.

My incredible readers, and my Hype Team—for sharing, messaging, commenting, reviewing, and generally loving on my books. It truly makes a difference, and I can't say how grateful I am for your support.

To the NHS and its staff—for helping and treating me when my knee decided to bend the wrong way... and all for free at the point of use. You are one of the most precious things in this country.

As always, I've saved the best for last, so, finally, thank you to Russ. The best. Just, the best. Thank you for accepting me always. <3

4I 2 2

ALSO BY CLARE SAGER – SET IN THE SABREVERSE

SHADOWS OF THE TENEBRIS COURT

Gut-wrenching romance full of deceit, desire, and dark secrets.

Book 1 – *A Kiss of Iron* – *Also available in audio*

Book 2 – *A Touch of Poison* – *Also available in audio*

Book 3 – *A Promise of Lies* – *Coming soon to audio*

BOUND BY A FAE BARGAIN

Steamy fantasy romances featuring unwitting humans who make bargains with clever fae. Each book features a different couple, though the characters are linked.

Stolen Threadwitch Bride (Ariadne & Lysander)

These Gentle Wolves (Rose & Faolán)

MORTAL ENEMIES TO MONSTER LOVERS

Five fantasy romances each by different authors, set in their own worlds. These enemies to lovers stories are united in their promise to deliver "I came to kill you" angst, scorching romances with inhuman, morally grey heroes, and happily ever afters.

Slaying the Shifter Prince, by Clare Sager (Featuring Zita and Sepher) – *Also available in audio*

Discover the full series here:

www.mortalenemiestomonsterlovers.com

BENEATH BLACK SAILS

An enemies-to-lovers tale of piracy, magic, and betrayal.
Featuring Kat's sister Vice. Complete series. Coming to audio in 2025.

Book 0 – *Across Dark Seas* – *Free Book*

Book 1 – *Beneath Black Sails*

Book 2 – *Against Dark Tides*

Book 3 – *Under Black Skies*

Book 4 – *Through Dark Storms*

Made in United States
Troutdale, OR
01/07/2025

27706692R00336